SH
THEY
RUN

ALSO BY TOM BALE

ALL FALL DOWN
SINS OF THE FATHER writing as David Harrison
EACH LITTLE LIE
SKIN AND BONES
TERROR'S REACH
BLOOD FALLS
THE CATCH

SEE HOW THEY RUN

TOM BALE

Bookouture

Published by Bookouture

An imprint of StoryFire Ltd.
23 Sussex Road, Ickenham, UB10 8PN
United Kingdom

www.bookouture.com

ISBN: 978-1-910751-69-5
eBook ISBN: 978-1-910751-68-8

For Niki, Graham, Neil, Pauline & Luke,
in memory of Jackie Spencer.

ONE

Any noise in the night could wake him now. Eight weeks since the birth of his daughter and Harry barely remembered how it felt to sleep for seven hours straight and wake naturally, refreshed and ready for a new day. All the warnings from their friends about the misery of sleep deprivation had turned out to be spot on.

The sound had come and gone by the time he registered he was awake, eyes glued shut, heart beating fast. Not the baby, he was sure of that. It must have been something outside, perhaps in the alley along the back where urban foxes prowled.

Harry waited, trying to recreate the feeling he'd had, the sense of a dream interrupted by a ... a thud, a scrape: a surreptitious noise, as though something – *someone* – was trying to go unheard.

Or maybe it had just been part of the dream itself. Either way, now he was awake he ought to take a look out of the window; check on Evie and see how much time there was before her next feed ...

Harry knew he should do these things but he couldn't. He was frozen in place, eyes tightly shut, not even daring to breathe.

There was an intruder in their home.

It wasn't a rowdy neighbourhood by any means, their tidy terraced street. Although modest in size, the houses were highly valued for their proximity to the railway station, to good schools and friendly corner shops and vibrant pubs, to all the pleasures that Brighton had to offer. Not quite in the heart of the city but close to one of its main arteries, the Port Hall district between Dyke Road and Stanford Road was arty, upmarket and conservatively bohemian – so letterboxes bore stickers refusing junk mail on environmental grounds, even while the parking bays were choked with 4x4s.

A lot of young families lived here, Harry and Alice's being one of the youngest. There weren't too many people coming home in the early hours, although a woman over the road worked shifts at the hospital. In the city beyond there was always the drone of traffic: sirens, car horns, slamming doors and screeching tyres, and sometimes the distant, deep rumble of trains leaving Brighton station. Depending on the season, there was birdsong to a greater or lesser degree, most of it charming and rarely disruptive, the exception being the caustic screech of the seagulls – or the *bloody* seagulls, as they were known round here.

All these things contributed to the soundtrack of Harry's sleeping hours; all were familiar and expected and unthreatening. What he'd just heard was of a different nature altogether.

But no one could have broken into the house without waking him, could they? Even if they had, they'd be satisfied with stealing what was on offer in the living room: the Blu-ray player and the PS4. Some cash, maybe a phone or an iPad. Harry couldn't recall precisely what was lying around, but he was sure of one thing: thieves were opportunists. There was no way they'd risk climbing the stairs or waking the occupants of the house.

So why, then, did Harry feel there was somebody right here, in their room?

Slowly, very slowly, he let out the breath that had caught in his lungs. He opened his eyes, remembering how next door's cat had given him a few scares in the past: that kettle drum *boom* when it leapt on to the dustbin; and its plaintive wail, like the cry of a tortured child. Harry willed it to make a noise now, to break the illusion of danger.

Nothing.

Because it wasn't an illusion.

His focus switched to the space around him. Alice was sleeping heavily and so, for once, was the baby. When the time was right they planned to move Evie to the nursery next door. For now she slept in a Moses basket on a fold-out stand, positioned close enough to Alice's side of the bed that she could reach out and soothe her back to sleep at the first hint of a restless murmur.

Evie had her own breathing pattern, a rate so rapid it brought to mind someone panting to complete a race, and a distinctive snore that managed to sound enchanting even on the nights when Harry was so tired he wanted to claw out his eyes and fill the sockets with concrete.

There was always a smell of milk in the room, Evie's signature fragrance, but now Harry realised it was competing with something else: a sour top note of male sweat and stale clothing that had no place in here.

And other breathing. Was he imagining that?

He locked up every muscle, devoted his full attention to listening, listening …

And then the voice of a stranger spoke from the shadows.

'Wake up, sleepyhead.'

Alice reacted with an urgent flailing of limbs. She probably thought she'd overslept and missed a feed. Harry tried to speak, wanting to find a way to keep her silent and still, because it had occurred to him that Alice's best hope of safety – of *survival* – was if the intruder believed Harry was alone in the room. But the words wouldn't come, and his rational mind knew it was a ludicrous idea. The street light filtering through the curtains was more than sufficient to see how many people were present.

Three.

And that thought – the knowledge that his baby daughter was here too – made him sit up in a panic, his mind racing. The bed trembled and Alice groaned and stretched, turning towards the Moses basket.

'Harry …'

'Ssshh.'

He rubbed his eyes, trying to make sense of a shadow, a shape, just to the right of the door. It took a step towards the bed as Alice, twisting in his direction, said, 'She's sound asleep. Why—?'

'Look.' Harry lifted his arm to point, wondering vaguely if he was hallucinating from sleep deprivation. *Oh yes, please: to hear Alice laugh and say there's no one here but us.*

But Alice didn't laugh. She sucked in a breath as if to scream, then choked it off, probably acting on the same instinct that had driven Harry's response: to keep Evie asleep, to protect her, no matter what else happened.

And still the figure waited at the end of the bed. It was a man, tall and broad, but there were no features apparent, nothing visible in the silhouette.

'Get out of here.' Harry barely recognised his own voice. He was ashamed of the tremor in it, as if such a weak command could send a burglar packing.

In response the man turned slightly, checking over his shoulder. There was another trickle of laughter. That was when Harry knew this wasn't a burglary at all.

It was something much, much worse.

TWO

In what seemed like an act of dark sorcery, the bedroom door swung open. The overhead light snapped on, a cold dose of reality on a bleak November morning. Both of them jumped at the shock, and Alice just managed to stifle a shriek.

A second man entered the room. He was shorter and thinner than the first, but otherwise looked the same. They were dressed in black overalls, along with thin leather gloves, and latex masks – a clown face on the first man, and Freddy Krueger on the second.

Their footwear was covered with plastic bags, secured around the ankles with rubber bands. When he saw that, Harry's terror jumped to a whole new level. The fact that they'd covered not just their hands and faces but their *shoes*, their entire bodies wrapped up to avoid leaving traces of DNA: these men weren't amateurs. They knew exactly what they were doing.

Maybe Alice had picked up on that; maybe she was choosing to ignore it. 'J-jewellery box,' she stuttered. 'On the dressing table. T-take it, and go.'

The second man snorted, the noise muffled by the mask into a weak impression of Darth Vader. In her crib Evie gave a snuffle, and slowly the man turned his head in her direction.

Harry tensed, ready to throw himself across the bed if either of the intruders took a step towards his daughter.

The first man said, 'Where is he?'

Silence.

Harry cleared his throat. 'What?'

'Renshaw. Where is he?'

Alice shook her head, perplexed. 'Who?'

'Renshaw. Edward Renshaw.'

The tone was impatient, but not particularly nervous. And quite well-spoken, rather than the gruff Estuary accent that Harry had instinctively expected.

He and Alice stared at the two men, then exchanged a baffled glance. It flashed through Harry's mind that years from now this event might form the basis of a humorous anecdote. They'd make new friends on holiday, and in the course of a boozy evening Alice would say, 'Tell them about the time those thugs invaded our house in the middle of the night, and it turned out they'd got the wrong address!'

Surfing a wave of relief, he said, 'We don't know anyone of that name,' and Alice overlapped with: 'Never heard of him.'

The first man looked at each of them in turn. His eyes were barely visible behind the mask but the intensity of his gaze was unmistakable.

'Edward Renshaw. Early sixties, Middle Eastern. Dark skin, dark hair.'

'And he's a fat fucker.' The second man's voice was coarser than his partner's. He held his hand up at shoulder height. 'About this tall.'

'He uses other names. Grainger. Miller. And he might call himself Doctor, not Mister.'

'We don't know him.' Harry felt sick with the desire to be believed. 'This is a mistake.'

'How long've you lived here?' the second man demanded.

'Two years, next February.' Alice sounded so confident that it gave Harry extra strength.

He added: 'Before us, it was a woman in her eighties. She had to go into a home. Mrs …'

'Stevens,' Alice finished for him. 'Beryl Stevens.'

Harry nodded vigorously. He felt sure they were coming across as honest, genuine people, doing their utmost to be co-operative in extremely stressful circumstances.

Alice was saying, 'Beryl was a spinster. She lived alone—'

The first man cut her off: 'You had a parcel.'

Harry felt Alice flinch at the interruption, her knee jerking against his leg. He glanced at her, worried that in desperation she'd invent a lot of nonsense to send them away. She was staring rigidly at the man in the Freddy Krueger mask, who had taken something from the pocket of his overalls.

A knife.

'Some time this week,' the first man said. 'The parcel was addressed to Mr E Grainger.'

Evie was stirring, kicking at her blankets. The bright light and the noise must have woken her. In any case, she was due a feed pretty soon: according to the bedside clock, it was a little after three a.m.

'Why would we get a parcel for this Grainger, or Renshaw?' Harry tried to sound defiant rather than angry. 'He doesn't live here. We have no idea who he is.'

'It came to this address. 34 Lavinia Street.'

Alice raised her hand, as if in a classroom. 'You realise there's also a Lavinia *Drive* in Brighton? And a Lavinia Crescent. The post can get mixed up. We've had junk mail for 34 Lavinia Crescent before now.'

The first man sighed, as though she and Harry were testing his patience. 'I don't think you appreciate how serious this is.'

His partner nodded. 'They need a lesson.'

For a moment Harry didn't understand: in the shock, his brain had seized up. It wasn't until the second man took a step towards the Moses basket that he got it.

Hurting Evie: that was the lesson.

THREE

'Don't you touch her!' Harry yelled. He flung himself forward, colliding with Alice as she made the same attempt to protect the baby. The man jabbed the knife in her direction, warning her off.

'Relax,' the first man drawled. 'He's good with kids.'

He chuckled at his own joke, sounding absurdly relaxed. Harry looked round and saw that he now held a gun, a small black pistol.

'Back where you were,' he told Harry. 'And lie still. A dead hero is no use to anyone.'

Harry had little choice but to comply, but the sense of his own impotence was like a fist clenched around his heart. Alice was ordered to lie alongside him and she obeyed, both of them shaking so hard they could feel the vibrations through the mattress. From Evie came a mewling cry of protest: *I didn't wake you. Why have you woken me?*

The man with the knife grabbed her blanket and whipped it out of the crib, like a magician unveiling a glorious surprise. And now Evie lay exposed, so tiny and vulnerable in her pink floral sleepsuit that the terror Harry felt – the terror of losing her – was almost more than he could bear.

Alice reached for his hand, squeezing it as intensely as she'd done in the closing stages of a long and difficult labour. Harry felt even more useless to her now than he had then.

'A lesson,' the knife man said, and in one swift movement he clutched the front of Evie's sleepsuit and hoisted her into the air, as though their precious daughter was a tatty old ragdoll, something to be tossed aside and forgotten.

Harry felt Alice slump against him. After a second or two when she must have been struck dumb with shock, Evie let out a wail that seemed to split the air like a klaxon. But despite the effect it had on her parents, it wasn't the first time she'd cried out in the night, and Harry knew it wouldn't be enough to alert their neighbours to what was happening here.

The cry galvanised Alice into action. She made a lunge for her daughter, ignoring the man with the gun, but his partner dodged back and dangled Evie out of reach, her sleepsuit stretching like a bungee rope. He lifted both hands to chest height, bringing baby and blade within touching distance.

'No sudden moves or I'll slit her throat. Kid this size, there ain't much blood to spare. You wanna see it draining out on your carpet?'

Alice whimpered, helplessly. Harry thought he did as well: the image too horrifying to contemplate.

'Be a waste, though,' the knife man went on. 'What d'ya reckon, on the open market?'

The question was directed at the gunman, who gave a curt shake of his head. He moved to Harry's side of the bed. Point blank range.

'My friend here – let's call him "Freddy" – is a psychopath. He could skin your baby like a rabbit and whistle while he did it. But he won't need to, because you're going to co-operate. Aren't you?'

Harry couldn't speak. His mind had snagged helplessly on the idea of Evie being killed or disfigured because her parents had failed to protect her. It was only when Alice let out a sob that he managed to nod. *Yes, we'll co-operate.*

*

'Let's relax, shall we?' The gunman signalled to 'Freddy', who dragged the Moses basket a safe distance from the bed and dropped Evie into it. Her sharp scream was followed by frantic uneven gasps, as if she had forgotten how to breathe.

'Please,' Alice cried. 'She's only eight weeks old. Let me take her.'

'Can't do that,' Freddy said.

'I'm begging you. She doesn't deserve this.'

'You're right,' the gunman said. 'Your loyalty to Renshaw isn't worth the life of your daughter.'

Harry opened his hands, the sort of gesture you make to appeal for reason. Deep down he knew it was futile, but it was ingrained in him to be sensible, and polite, and it was equally ingrained to hope others would treat him in the same way.

'We can't tell you anything about this man Renshaw because we have no idea who he is. No idea at all. So it's impossible to give you what you want. Don't you see that?'

The silence that followed had a different quality to it. Harry wondered if these men had been expecting such a deadlock; hoping for it, even. This felt like silence as a cue to action.

He was right. The gunman darted forward and shoved the muzzle of the gun against Harry's chest. His other hand came down hard on Harry's face, forcing his head back on the pillow. Alice tried to scream but Freddy used the baby's blanket as a gag, shoving a fistful of it into her mouth. Startled by the movement, Evie began to sob again.

Then he pulled the duvet off their bed and flung it in the corner. He turned back, a hungry gleam in his eyes as he studied Alice's body in her silk pyjamas.

'Undress.'

The order was emphasised with a casual swipe of the blade, which pierced the skin on Alice's neck, drawing a few bright beads of blood. Harry writhed in fury but the gunman held him firm, pinning his head to the side to make sure he had a clear view of his wife.

Her face rigid with fear, Alice had started to unbutton the pyjama top when Freddy lost patience and ripped it open. She was wearing a nursing bra, which he cut with savage haste. At the sight of her exposed breasts he made a noise in his throat, an involuntary purring that turned Harry's stomach.

'I'll give you another chance to tell us,' the gunman said. 'But not until my friend here has had a taste.'

Freddy sniggered. 'Taste. Got that right.'

Alice was shivering, arms flat at her side; too scared to try and cover herself. The man crouched by the bed, and Harry saw his wife's legs twitch, her instinct urging her to move. Fight or flight – but neither was possible.

Harry had to resist the impulse to shut his eyes. Hiding from this would be even more shameful than watching it happen. Freddy was leaning over, his head a few inches from Alice's stomach. He seemed to be inspecting the effects of childbirth: the loose folds of skin, the silvery stretch marks that were – as Harry kept assuring her – fading a little more each day.

Freddy nudged the mask up over his chin. Harry caught a glimpse of jowly stubble and wet lips; a fat pink tongue lolling over the bottom lip as his mouth opened, then clamped down on one of Alice's milk-heavy breasts. She cried out again, but it was muffled by the blanket. The sound of the man sucking greedily – feeding on her – was far louder, and it was revolting.

Harry bucked and fought, pushing the other man's hand away to free his head, not caring in that moment if he was shot. Death seemed a better option than this, to lie helpless while they—

Except that Alice's gaze was locked on to his, pleading with him not to fight, not to die. Then the gunman rammed a fist into Harry's stomach and for a second the pain was everything. He groaned and coughed, tasted bile and swallowed it down and finally lay still in shame and surrender.

Freddy pulled his mouth away from Alice's breast with a loud smacking noise, milk dribbling over his lips as he stood up and put the mask back in place. 'Weird taste.'

'You wouldn't want it in your tea?' the gunman asked.

'Nah. But I'd still do her.' Freddy sniffed, indicating Harry. 'Tie him up and we can both have a go.'

'No!' Harry cried. 'You've got the wrong house. The wrong people. For the sake of my wife and daughter I'll tell you anything. Anything at all. But it won't be the truth. Because the truth is that we don't know the man you're looking for, and I think you realise that.'

The speech rolled out of him like the last desperate plea of a condemned man. It was accompanied by visions of a funeral procession. Three black hearses, three coffins, one of them so tiny that it looked like a toy …

Harry waited. It was the longest, most agonising wait of his life. He had no idea what their response would be. Perhaps no words at all. Perhaps just a gunshot or the slash of a blade. And all the time Evie was crying, needing to be comforted, and there was nothing he or Alice could do to help her.

Finally the gunman walked round to where his partner was standing, spotted something on the floor and bent to pick it up. As he did, he began to speak.

'These are the rules. You don't go to the police. If you do, *we'll know*. However you go about it, we'll find out.'

He was holding a pack of wet wipes. He fumbled with the package, hampered by his gloves, then pulled out several wipes in a thick clump.

'You won't see us, but we'll be watching. You report this, and your baby will die. The police won't protect you. No matter what they claim, they can't. Not twenty-four hours a day. Not week in, week out, month after month. Do you understand?'

Harry nodded. Alice didn't. She seemed too traumatised to move.

The gunman turned to her and first tugged the makeshift gag out of her mouth, then used the wipes to clean her breast. Removing DNA.

'When we find Renshaw – which we will – he'll be questioned. If it turns out you knew him, or helped him in any way, the same thing applies. We'll take your daughter when you least expect it. Then we'll come for your wife. Then you. Am I clear?'

Harry nodded again.

'Say it.'

'Yes. I get you.'

The gun was aimed at Alice. 'You?'

'Yes.' The gun didn't move, so she said it again. 'Yes. I understand.'

A snort from Freddy, but Harry had the impression that he wasn't completely in agreement. Unlike his partner, Freddy was in no hurry to leave.

Harry realised he'd been too quickly seduced by the prospect of release. This man, this *psychopath*, could so easily reach out and cut Evie, by way of a parting shot, and there would be nothing they could do to stop it happening.

Then the gunman said, 'Give it back to them,' and Freddy scooped Evie up with one hand, provoking a fresh howl of anguish from the baby. He dumped her down on Alice, who immediately wrapped her daughter in a protective embrace, pulling the duvet up and turning away from the two men.

'Stay exactly where you are for ten minutes. And no police.'

'Yeah, and don't wake up tomorrow and remember this any different from how it was,' Freddy snarled. 'Right now you're both shitting yourselves at the thought of what we could do to you. Keep that in mind, all right?'

They backed up to the door, the gun still raised, and then they slipped out.

Harry and Alice could barely have moved if they'd wanted to. They listened to the intruders descending the stairs, the rattle of a bolt being drawn back. The front door opened and then shut, firmly, and the men were gone.

It was over.

It was only just beginning.

FOUR

Harry took a deep breath and rolled out of bed, prompting a cry from Alice. 'What are you doing?'

'Ssh.' Crouching, he hurried out of the bedroom. His legs felt rubbery, unreliable, but they just about got him into the nursery, where a small window offered a better view of the street.

With the room in darkness, he didn't think they'd notice him peering through the blind. He could see a van waiting in the road outside, without its lights on. A Renault, possibly. The two men clambered aboard, sliding the side door shut as the van pulled away.

He risked a better look, his face pressed against the slats in the blind. The van reached the end of the street, too far away for him to read the number plate. Brake lights flashed. A left turn into Port Hall Road would take it towards Dyke Road, which offered the quickest way out of the city, but the van went right, perhaps intending on a more complicated route over the railway lines and down to Preston Park.

Or maybe it wasn't going anywhere. Maybe it was just circling the block.

What had the gunman said? *We will be watching you.*

As Harry moved away from the window he heard Alice coughing and retching. He ran into their bedroom and found her sitting with her head tipped forward, awkwardly holding Evie clear of the vomit which covered the duvet.

'Are you okay?' He shook his head: stupid question. 'Here, let me take—'

'No!' The venom in her response made him recoil. Only then did her expression soften. 'She's feeding. She's calm.'

Harry fetched a couple of flannels and a towel, then stripped the bed and put on a new sheet and duvet while Alice stood for a minute, wiping her face as Evie continued to feed.

'How's your neck, where he cut you?'

She dabbed the flannel against the wound, then inspected it for blood. 'Just a scratch. It's fine.'

Harry grunted, but said nothing. The reluctance to discuss it was like a wall of sandbags piled up between them.

Dumping the dirty bedding in the bath, there was a moment when he had to grip the side of the tub while jagged lights and colours tore at his vision. He realised he had a pounding headache, hardly surprising given the lump coming up where he'd been hit with the gun. Briefly, he fantasised about swallowing half a box of paracetamol and then lying down somewhere dark.

Except that the van might be circling the block.

He checked on Alice again, and only just stopped himself from repeating that dumbest of questions: *Are you all right?*

Never better, thanks. You?

Instead, he said to her, 'I need to go downstairs.'

'Be careful.'

He shrugged off her concern, but at the top of the stairs he hesitated. Double switches controlled the lights on the landing and in the hall. He turned both of them on and hurtled down the stairs, his bare feet sliding over the carpeted treads. At the bottom he came to a sudden halt, perhaps hoping to trick another intruder into revealing himself.

But there was no one to trick. They'd been and gone.

The front door was shut. Harry slid the top bolt back in place and added the security chain. He opened the cupboard under the stairs, where his meagre collection of tools was kept. He might have been a reluctant DIY-er at best, but every home needed a claw hammer, didn't it?

Right now it seemed like the wisest purchase he'd ever made. Not much use against a gun, but he wouldn't dwell on that. It felt good and hefty in his grip, and he allowed himself a brief fantasy where he used it to smash the skulls of his tormentors.

Then he checked the downstairs rooms: the modest kitchen and long, narrow lounge-diner. Nothing was broken or ransacked, but he had the impression that some items had been moved since last night, as if during a cursory search. Had the intruders been looking for the parcel? Or for evidence that the mysterious Renshaw lived here?

In the dining room he discovered that the patio doors had been forced. There was no visible damage to the timber frame, and the doors could still be closed, but the latch wouldn't hold them in place. As a short-term measure he wound some parcel string round the handles, binding the doors together. That wasn't robust enough, he decided, so he wedged a dining chair under them as well.

The kitchen window was another concern: too easy to break and climb through. His answer was to shut the internal door and stand the ironing board against it: a crude but effective early warning device. Anyone opening the door would tip the ironing board over, and the resulting clatter was bound to wake him.

Huh. As if he'd ever sleep again, after this.

He carried the claw hammer upstairs, unsure whether it represented a show of strength or an admission of weakness.

Alice was lying on her back, eyes shut, so she didn't see him slip the hammer under his pillow. Evie was nestled against her, awake but sated. The aura of calm struck Harry as absurd. Surely it was better to acknowledge that something fundamental had occurred? Confront the turmoil that lay just beneath the surface?

Easier said than done. The only saving grace was that Evie, at least, would carry no memory of this into her future. He and Alice, on the other hand, were indelibly marked by it. He knew that by the way she opened her eyes, regarded him for a moment then quickly looked down. An image popped into his head – of the man in the Freddy Krueger mask sucking on her breast. He forced it away.

'Have they gone?' she asked.

He nodded. 'Drove off in a van – maybe a Renault. I couldn't get the number.'

He decided not to mention which way it had turned. Instead he told her about the patio doors, and how he had made them secure. While he was talking Evie began to wriggle, her eyes fluttering.

'This light's too bright,' Alice said.

Harry put his bedside lamp on, then switched off the overhead light. He climbed into bed and lay on his side, gently stroking tufts of Evie's light brown hair.

'Is she definitely all right? The way he was holding her …'

'I checked. I think there's a bruise on her stomach—' She choked up. Harry reached over Evie and rested his hand on her shoulder.

'We'll be okay,' he said. But when he heard the tone of his voice he wasn't completely sure that he believed it.

Alice said nothing, and Harry had no idea what she was thinking. He lay beside her and fretted, afraid that anything he said would make it worse. Then a tiny snore caught his attention; Evie was sound asleep.

'Shall I put her in the crib?' he whispered.

'Not yet.'

Alice's voice didn't sound quite right; Harry sat up and saw there were tears streaming down her cheeks. She looked like someone in the grip of an uncontrollable grief, and yet she wasn't making a sound.

'Alice—'

'Ssh! Please, I'm not ready …' She sniffed. 'I'll be fine. This is how I'm dealing with it.'

Harry had no choice but to give her that space, if it was what she thought was best. But it worried him all the more. He wanted to be actively supporting her; not lying here like a mannequin.

Besides, there was one thing they *had* to talk about – and it had to be now.

FIVE

'We haven't called the police.'

It felt safer, somehow, to phrase it as an observation. Harry was aware that he didn't want to influence Alice's opinion in any way. He needed to know what she thought, because he had no idea what to think himself.

She'd stopped crying, and her voice sounded more like normal, though the tone was flat. 'You heard what they said. We can't.'

'I don't see how they'd know.'

'They're going to be watching.'

Still debating whether to tell her which way the van went, Harry said, 'Do you reckon that's likely?'

'I don't know.' Alice sniffed again. 'I hope not.'

'If they *are* watching us, that's more reason to go to the police, because it means they haven't finished with us. If we believe the threat is real, then we need to report it. Go to a police station and explain it all.'

Alice considered this carefully. A few strands of dark brown hair had adhered to her cheeks. She pulled them away and turned towards him. Her eyes were red and puffy.

'Yes, but we can't tell the police anything about them. We didn't see their faces. And they wore gloves, so there won't be fingerprints. It's pointless, isn't it?'

'We can describe their voices. The one with the gun, didn't he sound fairly well-spoken? Middle-class?'

'What's that got to do with anything?'

'Well, it doesn't really fit the profile for … whatever they are.' He threw up his hands. 'Oh, I don't know. I'm probably not making much sense.'

Alice raised her head to check the clock. 'Little wonder, at quarter to four in the morning.'

'So what do you want to do?'

'This.' Shifting position to face him, her hand appeared beneath the duvet, seeking his. 'If we did, we'd need to describe all of it. So I'd have to tell the police exactly what that man did to me.' She shut her eyes tightly for a moment. 'And then it'll be all over the news.'

'Not necessarily. We can probably insist they keep our identities secret.'

'In this day and age? Come on, Harry. It'll be out there eventually, you know that. And the thought of having something so personal plastered across the *Argus*, or on the local news. I couldn't bear the idea of walking down the street with people looking at me, knowing all the details …'

'Okay.' Harry wasn't sure if he agreed, exactly, but in her place he knew he'd probably have the same reaction.

'And for Evie's sake. The past doesn't fade away like it used to. Imagine her going online, ten or fifteen years from now, and being able to read all the news reports.' She sniffed. 'I don't see how we can go for that option, when we have the chance to forget it ever happened.'

He nodded sadly. 'But can we forget?'

'We can try.'

For a minute or two there was a companionable silence. The real communication was in the physical connection, their fingers gently twisting together.

Harry sighed. 'I can't understand how they forced the lock without us hearing. To get upstairs and into our bedroom …'

'Because we're exhausted. Think how long it's been since we had a good night. When we do sleep it's probably much deeper than we realise.'

'Hmm. We'd better see about getting an alarm fitted.'

Alice agreed. Then she said, 'The threat that they're watching us, would it be a bluff? I mean, they got the wrong address, so what reason do they have to stick around?'

'They don't. Unless …'

'What?'

'Well, suppose they find this guy, Renshaw or whatever he's called, and to save his own skin he tells them what they want to hear – the way we might have done. He could claim that we *are* part of some conspiracy. That we *did* lie to them.'

Alice tightened her grip on his hand. 'I hadn't thought of that.'

'It's unlikely, but not impossible. Then again, they got the wrong house, so maybe they're not as smart as we think.' He mused on it. 'What could be in the parcel that's so important?'

'I don't want to speculate. Look, Evie's zonked out. We ought to try and sleep.'

'Okay. But are you sure about not calling the police?'

'Not really.' She shivered. 'I feel like I'm being a coward. But I just don't see what it would achieve. Do you?'

He half sat up, leaning over Evie to plant a kiss on Alice's forehead. She gave him a brief, taut smile in return. Harry switched off the bedside light and winced at how menacing the darkness now seemed.

Got to get used to it, he thought. But his hand slipped beneath his pillow, seeking the reassuring weight of the hammer.

*

He lay as still as possible, trying to clear his mind and focus on breathing slowly. It didn't work, of course. At best he was able to avoid fixating on the ordeal itself, but he couldn't drag himself away from other questions. *Why us? Why our address? Why tonight?*

He thought about the parcel, and the man they were hunting. How long had Renshaw eluded them, and where was he now? Harry found himself wondering if the man did, in some way, deserve what was coming, should his pursuers catch up with him.

Alice, in the quietest of whispers: 'You asleep?'

'Sparko. You?'

A well-worn joke; normally it prompted a smile, at least. Tonight all he got was a tired exhalation.

'You know,' she whispered, 'when Evie was born I felt almost overwhelmed by all the new terrors that seemed to accompany her into the world. That she'll catch an infection, some horrible disease that won't respond to treatment. That we'll drop her in the bath, or she'll poke her fingers into a plug socket. That somewhere out there is the person who one day is going to run her down as she's walking home from school on a winter's afternoon ...'

A pause to catch herself left an unearthly silence in the room; the only thing that moved was a tear, rolling down Harry's cheek.

'I worry that she'll have spots, like I did for a while, and be convinced that she's ugly. That she'll be bullied or excluded by the in-crowd, the bitchy girls. That she'll grow up to be too fat, or too thin, too tall or too short. Too clever by half or not clever enough. That boys won't fancy her – or that they will ...'

Another pause. Harry knew what was coming now, and he had to let her say it, no matter how much it hurt them both.

'But I *never* would have dreamt that at eight weeks old a man with a knife would hold her in his fist and threaten to cut—'

'It's okay. It's okay now.' He managed to reach over and hold her as she wept. Conscious of Evie between them, she barely made a sound.

When she'd recovered, she faced him and said, 'What if we look back on this one day and wish we'd done something differently? Rung the police, or gone after the van, or … or sold the house.'

'You want to sell the house?'

'No … I don't know. That's just it. I haven't got a clue.'

'There's no real answer, other than what you said earlier. Try to put it behind us. We go on with our lives and hope that, in time, the memories of it will fade.'

She knew Harry was right. Probably. Possibly. So Alice assured him that she was fine now, and it really was worth trying to get some rest.

Then she lay very still, and waited, and only when Harry was sound asleep did she ease Evie into her arms, kissing her cheek and delighting in the little squirm she got in response. She set her daughter down in the Moses basket and tucked her in, making slow shushing noises until she was satisfied that Evie was going to stay asleep.

Then she climbed back into bed and stared up at the ceiling and knew she would be counting the minutes till dawn. Plenty of time to re-live the terrors of the night, over and over again.

Plenty of time to wonder why she hadn't been entirely honest with her husband.

Plenty of time to wonder if she'd just made the worst mistake of her life.

SIX

Daylight. Too much of it for six thirty, even in mid-November.

Harry struggled awake as the memories came crashing back. He might have dismissed it as a morbid nightmare if his hand hadn't shifted on the mattress and struck solid metal. The claw hammer.

But they were all right. They were safe. Thank God.

He rolled over. Alice was sitting up in bed, feeding Evie. Her eyes were shut, and she was frowning so intently it was almost a snarl; far from her usual expression when breastfeeding.

He always found it a humbling experience to watch mother and baby locked together like this, though right now it just emphasised how superfluous he was. For nine months Alice had nurtured this baby inside her; now she was nourishing her child with a diet that only nature could provide, while Harry's own contribution to this miracle had begun and ended, nearly a year ago, with a tiny spurt of fluid.

He groaned quietly. 'What time is it?'

'Nearly half-seven.'

'*What?*' He'd overslept by an hour, which meant he would miss out on the best part of the day. It was after her morning feed that Evie was at her most receptive to the faces he pulled, and had lately begun to reward him with a smile or a phlegmy giggle.

Then again, shouldn't he be counting his blessings that they were here at all?

'She slept later than normal. And you were out cold.'

'Was I? Sorry.' He sat up and put his arm round Alice. When he kissed her cheek he thought she flinched slightly. 'Did you manage to sleep?'

'Not really, though I can't say I feel any more exhausted than usual.'

'Do you want me to stay home today?'

'You, throw a sickie?' She snorted. 'It's tempting. But it won't really help.'

'I can have Evie while you sleep. And there's the patio doors to sort out.'

'I've already texted Steve.' This was Alice's uncle, a self-employed joiner. 'He's coming round this morning.'

Talk about superfluous, Harry thought. 'What did you tell him?'

'Just that someone tried to break in, and because nothing was stolen we didn't bother to report it.' Her voice had taken on a chilly tone, as if she stood by the decision but disliked herself for doing so.

'Once we've had the doors repaired, we can't change our minds about the police,' he pointed out.

Alice nodded. If anything, she looked heartened by the thought. As if a new lock might be all they needed to make the whole thing go away.

Harry showered, then dressed in jeans and a thick winter shirt. It had been a day or two since he'd shaved, but his was an industry where the dress code wasn't so much smart casual as *casual* casual; facial hair had been almost *de rigueur* even before the dreaded rise of the hipster.

He trudged downstairs and made sure everything was as he'd left it. After opening the living room curtains he stared out at the street for a minute. There were no vans in sight. No pedestrians other

than a couple of dog walkers, a few teenagers dawdling to school.
What little sky he could see looked dull and heavy with cloud.

The cold light of day. Not that it helped him make sense of
what had happened last night.

He made coffee for them both. Evie had finished feeding,
so he coaxed the wind from her while Alice had a shower and
washed her hair.

'This is going to make you late,' she said as she returned,
wrapped in a towel. The hot water had restored some colour
and vitality to her skin, but she was still far from her normal self.

'Doesn't matter. I still feel I should stay here.'

'Better that we stick to our routine, if we're serious about
putting this behind us. Anyway, you're snowed under at the
moment.'

Harry couldn't deny that. He was still dealing with the backlog
that had built up during his paternity leave.

'You're sure you'll be okay here on your own?'

She nodded. 'I've got to be, haven't I?'

'So we're not going to the police? That's definite?'

'Definite.'

He asked her again, just before he left the house. Evie was sleeping
in the Moses basket, which he'd carried down to the living room.
Alice was eating toast and watching breakfast TV, gently scolding
the pompous presenter.

'"I *am* willing to interview you,"' she said, in an eerily accurate
impression of the man, '"so long as we're both clear that nothing
you've achieved in your life compares with my ability to get up
early and read from an autocue."'

Harry laughed. This was an encouraging sign, he thought: the
return of her sarcastic humour.

He kissed Evie one more time, then stepped into the embrace that Alice offered him. Only when she'd nestled her face against his chest did he speak.

'You're absolutely certain about this?'

'Harry, I spent all night going through our options. Imagine if we report it, and then the police catch them? I'm in the witness box, being cross-examined by some smartarse lawyer who says, "Can you be sure that this is the man who sucked milk from your breast, Mrs French?"'

He felt her shudder and said, 'No. Okay.'

'Even if they were convicted, how long would they be in prison? A couple of years at most. And they'd come out far more determined to get revenge on us than if we just … let it go.'

Harry nodded. It sounded like a pretty solid argument.

Alice said, 'So promise you won't change your mind and call the police without telling me.'

'I promise.'

'And you won't say a word to anyone at work?'

'No, of course not.'

She backed out of the embrace, one hand lingering against his cheek while she kissed him, then pushed him towards the front door.

'Off you go, then, breadwinner.'

Harry went, but it felt wrong. Before he reached the end of the street he'd looked round four or five times, studying the traffic, checking the house in case Alice had come to the door to call him back.

But if he stayed home today, he knew that going to work tomorrow would be just as difficult. Maybe Alice was right, and they had to put this behind them. It was certainly understandable that she would want to blot out the memory of such a hideous assault. Even so, a disquieting voice in his head went on muttering that silence wasn't necessarily the best option, and that they shouldn't be dealing with this alone.

It was a grey, oppressive November morning, not particularly cold, the air like a damp sponge. A stiff breeze carried the scent of the sea and a few spent fireworks, as well as an unseasonal but welcome aroma of freshly cut grass.

In Dyke Road the traffic was nose to tail in both directions. Harry could just make out the upper deck of a bus, up by the Booth Museum. He turned the other way, walking past the sixth-form college, BHASVIC, that he'd attended himself some fourteen or fifteen years ago. It was here that his talent for art and design had blossomed and been skilfully directed towards a future career.

At the age of thirty-two Harry was the co-owner of LiveFire, a design company that specialised in animation and visual effects for the film, TV and advertising industries. After six years of gathering experience in a range of roles – including a brief but invaluable spell at the legendary Industrial Light & Magic – Harry and a friend from university had set up their own business. They had quickly gained a reputation for stunningly innovative work, winning a BAFTA and two Visual Effects Society awards within the first three years.

Harry and his partner, Sam, now employed almost a dozen people, working out of offices on the second floor of a building in Middle Street, in the heart of what had once been the fishing village of Brighthelmstone.

Most days Harry either walked or cycled into town, but today there wasn't time. He liked to set an example by being in at eight, if not earlier, and until Evie's arrival he'd often worked till six or seven in the evening. Finding a way to compress his duties into a shorter working week was a challenge he hadn't yet been able to meet.

The simple fact was that Harry loved what he did. As a child he'd been addicted to drawing, spending whole days immersed in the world of his imagination. He'd dreamed of turning his hobby into a living, but had hardly dared believe it would come true on this scale.

Maybe that was the problem? He'd had far more than his fair share of good fortune, and last night was the payback.

At the bus stop he paid close attention to the people around him, and to the traffic crawling past. If the threat about watching them was real, wouldn't someone be following him now, to make sure he didn't go to the police?

Several people joined him at the stop. One or two sensed his scrutiny and met it with a frown or a glare. Harry was a tall, slender man with light brown hair, green eyes and an easy-going manner. Attracting any kind of hostility from strangers was completely alien, and made him see just how easily his suspicion could spill over into paranoia, even aggression.

When the bus arrived it was standing room only. Harry shuffled to the back, wondering if he'd recognise the men from last night. Probably not, unless he heard their voices. The well-spoken one had pronounced the street name, Lavinia, with a slight flourish on the *L*.

34 Lavinia Street.

And that was when the idea struck him. But there was nothing he could do until the bus reached the Clock Tower. This wasn't a conversation he could have in public.

He found a quiet spot on the steps up to the top floor of the Boots building. Alice answered on the first ring: 'What is it?'

'I was just mulling over our address, and whether, after they left us, they went in search of Lavinia Drive and Lavinia Crescent. And then it got me thinking: we're hoping it was a mistake, but what if it wasn't?'

'Harry, I can't see … I mean, it *has* to be a mistake.'

'From our point of view, yes. But what if that really was the address they were given?'

'Why?'

'I don't know. Maybe Renshaw was trying to throw them off the scent. Send them looking for him in the wrong place.'

There was a heavy silence. Harry felt a pang of self-disgust. Alice couldn't explain their predicament any better than he could. Why was he scaring her with this futile speculation?

'Sorry,' he said. 'That was silly. Forget it.'

'All right, but don't spend all day worrying about me. I'll be fine.'

Harry could hear the effort she was making to sound upbeat, so he agreed that he wouldn't. Then he told Alice that he loved her, said goodbye, and set his mind to the day's next test. Because now he had to stride into the office with a smile on his face and pretend that his world hadn't very nearly been torn apart.

SEVEN

The phone call was a terrible setback. Just when she'd convinced herself that sending Harry to work had been the right thing to do.

You can cope here on your own, Alice.

You are not *afraid.*

And then he'd broken the spell with that one suggestion: *Maybe Renshaw was trying to throw them off the scent.*

Alice had felt her throat closing up; for a few seconds she couldn't speak. Luckily Harry hadn't picked up on it. But after the call she collapsed on the sofa, dizzy with fury and shame.

How could she have been so stupid, not to have seen that possibility herself?

Evie slept until ten, a gift of freedom that Alice foolishly squandered; her mind was occupied by a fleeting encounter from two days previously: one she had thought nothing of at the time and now struggled to recall in any detail.

When her daughter woke, it came as a welcome distraction. They chatted together: a lot of meaningless burble that seemed to give them both great pleasure. Then a feed, a nappy change and burping – accompanied by a singalong to some cringeworthy kids' TV show with graphics that would make Harry weep. All the normal routines, but today they felt hollow.

Until a couple of months ago Alice had regarded herself as a career woman. She was a dental hygienist, self-employed and attached to three different practices in and around Brighton. Although she had dearly wanted children, she'd been certain that this career would remain of equal importance, and she would simply have to find a way to juggle both, the way most mums did.

Then Evie arrived, and Alice was almost scared by the extent to which she adapted to motherhood; how natural, how gratifying it felt. What that meant for the future, she had no idea. And it was still far too early to feel she knew what she was doing, of course – her own mother had virtually said as much, in the gloriously tactless tradition of a new grandparent. But that would come with practice, not to mention generous dollops of advice from the older generation (both of Evie's grannies had been an enormous help over the past few weeks, but at times they'd also driven Alice and Harry to distraction).

So what would Granny Barbara think now, Alice wondered, if she could see how her daughter jumped every time she heard footsteps on the pavement? A chair wedged under the patio doors like there was a siege in progress.

Face it head on, her mum would probably say. There aren't any monsters lurking out there, but you won't accept that until you prove it to yourself.

You have to go out.

She was all but decided when Evie intervened with a bowel movement that had somehow leaked from a brand new nappy. She had to be stripped, then dressed in a new outfit: bodysuit, tunic and leggings, plus a thick hooded pramsuit for venturing outside.

While changing her, Alice examined Evie's stomach. There was a very faint discolouration of the skin, but she detected no

tenderness resulting from last night's mistreatment. A miracle
escape, perhaps, though it did nothing to reduce Alice's burning
hatred of the men who had threatened them. She'd spent much
of the night crafting dreams of bloodthirsty vengeance – gouging
out their eyes, tearing off their balls – and she meant it, too.
Becoming a mother had changed her in many fundamental ways:
a willingness to maim or kill for the sake of her child being only
one of them.

Another twenty minutes slipped by before she was ready to
leave the house. Her final preparation was to check the street
from each of the bedroom windows. Mid-morning, there wasn't
a lot of activity. A van trundled past, but it bore the livery of a
local plumbing firm.

'It's safe,' Alice murmured to herself. 'Perfectly safe.'

Manoeuvring the flashy iCandy buggy through the narrow front
door was a pain. Sometimes the bumps and jolts made Evie cry,
but this morning she endured them with what seemed like an air of
benevolent curiosity, as if the discomfort was a price worth paying
to experience the rich sensory bombardment that was 'outside'.

Alice pushed the buggy along the street until she found a gap
between the parked cars. There was no traffic but still she paused
before crossing, her gaze drifting to the houses opposite as she
tried to place which one was likeliest.

No. Too dangerous.

She decided on a walk first. Once round the block: Port Hall
Road, right into Exeter Street, then Buxton Road and back to
Lavinia Street. It wasn't a bad day for a stroll, milder than she
expected, with the sort of blank white sky that brought to mind
a dust sheet – as if behind it the real sky was getting a fresh coat
of paint.

Today's dogshit count was disappointing: two fresh piles since yesterday morning's walk. Alice thought last night's torment might have given her a new perspective on such misdemeanours, but no: in AliceWorld there would be snipers on rooftops to counteract such disgusting anti-social behaviour. *Clean it up right now, buster, or we open fire …*

At the corner of Port Hall Road, Alice glanced back and noticed a man at the far end of her street. He had something in his hand – must be a phone. He lifted it, turning away from her as if uninterested, but it seemed a slightly calculated move. He was about the right size to be one of the men from last night. The one with the knife.

The one who'd threatened to slit my baby's throat.

Alice froze. She'd never make it back home before he intercepted her. She could run in the other direction, but to where?

Her legs felt weak. To stay upright she had to lean on the buggy, which threatened to tip backwards. She took a step towards the house on the corner and rested against the wall while she fought to rein in her panic.

A car drew up at the corner of Buxton Road. The man walked towards it and climbed in, never giving her a second glance.

You're a fool, Alice French.

There was an impatient cry from Evie. Alice set off again, peering into every parked car, every doorway. By the time she'd completed the circuit she was convinced it had been nothing more than her overcharged imagination.

Halfway along the street she stopped. Home was just across the road. She moved to the front of the buggy and knelt down, pretending to adjust Evie's blanket while casting her mind back to Tuesday morning.

41? 43? 45? What did she think?

43, she decided, was the most likely address.

Her heart was thumping madly. She took hold of the buggy and began pushing it towards the house, a couple of doors along. It felt unreal, as though she was floating. Was she really going to do this?

Number 43 had little to distinguish itself from any other home in the street. A narrow three-bedroom Victorian terraced house with the front door on the right-hand side and bay windows top and bottom on the left. White stucco on the wall, overdue a fresh coat of paint. Net curtains in the lower bay, and thick curtains drawn upstairs. No lights on, as far as she could tell.

The short path was paved rather than tiled. A single step led up to the front door, which sat in a shallow recess. The door was solid timber, painted dark grey and in better condition than the rest of the property. A tiny letterbox sat neatly in the centre.

After scanning the street again, she stepped on to the path, pulling the buggy behind her. She rang the doorbell and waited, her breath coming in quick gasps.

There was no hint of movement within the house, so she knocked on the door. The sound echoed along the street and seemed to broadcast her presence to the world. But still no one answered. The net curtains didn't twitch.

She checked the street, then rang the bell and knocked again. With every second the urge to flee was growing stronger.

Maybe this wasn't the house. Although Alice knew most of the local residents on a nodding acquaintance at least, she couldn't say with any certainty who lived where.

She wasn't sure what made her do it, but some reckless impulse sent her next door to number 45. She knocked and almost immediately heard footsteps. Now it came to her, who might live here. The ageing hippy.

Sure enough, the man who opened the door was in his early sixties, tall and thin, with long wispy grey hair and white stubble on his chin. Moist brown eyes, bisected by a pair of half-moon glasses. He wore yellow chinos and a pale blue collarless shirt. He was barefoot.

'Hi!' She gave him a bright smile. 'It's, er, Maurice, isn't it?'

'Lawrence,' he corrected her. 'Lawrence Wright.'

'Yes, er, sorry to bother you. I just wondered if you know anything about the people next door?'

'Next door?' His voice was crisp and considered. 'What's the problem?'

'No problem. Is it empty, do you know?'

'I believe so. Occasionally there's a noise, but that could be attributed to vibrations from the next house along.' He tutted. 'The perils of terraced accommodation.'

'Yes, exactly.' She was grinning like an imbecile. 'Well, it was just me being nosy. Sorry to have bothered you.'

She retreated, cringing at the way he was appraising her. His cheek bulged as he worked his tongue thoughtfully in the corner of his mouth.

'Do you like wine?'

'I – yes, well, I drink enough of it!' She heard herself laugh and thought: *oh, good grief!* Thankfully Evie chose that moment to issue a little yelp. 'Must get going, sorry.'

'I make my own, you see. Why not pop over one afternoon for a glass or two? Tuesdays or Fridays are best for me.'

'I'll, um, have to check my diary. But thanks.' She moved away, leaning over the buggy as if Evie was demanding her attention. She'd gone a few paces before she realised she was heading in the wrong direction. And now there was a van turning into the street. It accelerated towards her, flashing its lights a couple of times.

Alice froze. Should she run back to Lawrence Wright and plead for help?

The van was slowing as it closed in. A plump hand emerged from the driver's window to gesture at her. Alice looked carefully and experienced a relief so profound, it rivalled the moment when the midwife confirmed that her newborn baby was intact and in perfect health.

It was Uncle Steve, riding to the rescue.

EIGHT

The offices of LiveFire were comprised of four rooms, one of which housed a studio for stop-motion animation that also doubled as a screening room. As the business expanded, Harry and Sam had ended up squeezed into a single office, with the other kept for meetings. The remaining area formed an open-plan workspace. At any one time there were several people out with clients or working elsewhere, so they just about managed to cope with the space available.

Harry was extremely glad that Sam was starting the day at an advertising agency in London, pitching for some work on a series of phone commercials. Had they been together in such close proximity, Harry would have found it impossible to conceal his anxiety.

He knew he looked pale and wrung-out, his eyes bloodshot, his hands trembling. Then again, since returning to work as a new father it had become a running joke that he was now a crumbling ruin of a man, so his current state didn't arouse any undue curiosity. Another saving grace was that deadlines were approaching on a couple of major projects, so no one had time for long conversations. After a quick tour of the desks Harry was able to retreat to his office for some much-needed solitude.

He'd feared that last night's ordeal would prove too much of a distraction, but once he'd got the Maya software running he was soon immersed in another world. He'd been sent a basic storyboard for a big sci-fi movie and asked to create a digital animation to accompany the key set-piece scenes. As Harry understood it, the picture was assured of a green light, but not at the budget the producers wanted. Harry's task was to wow the studio executives into pledging more cash.

He had intended to call Alice around ten o'clock, but became so engrossed that when he finally broke away from the screen he discovered it was gone eleven.

'Sorry,' he said when she answered. 'Really didn't think I'd get caught up in work.'

'That's a good thing. Anyway, Steve's here, so I'll talk to you later.'

She'd ended the call before he could say goodbye. Harry stared at the phone for a moment, trying not to read too much into her abruptness. It was a standing joke among their friends that he and Alice had a relationship that was, if anything, *too* harmonious. Harry didn't think that was true – friends didn't always get to see the little everyday squabbles and disputes – but he would happily concede that the bedrock of their marriage was their friendship: something that he believed would endure even if they were not together as partners. But now he was left with a disturbing sense that this event could turn them into strangers, forced to rebuild their relationship from the ground up, one brick at a time.

And who was to say they'd fit together so perfectly the second time around?

Alice had crossed the road without looking back at either number 43 or 45. Once Steve had parked, she greeted him warmly and led him indoors, all the while making light of the attempted break-in.

'Harry heard them, thank God. He switched the lights on and went downstairs, and by then they'd gone. Probably just kids.'

Steve took Evie and wandered into the living room. Alice was filling the kettle when he returned, frowning.

'I was expecting to find some yobbo had kicked the door in, but this is pretty clean. They forced the lock without damaging the surround.'

'That's good, then. Easier to repair?'

'It is. But I don't think kids would have done that. Looks more like a professional job.'

Alice forced a laugh. 'Are you trying to scare me?'

'Sorry, love. I just thought you'd have called the cops.'

'What's the point? It's not like we can tell them anything.'

'I suppose not.' Still troubled, he scratched his head. 'I'll have a cuppa, then pop out and get you a new lock. Wickes all right for you?'

'Yes, I assume so.'

With a sly grin, he said, 'I mean, round here you're probably no one unless you've got the latest designer fittings …'

'Very funny. For that you're only getting one sugar.'

They were chatting over tea and biscuits when Harry rang. Alice kept the conversation brief, not wanting Steve to pick up on any tension. Afterwards she announced that Evie was due her lunch. Steve looked blank for a second, then went slightly red.

'Got you. I'll make myself scarce.'

He was gone for about twenty minutes, returning while she was in the middle of a feed. Breaking off to let him in, she carried Evie into the kitchen so that Steve could work undisturbed. It was as she transferred the baby to her other arm that Alice made sense of her vague reluctance to continue.

So far today she'd only fed Evie from her right breast. She didn't want to use her left: the one that had been mauled last night. Just the memory of that man's filthy mouth caused waves of nausea.

But she couldn't let it haunt her. The build-up of milk would quickly become uncomfortable – and Evie certainly wasn't going to differentiate. To her, food was food.

She steeled herself to get on with it, staring fixedly out of the window until her mind went blank. When it was done, she carried the baby into the living room and set her down on the change mat. Steve had needed to make a few minor alterations to the door frame, enlarging the cavity to accommodate a sturdier lock, so the room was filled with the sweet aroma of wood shavings.

'I love that smell,' Alice said. 'But I'm about to ruin it. Evie's got a full nappy.'

'Aw.' Steve pinched his nose in mock disgust. 'I'm almost glad mine have grown up.'

'If it doesn't put you off too much, you're welcome to stay for lunch. Pasta salad …'

'Sounds a bit too healthy for me.'

'I can do garlic bread with it?'

'Deal.'

In a clean nappy, Evie sat in Alice's arms, watching Steve with the same look of wonderment that greeted almost every sight that was placed before her.

'Can't imagine what it's like, can you?' Steve said ruefully. 'Seeing the world through her eyes, everything so new and exciting.'

Alice nodded but had to suppress a shudder, thinking of what Evie had witnessed last night. She hesitated, then said, 'After lunch, would you watch Evie for me while I pop along to see a neighbour?'

She thought she'd sounded perfectly casual, but Steve was studying her carefully.

'Sure. But I hope nothing's wrong, is it?'

Alice considered laughing off his concern, but wasn't sure if she could make it sound convincing. Instead she went for the sombre approach, slowly shaking her head.

'Everything's fine, honestly. You don't need to worry about us.'

Harry lost track of time again, until he registered movement in the main office and realised that people were heading out to lunch. He wasn't intending to take a break himself, but by half twelve his stomach was rumbling. He decided that a sandwich and a short walk would do him good.

He hurried out, offering a quick nod to a couple of colleagues on their way back in. Crossing the road, he set off towards Duke Street, the air ringing with the joyous clamour of children at Middle Street Primary. He was hardly able to credit that in just a few years Evie would be running around a similar playground, already living her own life, away from her parents' protection—

At the corner of Dukes Lane he stopped abruptly. Something had spooked him: he could feel the hairs standing up on the back of his neck.

A lot of people were streaming past, paying him no attention. The slow-moving traffic included a couple of vans, but none that resembled the vehicle he'd seen last night. He was about to dismiss his reaction when he noticed a woman in a beige raincoat wandering towards him, a mobile phone at her ear.

He heard her say, quietly but clearly: 'Stay there a second.' Although she wasn't looking in his direction, Harry had the bizarre feeling that the words were intended for him.

She was in her forties, he guessed, slim and well-groomed, wearing jeans and leather boots. Long dark hair spilled over the collar of her coat, but something about it didn't look quite right. She drifted closer, still apparently focused on her phone conversation, and said, 'Two men broke into your house last night.'

As Harry's mouth dropped open, she hissed: 'Ignore me. Look away.' Her accent was difficult to place – northern, possibly, but it also had a vaguely mid-Atlantic tone.

She continued past him, then paused as if distracted by the call. Harry realised he had to do something, so he wandered towards a clothes store in Dukes Lane and pretended to gaze at the window display. With so many pedestrians passing by, the woman made it look like a natural choice to move clear of the stream, easing into a space close to the shop. Turning side on to him, she spoke rapidly.

'Before we talk I've gotta be sure it's safe. Take a walk through the Lanes towards the Old Steine, then double back through the bus station and cross the coast road.'

'I'm not—'

'Uh uh, don't argue. You need to vary your pace, okay? Dawdle, then speed up. I'll meet you by the aquarium, on the boardwalk outside the Harvester pub. Now go.' Then she laughed, and in a much lighter tone she said: 'Good idea, Bob! But I don't see it happening this year …'

As her voice faded, Harry turned and watched her heading towards West Street. For a moment he was so confused that he wanted to run after her and demand an explanation.

Then her message hit home. He strode off in the opposite direction. He had no idea who she was or whether he could trust her, and yet he'd already decided to follow her instructions.

She knew about last night. That was enough to capture his attention.

She knew.

NINE

The questions began to mount up as Harry threaded through the narrow pedestrian streets and twittens, which despite the profusion of high-end boutiques still retained a medieval feel. Although visitor numbers tended to dwindle during the autumn, the Lanes were always busy in the middle of the day, making it impossible for Harry to move quickly or smoothly. Where he saw a gap he dashed forward; at other times he let himself get snarled up in the crowds.

When he reached East Street he was able to accelerate, although once or twice he ducked into shop doorways, glancing back to see if anyone had changed direction or tried to dodge out of sight. It made him want to laugh, almost. How had his life turned into a corny spy movie?

He wondered if he should let Alice know where he was going, but got stuck on his motive for doing so. If he truly feared being lured into a trap, he shouldn't be meeting this woman at all. Phoning Alice now would only alarm her for no good purpose.

Besides, the suggested rendezvous point was every bit as public as Middle Street, and the vibe he'd got from the woman hadn't been threatening. He concluded that the risk was worth taking, if there was a chance she could shed some light on what had happened.

A few doubts surfaced as he entered the canyon-like space of the bus station at Pool Valley. Apart from a couple of long-distance coaches parked in their bays, there was hardly any sign of life. The area had a desolate, slightly threatening feel. Litter swirled around his feet as he quickened his pace, suddenly fearful of an ambush. Two men in chef's whites were smoking outside the back door of a restaurant; staring at Harry as if they knew something he didn't.

Just paranoia, of course. He cut through to the seafront and used the crossing by the Royal Albion Hotel. Tourists were milling around the entrance to the pier, eating fish and chips and candyfloss and even ice cream. The air reeked of vinegar and made his stomach lurch.

Up ahead, the Brighton wheel was turning against the murky sky. Most of its pods were empty: not much to see up there today. Harry crossed the road, scanning the pavement in front of the Sea Life Centre. Further along, a coach party had just disembarked, the crowd swarming in his direction. He darted in front of them and was climbing the steps to the terrace when someone whistled quietly and said, 'You're clear.'

The woman was right behind him.

Clare McIntosh at number 48 was one of Alice's closest friends in the street. Clare was in her late fifties, a former civil servant who now worked part time in one of Brighton's many small theatres. She'd also founded a book group, the Lavinia Luvvies, which was attended by more than a dozen women in the Port Hall area, and had another half dozen angling to join. Widowed and childless, she'd been a resident here for nearly thirty years, and as such she was a goldmine of information.

Alice couldn't recall which days her friend worked, but she was in luck. Clare answered the door within a few seconds – though not before Alice had spotted Lawrence Wright peeking at her from his bedroom window. She pretended not to notice.

Clare was dressed in tatty jeans and an old painting smock, and minus her usual beads and bangles. She had a scarf tied around her hair, and dabs of what looked like white emulsion on her cheek and forehead.

'Alice! How lovely to see you. Where's the little one?'

'My uncle's babysitting. Look, if you're busy …'

'Oh, no. Glad of a break. I'm just tackling the bedroom ceiling.' She wiped the back of her hand across her face, leaving another smear of paint. 'Come in, come in.'

Alice followed the other woman into the kitchen. The house was identical in size to her own, but made cramped by the profusion of books and pottery, glassware, clocks and tapestries – not to mention the shelves and cabinets required to store them.

'Forgive the chaos.' Clare scrubbed her hands, then moved a stack of newly washed clothes from one of the kitchen chairs. 'Drink?'

'I'm fine. Can't stay long.' Aware that she was probably blushing, Alice came straight to the point. 'I'm curious about some of the other residents along here.'

'Oh, yes? And you thought: who better to ask than the nosiest old bat in Lavinia Street?'

Alice had no choice but to grin. 'Something like that.'

Harry was astonished by the way the woman had just appeared. 'You can't have followed me.'

'I'm good at this. I have to be.' She offered her hand. 'Ruth Monroe.' And when Harry had introduced himself, she nodded towards Madeira Drive. 'Let's walk.'

'No, hold on. How do you know about last night?'

She took a few steps, saw he wasn't following and muttered: 'I'll do my best to explain. Come on.'

As they set off along the pavement he was able to give her a quick appraisal. She was four or five inches shorter than him, maybe five seven, allowing for the low heel on her boots. Her coat and jeans were good quality but anonymous. She wore a plain gold band on her wedding finger, but no other jewellery that he could see. Again that long, glossy hair caught his attention.

'So you knew about the break-in, and did nothing to stop it?'

'Not really. I saw them going into the alley along the back. It was too dangerous to follow, so I couldn't tell exactly where they were heading. Approximately thirty minutes later I saw them leaving your house—'

'What?' He was breathless with shock. 'They were in my home for *half an hour?*'

'Twenty-eight minutes, to be precise.' She registered his astonishment with a raised eyebrow. 'If they woke you, it was because they wanted you awake.'

Harry couldn't speak. Bad enough that the intruders had materialised in his bedroom, but to think of them prowling through the house for all that time. What if he or Alice had got up and blundered into one of them on the landing?

'I know how traumatic this must be—' Ruth began, but Harry was jumping ahead of her.

'Do you know where they went? Did you get the van's number? Where are they now?'

She raised a hand. The nails were short, painted a dark purple. 'I didn't follow them. My priority was to see what had happened to the occupants of the house. I half expected the police to show up. When they didn't, I considered calling them myself.'

'Why didn't you?'

'Lights going on told me someone was alive. No police or ambulances meant no casualties.'

'No cas—' His voice was thick with indignation. 'They terrorised us. Threatened to cut our baby's throat.'

Ruth gave a matter-of-fact shrug. 'You might not think so, but you got off lightly.'

Alice hid her interest in number 43 by beginning with a question about Lawrence Wright.

'He's something of an acquired taste – as is his homemade wine,' said Clare, with a dry chuckle. 'He was a teacher, retired early for medical reasons. Possibly a breakdown, though don't quote me. Quite highly strung, and he can bore for England. Still, I'd run him close on that score.'

'Don't be silly. What about next door to him?'

'The Walkers? She's a snotty mare, which is why I haven't let her join the book group. And hubby's a bit of an arse, too. Works for one of those cable TV channels that endlessly regurgitate the dross of yesteryear, but to hear him pontificating you'd think he was Lew Grade.'

'Who?'

A wince. 'Oh, you're cruel. Am I really that ancient?'

'Of course not. Actually, I meant the other side. Number 43.'

Frowning, Clare said, '43? That belongs to Mrs Beckerman. She must be, ooh, ninety-something by now.'

'Is she a recluse?'

'Oh, she doesn't live there. She emigrated to Israel at least fifteen years ago. Kept the house as an investment, I believe. It's been rented out several times, but not recently. Certainly not since you and Harry joined our little community.'

'So it's empty? Or perhaps someone lives there who wants to keep a low profile?'

Clare pursed her lips. 'Not impossible, I suppose. Why?'

'I thought I might have seen someone, that's all.' As Alice stood up, she realised she was anxiously twisting her wedding ring and had to make a conscious effort to relax. 'I'd better get back.'

'You've intrigued me now. Could be squatters, I suppose.'

'Squatters! I hadn't thought of that.'

'It's not always the orgy of destruction that the media claim. I did it myself when I was eighteen or nineteen.' Clare smiled at the memory. 'Shacked up with a beautiful boy and his friends in a townhouse in Richmond. We actually took great care of the property. In fact, I painted *that* bedroom ceiling as well ...'

Her reminiscences followed Alice along the hall; before letting her go she secured a promise that next time Alice would bring Evie for a visit.

'And I shall keep an eye on that house,' Clare told her. 'I do like a good mystery.'

Alice grinned and nodded, but in her heart she couldn't agree. Mysteries had their place, but what she needed was a solution.

TEN

You got off lightly. The words, delivered in such an offhand tone, had him reeling.

They set off along Madeira Drive in the direction of the marina, passing an array of small businesses housed within the colonnaded walkway: cafes, galleries and gift shops, some of them already shuttered for the winter. From the mess of anxiety and confusion that currently passed for his brain, Harry plucked his next question.

'How did you find out where I work?'

'I followed you this morning, and got on the bus at the stop before yours.'

'What, you camped outside my house all night?'

'No. From about six thirty.'

'Who are you? Or what, I mean? A cop? A private detective.'

She flapped her hand, as if the answer wasn't important. 'Close enough.'

'Which one?'

'Either. Both.' She turned away and marched across the road. There were fewer people on this side, and the pavement was wider, divided into lanes for pedestrians and cyclists. The wind buffeted them as they walked towards the old Volks railway line and the beach beyond. The rhythmic crash of the waves against the shore managed to sound both violent and strangely soothing.

Ruth leaned on the railings and gazed straight ahead, ignoring Harry's scrutiny as he tried to decide whether her presence was harmful or benign. He stuck with his initial assessment of her age: early or mid-forties. She had a striking, photogenic face with high cheekbones and clear blue eyes, and a dimple on her chin. Her skin was pale, with fine smile lines around her eyes and at the corners of her mouth. Her lips were full and very symmetrical, with what he decided was a sardonic edge to them. And then there was the oddity of her hair.

'Are you wearing a wig?'

Sounding mildly hurt, she said, 'I think it looks very realistic.'

'It does. But the colour isn't quite right for the tone of your skin. And there's something about the shape – the way it sits against your temple isn't completely natural.'

'You sound like an expert.'

'I work in visual effects. Hair and fur are some of the trickiest things to animate. Every single strand has its own weight and shape, its own way of catching the light as it moves.'

She nodded. 'But it's good enough to fool a casual observer?'

'Absolutely. I'm just curious to know why you're wearing a disguise.'

'Isn't that obvious? These are very dangerous people.'

Harry wasn't about to dispute that. Her next question was whether they'd taken anything.

'Not as far as we could tell,' he said.

'They woke you, though, so they must have wanted something. What was it?'

Harry opened his mouth, then hesitated, turning away from her. The sea today was the rich green of a weathered copper roof; green and churning, its white peaks spitting up to taunt the darting gulls.

'I get it, Harry. You're not sure if you can trust me. Well, you should know that I'm equally wary of you.'

The comment startled him. 'What?'

'I didn't actually *see* a break-in. For all I know, you could be in league with them.'

'You seriously think …?' he spluttered, and went to add: 'You approached me—'

She shook her head. 'My point is, there's an element of risk here, on both our parts. I need to know what happened. Are you gonna tell me, or not?'

Harry fumed for a second before relenting.

'They were looking for a man called Renshaw, also known as Grainger or Miller.' He studied her closely as he said the names, but she gave nothing away. 'Do you know who he is?'

'I take it you don't?'

'Never heard of him.'

'But they expected to find him at your house?'

Harry nodded. 'It's a mistake. We've been there nearly two years. He wasn't the previous owner, either.'

'So how did they come by your address?'

'No idea. They said something about a parcel.'

A spark of interest in her eyes. 'Go on.'

'They said we'd been sent a parcel – for Renshaw, I mean, although it was addressed to Grainger.' He sighed. 'This is like trying to describe a dream. It had a kind of logic at the time, but now it makes no sense at all.'

Ruth shrugged. 'So you denied knowing anything. What happened then?'

'They kept insisting the parcel had been sent to us.'

'And had it?'

'No.' He said it too loudly, attracting the attention of an elderly couple walking past. After waiting a second, he hissed, 'No, of course not.'

'But you say they were certain about it. Maybe they sent the parcel?'

'Why would they do that?'

'If they're searching for Renshaw, it could have been a way to flush him out.'

'But I just told you, Renshaw doesn't live at our address. He never has.'

'Did they say what was in the parcel?'

'No. And we weren't about to ask.'

It was a curt response, and Ruth chose that moment to push off from the railings and start back towards the pier. Assuming he must have offended her, Harry said, 'Hey, how about answering some of my questions?'

'Not yet. Mine are more important.' The brusque tone was tempered by a playful smile. She waited till he was alongside her, and said, 'Is there any chance that you had something through the post? A failed delivery, maybe, where they leave one of those notes?'

'I doubt it. The baby's only a few weeks old, so Alice – my wife – is at home virtually all day.'

'And was she just as sure about it? No deliveries at all?'

'Yes. No.' In trying to answer both questions, Harry sounded muddled. He recalled the moment clearly: how Alice had flinched, because the man with the knife had been moving in on Evie.

'No parcel, no failed delivery,' he said. 'It was a mistake. As well as Lavinia Street, there's a Lavinia Drive and Lavinia Crescent in Brighton.'

'And you told them that?'

He nodded. 'It occurred to me afterwards, perhaps they went there, too?'

'I'll check it out.'

'If you know who these men are, isn't it your duty to report this?'

She turned towards him, one eyebrow sceptically arched. 'You had the opportunity to call 999 last night, yet you didn't. Why was that?'

Harry swallowed. 'Because they threatened us. They said our baby's life was at stake if we went to the police. Rightly or wrongly, we decided to take that threat seriously.'

'Probably a good decision, then. The authorities wouldn't have been much help.'

'Why not?'

A dismissive gesture. He was about to protest when his phone buzzed. Thinking of Alice, he quickly checked it and found he had three texts from Sam, the last of which said: *Where r u, mate!? Transat meeting at 2!*

Harry swore under his breath. Ruth was studying her own phone, as if to make the point that he wasn't the only one in demand.

'I have to go,' he said. 'But I can't leave it like this. At least tell me who those men were.'

At first she seemed to ignore him, stepping back to avoid a group of bored-looking teenagers on a school trip.

'All I can say is that they're career criminals, and they're every bit as unpleasant as your experience would suggest.'

'And Renshaw?'

'The obvious conclusion is that he crossed them in some way. Or he's got something they want.'

'Right.' Harry felt a peculiar sense of relief. None of this was good news, but at least the bigger picture was slowly being revealed.

They reached the wheel. Ruth started moving towards the crossing by the aquarium. There was no farewell, no glance back to see if he was following.

'Hold on,' he called. 'Are we going to meet up again?'

'Depends what happens next.'

'Hopefully nothing, from our point of view.'

She gave him a quick, bitter smile. 'In that case, you won't need to contact me. But I can leave you a number, in case they come back.'

He was horrified. 'Do you think they will?'

'Unlikely, but you can't rule it out. Especially if they believe you kept something from them.'

'We didn't.'

'Good. Let's hope you convinced them of that.'

ELEVEN

She read out her mobile number. Harry keyed it into his phone and confirmed it with a text. Then Ruth crossed the road and was soon lost from sight in a crowd at the gates to the aquarium. Harry was reluctant to see her go: there was so much more he needed to know. But he was late for an important meeting.

He ran most of the way back to the office, arriving breathless and perspiring heavily. He longed to clean up but there was no time even for a quick detour to the gents. In the meeting room Sam was already running through the introductions.

Their project manager and a couple of lead animators were sitting along one side of the table, facing a large interactive whiteboard and several monitors used for video conferencing. The screens showed two men and a woman sitting inside another meeting room, this one in Los Angeles. All three were suited and serious and perfectly still: a modern art installation entitled *Time is Money*.

Sam disguised his genuine relief by beating his chest in mock relief. 'Phew! And here, by the skin of his teeth, is my partner, Mr Harry French.'

As Harry entered the range of the camera on the table, one of the Americans nodded and said, 'Glad you could make it, Harry.'

Out of view, Sam was mouthing a question: '*Where the fuck were you?*'

'Sorry about that.' Harry settled into his seat, then realised his notes were still on his desk. He'd have to wing it. Difficult enough at the best of times, but right now, with his thoughts in turmoil ...

But he had no choice. So he smiled broadly, rubbing his hands together to communicate his eagerness to begin, and said, 'Guys, hello! I can't tell you how excited we are to have the chance to pitch for this. We're convinced that LiveFire have exactly the right qualities to make this project a success ...'

And after the meeting, once he and Sam were back in their office, came the tense exchange that Harry both expected and thoroughly deserved: 'Jesus, H. If there's one thing we've learned it's that you do not keep the money men waiting.'

'I know. I was only thirty seconds late.'

'And what about a chance to touch base before we went in? You were the one that kept reminding me to get back from London in good time.'

'It totally slipped my mind. I'm sorry.'

'Your brain's turned to scrambled egg lately. Puts me right off having sprogs, if this is what it does to you.'

Harry grinned. 'When Pete wanted to discuss adoption, you said you'd rather share the house with a boa constrictor.'

'I think it was a python.' Sam snorted, looking Harry in the eye. 'Seriously, mate, are you all right? Because you look like shit warmed up.'

Harry had to bite his lower lip, resisting a powerful desire to tell him everything. 'Just knackered.'

'You came back too soon. You're not ready to be doing four-teen-, fifteen-hour days again.' Sam scooped up his cigarettes and lighter. 'Why don't you get off home?'

'Yeah, I might, in a bit.'

He called Alice the moment Sam had left the office. She had good news: the patio doors had been repaired, with a stronger lock than before. Her uncle had also recommended a firm who could fit a burglar alarm.

'Great,' Harry said. 'And are you feeling okay?'

'Yes. Fine.' Which, from her tone, meant: *not really*.

'I'll be home soon. I'm finishing early.'

'Oh?' His wife's laughter was refreshingly normal. 'I'll believe that when I see it.'

'Well, I might just surprise you for once.'

'Lucky me.'

But the positive attitude he'd adopted for Alice's sake didn't last long. As he tried to write up some notes on the meeting, the doubts and fears came flooding back. They should have called the police. They'd been fools to be intimidated by threats. Going it alone meant they had no protection whatsoever – and what was it Ruth had said? *You got off lightly.*

He shivered. Tonight he would have to barricade the house again, and still he doubted that he'd feel safe enough to sleep. Perhaps he and Alice would have to take it in turns to sit up, keeping watch, the way people had in more primitive times.

And then what? If they made it through tonight, what about tomorrow? And the night after that?

He was out of the building by ten past four. He thought about letting Alice know, then decided it would be nicer just to appear. He caught a 27 bus in North Street and took a window seat. Normally he loved the slow fading light of late autumn: soft and silvery grey; no glare, no shadow. On camera he would add a blueish tint, perfect for romantic cityscapes—

His phone rang. It was Ruth Monroe.

'I've ruled out those other addresses. Lavinia Drive only goes up to 28, and 34 Lavinia Crescent is a dry cleaners. No living accommodation.'

'Okay. Is that good or bad, do you think?'

'From your point of view? I don't know. But I'd urge you to stay on your guard.'

Sound advice, probably, but it made him feel despondent as he walked down the hill from Dyke Road. He turned into Lavinia Street and surveyed the rows of tidy charming homes, rendered in various shades of white and cream and beige, and nothing about the area seemed charming or homely any more. It was now an alley with death traps on either side, each blank pane of glass concealing a possible threat to his family.

Only the prospect of seeing Evie could lift his spirits. He was suddenly desperate to hold her in his arms. He let himself in, calling out to Alice, and immediately heard movement from the living room; an odd sense of a conversation stifled in mid-flow.

Then Alice appeared, scowling furiously. Harry's first thought was: *Someone saw me with Ruth Monroe* …

'You're home early!' Her voice, bright and cheerful, was in stark contrast to her expression. She stepped into the hall, one foot hooked around the door to pull it closed behind her, and hissed: 'The police have just turned up.'

Harry froze in the act of removing his jacket. '*What?*'

'Did you call them?'

'No. We agreed that we wouldn't.'

'Well, they're here. So somebody's told them.'

Harry knew that tone of barely concealed hostility: he'd heard it quite a lot over the past few weeks, as their tempers were frayed by lack of sleep. He resented the fact that she didn't believe him, but before he could say another word the living room door was pulled open by a thickset man in a grey suit. He was in his thirties, with dark curly hair and a blotchy complexion. He flashed a warrant card at Harry.

'DI Dean Warley. You're Mr French?'

As Harry nodded, Alice said, 'They just got here, so it's quite handy you're home.'

'Knocked off early?' the detective asked, but Harry still hadn't found his voice.

'It's a rare treat, believe me,' Alice said on his behalf.

DI Warley backed into the living room, allowing Alice and Harry to follow. Evie was on her playmat, cheerfully kicking and waving. A young woman was kneeling beside her. She wore a blue suit, and shoes with stiletto heels that jabbed into the sofa as she leaned over and cooed at the baby. Warley introduced her as DC Cassell.

'Sian,' the woman said. She was pale and thin, almost malnourished. She had long red hair pulled back in a ponytail. Her features were sharp and severe, and seemed designed to portray hostility.

Harry remained standing, as did DI Warley, while Alice took a seat close to Cassell. It was Warley who spoke first.

'We were just asking your wife what she could tell us about the men who broke in last night. Very little, it appears?'

'I'm afraid so. They wore masks and gloves.' Harry turned to Alice. 'Did you mention their feet?'

'What? Oh, no.'

Harry explained: 'They'd tied plastic bags over their boots. I assume it's so they didn't leave any trace evidence.'

'Could be.' The detective looked faintly amused. 'Sounds very thorough. What about their voices? Would you recognise either of them, if you heard them again?'

Harry was deliberating when Alice said, '*Yes.*' It was so vehement that they all looked in her direction. 'When somebody puts a knife to your baby's throat and says he'll drain the blood out of her, you don't tend to forget it.'

Warley sucked his teeth, as if affected by this show of emotion. He wandered across the room, peering at a couple of family portraits on the wall, eased past the dining table and came to a stop by the patio doors.

'And this is where they got in?'

Harry nodded, and Alice said, 'We thought it best to fix it quickly. My uncle replaced the lock this morning.'

'That was handy.' DC Cassell grinned, and after a second so did Alice, but rather uncertainly. She glanced at Harry and her expression changed. It was like watching a cloud passing over the sun.

Almost to herself, she said, 'How did—?'

TWELVE

She broke off mid-sentence. Harry saw the panic in her eyes and guessed what it was. If the detectives had only just arrived, Alice wouldn't have had time to describe the break-in.

So how could they know this was the point of entry?

Harry saved her with a question of his own, phrased in the same way. 'How did you hear about this? We didn't report it.'

DC Cassell, who seemed just as eager to dismiss the awkward hesitation, said, 'We're acting on information received from, uh, a confidential source ...'

A sharp look at DI Warley, who nodded. 'This is part of a wider investigation.'

'Into what?' Harry asked.

'I'm afraid we're not able to say.'

Harry pretended to look annoyed. He sat down next to Alice, his mind working frantically to get a grip on this situation. The crucial thing to avoid was the sort of accusation that Alice's question had nearly provoked.

You're not detectives.

It would be so easy to say. So easy to demand a closer look at their warrant cards, and call the local police station to verify them.

And then what?

The woman, Cassell, was kneeling beside Evie. One wrong word and she could snatch their daughter into her grasp, just as the man with the knife had done last night.

Harry nudged against Alice, his hand finding hers and squeezing it. He was praying that she too understood the danger they were in.

DI Warley wandered towards them. Maybe it was just Harry's imagination, but he thought the so-called detective looked more tense than before; aggressive, almost. Without being invited, he grabbed a dining chair and swung it round so that he could sit facing them.

'Now,' he said, 'we know they didn't come here to rob you. We think they're searching for a man by the name of Renshaw.'

Harry knew they had to go on acting naturally, so he nodded.

'They said he's also known as Grainger, or Miller. But we don't know any of those names.'

'Who is he?' Alice asked.

'An associate of theirs. That's really all I can tell you.'

Harry sensed Alice was going to speak again. He squeezed her hand, but of course she wasn't to know what he meant by it.

'So he's a criminal as well?' she asked. 'Does that mean you're trying to find him?'

Warley nodded. 'For his sake, it's vital that we get to him before they do.'

The woman turned her gaze upon Alice. 'If you know where he is, if you have any information at all …'

'We don't,' said Harry. 'We've been here nearly two years. Before that it was a widow, Mrs Stevens. Renshaw's never lived here, or had any connection to this address.'

'So why did they think he had?' Cassell asked. She was still staring hard at Alice, and so was Warley. Harry remembered what Ruth had said: it's unlikely that they'll return, but you can't rule it out.

Especially if they believe you kept something from them.

*

Alice knew she had to answer the question, but it felt like her throat was slowly filling with sand. She was trying to work out how Warley could have known about the patio doors. Her first thought was that he had spotted Steve's handiwork – and perhaps there was still a lingering smell of sawdust in the air – but as she'd gone to ask him the other possibility had suddenly occurred to her.

These people were imposters.

Then Harry had changed the subject, and now he was squeezing her hand, a gesture of support but also, she realised, as a warning. Once again he came to her rescue, answering the query that had been directed at her.

'Because of the parcel. They seemed to think we'd had a parcel, addressed to Renshaw.'

Grainger, Alice wanted to correct him, until she realised that Harry's error might be deliberate. He was testing them.

'And had you?' Cassell asked.

'No, absolutely not,' Harry snapped.

Warley bowed his head, examining his shoes for a second. They were dirty and scuffed, Alice noticed, whereas the suit was brand new. It looked cheap, didn't fit him very well. Had it been bought in a hurry, to enable him to play this role?

He looked up. 'Why don't you take us through it, from the moment you first became aware they were in the house? Tell us everything you can remember.'

Harry did most of the talking, and quickly saw how this irritated them. There were frequent suspicious glances at Alice, as if they felt she might know more than Harry did. Or maybe they viewed her as the weaker link.

The detectives were particularly interested in the parcel, though to an extent they tried to disguise that fact. Lots of unrelated questions were thrown in, but by paying attention to their body language Harry could see how they relaxed slightly, then grew more alert whenever they returned to the key issues.

He gave them an accurate account of what had happened, mindful that everything he told them might later be compared with the report from last night's intruders. He maintained that he and Alice knew nothing about any parcel. The whole thing was a dreadful mistake: nothing more.

When Harry described in detail how the man with the knife had assaulted his wife and child, Alice's face flushed and she began to weep quietly. Harry felt horribly callous for thinking it, but he knew her reaction didn't harm their case at all. Warley and Cassell listened impassively, though the woman was a bit twitchy, and once or twice seemed to be suppressing a smirk.

After a few minutes Evie began to get restless. There was a tense moment when Alice went to rise from the sofa and Cassell blocked her path.

'I can take her.'

'No!' Alice almost shrieked the word as she squeezed past the other woman. 'She's due a feed.'

Warley looked as though he might object when Alice made to leave the room, but Harry caught Cassell signalling at him not to intervene.

Feeling slightly bereft once she and Evie were gone, Harry answered their questions for another ten minutes, emphasising that they had taken seriously the threat not to report the break-in to the police.

'That's understandable,' Warley said. 'As I say, we're coming at this from a different angle.'

Finally, with a neutral glance at his colleague, he slapped his hands on his legs and declared that they were done. Harry jumped up, unable to disguise his eagerness to see them leave.

He opened the front door and shivered at the rush of cold evening air.

'Will we have to make formal statements?'

Warley shrugged. 'We'll be in touch if we need anything else.'

'And you'll let us know if there are any developments?'

An eyebrow went up. 'Developments?'

'If you manage to catch these men.'

'Oh.' Warley had the ghost of a smile on his face. 'Certainly will.'

'We won't let this drop,' Cassell added. 'You can be sure of that.'

THIRTEEN

Harry locked and bolted the door, rested his head against it and slowly exhaled. He was dimly aware of a car starting up, and knew he should be checking the make and model, perhaps taking the number if he could get it. But he lacked the will to move.

Worse than that, he didn't see what it would achieve.

He turned as Alice emerged from the kitchen with Evie at her breast. She'd stopped crying but her face was still raw with emotion.

'You hadn't mentioned the patio doors, had you?' he asked.

'No. I suppose he might have noticed it was a new lock?'

'More likely they were fake, which is why I didn't push them for a contact number.' Harry gave a sigh, before clutching at the only thread of optimism in sight. 'At least we didn't let on that we suspected them. And we were honest about what happened, so there's no reason for them to doubt us.'

'So why were they glaring at me as though they knew it was a pack of lies?'

'I don't think they did.' He held her by the arms and could feel her trembling. He'd expected to come home and sit calmly while he told her about the mysterious woman who'd approached him. Now he was only going to add to her misery—

'I'm sorry.' Alice sniffed, and with a free hand brushed at a stray tear. 'It wasn't intentional, Harry, but I haven't been straight with you.'

'What?'

'I … I think there *was* a parcel for Renshaw.'

Harry stepped away from her, unable to believe what he was hearing. And then he remembered.

'Last night, I felt you jump when they first mentioned it.'

'Did I? I'm not sure. I was so petrified.'

'Jesus, Alice. If they'd realised you were lying, they could have killed us.'

'I know. Please don't say that.' She held his gaze, pleading with him. 'Everything happened so quickly, it wasn't really a conscious decision.'

'So where is this parcel?'

She shook her head. Evie had finished feeding. 'Let's go and sit down.'

First, Harry decided that he needed a drink. And not beer or wine, either. He rummaged in the kitchen cupboard where they kept the spirits and found a bottle of vodka. Alice was persuaded to join him – 'A very small one' – and took her glass in exchange for Evie and a muslin cloth to drape over his shoulder: Harry was on burping duty.

Settling on the sofa, she took a sip of vodka and briefly wrinkled her nose, like a child forced to eat some exotic fruit.

'Tuesday morning, the postman knocked because of a package that was too big for the letterbox. There was some other post as well. I took it and shut the door, and then someone else knocked, literally a few seconds later.'

'Okay.' Harry could feel his heart pounding. He thought of Ruth pressing him: *No deliveries at all?* And that produced another jolt.

Who was Ruth, really?

Alice went on: 'It was a man of about sixty, sixty-five. Not exactly like the description we got last night. He was plump rather than fat, nearly bald – just that kind of white fuzz – and he had a thick grey beard.'

'Was he Middle Eastern?'

She shrugged. 'I suppose he had a slight accent. He told me his name, but I honestly can't remember what it was. All I know is that it matched what was on the envelope. He said something about his sister-in-law – he'd spoken to her that morning and found she'd got her numbers mixed up.'

Harry couldn't help snorting. 'Right.'

She glowered. 'I had no reason to be suspicious.'

'But didn't you ask him to prove his identity?'

'Why? If the parcel was addressed to Grainger, or whatever it was, and he said his name was Grainger, what reason would I have to question it?'

Harry conceded the point. 'Sorry.'

'It's not like we don't get the wrong mail from time to time. If he hadn't knocked I've have scribbled, "Not known at this address" and stuck it in a post box.'

'Did you see where he went?'

'I think he crossed the road, but I didn't stay and watch. Evie needed changing. I shut the door and never gave it another thought.'

Harry took a gulp of vodka, already aware that one glass wouldn't be enough.

'He said the numbers got mixed up? We're 34. Does that mean he lives at number 43?'

'Possibly.' Alice hesitated. 'I had a word with Clare McIntosh today. I didn't say anything about the break-in – just had a general chat about neighbours. 43 is owned by a woman who emigrated years ago. Clare says it's been rented out in the past, but she thinks it's empty at the moment.'

Harry pulled a face. 'Can't say I've ever seen anyone coming or going.'

'Me neither. But now it's got me wondering if he's in there. Hiding.'

Harry mulled it over while automatically rocking Evie in his arms. He glanced down and found she was asleep.

'Her routine's in chaos,' Alice said. 'We'll pay for that tonight.'

'Can't be helped.' Harry set Evie down in the Moses basket, then refilled his glass and sat beside Alice. She had barely touched her vodka, having vowed to drink sparingly while breastfeeding.

'I'm sorry.' Tentatively, she placed a hand on his knee. 'Last night I just froze. But even if I'd told them, it wouldn't have been enough to stop them hurting us – or worse.'

'Maybe not. Or maybe they'd have gone storming over to number 43.'

Alice shivered. 'After what you said this morning, I've been wondering if Renshaw did it deliberately. Arranging to have the parcel sent here, knowing he could collect it and keep his own address a secret.'

Harry had to think about that for a moment. He felt sick. And a little angry, too, if he was honest. But he had no right to be: would he really have acted any differently, in the circumstances?

'There's another reason I didn't tell you,' Alice said quietly. 'It occurred to me during the night that we were more convincing – or you were, I mean. Because you didn't know about a parcel.'

'Maybe.' He frowned. 'You're saying you were going to keep it secret, in case they came back?'

She gestured weakly at him, as if exhausted by this conversation. 'Well, didn't you think they might? Isn't that why you kept asking if I'd be all right here today?'

'I suppose. So what's in this parcel, do you reckon?'

She shrugged. 'It was just an ordinary padded envelope. A bit bigger than A4, quite thick and heavy. But it felt like paper inside, rather than something solid. Quite … supple.'

'Like money? Bundles of money?'

'Could be. Which means he must have an accomplice somewhere.'

'And you think he gave this accomplice our address, as a kind of drop-off point?'

'The timing has to mean something. To knock at the door within seconds of the delivery, he must have been watching for it. And you can see our front door from the windows at number 43.'

Harry leaned forward, wearily rubbing his eyes. 'All we've just done is make a series of logical deductions. And if we can do that, so can they. Sending the fake cops – if that's what they were – was a pretty astute way to verify what we said last night.'

'Thank God we kept our story consistent,' Alice said, with a heartfelt sigh. 'Hopefully this might now be the end of it.'

'Unless they reach the same conclusion we just did – that Renshaw used us. Used our address, anyway. That means he's got to be hiding close by, in which case the smart thing for them to do would be to hang around for a while, until he resurfaces.'

'If Renshaw's got his parcel he's probably miles away by now.'

'Hmm. But the men chasing him won't know that for sure. They might go on searching for weeks. Or watching *us* for weeks.' He thought about Cassell's parting comment, which now seemed loaded with menace: *We won't let this drop. You can be sure of that.*

There was a burbling moan from Evie: waking far too soon from her nap. Alice frowned but Harry, as usual, welcomed any opportunity to spend time with his daughter. He lifted her to eye level and rubbed noses; Evie responded with a sound halfway between a cough and a giggle. Her eyes shone with such delight, such overwhelming love and trust that Harry was in no doubt about how she felt.

As far as their baby was concerned, he and Alice were the entire world; the universe itself.

But would that be enough to protect her?

Both of them seemed glad to take a break from the conversation. Harry carried Evie upstairs and ran her a bath, while Alice took care of some chores. But even with Evie in a happy splashy mood, Harry was too preoccupied to fully enjoy the time with her.

If the cops were fake, then what about Ruth Monroe? Had her approach been yet another attempt to worm information out of him? Reflecting on it now, he saw how she had remorselessly pumped him for information while revealing practically nothing about herself.

There was one positive aspect, of course, and ironically it was thanks to Alice. If she *had* told him about the parcel any sooner, he might have mentioned it to Ruth.

But was she one of the gang? Harry didn't want to think so. He regarded himself as having pretty good instincts about people, and she hadn't triggered anything like the same unease that he'd felt when he was talking to Warley and Cassell.

He decided to contact her tomorrow and suggest another meeting. If she was working with the fake cops she'd be expecting Harry to get in touch. But this time, if he played it skilfully enough, he might be able to tease a little more out of her.

And then, when he came home tomorrow, he would tell Alice all about it. He didn't want to add to her fears right now. Better to wait until he had a clearer idea whose side Ruth was on.

FOURTEEN

First, the phone call. It was not a success.

The voice in her ear was young and sweet and warm as honey. 'This is Keri. What can I do for you?'

'Keri, please don't hang up—'

'Who's …?' Then a snarl, her voice unrecognisable from seconds before. 'Leave me the fuck alone!'

'I can't. I need to see you.'

'You must be joking, psycho bitch.'

'Keri, listen, I don't care about you and—'

'*Just leave me alone!* Fuck off and die, will you?'

The line went dead. Ruth dropped the phone on the bed, the air suddenly warmer, the four walls close and stifling. She had to get out.

No destination in mind. No purpose other than to lose herself in the only way she knew how.

Her knowledge of Brighton was limited to a handful of day-trips and a couple of hours' internet research. She headed east, only because she knew that to the west lay Hove, with its genteel reputation. She wanted anything but genteel.

She followed the upper pavement of what quickly became a two-tier coastal road. Eleven p.m. and there were cars and buses thundering past; to avoid the noise and fumes she took some steps to the lower road, Madeira Drive, and found that a terrace ran between the two levels. There were benches at regular intervals and she sat for a while and studied the view, the Brighton wheel and the pier both dressed in gaudy lights, reflected on the water in shining dabs of colour.

From this vantage point the historic Volks railway seemed both cute and slightly ridiculous, given that it seemed to run for about the length of a bowling alley. Beyond the tracks, vague shadows flitted over the beach. It was a mild, cloudy night, no moon or stars, but the wind was light, and above the crunch of stones and the wash of the sea Ruth made out the occasional moans of pleasure and pain. Life in the raw, here on the beach in the dark: drinking, swearing, shooting up, dancing and fighting and fucking. None of it meant anything to her and none of it ever would; not while she could whisper his name and hear nothing in reply.

Would you be here, on this beach?

She listened, watched, staring straight ahead, her peripheral vision alert.

Waiting, waiting …

Edging towards midnight, when predators come a prowling.

Oh, yes please.

But, tonight, nothing.

FIFTEEN

Harry was sound asleep until someone grabbed him. His precautions had failed; the intruders were back in the house and it was too late—

No. It was Alice whispering his name. He rolled towards her, listening hard for other sounds or movement.

'What woke us?' he asked.

'Me, I think.' She was barely audible, but he could feel the puff of her breath on his skin as she talked. 'I had a nightmare. The whole thing again. They question us. This time I admit to the delivery.'

'That's just because—'

'No, Harry. Listen. I tell them, thinking it'll make them go away, but it doesn't. The one with the gun stays here and the other goes to find Renshaw.'

Harry moved back so he could see her face. A warm, soft glow from the nightlight she'd insisted on using tonight; enough to make out the tears glistening in her eyes.

'He's gone for what feels like hours. When he comes back he says there's no sign of Renshaw, so he … he …'

'It's just a dream. Don't torture yourself.'

'They kill Evie. Right in front of our eyes, Harry. They murder our little girl, and there's nothing we can do to stop them.'

She refused to be consoled. Harry was almost grateful when Evie cried out.

'I'll see to her,' he said. 'You get back to sleep.'

It was twenty past three; about the same time they'd been woken the night before. Maybe a cuddle and a bit of rocking would be enough to get her back off.

He peered into the Moses basket and saw Evie's face light up, arms and legs thrashing with excitement. He could almost read her mind: *Hey, Dad! Thought we could hang out for a while, burp and burble some of the night away: you're cool with that, aren't you?*

He returned her smile. 'Nothing I'd rather be doing, kiddo.'

He took her downstairs, where he had to move the ironing board to get into the kitchen. He switched on the light, checked the window was intact, then prepared a bottle of formula milk that they'd agreed to use in emergencies or at times of exhaustion. Harry felt it was the least he could do, given how guilty he was feeling.

He had passed a long, tense evening without mentioning Ruth Monroe. Having begun to doubt the wisdom of his decision to say nothing, he realised that he'd already delayed too long. Telling Alice now wouldn't just freak her out: it might cause her to question his motives for holding back in the first place.

It got him thinking about timing, and chance, and how the significance of those small, often innocuous decisions never became clear until you looked back and saw how your life had been nudged, irrevocably, in one direction or another, for better or worse.

The way they'd met was a perfect example. Harry had been twenty-one, in his second year of a fine art degree at Central Saint Martins, while Alice, a year younger, was studying dental hygiene at Barts. Sadie, a fellow student of Harry's who prided herself on her matchmaking abilities, happened to land a part-time job in the cafe where Alice worked at weekends. She decided to connect them after discovering that they both came from Brighton and shared a love of the Channel 4 sitcoms *Spaced* and *Peep Show*, and a violent aversion to TV talent shows.

The venue was a birthday party at an enormous but dilapidated rental property in Dalston, occupied by some thirty undergraduates from universities across London. When Sadie warned him that she was running late, Harry nearly bailed out – he had a painting to finish. But he'd wandered in on his own and immediately hit it off with a cute, dark-haired girl who he mistakenly believed was the friend that Sadie wanted him to meet. The fact that the girl, Mia, had so readily given Harry her phone number was something Alice still ribbed him about, eleven years later.

The close call had been discussed on their first proper date, and Alice had brought up the film *Sliding Doors*, where the life of a character played by Gwyneth Paltrow divides into two parallel realities. 'Imagine if that had happened to you: one where you stayed all loved up with Mia, and one where Sadie barges in, punches her in the face and steers you off in my direction.'

'It wasn't quite like that. And multiple universes may well exist, but if we can only see the one we're in, it's a moot point.'

'You don't think you missed out on a perfect life with Mia?'

'Not really. She'd never heard of Nick Frost.'

'So you weren't even slightly tempted to call her?' At this juncture Alice liked to tut, as if Harry were a hopeless innocent. 'You could have got laid that night, instead of waiting ... ooh, what was it, *weeks* of agonising abstinence before I—'

'Eleven days, three hours and six minutes.'

Fortunately it seemed to delight her that Harry remembered precisely how long it took for them to tumble into bed. But it was true that on the night of the party Mia had been far more interested in him than Alice.

Harry, naturally, had been drawn to the girl who played it cool, and made him work for the reward of her interest. Alice was smart, and funny, and came across as unusually comfortable in her own skin. And yet it had bothered him ever since, these jokes about *Sliding Doors* and alternate realities. He didn't see any reason why she should feel insecure about the choice he'd made, and yet the doubts were there – and now motherhood appeared to have pushed them closer to the surface once again. So any mention of Ruth Monroe had to be handled very delicately …

After taking a few ounces of milk, Evie's eyelids grew heavy. She began to wriggle, slapping her hands against the bottle in frustration.

'I feel for you,' Harry murmured. 'Stay awake and go hungry, or feed and be sent to sleep. It's a tough dilemma.'

She struggled for another ounce before surrendering. When Harry carried her back upstairs, a couple of treads creaked. He wondered how the men last night had managed to move so stealthily through the house. And where were they now?

Did Ruth know?

Was she part of the gang?

He'd have to try and find that out once and for all. And then he would come clean to Alice.

He settled Evie in her crib and climbed into bed. He was just getting comfortable when Alice spoke.

'I keep asking myself: why us?'

'There's no answer to that. Lots of bad things happen to people who don't deserve it.'

'I'm so scared, Harry. I don't see how we can ever be safe now. Whether we go to the police or not, it makes no difference. Whatever we do, we're at their mercy. Because we obey the rules, and we're up against people who don't.'

'I won't let them hurt you or Evie. I promise you that.'

Alice moved closer and caressed his cheek. 'Thank you,' she said. Then, as she turned away, he thought he heard her whisper, 'But you can't.'

Harry lay awake, pondering that, for a long time. She wasn't taunting him, wasn't trying to hurt his feelings: she was simply stating a fact. No matter what assurances he gave, it wasn't within his power to prevent them from coming to harm.

We obey the rules, and we're up against people who don't.

He tuned in to Evie's steady breathing, and thought about Alice's eloquent description of the terrors that accompany your firstborn into the world. He considered what it meant to have something so precious that it was worth more than his own life. From that came a profound anger and determination. His promise to Alice had been sincere, and he intended to keep it.

Whatever it was they tried next, Harry would be ready for it. And he would fight back.

SIXTEEN

On Friday morning Harry left the house with two questions uppermost in his mind. Would Ruth Monroe be following him again – and could he trust her?

The weather was unexpectedly glorious for November: mild and still, the sunlight diffused by a gauze of morning mist. Harry took a bus to Queens Road, then strolled down the hill to Middle Street. He saw no sign of anyone watching him.

He made the call as he walked. Ruth answered on the fourth ring, her voice thick with sleep.

'What's happened?'

'Probably nothing, but I'd prefer to discuss it in person.'

'Yeah, okay.' A groan; the creak of bedsprings. 'Give me twenty minutes.'

'I've got to work this morning. How about lunchtime?'

'Can it wait till then?'

'Yes, I think so. Same place as before, at twelve o'clock?'

'No. Let's meet on the lower esplanade, near the Pump Room cafe. Make sure you use the same evasion techniques as yesterday.'

'Is that really necessary?' The scornful tone was deliberate. He figured that if Ruth was part of the gang, she'd be less inclined to persist with this rigmarole.

'If you don't do it, I won't be there to meet you,' she said, and rang off.

*

Sam was at his desk when Harry got in, a half-empty jug of coffee on a hotplate beside him. He was wearing his Harman Kardon noise-cancelling headphones: a sure sign that he needed to work without being disturbed. A quick nod and a smile, then he was back to his screen. That was fine with Harry.

After clearing his emails and dealing with some of the usual administrative crap, he tried to focus on his storyboard project. During the night he'd thought up a couple of great sequences, but now he struggled to see what had made them so special.

He felt exhausted. He hadn't slept more than an hour at a time, and by six a.m. he'd been back downstairs, roaming the house to check it was secure, then drifting and dozing on the sofa until he heard movement in the bedroom.

After making tea for Alice, he'd sat on the bed while she fed Evie. Alice hadn't slept well, either, so they were both a bit grumpy and uncommunicative. Only when it was time for him to leave for work did the barriers come down. They shared a long embrace, and then a kiss that became a little more than a gesture of farewell.

'Mmm,' Alice had said. 'This is a bad time to feel horny.'

'So when's a good time any more?'

'Ah, come on.' She gave him a playful swipe. 'Tomorrow morning, if Evie permits?'

'Evie never permits. She's got a built-in nookie detector. A sibling preventer.'

Alice laughed. 'Okay. Then we'll see if one of the grannies will have her for a bit.'

Harry was sceptical: on the only occasion they'd tried it, his mother had phoned in a panic after less than an hour, his dad trying gamely to sing a lullaby in the background while Evie bawled her little lungs out.

'It must eventually get easier.' Alice ran her hand over his buttocks. 'One way or another, we're due for a bit of fun this weekend.'

'Deal.' Solemn again, he said, 'I'm still not sure I should be leaving you ...'

'It's *fine*.' What followed was a rerun of yesterday's debate about the wisdom and practicality of Harry neglecting his work to look after his family. Making light of what she called her 'night terrors', Alice insisted that she really didn't need him cluttering up the house.

'All right,' he agreed ruefully. 'But keep the doors locked and bolted. If anyone comes round, call the police.'

She looked amused. 'And say what? "Hello, yes, our lives were threatened two days ago. We couldn't be arsed to report it at the time, but we'd still like you to take it seriously, please."'

'It's not like that—'

'It *is* like that, Harry.' She shrugged. 'That was the choice we made. For better or worse, we're on our own now.'

Well, maybe they were and maybe they weren't. Hopefully Harry would find out soon whether Ruth Monroe could be trusted. And then, tonight, he'd face the awkward task of explaining her involvement to Alice ...

At ten o'clock he had a meeting with three of the animators to review progress on a commission from an ad agency on behalf of a major car manufacturer. It was a sign of how bad Harry looked that his team expressed sympathy for once, rather than just teasing him for his lack of sleep. He felt like a rat, going along with their assumption that Evie was to blame.

The brief called for a volcanic eruption, and Harry came up with some suggestions to improve the flow and thickness of the lava; some tweaking to the play of light which should make the stream appear hotter and more viscous. Other than that, it looked good to go.

Back at his desk, he thought about calling Alice but decided it might unnerve her if he showed too much concern. He settled for a quick text: *Everything ok? xx*

She replied immediately: *Fine x*

He could almost picture her irritation that he was fussing. That shouldn't stop him from phoning later, though. After his meeting with Ruth.

It wouldn't have made any difference if they *had* spoken. It wouldn't have altered how things turned out. But Harry would come to despise himself for that decision all the same.

SEVENTEEN

Alice was beginning to question whether she was losing her mind. Three times she found herself at the bedroom window, with no recollection of the thought processes that had led her there. Was this how she was cursed to spend her days? A curtain-twitcher, compelled to waste every free moment observing what had once been her lovely, ordinary street?

Evie certainly wasn't impressed: she kicked and squealed in her mother's arms, and fought against sleep. It left Alice feeling even more exhausted, and doubtful of her abilities as a mother.

She held the baby at eye level and spoke quietly but firmly, Evie gazing at her with a sense that she knew this was important.

'Listen, my darling. If I was as tired as you are – which I am – and someone was offering me the chance to sleep, I would bite their bloody hand off. So why stay awake, baby? Why do you do this to me?'

Evie smacked her lips together, as if formulating a reply; then she made a cooing noise and solemnly expelled a bubble from her mouth. Alice burst out laughing.

'You win me over. You always find a way to win me over.'

Finally, Evie slept. Alice tidied up, then made tea and was carrying it through to the living room when the phone rang. Not Harry, but Uncle Steve, wanting to make sure she was all right.

'You've not seen any sign of the scrotes that did it?'

'No. Harry didn't get much sleep last night, listening out for them, but we're good, thanks.'

By the time she rang off she was back at the window, but her view of number 43 was obscured by parked cars. It would be better upstairs …

She was thwarted by a cry from the Moses basket next to the sofa. Alice managed a few gulps of tea and a single chocolate digestive before the cries grew too heart-rending to ignore. She put a hand over her mouth, stifling the response that had popped into her head: *Give me five minutes, can't you?*

It was stress, of course, brought on by the events of the other night, as well as the wearying grind of coping with a new baby. And Evie was overjoyed to see her, kicking and waving with an enthusiasm that shamed Alice to her core.

Catching a familiar whiff, she checked Evie's nappy and pulled a face. 'Let's clean you up, then maybe we'll lie on the bed and play, shall we?'

Not just an excuse to go upstairs, she told herself. Besides, the Metanium ointment was in the bathroom.

First a quick look out of the bedroom window. Nothing different about number 43 today, although she was in time to see Lawrence Wright emerge from his home and make for a Toyota Yaris parked a little further along the road.

Her phone buzzed: a text from Harry. She replied, feeling slightly disappointed that he hadn't bothered to call, even though she knew how engrossed he became. *You were the one who persuaded him to go to work in the first place, remember.*

Crouching by the bed, she removed Evie's leggings, undid her bodysuit and opened the nappy. 'Ugh, baby. You've put me off refried beans for life!'

Her tone prompted Evie to smile, as though accepting a fine compliment. Over the sound of her own voice, and some distant drilling that had been intermittently disturbing her all morning, Alice heard the familiar rattle of the letterbox, the soft thud of post hitting the mat.

She grabbed the wet wipes and started cleaning Evie at twice the normal speed. Her heart was thumping like mad; she realised she was steeling herself for a knock on the door.

Don't be silly. Lightning doesn't strike twice.

With Evie in a clean nappy, Alice washed her hands and then checked the window again. A blue Peugeot estate drove past from left to right. The driver didn't so much as glance in her direction, but she had a vague impression that she'd seen him before. Could he have been the man at the end of the street yesterday morning?

At number 39 the window cleaner was using a telescopic pole to reach the upper windows. He was a plump Latvian man who worked with his son, the pair of them gently bickering the whole time. From Port Hall Road she could hear builders at work: the boom and clang of rubble being tossed into a skip. Overhead the bloody seagulls were swooping and squawking, and there were distant screams of laughter from the playground at Stanford Infant school.

And cutting through all these distractions, a soft voice in her head: *Go and see what it is …*

Evie was probably safe enough on the bed, but Alice had heard too many horror stories about babies coming to grief when left for only a few seconds. She carried her downstairs, pausing at the bottom to scoop up the post.

Four items. She wasn't able to examine them until she was sitting on the sofa with Evie propped up on her lap.

Two white A5 window envelopes, one addressed to her, the other to Harry: financial stuff. An insulting item of junk mail from their internet provider, offering new subscribers a far better deal than Alice and Harry were getting. Finally, a small padded envelope, which contained something tiny and rectangular, but fairly rigid. Plastic rather than metal, she thought.

She turned the package over. The address was handwritten, in shaky capital letters, and the sight of it made her cry out. Her heart raced as she stared at the words in front of her.

Mr E Grainger, 34 Lavinia Street, Brighton BN1 5PD.

EIGHTEEN

Harry felt even more self-conscious than he had yesterday, weaving through the city streets on the way to his rendezvous with Ruth. Was she following him again?

As he'd got up to leave the office, Sam had slipped off his headphones and apologised for being so uncommunicative. Did Harry fancy a quick drink?

'Can't, sorry. Got some errands to run.'

'Shame. You look dead on your feet, mate.'

That morbid phrase seemed about right, Harry thought. Still, it felt good to be outside. The morning mist had dissolved and the city was bathed in bright autumn sunshine. There was a bracing chill to the air that tasted sweet in his mouth.

Having taken a detour along Russell Road, behind the Brighton Centre, he crossed the seafront road at the lights by the Hilton Metropole hotel and took the east ramp to the lower esplanade. The west ramp was closed while construction work continued on the city's new tourist attraction, the i360. The five-hundred-foot tower had been assembled during the summer and now loomed over the entire city; with its glass passenger pod not yet attached, Harry thought the sleek silver tube had a slightly malevolent presence. Dubbed the 'iSore' by critics, it had been likened to a gigantic chimney, or a missile, while Sam had joked it was only right that Brighton and Hove could boast of the tallest erection on the South Coast.

Harry was passing the volleyball court when he heard a whistle, and Ruth materialised alongside him. Today her hair was dark blonde, shoulder length, and she was wearing sunglasses and a black leather jacket.

'New look?' he commented.

'I try to vary my appearance. You never know who might be watching.'

'You honestly think that?'

'Yes, I do. Why?'

'This subterfuge; I can't help wondering if it's a bluff.'

She turned to study his face. 'What's happened?'

'Nothing.'

'Oh? Because the tension's coming off you like steam from a kettle.'

Unwilling to speak, he skirted around the volleyball court. There were too many people outside the Pump Room to have a conversation like this. He walked briskly, but Ruth had little difficulty in matching his pace.

'Let me guess,' she said. 'After giving it some thought, you're not sure if you can trust me.'

'Would you blame me if I don't?'

'Not really. Especially after I warned you that they might come back.'

Her words hung in the air. Before Harry was completely sure that he should confide in her, he found himself saying: 'I think they *have* come back.'

Harry headed for the beach and Ruth followed without protest. The crunch of their feet on shingle sounded like the cascade of coins from a slot machine. Fifty yards to their right, a few tourists were taking photographs of the i360, as well as the sad, skeletal remains of the West Pier, but the rest of the beach was deserted.

Stopping on a ridge overlooking the shoreline, he said, 'We had a visit last night. A man and a woman, claiming to be police officers.'

'And you don't think they were genuine?'

'One of them held out what appeared to be a warrant card, but I was too shocked to look at it properly.' He described the conversation they'd had; the possible slip-up over the point of entry. 'We didn't let on that we suspected them. It seemed safer not to say anything.'

'Did they tell you which station they were from? Were you given a card or a reference number?'

'No. Nothing like that.'

'Then I think you're right to be worried, Harry.' Her cool gaze skewered him with its perception. 'And now you're thinking that maybe I'm a phony, too?'

Harry didn't flinch in his answer: 'Well, are you?'

For a long moment there was no reaction. Then she shook her head. He caught a gleam of amusement in her eyes; perhaps even a little admiration.

'No, Harry. This is not another ruse to get information from you. But since I can't prove a negative, you'll either have to trust me or walk away.'

With a sigh, Harry stuffed his hands into his pockets and faced the sea. A few streaks of cloud drifted along the horizon like smoke from a distant war zone.

He heard Ruth moving, thought for a second she was abandoning him, but after inspecting the ridge for damp, she chose a patch of dryish stones and sat down.

'Were there any discrepancies between what you said during the break-in and what you told these visitors last night?'

'I don't think so, no.'

'And you didn't mention me?'

'Absolutely not.'

'What about your wife? Did she give anything away?'

'No, she—' Harry stopped, but it was too late. 'Alice doesn't know about you yet. I held off because I wanted to meet up today and …' He opened his hands and let them slap against his sides.

'Makes sense,' Ruth agreed. 'It would be one hell of a deception to send me in like this, but not impossible. Except they didn't, okay? I don't work for them.'

'So I trust you or walk away?' he said.

'That's about it. Your call, Harry.'

He couldn't walk away; not with that nagging voice saying it was a mistake to go it alone. If there was any chance at all that Ruth could help, Harry had to take the risk. Besides, he could also play it cagey: he didn't have to tell her about Alice receiving the parcel.

He sat down, and Ruth produced a small notebook and pen.

'Give me the names of those cops. I can get them checked out.'

'So you *are* a police officer? Or you were?'

All he got was a shrug. 'Names?'

'Uh, DI Warley. Dean. And the woman was … Sian. Sian Cassell.'

Ruth seemed to react to the name *Sian*. She asked him to describe them both.

'He was in his mid-thirties, about five ten, not fat but solid. Dark curly hair. Bad skin, with a lot of acne scars.'

'Accent?'

'South East. A deeper voice than the man on Wednesday. The woman was thirtyish, painfully thin with a narrow face, and sort of pinched features. Long red hair, pulled back in a Croydon facelift.' He cracked a smile but Ruth ignored the reference. 'Do you know who she is?'

'I think so. There's a Sian who's part of this organisation.'

Harry deflated at the news. He realised he'd been clinging to the hope that they were genuine detectives.

'And what kind of organisation is it, exactly? I know they're criminals, but what do they do?'

Ruth let out a long sigh, which seemed to signal that she had made a decision.

'It starts with an old-time villain called Kenny Vaughan. A serious face in his day. Armed robberies in the 1970s, then drugs in the eighties and nineties. A gang like Vaughan's is hard to bring down. The main men keep a safe distance from any incriminating activity. But one day Kenny let his temper get the better of him. He suspected one of his subordinates of cheating him, and beat the man to death with a crowbar, in a warehouse containing a shipment of heroin with a street value of forty million pounds. Unfortunately for him, the police had the warehouse under surveillance at the time.'

Harry whistled. 'I can't believe I didn't hear about this.'

'It was a while back. 2002. The first trial collapsed amid allegations of jury tampering, but Vaughan was finally sentenced to thirty years. Most of his key people went down with him. The gang collapsed, and rival operators moved in to carve up the territory for themselves.'

Harry was puzzled. 'So how does this relate to us?'

'Three men were absent when the police raid took place. A violent enforcer, Niall Foster, his sidekick, Darrell Bridge, and a young man called Nathan Laird. Nathan was just beginning a partnership with Vaughan, part of a plan to diversify, steering the business away from the high-risk area of drugs into something nearly as lucrative, but a lot safer.'

'Like what?'

Ruth shook her head: he was interrupting her flow. 'Once Vaughan was in custody, the other three melted away. Laird's whereabouts are still unknown, but Foster and Bridge re-surfaced a while back, along with another man, Mark Vickery. Vickery's also white-collar, a crooked accountant. He wasn't involved in the original set-up with Vaughan, but he does have a close connection to Nathan Laird. The two of them were childhood buddies.'

'So you think Laird is involved with these other three?'

'I'm certain of it. Foster and Bridge are a couple of Rottweilers, and Vickery doesn't have the power or charisma to keep them in check. More likely he's fronting for Laird.'

'Doing what?'

'I'm still trying to get to the bottom of that. There seem to be plenty of legitimate – or semi-legitimate – businesses. Bars, nightclubs, a hotel. Along with that, I think it's probably the same operation that Nathan embarked on back when he first started working with Kenny Vaughan. Prostitution. The flesh trade.'

There was a brief, sombre silence. Harry still wasn't sure whether to mention the parcel. First he wanted to know how this connected to him.

Ruth explained: 'The men I tracked to Brighton on Wednesday night were Foster and Bridge, along with a driver, who I didn't recognise.'

'And the fake cops?'

'I'm not sure about this guy Warley, but the woman is probably Sian Vickery, Mark's sister.'

'Okay, so why is this so important to you? That's what I can't work out. Why are you taking all these risks to follow them?'

He wasn't expecting a candid response to such a personal question, but this time Ruth replied without hesitation.

'They murdered my husband.'

NINETEEN

For nearly half an hour Alice knelt by the bed, singing songs to keep Evie entertained. Every few seconds she glanced at the houses over the road, specifically number 43 and the sliver of its front door that was visible from her bedroom.

The other mail had been opened and discarded. Only the tiny padded envelope remained untouched. Despite all the recent trauma, her social conditioning made it almost impossible to consider opening a letter intended for someone else.

But the minutes ticked by, and Renshaw did not come.

Alice wondered if he'd already fled. It might be that he knew nothing of this second delivery. But its presence forced her to make a decision: deliver it to 43 – because that seemed the likeliest place for him to be hiding – or keep it here. Open it or throw it in a bin. Call the police or stay silent.

None of these options seemed wiser or more appealing than any other. None offered the promise of a safe resolution. And if she were to hang on to the package, and the gang returned and found it in her possession, she might be signing a death warrant for her family …

She heard a car approaching, rose to take a look and glimpsed a slender woman at the wheel, a spray of long red hair over her shoulders. Was it Sian, from last night?

Alice gasped and ducked below the window. But as she waited for her heart rate to steady, it struck her that this might be a positive development.

Maybe – just maybe – the police officers were genuine, and DC Cassell was patrolling the neighbourhood in case the gang returned?

She weighed up that idea for a minute, then reached for her phone and Googled Sussex Police. The website didn't seem to list contact numbers for different departments, so she dialled the non-emergency number: 101.

A pleasant female voice answered. Alice asked if she could speak to Detective Inspector Warley.

'Do you know where he's based?'

'Um, Brighton, I think.'

'Transferring you now.'

A few seconds to wait, Evie choosing this point to let out a warning cry: *I'm getting bored, Mummy …*

A man answered this time. Alice repeated the request and there was silence for a moment: silence and an awful foreboding on her part.

'Name doesn't ring a bell.'

'Dean. DI Dean Warley.'

'Are you sure he's based here in Brighton?'

'Uh, that's what I thought …'

'Afraid not. What case are you calling about?'

'Oh, it's, uh, a personal matter. Sorry to have bothered you.'

He was speaking again as Alice cut the connection and dropped the phone on the bed, shuddering with pent-up fear.

A personal matter. Well, you got that right, she thought, shaking off an image of the man with the knife, his filthy mouth bearing down on her breast.

Back to the window: there was no sign of the woman who might or might not have been Sian Cassell. Alice picked Evie up, glancing nervously at the phone. She was almost expecting the detective – the *real* detective – to ring back and say he knew there was something wrong.

But he can't help you. It's too late for that.

Evie refused to be soothed in her mother's arms. Alice tried to laugh off the rooting mouth.

'Oh, baby, surely you're not hungry already?'

Evie met her eye, looking remarkably certain. *Milk on demand, buster: that's the deal.*

Alice fed her on the bed, the parcel still within reach. She was thinking that it represented evidence, so maybe there *was* still time to go to the police.

But what if it contained something illegal? Perhaps they'd believe what Alice told them, or perhaps, it occurred to her now, they would seek other explanations.

Like Harry, for example.

We appreciate that you reported this in good faith, Mrs French, but have you considered that your husband might be involved, without your knowledge?

She found herself questioning Harry's measured reaction last night, when she admitted to the delivery. Shouldn't he have been more shocked? Angrier?

Oh God, this was madness. How could she even think such a thing?

Evie fed ravenously for what seemed like an age, shook off her drowsiness while being changed, then fed again and finally went off to sleep. Alice stood up, rocking her gently as she moved to the corner of the window. Her gaze homed in on 43, just in time to catch a ripple of movement behind the bedroom curtains.

He was in there. Hiding.

Alice came alive with a sudden fury. How dare he do this to her!

And with that, the decision was made.

*

Evie grumbled in her sleep as Alice wrestled her into a pramsuit. The walk would soon send her back off, especially as she was going to be in her baby carrier rather than the buggy.

Alice checked the street before locking up, then made a cautious circuit of the neighbouring streets to be sure the car she'd seen wasn't waiting nearby. Back in Lavinia Street, her temper still high, she strode up to number 43 and knocked on the door.

No answer. Alice knocked again, hard enough to rattle the door in its frame. Luckily, Evie stayed asleep. Leaning out of the recess, Alice surveyed the street once more, then crouched down, being careful not to squash Evie, lifted the letterbox flap and shouted through the narrow slot: 'Mr Grainger! I have another letter for you.'

She waited, still squatting, ignoring the discomfort and the fact that she would present an ungainly sight to anyone walking past – the massive arse that Harry valiantly insisted wasn't massive at all – and although there was no sound from within the house, she was sure she could sense a presence.

He was listening.

She lowered her voice. 'We went through hell because of you, Mr Grainger, or should I say *Renshaw*? Now come to the door and face me.'

Still nothing. Her knees were aching. Evie's feet were digging into her abdomen. Holding the door for balance, Alice straightened up, her other hand reaching for the envelope in her back pocket. Perhaps she'd just shove the packet through the door and pray that was the end of it.

She could hear a car some distance away; in Buxton Road, maybe. She was turning to look when the front door was wrenched open to reveal the man from the other morning, a horrified expression on his face.

'Quickly!' He motioned her inside, but Alice had frozen in shock. When she failed to move he grabbed her by the arm. She tried to back away but saw a car at the end of the street and knew it was the same one from earlier – driven by the woman with long red hair – and it was this more than Renshaw's physical strength that pitched her through the doorway and into the house.

Like her namesake falling down the rabbit hole, she thought – except that Lewis Carroll's creation hadn't had the most precious human being on earth strapped to her chest. Alice was dimly aware of Renshaw pushing past her, still growling, 'Get in! Get in!' even as he slammed the door shut and slid a heavy bolt into place.

TWENTY

Harry didn't know what to make of Ruth's revelation. If it was true, it made his own family's ordeal seem trivial by comparison – but it also brought home just how much danger they were in: dealing with men who had killed before.

'When? I mean, how? And why haven't they been prosecuted?'

'Oh, Harry.' Her tone suggested that he was being hopelessly naïve.

'Well, if you were a cop—'

'I didn't say I was.' After a tense silence, she added: 'In any case, my husband was a police officer. He worked in Intelligence, though his investigation into Nathan Laird was off the books. That's one of the reasons his death couldn't be tied to the gang.'

'How did he die – if you don't mind me asking?'

'He was stabbed, in Ipswich, eleven months ago. It was staged to look like a mugging gone wrong. Late at night, in a bad part of town. The official investigation got nowhere fast.'

'But surely, with him being a police officer, his colleagues would go all out to find his killer?'

'Sure. But if there's no evidence, no witnesses, there isn't a lot more they can do.'

The question had obviously stung her, and Harry had the impression she was holding something back.

'If you told them about Laird ...' he began.

'Look, it's not like a normal homicide. If a member of the public is murdered, you rule out immediate family and friends, and then you ask who else might have wanted them dead. In most cases you're lucky to find even one or two people with a serious grudge. When it's a cop with nearly twenty years' service, you have the opposite problem. Way too many suspects. You have to look at practically everyone he ever investigated, everyone he helped to put away, as well as all their families and associates.'

Harry was happy to concede the point, but he said, 'In that case, how can you be so sure that Laird was behind it?'

'I know, all right.' Her voice was like steel. 'I just know.'

She changed the subject back to the visit by the fake detectives. She could make a few calls and hopefully get some information later today.

'Then you can put your wife's mind at rest – or not, as the case may be.'

'Probably not,' Harry said glumly. 'What you've told me about the gang is bound to freak her out.'

As he said it, he was thinking: *The parcel. Are you going to mention the parcel?*

Ruth gave him a quizzical look, as if she sensed there was something on his mind. In a clumsy attempt to divert her attention, Harry said, 'So, why no wig today? That's your real hair, isn't it?'

She nodded, shrugged. 'Wigs get itchy.'

'Okay. And since you're answering my questions for once, another thing that intrigues me is your accent.'

'It's a mess, that's for sure.' She fixed him with a sardonic grin. 'Don't think I can't see what you're doing.'

'Can you blame me for wanting to know more?'

'I guess not.' She glanced at her watch, then stood up. 'My father's American. He was in the military. He met my mother while he was stationed in Germany. That's where I was born. We transferred to the UK when I was thirteen, to Mum's home county of North Yorkshire. At eighteen I moved down south for university, so that's why it's such a godawful mix.' She snorted. 'Mostly I get mistaken for a Canadian.'

They walked back across the beach. The fine weather had attracted tourists and school parties, parents with young children.

Harry drew in a breath. 'Do you think I should even be here, leaving Alice and Evie alone when these people are still at large?'

'Only you can decide that. But you can't stay home forever, can you?'

'No, I suppose not.' He sighed, unable to dispel his unease; a sudden conviction that he had abandoned his family just when they needed him most. 'The worst thing is the uncertainty, the fact that there's no way of knowing when – or if – this will be over.'

'It'll be over when they get what they want.'

'Or when someone stops them?'

Ruth made a noise; not quite a laugh, not quite a cough.

'Sure,' she said. 'But that's my job to worry about. Not yours.'

TWENTY-ONE

After bolting the door, Renshaw produced a set of keys and used one to lock the mortice on the front door. Alice watched the keys go into his pocket and knew that her hopes of escape had just vanished with them.

'Why have you … ? Let me go.' She tried to make it sound like a command, but it came out as little more than a frightened croak.

'Have you any idea what you've done?' Renshaw was a short, rotund man, humming with nervous energy. He wore a grubby-looking suit with a thick sweater beneath the jacket. His accent seemed more distinctive than it had when he'd collected the parcel, the words thick and unformed.

He wouldn't be used to speaking, Alice realised. Not if he spent his days hiding in here.

She dug the envelope from her jeans, working hard not to let the fear show. 'This is for you. Now let me out.'

Still furious, he snatched it from her. 'If you have led them to me, we will be lambs to the slaughter.'

'They broke into our house,' Alice snapped back. 'They terrorised us, because of you.'

Renshaw acted as if he hadn't heard. 'Who did you see, just now?'

Alice shrugged. 'I'm not sure. A woman with red hair, maybe.'

'A young woman? Thin?'

'She came to the house last night, claiming to be a detective. DC Sian Cassell.'

He groaned. 'Sian.'

'You know who she is?'

Renshaw nodded, fear in his eyes. 'And she saw you come to this address?'

'I don't think so.' Alice found the courage to take a step towards him. 'You have to let us go.'

Her use of the plural confused him. Then his gaze dropped to the carrier and he gave a start, swearing under his breath.

'Please. This isn't anything to do with us—' Alice moved to go round him but he blocked her path.

'You are part of this now. You cannot walk away.'

It wasn't a threat: if anything, she thought, his tone was slightly regretful, as if he didn't wish her or Evie to come to any harm. Stepping back, he held out his palms in a placatory gesture. With the bushy beard and crinkly eyes, he reminded Alice a little of Anthony Hopkins.

'Forgive me,' Renshaw said. 'This must be very upsetting. But we are in danger here; that you must believe.'

'I do,' she said hotly. 'I told you, they woke us in the middle of the night. They wore masks, gloves. And they knew about the parcel.'

He winced. 'What did you tell them?'

'Nothing. I was so shocked, I didn't even make the connection to the other day.'

'Good. But if they are watching now …' Tutting gravely, he shook his head. 'I will see.'

As he turned to climb the stairs, Alice quickly took in her surroundings. The house was bitterly cold and had a damp, fusty smell. In the hall the Anaglypta wallpaper was peeling and dotted with mould; white gloss on the woodwork had faded to yellow. The carpet was threadbare, coated with dust and grime.

An instinct to flee propelled her along the hall. The kitchen was home to piles of cardboard packaging and empty cartons. Renshaw appeared to be living on baked beans, Pot Noodles and ready meals.

The back door looked less sturdy than the front, with a couple of glass panels, but Alice quickly spotted another mortice lock – the key doubtlessly in Renshaw's pocket. And something odd: above the door, on a narrow makeshift shelf, a bucket with a cord tied to the handle. The cord was stretched across the top corner of the door. A booby trap.

There was a second when she contemplated climbing out of a window, but with Evie in the carrier it wouldn't be easy. Then she heard Renshaw calling softly: 'Come. Please.'

She returned to the stairs, noticing that folded towels had been laid on some of the treads. Soundproofing.

On the landing, Renshaw waited with a grim smile. 'You are safer with me than out there.'

Alice didn't trust him, particularly, but on this issue she didn't doubt him, either. She climbed the stairs to find the narrow landing was made more cramped by the presence of a pull-down loft ladder. The opening to the roof space yawned above her.

Renshaw had moved into the front bedroom. It was empty except for a broken chest of drawers, the panels of laminated chipboard slowly regressing to their flat-packed state. The curtains were drawn but pinned at each side to leave a sliver of glass visible. Moving closer, Alice noticed a strange dullness to the window and saw it had been coated with a layer of what looked like cling film.

'Tell me more about Sian.' Renshaw was standing to the left of the window, examining the street in the direction of Alice's home. 'A detective, did you say?'

'She was with a man called Warley. They knew about the break-in, even though we hadn't reported it. I think they were trying to check if we'd been lying the night before.'

'And they were satisfied with your answers?'

'I think so.' She gestured at the window. 'I'm not even sure if that's who I saw just now.'

'We have to pray it was not.'

'Look, what is this about? Why are they searching for you?'

He shook his head, then Alice saw his shoulders jerk. He swore under his breath.

'It is them. A blue Audi.'

'I don't think that was—'

'There will be several people. More than one car.'

Alice tried to remember the man on the phone who'd spooked her yesterday morning. He'd got into a blue car, hadn't he?

Renshaw made a fist of his right hand and turned towards her. Alice wrapped an arm around the carrier to protect her sleeping baby, but with a dismissive sigh Renshaw hurried out of the room.

That was when Alice realised she wasn't completely helpless. She had her phone.

Before she could do anything, there was a distressed moan from a room at the back. Alice eased past the loft ladder and found Renshaw in his bedroom. There was no furniture except a single bed. The floor was littered with clothes and dozens of tatty paperbacks: Robert Ludlum, Tom Clancy, John Grisham. The same curtain arrangement as in the front, Renshaw peering through the narrow gap.

'They have us penned in.'

'Are you sure?'

'See for yourself.'

Alice made sure her phone was hidden as she picked her way across the room. The gardens on this side of the street were deeper than her own, backing on to an alleyway with another set of gardens beyond that. Renshaw's property was bordered by a high wall, but Alice glimpsed the head of a man in the alley. He had a phone at his ear.

Renshaw moved alongside her, his breath foul on her face when he spoke.

'He will summon others. When they have enough people, they will come for me. Do you see?'

Ending the call, the man placed his hands on the wall and boosted himself up. Alice gasped, taking a few steps away from Renshaw before she lifted her phone into view.

'We've got to call the police.'

Renshaw gave her a look of withering contempt, but she ignored him, tapping in the number.

'No!' He made a grab for her. Alice dodged back but tripped on a book. Her free hand went round Evie, and Renshaw caught her other arm, fingers pinching tight, and pulled the phone from her grasp. He checked that the call hadn't connected, then shoved the phone into his pocket.

'The police will not help. You know that, or you would have gone to them before.'

'But we have to. We're trapped in here.'

'No. Not trapped.' He made an effort to calm himself. 'If the police come, it only delays the end. They cannot protect me forever. Nor you.'

'Then what are we going to do?'

Renshaw was staring at the carrier, his lips pursed. 'There is a way. It will not be easy, but if you stay here you will die. Your baby will die.'

*

A loud noise made them both jump: someone thumping on the front door. Renshaw picked up a bulging Nike rucksack and returned to the landing. He indicated the ladder. 'You must go first.'

'I can't get up there. Not with Evie.'

'If they capture us, we are finished.'

'But what good will it do, hiding up there?'

'This is not to hide. I have prepared for this day.'

Another heavy thump on the door. Alice cringed at the sound, then stepped gingerly on to the bottom rung. It was a steep climb, and there wasn't a lot of room to get through the hatch.

'Hurry! You must hurry!' Renshaw was struggling to contain his frustration. Alice understood the urgency, but she had to take extra care that Evie didn't bump her head on the hatch. The baby was at least facing Alice, nestling close against her chest.

As she climbed into the loft space, she saw that sheets of plywood had been laid over the joists to form a basic floor. The beams and rafters crowded around her like a primitive cage. As she moved off the ladder, her hand caught the head of a screw protruding from the floor, and she gasped at the pain.

Renshaw clambered up behind her, his breath whistling in his nostrils. He shoved the rucksack across the floor, hauled himself into the loft and reached over Alice's shoulder to press a switch.

A light came on, a single bulb caked in dust. Now she could see how small the space was; how exposed. Apart from a few mouldy cardboard boxes and a couple of old deckchairs, it was empty. Nothing to hide behind. Nothing to use for self-defence.

'This isn't going to work.'

'Bring the ladder up. You pull on it here, see?' He showed her the retracting mechanism. The ladder was designed to fold as it slid into runners on the joists, with a cord that pulled the loft hatch up after it.

Not easy to operate in a cramped space, while wearing the baby carrier, but Alice did her best. She noticed a large bolt, fixed to the edge of the opening. Once the hatch was in place, she slid the bolt home and allowed herself to breathe a small sigh of relief.

From downstairs came more hammering on the door. The sense of relief was gone in an instant.

There was no way out. All she had done was entomb them up here.

TWENTY-TWO

'Be ready,' Renshaw said. 'I planned to do this alone. It may not work with two— three,' he corrected himself.

Twisting round, Alice saw that he'd moved the deckchairs aside and was scrabbling at the brickwork as if hoping to claw out a hiding place. She crawled towards him, arching her spine to keep Evie's carrier from catching on the boards. Taking a second to orient herself, she realised this was the party wall with number 45. Lawrence Wright's home.

There was a grunt of exertion from Renshaw, and to the sound of bricks shifting and sliding a shadow opened in the wall. He removed half a dozen in a single block, and now she could see an outline where the mortar had been pre-cut.

'When did you do this?'

'Months ago. Today we have some good fortune,' he added drily. 'The man next door is out.'

Alice leaned closer to the cavity and saw that Lawrence Wright's wall had been cut the same way, the loose bricks sitting in place like tins on a shelf. Renshaw got to work, his upper body disappearing into the space between the walls. A sudden impact reverberated through the building and he backed out, cursing, his face and hair clouded with dust.

'Too heavy. It slipped from my fingers.'

'They'll have heard that.'

'All the more reason to hurry. It is a tight fit. Remove the papoose.'

'No.'

'You must. I will pass the baby through to you.'

Alice knew it was probably the right thing to do, but the thought of leaving her daughter in Renshaw's care, even for a few seconds, while she crawled into the unknown …

'Now!' he hissed, and made to grab at one of the straps. Alice batted his hand away and removed the carrier herself, only to discover that Evie was wide awake and gazing at her with an absurdly placid curiosity: *What's this strange adventure we're having?*

The next sound from downstairs was a muffled impact, followed by a long groan from the woodwork, as if someone was testing the strength of the front door. Putting aside her misgivings, Alice handed the baby over and prepared to crawl through the wall. Even without the carrier, there was only just room to squeeze through. As she moved forward, Renshaw warned her to take care.

'The other side is not boarded.'

'Right.' She had a vivid childhood memory of her dad slipping in the loft and putting his foot through the ceiling. He'd sprained his ankle and taught her several new swear words in the process.

It took only a few seconds but it was a gruesome experience, the air cold and foul, dust and soot choking her nostrils. Her hands were stung by loose grit, and dead insects crunched beneath her skin. A narrow void separated each skin of brickwork, hung with grimy cobwebs like the entrance to a monster's lair. Alice was plagued by an image of the blackness suddenly widening to swallow her whole – and Renshaw, with her daughter in his possession, cackling gleefully as he bricked up the wall and sealed her in …

The neighbouring loft was in darkness, with only a faint square of illumination around the hatch. As her vision adjusted to the gloom, she saw there were half a dozen plastic storage crates sitting on the joists, filled with what looked like papers and books.

The timbers were rough with splinters and difficult to grip firmly. She was pulling herself forward when a slapping noise caused her to freeze. It was followed by a creak of movement. Her first thought was Lawrence Wright, now home and on his way upstairs to investigate the disturbance.

Then the sound repeated, echoing in the confined space, and she realised it came from overhead. Something on the roof.

A seagull, she hoped. Just a bloody seagull.

She wriggled and kicked, scraping over the joists while trying to avoid contact with the ancient rockwool that was packed between them. She knew it was an irritant to the skin, and also dangerous if inhaled. A terrible environment for a baby.

It seemed to take forever to bring her legs through, then clamber up into a crouching position, so that she could turn back to face the opening. There was another stab of pure terror that Renshaw would refuse to hand Evie over to her.

But he was urging her to go faster. He thrust the carrier at her, barely giving her time to retreat with Evie before he shoved the rucksack through. Then he surprised her by turning, pushing his feet towards her and squeezing himself backwards through the gap. That way he was able to drag the deckchairs back into place, he explained as he straightened up. To buy them a little more time.

Alice had fastened the carrier and was trying to pacify Evie, who hadn't been impressed by their brief separation and looked on the verge of a tantrum. Renshaw brushed past her on his hands and knees, moving towards the hatch. As he reached it, Alice saw what was missing.

'No ladder.'

A brusque noise from Renshaw. 'We jump.'

'But I can't—'

'I did not plan this with you in mind. Or the infant.'

He moved the hatch aside, throwing light and shadow into the loft. Alice saw a patch of grey carpet, far below, and felt like a parachutist peering from the aircraft door.

'This is crazy,' she muttered, to which Renshaw took offence.

'You should thank me. You brought this about. Now I am saving your life.'

It was an outrageous distortion of the truth, but before she could protest he had twisted and put his legs over the edge. The rucksack went first, dropped like ballast, then Renshaw leaned forward and fell.

He landed heavily, collapsing on the floor. Alice wondered about the odds of Lawrence Wright having returned within the last few minutes. Supposing he popped up now and confronted them, what would Renshaw do?

Fortunately no one appeared. Renshaw climbed to his feet, wincing as he tested his ankles, and beckoned her to follow.

Alice looked down and was suddenly paralysed. 'I can't.'

'You must. Or else I leave you to your fate.'

Alice shut her eyes, swallowed, and told herself: *This is just a dream. A crazy dream. In which case, it can't hurt to jump, can it?*

She nodded, but told him she wanted to hand Evie down first. It meant another delay while she removed the carrier once more, Renshaw muttering crossly. Then a horrible moment, leaning over the hatch, when her knee slipped partly off the joist: she nearly dropped Evie, and could have tumbled out after her and injured them both. She realised she was shaking; her system so flooded with adrenalin that it was almost impossible to keep still.

Stretching up on tiptoe, Renshaw just managed to reach the carrier. 'Let her go,' he said crossly.

'You don't have her properly.'

'Let. Her. Go.'

'You'll drop—' Alice yelped as Renshaw somehow gained a little more height and snatched the baby from her grasp. Then he enraged her by setting Evie down on the floor at the end of the landing, abandoning her while he strode into one of the bedrooms.

Alice swung her legs round and virtually leapt from the loft, all fear for her own safety forgotten in her haste to get to Evie.

Renshaw was hurrying back as she picked up the carrier and fixed Evie to her chest. Ignoring her, he crossed the landing into another bedroom. Alice followed him to the doorway and saw him staring down at the street.

'There's a man out front, preparing to break in next door. The woman, Sian, is keeping watch, across the road.'

Alice gestured behind them. 'And the man out back?'

'I can't see him. Probably he waits in my yard, by the back door.'

He put the rucksack on and made for the stairs. He moved with such an easy familiarity that Alice wondered if he'd been in here before.

Despite the danger, there was a foolish but undeniable thrill to know she was trespassing in someone else's home. Passing a spare bedroom full of bottles and wine-making paraphernalia, she followed Renshaw downstairs. He paused at the kitchen door and gave the carrier a scornful glance.

'The baby must stay quiet. If they hear us, all this will be for nothing. We must wait now in silence.'

'Wait? But you've been rushing me—'

'To be ready.' He gestured with his thumb. 'Out there, they are waiting, too. Probably for another car. And when they go in, we go out.'

Alice frowned. 'You mean, sneak past them?'

'Yes. So the baby …' A finger at his lips. 'No noise.'

Lawrence Wright's kitchen was compact but modern, with gleaming white cabinets and black speckled Corian worktops. The tiled floor had been recently cleaned: there was a sharp tang of disinfectant in the air, which reminded Alice of something.

'That bucket in your kitchen … what's in it?'

'Nothing to concern you.'

Gesturing for silence again, Renshaw approached the back door, his battered brogues sliding on the damp tiles. The door was half-glazed, with a bolt at the bottom. There was a Yale lock, and a key which presumably corresponded to it, hanging from a hook next to the door.

Renshaw moved cautiously towards the window, looked out for perhaps half a minute, then slipped the key off its hook and unlocked the door. With another warning glance at Alice, he knelt down and drew back the bolt.

Alice waited, sure that the tension in her must be apparent to Evie. She'd begun to rock her, gently, without being aware that she was doing it; she'd found before that the carrier seemed to work wonders, and now the combination of movement and body heat was sending Evie to sleep again.

Slowly Renshaw eased the door handle down. Alice risked moving closer to him, wanting to scout out the route they would take. Lawrence Wright's garden had been imaginatively laid out in a diamond pattern of flagstones and loose gravel, bordered by a colourful variety of plants in raised beds enclosed within old railway sleepers.

Renshaw opened the door a fraction, letting in sounds from outside: traffic noise and seagulls, and then a voice. The low murmur of a phone conversation.

And the voice was familiar. The man in the Freddy Krueger mask. The one who'd—

'Got it,' the man said, and Alice felt her legs go weak at the thought of how close he was: three or four feet away, hidden by nothing more than a flimsy wooden fence.

They heard a dull thud, then a splintering noise. He was forcing the lock.

Renshaw used the sound to cover them, opening the door a few more inches. Then he froze as a low buzzing noise filled the room. He glared at Alice: *What is it?*

The second buzz was louder. It seemed to originate from Renshaw himself.

'My phone,' Alice mouthed at him. 'In your pocket.'

In a panic, Renshaw scrabbled for the phone, almost dropping it as he tried to figure out the controls. The ring tone was set to increase in volume, and it was doing that very effectively. Alice was about to grab it from him when he located the power button and switched it off.

He shoved the phone away, glared at her again, and turned to the door. Once she'd recovered from the shock, Alice realised that it now seemed incredibly quiet.

The man next door had stopped what he was doing.

He'd heard them.

TWENTY-THREE

'What will you do now?' Harry asked Ruth, when they'd walked back to their original meeting point by the Pump Room.

'Probably stick around for another day or two. See what I can find out about these visitors you had last night.'

He nodded. 'And then what? Assuming they don't reappear … ?'

'Back to East Anglia, I guess. There's someone I need to see.'

She stopped, a little abruptly. Harry touched her arm, and said, 'Go on. Please.'

Ruth sighed. 'Greg had a source with links to the gang. Since his death she's kept a low profile. Keeps changing the name she works under. I only tracked down a number for her a couple of weeks ago.'

'Why haven't you spoken to her before now?'

'She's refused to talk to me. I need to meet her face-to-face.' Ruth was avoiding his gaze; she looked subdued, almost embarrassed. 'She's an escort. A call girl. She slept with my husband while he was trying to get information about Laird.'

Harry had no idea what to say. 'I'm sorry.'

'Yeah, well. Shit happens.' Her shrug was too casual to be genuine; this cut her deeply, Harry was sure.

He frowned. 'So, uh, why was your husband investigating Laird in the first place? Didn't you say it was off the books?'

'That, Harry, is definitely something you don't need to know.'

It was a blunt response, and it came just as he was convincing himself that he should tell her about the parcel. Insulted by her manner, he changed his mind in that instant. If she wasn't prepared to open up to him, then why should he confide in her?

They shook hands like a couple of politicians, cordial but each a little wary of the other.

Ruth said, 'Goodbye, Harry. Stay alert, okay, but don't drive yourself crazy, either.'

He nodded grimly. 'Easier said than done, but I'll give it a try.'

Ruth turned and walked away in the direction of Hove Lawns. He knew he might not see her again, and it struck Harry that this would be a good thing if it also meant there was no further contact from the gang.

So why, then, was there a sense of regret?

Pondering that, and unable to find an answer, Harry climbed the ramp to the main road and waited to cross at the lights. He took out his phone, saw there were no missed calls or texts, and rang home.

There was no answer on the landline, but that didn't worry him unduly. It was just gone one o'clock. With such lovely weather, Alice could simply have taken Evie for a walk after lunch.

He tried her mobile. It rang three, four times, then abruptly cut off. Harry stared, uncomprehending, at the display. Why would Alice do that?

He went cold inside. The traffic lights had changed but he ignored the bleeping of the pedestrian crossing as he considered the only answer that made sense to him.

She wouldn't.

Alice thought she could almost *feel* the man next door listening for them. Renshaw was glowering at her but she ignored him.

Her focus was on Evie, praying her daughter wouldn't choose this moment to make her presence known.

A few seconds of agonising silence, then a grunt as the man got back to work. Renshaw took a deep breath, eased the door open and signalled to Alice.

'Once he's inside,' he mouthed. She nodded.

Breaking in was evidently a tough prospect. It took another minute before they heard the timber splitting; a clatter as the door flew open and hit a kitchen unit.

Alice was aware of the anticipation on Renshaw's face: a faint smile forming.

Next came a scream, the dull thud of a bucket hitting the floor. Frantic activity in the kitchen; cries of pain and then the sound of water splashing.

By then Renshaw was moving, in a fast scuttling action, crouching below the line of the fence. Alice followed, taking careful strides to avoid the patches of gravel. At the end of the garden there was a waist-high wall with a wooden trellis mounted on top. Thankfully, the railway sleepers formed a step, and the top of the wall looked wide enough to stand on while they climbed over the trellis.

The only drawback was that they would be visible to anyone looking out of Renshaw's windows. That was where the booby trap had come in, she realised. To divert attention.

Renshaw had charged the wall with too much momentum. He grabbed the trellis to keep from falling backwards, but it wasn't strong enough to take his weight. Alice saw him teetering and managed to brace him, buying a vital second in which he grabbed a post and regained his balance.

Alice hurried after him, faster and more agile, but hampered by the baby carrier. The knowledge that the gang had guns was never far from her mind. From one of the back bedrooms it would be like shooting tin cans at a fairground.

Lifting her leg over the trellis, she felt a sudden cold sensation along her spine. She glanced back at Renshaw's house and caught a man staring at her from an upper window, just as she'd feared. For a moment he looked bewildered; then he shouted something and disappeared.

'They've seen us,' she cried.

'Hurry, then.' A note of distress in Renshaw's voice. He'd snagged his trousers on a nail, and had to wrench himself free before dropping into the alley.

Alice had to jump while trying to hold Evie steady. She landed inelegantly, falling to her knees on the narrow weed-strewn path. She felt a sharp pain as one hand slapped against the ground. A sliver of glass had embedded itself in her palm.

'This way.' Renshaw gestured in the direction of Port Hall Road. They ran in single file, Renshaw taking the lead, Alice desperately soothing Evie and trying to ignore the throbbing in her hand.

At the end of the alley Renshaw checked the way was clear, while Alice looked behind them. There was no one on the path, but she thought she could hear voices and movement from one of the gardens.

Renshaw made for an old Seat Ibiza parked a few yards away. Alice dimly recalled having noticed it before; a permanent fixture in the street.

'Will it start?'

'Yes, it will start.' He shrugged off the rucksack and slung it on to the back seat. 'Get in.'

Alice gripped the handle of the passenger door, then hesitated for a moment. She didn't have to obey him. Renshaw would probably drive off without another thought for her safety. And yet, strangely, it was his indifference to her fate that made the decision for her.

The men chasing them would be here within seconds. On foot, Alice could never escape.

It was Renshaw who had put her in this danger. Now he had to get her out.

TWENTY-FOUR

Harry sprinted to the railings and scanned the esplanade. No sign of Ruth among the pedestrians strolling back and forth below him, but by now she was probably hidden from view by the i360 site. Then some instinct caused him to look in the opposite direction, and he spotted her walking briskly towards Brighton pier. She must have doubled back once he was out of sight.

Dashing for the ramp, he started to feel foolish. Wasn't this a silly overreaction, going into panic mode because of one missed call?

He was closing the distance when Ruth turned and gazed straight at him: a brief, unsettling act of telepathy.

'Harry?'

'I just tried to phone Alice. There was no answer, but it didn't go to voicemail. It's like she cut the connection, or someone did—'

She raised her hand. 'Calm, Harry.'

'Look …' He took a deep breath. 'I'm sorry. I probably should have mentioned this sooner, but there *was* a parcel.'

He quickly relayed Alice's account of an elderly man collecting what had appeared to be an innocently misdirected delivery. Ruth shook her head, as if sorely disappointed. 'I wish you'd said.'

'But *I* only found about it last night. And after those cops came round I wasn't sure who I could trust.'

She considered this, blinked slowly a couple of times, then said, 'Okay. I can see that.'

He called Alice's number three times, with no success. On the third attempt he left a message: 'Alice, can you ring me when you get this? Straight away, please. I need to know you're all right.'

'Maybe you just caught her at a bad time,' Ruth offered, but her expression was almost as tense as his own.

'I hope that's all it is. What do you think?'

'I think you need to get home, to be sure.' Ruth was already turning back the way she'd come. 'We'll take my car. Come on.'

The Seat was moving almost before Alice had shut her door. She clung to the seatbelt as the car lurched out of the parking space.

Renshaw's attention was focused on his mirrors rather than on the road ahead, so he didn't react when a lorry nosed out of a turning to his left. Alice's scream came just in time, causing him to jerk the wheel and avoid a collision.

He braked sharply at the approach to Dyke Road. As the car came to a halt Alice wrestled the belt buckle into its clasp, adjusting the strap so it went to one side of the baby carrier. It shocked her that she could even think of transporting Evie like this, flouting the law and taking a dreadful risk, but it was only because the alternative was so much worse.

Mercifully there was a gap in the traffic, so Renshaw was able to turn right without a delay. Just ahead, the pedestrian lights by the cafe were changing to red. He stamped on the accelerator and sped through them. Checked the mirror again, and let out a grateful sigh.

'Where are we going?' Alice asked.

'Just away from here. That is what matters for now, yes?'

She said nothing. At the junction with The Upper Drive the road was empty and the lights were green. Alice inspected her hand, plucked out the fragment of glass and found a tissue in her pocket to stem the bleeding. She felt she could think clearly now, for the first time since she'd been dragged into Renshaw's house.

'If you can drop me off near the top of Dyke Road, I'll walk to Hove Park and get a bus.'

'And then where? You cannot go home.'

'I've got friends, family—'

'And you know for sure that you will be safe?' Before she could object, he added: 'They saw you, remember, climbing over the fence with me. Their next step will be to search your home, as well as mine. If you have an address book, they will find it. They will be looking for *you* now. To lead them to *me*.'

'But I've got nothing to do with this …' She tailed off, recognising the absurdity of her statement. 'And there's Evie. She has to be fed, and changed, and I don't have—'

'This is far from perfect,' he said irritably. 'But I will try to find a solution.'

A moment later he swore. There was a line of about a dozen cars waiting to enter the roundabout at the top of Dyke Road. Alice felt a spasm of panic. There were no other junctions, nowhere they could turn off the main road.

Sitting ducks.

She reacted without thinking, throwing open the door while simultaneously releasing the seatbelt. Renshaw clawed at her, pulling at one of the carrier straps as Alice struggled to climb out of the car. Whether deliberately or not, he feathered the accelerator and the car rolled forward, almost bringing her down as she broke free of his grasp.

Stumbling, she made it to the pavement and straightened up. Evie was wailing so loudly that it drowned out Renshaw's protests. In the car behind, a middle-aged man was gaping at her, open-mouthed. Should she ask another motorist for help? Beg someone to give her a lift?

The sound of car horns from further down the hill caught her attention. She moved closer to the road and saw two cars driving aggressively, leapfrogging the slower traffic and accelerating fast towards them.

The queue for the roundabout began to move. Renshaw's car jerked forward, causing the passenger door to swing shut. The car behind followed, the driver now studiously ignoring Alice. Whatever was going on, he wanted no part of it. That small act brought home to her how vulnerable she was.

'Wait!'

She ran to catch up with the Seat. Renshaw only slowed when the traffic came to a halt. Once again his indifference was oddly reassuring; she had little to fear from him, whereas there were very good reasons to be afraid of the people chasing them.

She opened the door and dropped into the seat. Renshaw winced at the sound of Evie crying.

'Mad woman! What did I tell you?'

'All right. Just go. They're only a few seconds away.'

'Then keep the baby quiet. I must concentrate.'

Doing her best to calm her daughter, Alice fastened the seatbelt and grabbed the door handle as Renshaw pulled on to the roundabout without any regard for the traffic coming from his right. Somehow he managed to weave between a lorry and two other cars, sped across the road bridge and took a right at the smaller roundabout on to the eastbound carriageway of the A27.

Now they had a chance, Alice thought, keeping a close eye on the wing mirror. With any luck their pursuers would assume they'd gone left, on the westbound route.

As the familiar landscape slipped past – the playing fields of Waterhall, nestled within the dramatic sweep of hills that led to Devil's Dyke – she felt a stab of self-loathing. *This is all my fault.*

I didn't have to take that second parcel across the road. Now I'm getting what I deserve …

But Evie shouldn't have to suffer for her mother's stupidity. Neither should Harry.

'I need to call my husband.'

Renshaw nodded. 'Of course. Later.'

'Why later? If it's not safe at the house, I've got to warn him.'

Silence. Alice twisted round in her seat, preparing for a confrontation. It dimly registered that Renshaw was still on the slip road, which would take them north on to the A23.

'Give me my phone, please.'

'I cannot have you call the police.'

'I won't. Just one quick call to my husband.' She paused. 'If I don't get in touch he's bound to go to the police. And he knows about the parcel – he can tell them enough to cause problems for you.'

Renshaw fumed. 'You are an obstinate woman.' But his hand was moving towards his pocket.

Ruth's car was a brand new Vauxhall Corsa. A hire car, she explained: something else she varied, for the sake of anonymity.

It took a few minutes to exit the car park beneath the town hall. Harry was frantic by the time they turned into West Street. Although his home was only about a mile away, all the city centre routes were choked with traffic.

'Maybe I should call the police?' he said, as they endured an interminable wait at the lights outside Waterstones.

'I'd prefer it if you didn't. But I can't ask you not to.'

Harry was turning his phone over in his hand, trying to work out what he'd say.

'There's still a chance it's something mundane,' Ruth said. 'Could be her phone's out of battery.'

'It shouldn't be. She charges it every night.'

'Okay. Then go ahead, if you feel that's best.'

He nodded. Swiped to unlock the phone, and as he did the display lit up and he saw the magic words: *Alice calling*.

'It's her!' He connected, realising how close he'd come to making a fool of himself. 'Hi, darl—'

'Harry, listen. I can't explain it all now but something else has happened. Those people are still here. It's not safe to come home tonight.'

'What do you mean? Where are you? Is Evie all right?'

'We're both fine.' A little catch in her voice gave the lie to that assurance. And Evie was moaning in the background, a wretched sound that tore at his heart.

'Where are you? At home?'

'No. But we're safe, honestly.'

He caught a worried glance from Ruth, then had a terrible thought. Lowering his voice, he said, 'Are you being coerced?'

'No, it's not that.' She was crying openly now. 'I'm sorry. This is all my fault.'

'Please, just tell me where you are.'

'On the A23.' There was a pause, a heavy sigh. 'I'm with Renshaw.'

'With Renshaw? Why? I mean …'

'There was another package. I took it to number 43. I thought it was safe, but they saw me. We only just got away.'

Ruth was leaning at an odd angle, trying to listen in. She tapped his leg. 'Find out their destination, and whether she trusts him.'

'Alice, is this definitely okay?'

'Who's with you?' Alice cut in. 'I heard a woman's voice. Have you told someone about this?'

'No. It's not—'

'Who is it, Harry?'

He glanced at Ruth, who gave an apologetic shrug. 'Just … someone who knows about this. Someone who can help us. I was going to tell you tonight …'

He tailed off as they reached Seven Dials. It was a complex junction, and Ruth needed to know which exit to take.

Alice, with an angry sob, said, 'Is this because I didn't come clean about the parcel?'

'No, of course it isn't.'

'How do you know you can trust her, Harry? For God's sake, she could be working for *them*.'

'Look, you have to forget that and tell me where you are, where you're go—'

It was no use. The line had gone dead.

He'd lost her.

TWENTY-FIVE

Renshaw made a couple of attempts to seize the phone while she was speaking, but each time Alice twisted away from him. More worrying was how the car veered dangerously whenever he took his hand off the wheel.

In the end she gave in, cut the connection and let him take the phone. She saw him trying to switch it off, but said nothing. In that moment he could have thrown it out of the window and she wouldn't have cared. She felt numb. Sickened.

'What is this?' Renshaw muttered crossly, pushing the car to seventy, then eighty miles an hour, carving a track into the outside lane of the A23. 'Who is with him?'

'A woman,' Alice sighed. She didn't want to believe that Harry had been conned by a member of the gang, but she hated herself for the other possibility that slipped into her head: *He has a lover. Because you got fat, you're always tired, you're no fun—*

'Working for them, that's what you said?'

'I don't know that for sure. I just wanted to remind him to be careful.'

'But this woman, she is a stranger?'

'I didn't recognise her voice.' Alice shut her eyes for a second. She'd barely heard the woman, but if it was someone they knew, Harry would have identified her, wouldn't he?

Not if it's his lover. Molly from the office, with the sexy gap between her front teeth and a bum like a pair of apples.

'Oh God, this is such a mess. It can't be happening.' Wearily she scrubbed at her face with both hands, then let out a slightly manic laugh. '*Is* it happening, or am I going to wake up soon?'

Renshaw only grunted, as if such a stupid question didn't warrant an answer.

'Where are we going, anyway?'

'Better that I do not say.'

This fired her up again. 'No way! I bloody well want to know, otherwise—'

'Otherwise what? You will throw yourself from the car again?' He jiggled the wheel, a malicious reminder of the speed they were doing. Then he shook his head. 'I joke with you, yes? Right now I have no answer. I have to think of somewhere safe. Until then we just drive.'

Harry stared at his phone in horror. For a second or two he couldn't quite believe what he'd just heard. His wife and daughter were in a car with *Renshaw*?

He redialled but there was no answer. Was Renshaw refusing to let her take the call? Or had Alice decided that she couldn't trust him?

He thumped his leg. 'Fuck!'

'I'm sorry,' Ruth said. 'I shouldn't have butted in.'

Harry said nothing, still trying to make sense of this development. A moment later Ruth pulled into a lay-by outside a parade of shops at Seven Dials. She kept the engine running, but turned to face him.

'Did I hear that your wife's with Renshaw, and they're running from the gang?'

'Looks like it.' Conscious of what else Ruth might have overheard, Harry was reluctant to say any more. But Ruth read his hesitation correctly.

'And now she's got you doubting me again. *How do I know you're not the enemy?* That's what you're thinking.'

'Well, it's not impossible, is it?'

'No, it's not *impossible*, Harry.' She gave him a quick, humourless smile, making him feel like a child, trying to justify some ridiculous notion to a grown-up. 'Why didn't you tell your wife about me?'

'I'd intended to. But then I got home to find those detectives at the house. Afterwards I was so worried about who to trust ... I didn't want to add to her stress.'

Ruth nodded. 'Fine, but it's no wonder she freaked out.'

'And now I have no idea where she is. That's what really matters.'

There was a lot of emotion in his voice. Ruth reached out and placed a hand on his shoulder.

'Back there on the beach, you made a decision to trust me. And that's a smart decision, Harry. The right decision. Okay?'

'Perhaps it is, but what are we going to do? If I call the police I can't even tell them what make of car she's in.' He sighed. 'This is all because we didn't report the break-in when it happened.'

'You had good reasons not to, and reporting it might have got you in even bigger trouble. You can't change the past, so focus on now. The important thing is that they got away from Laird's people.'

As far as we know, Harry thought. 'But what should I do? She said it's not safe to go home.'

'We can probably risk a drive past, maybe.' She signalled, then pulled out on to the road. 'But we have to be careful. They'll want to search Renshaw's house. And they'll be sure to leave a couple of guys in the area, in case he comes back.'

'He's got to come back!'

'You've seen the people that are chasing him. It's suicide to return.'

'So what about Alice and Evie? How do they get home?'

'I expect he'll drop them off somewhere.' Ruth seemed to be choosing her words carefully, and Harry sensed the weight of what went unspoken.

'But that's not the only possibility?'

'No,' she admitted. 'He may decide to keep hold of them for the time being.'

'So they could end up as hostages, effectively?'

Ruth kept her eyes on the road. 'Effectively, yes.'

They turned into Port Hall Road, went past Lavinia Street and drove around the block. Harry could barely concentrate on anything other than the idea of Alice and Evie being held by someone in desperate trouble, someone willing to use them as pawns. And not only was he unable to help them, he'd probably left Alice with the impression that he was cheating on her.

'Fucking disaster,' he muttered, not realising he'd spoken aloud until Ruth responded.

'Put that aside for now. Have you noticed anything different along here? Anything out of place?'

'Uh, no. I don't think so.'

'Good. Keep low and we'll take a look at your street.'

She made the turn, and Harry felt anxiety clawing at his stomach. The sight of a woman pushing a buggy across the road produced a savage longing to see his wife and daughter, quite safe, enjoying a leisurely afternoon stroll.

At number 43 there was no obvious sign of a disturbance, but as they rolled past Harry sensed that something wasn't quite right: too much shadow around the frame, as if the door was slightly open.

A moment later they were level with his own home. Here the front door was firmly shut. No movement at the windows.

'Keep an eye on parked cars,' Ruth told him. 'If anyone's just sitting there, we've got a problem.'

They reached the end of the street. Ruth decided on another circuit, finally parking in Port Hall Road, facing towards Dyke Road for a quick getaway. His home was about thirty seconds' walk away; half that time if he ran.

'I think it's clear. I'll keep watch while you go in.' She saw the alarm on his face. 'I take it you want to check out the house?'

'Of course.' He swallowed, hurriedly opening the door so that she wouldn't see how nervous he was.

But I'm allowed to be nervous. This isn't my life. This isn't what I do.

He took out his keys and caught Ruth giving them a thoughtful look.

'Hold them in your fist, with a couple sticking between your fingers. Works like a knuckleduster.'

Harry stared at her, appalled.

'Oh, and pack a bag. Enough for a couple of nights away.'

'What? Why?'

'Precautions.' She flapped a hand. 'Go.'

The afternoon sun had a brittle warmth to it: fine weather for yomping over the Downs in jeans and a thick sweater. For a few seconds he indulged in a fantasy where bunking off early on Friday was a delicious treat, rather than this nerve-wrenching ordeal.

He walked jerkily along the street, feeling about as natural as he had on the red carpet at the BAFTAs. He reached the front door and fumbled the key into the lock.

Once inside he stopped, the keys gripped in his fist in the way Ruth had suggested. His instinct told him the house was empty, but he had to be sure.

First he checked the kitchen. Nothing out of place. Breakfast dishes in the sink; an empty mug on the worktop. He touched the kettle and felt a hint of warmth; again came that awful craving for normality.

In the living room Uncle Steve's new lock was intact. The handset for the landline phone was sitting on the arm of the sofa, and he snatched it before climbing upstairs, dialling 1571 to check for messages. There were none.

The bedrooms were undisturbed, but the sight of Evie's change bag jolted him in a way he could never have foreseen. Her change mat was on the floor, together with a pile of clean nappies and a packet of wipes. The house was like the *Marie Celeste*: everything left as if Alice had merely intended to pop out for a minute or two. And yet he had no idea where she had gone or when he would see her again.

The phone was still in his hand. Impulsively he pressed the green button for a dialling tone and then stabbed out the number.

9.9.9.

As it began to ring, he turned his head to the window. There was a blue car drifting past. An Audi.

He felt his mobile buzz but had to ignore it, because a voice was asking which service he required.

'Er, police.'

A second's delay while he was connected. In this time his mobile appeared in his other hand, though he hadn't consciously reached for it. He had a missed call from Ruth. As he stared at the display, a text came in.

A steady female voice said, 'Hello, you're through to the police. What's the emergency, please?'

'They've, uh … it's my wife.' Harry's mind had gone blank. He knew what he wanted to say but the words couldn't be assembled in order.

'All right, sir, just take it calmly. Can you tell me your name?'

'Harry. Harry French.'

'And this is your home you're calling from, Mr French?' She asked him to confirm his phone number and address, which he did, and then he found himself suddenly babbling:

'My wife's gone, with my daughter. She's only eight weeks old. They don't have spare clothes, no nappies or wipes or anything …'

'I see. And are they in danger?'

'They might be. We had these … these men. Came to the house, the other night.' He heard himself laugh, as if from a distance, and wondered if he was losing his mind. 'Sorry, this probably isn't making much sense.'

'Like I say, Mr French, nice and calm. What's your wife's name?'

'Uh, Alice. But that's not …' He tailed off, because his fingers had taken it upon themselves to operate his mobile phone and open the text. It said:

They're watching your house. Call me.

TWENTY-SIX

'Mr French? Harry? Are you there?'

'Sorry. Yes. I think those men are back. Can you get someone round here now?'

'We'll have a car on the way, but I need to know a bit more about the nature of the emergency. Now, these men. Where are they right now?'

'Uh, they're outside, I think.'

'So you've seen them? Can you describe—'

'I can't actually see them. But they're watching the house.'

'And is it these men that have your wife and daughter?'

'No. She – they – went off with someone else …' He faltered, aware that it was impossible to explain it coherently.

'All right, Mr French, let's go back to your wife and little girl. When were you last in contact with them?'

To Harry the question seemed to be coming from the end of a long tunnel. Much closer was the sound of his mobile.

'I'm sorry,' he blurted. 'This is a mistake.'

He cut the landline over the operator's protest, answered his mobile and Ruth said: 'Jesus, Harry, where were you?'

'I thought …' He felt his body slump. 'Doesn't matter.'

'It does matter. They're here, right now. Luckily it doesn't look like they're preparing to break in. My guess is they want to follow you, hoping you'll lead them to Renshaw via your wife. That means we need to lose them, okay?'

Harry shuddered, thinking: *I don't want to play this game …*

'Harry?'

'I'm here.'

'Good. Now focus. Be ready to move when you get the signal. Right?'

'All right.'

The signal was the bleep of a horn, and it came only a few minutes after they'd agreed on a plan. While he was waiting he received a text from Sam, asking if he was okay. Harry realised it was now past two o'clock: he should have returned from lunch more than an hour ago. He texted back, saying he'd been forced to take the afternoon off because Alice had come down with a migraine. A feeble excuse, but it would have to do.

When the taxi pulled up outside, Harry locked the house and got into the back seat, trying not to scan the street for the vehicle that was set to follow him.

'Station?' the driver queried, as if such a short journey wasn't worth his while.

'Please. And I'm late. Can we hurry?'

The man scowled, slotted the car into gear and pulled away. Harry didn't risk glancing back until they were turning the corner, but when he did he saw the blue Audi on their tail.

In the brief time it took to reach the railway station, Harry tried to steady his nerves for what lay ahead. Already he was at a loss to understand why he'd called the police. But it was equally chilling to consider how isolated he was, despite being in his home town. He couldn't approach his family or friends without placing them in danger.

Like it or not – and even though he still didn't trust her fully – Ruth Monroe was his only hope right now.

*

The taxi pulled into the station's main entrance. Harry found a ten-pound note and reluctantly handed it over, knowing there wasn't time to wait for change. The driver's scowl was now tinged with disbelief at the scale of the tip.

Harry got out and hurried towards the concourse. The blue Audi was several cars back, queuing to turn into the station. There was a man in the passenger seat: grey-haired, a rounded, reddish face and a piercing gaze. Eye contact lasted less than a second but Harry felt sure this was the man from Wednesday night – the one with the gun.

Niall Foster, if Ruth was correct.

As the Audi came to a halt, the passenger door was swinging open. Harry had guessed they would pursue him on foot, to see which platform he made for.

He picked up his speed, muttering apologies as he bumped shoulders with other passengers. He spotted a large party of students and used them for cover, cutting away from the barriers and instead making for the station's rear exit.

Once he'd passed the row of ticket machines there were fewer people around and he could run properly. This felt like the closing straight, his footsteps thudding on the timber boards of the long walkway that led out to Stroudley Road. In seconds he'd reached the roundabout next to the short-term parking bays.

He looked back and saw an elderly couple on the walkway, veering to one side as someone came up behind them. The man from the Audi was hurrying forwards, but with his head turned towards the station platforms, as if he wasn't certain which route Harry had taken.

Dashing past a rack of pushbikes, Harry grew frantic as he realised there were very few places to hide. A few more seconds and he was going to be in plain sight.

He sprinted faster still, detouring on to the road because of a construction site that had swallowed up the pavement. Just beyond that was a hotel, the Jurys Inn, and slotted between that and the building site was a narrow walkway with steps leading down towards the lower section of Stroudley Road. In other words, a valuable shortcut – but only if Harry could move a lot faster than the man behind him.

He reached the walkway and darted along it, not even daring to look back. There were four flights of steep concrete steps, and he descended them at a reckless speed, using the handrail in the centre for balance and leaping five or six steps in one go.

By the time he reached the bottom his ankles were in agony. He'd agreed to meet Ruth at a bus stop just round the corner, but as he ran down the hill he heard the whine of an engine being pushed to the limit. The Corsa burst into view and he dashed towards it, waving at her to stop before she turned into Stroudley Road, which went nowhere other than the station.

As she screeched to a halt, Harry grabbed the door, threw himself in and they were moving again, Ruth in the midst of a rant about the city's road layout, its idiotic twenty mph speed limit, the endless fuckwittery of other motorists. Harry had to interrupt after checking the junction as they drove past: 'No sign of Foster.'

'That's something,' Ruth muttered. 'Much better if they don't know I'm involved.'

She floored the accelerator to beat the lights at the junction with New England Road, but didn't spare him a glance until they were on Preston Road, heading north out of the city.

'You haven't brought any stuff.'

'Wasn't time – uh, speed camera coming up.'

She braked hard enough to pitch him forward, crawled past the camera and then accelerated once they were beyond its range.

'What do you mean? You had plenty of time.'

'Sorry.' He felt foolish now; ashamed. 'I called the police.'

Ruth groaned. 'And told them what?'

'Nothing that made any sense.' He thought back over his garbled explanation. 'In fact, I bet it sounded like my wife had run off with someone, and I'd cracked up as a result.'

'Did they say if they were sending a car?'

'I'm not sure if it got that far. Shame, though. If they'd turned up and seen those guys acting suspiciously—'

'I'm glad they didn't. Would you want a couple of dead police officers on your conscience?'

Abashed, Harry shook his head. 'No.'

'I understand why you were tempted, but you can't do anything like that again. No unilateral decisions whatsoever, you hear me?'

The dressing-down made him bristle for about six seconds, until he accepted that she was right. If he'd wanted help from the police he should have called them at four o'clock on Thursday morning.

Belatedly he recognised that they were making for the A23, following the route that Alice and Renshaw had taken, though by now there was no chance of picking up their trail.

He glanced at Ruth. She had a quiet, unshowy driving style, quick to read the traffic, controlling the vehicle with small, deft movements. She looked relaxed but alert, in a way that hinted at professional training. He pictured her driving down this road on Wednesday night, in determined pursuit of Laird's men.

He frowned as a thought came to him. 'When you followed them down here, did they go anywhere else?'

'Say again?'

'You told me you followed them to Brighton. Did they head straight to Lavinia Street, or did they go anywhere else first?'

Now there was a grin, little more than a twitch of her mouth. 'Where do you think we're heading now?'

TWENTY-SEVEN

They drove on past Hickstead, the Seat labouring through the long climb up Handcross Hill. Evie had quietened at last, and her eyes were growing heavy. She didn't seem uncomfortable in the carrier, although various limbs kept prodding into Alice's stomach and legs. Alice wondered how long she could stave off the next feed, if Evie grew hungry.

The conversation with Harry had left her feeling sick with worry. As a new mother her emotions were volatile enough already: the last thing she wanted was to turn into a weepy, raging nut-job while she was in a car with a stranger. But Renshaw would fall silent for a minute, only to worry away at the issue once again.

'You cannot say who this woman might be?'

'No.'

'But she was with your husband? Alone with him?'

'I think ... I think they might have been in a car.' She frowned as this occurred to her. Why wasn't he at work?

'The woman knows about me. That I do not like.'

'I don't understand – we promised not to say a word.' She fretted over it, trying desperately not to let her imagination run wild. 'He said she could help us.'

Renshaw's snort might have been cruel, except that Alice now found it all too easy to see it the same way he did: *As if anybody could be that gullible ...*

The A23 became the M23, and the motorway traffic grew heavier once they were past the junction for Gatwick airport. A plane was coming in to land, crossing the carriageway just seconds before them. It was a sight that normally made her dream of holidays, of foreign travel and grand adventures, but now it made her yearn to be home.

The periods of silence grew longer. Alice had any number of questions but Renshaw seemed dangerously out of his depth on the busy road, often failing to anticipate the actions of other motorists. Whenever a vehicle nearby changed lanes, he braked and swerved unnecessarily.

'Is anyone following us?' she asked.

'I cannot say for sure. I think not.'

'In that case, can you pay a bit less attention to your mirror and a bit more to the road ahead? Otherwise we're going to crash.'

'We will not crash,' he said, but he seemed more offended than angry that she had criticised his driving.

She yawned. 'Do you know where we're going yet?'

'All I can say is this: when I know, you will know.'

His tone was gentler than before: perhaps a conscious effort to be more civil. She thought of all the time he must have spent holed up alone. His social skills were bound to be rusty.

'Surely we have to go to the police?'

'Probably, yes. But later. Please relax, try not to worry. You are safe.'

Alice yawned again, overcome by a sudden weariness and an almost reckless disregard for the future. Right now, wasn't it enough to be away from those men? Away from Harry and his mystery woman friend?

Actually, she thought, what she craved was oblivion.

She looked down. Evie was asleep. Good for her.

A moment later Alice closed her eyes, too.

*

It was a struggle to keep his temper in check as Ruth revealed that she'd known the whereabouts of their intruders – and she, of course, was sharp enough to see it.

'If you're pissed off with me, Harry, just come out and say so. You feel I could have done more to help. If I knew where Foster and Bridge had gone after they invaded your house, I should have called the police and had them arrested at the hotel—'

Harry was nodding emphatically. 'Yes. So why didn't you?'

'Because it sounds fine, in theory. The reality would have been very different.'

'So you keep saying. I just wonder if it isn't an excuse.'

'An *excuse*?'

'Yes. If you really want to see these people brought to justice, how many more crimes are you prepared to witness and do nothing about? At what point will you decide that enough is enough?'

In barely more than a whisper, Ruth said, 'When that time comes, Harry, I want as few people as possible caught in the crossfire. People like you. Alice. Your daughter.'

'That's not fair. You can't claim we're the reason you haven't—'

'I'm choosing to help you, remember? I could have abandoned you back there. And once they figured out that Renshaw had got away, their next target would have been you.'

She checked her watch, but the pause was clearly designed to let the warning sink in.

'Round about now you'd be lying in a pool of your own bodily fluids, begging to tell them how long Renshaw and your wife have been conspiring together.'

It sounded horribly plausible. Harry crossed his arms and lapsed into silence. They left the A23 at the Hickstead junction, crossed the bridge over the main road and turned into the services car park. Ruth drove slowly, on the look-out for Laird's men, and finally steered into a space close to the Little Chef restaurant.

'They're not here,' she said.

'Did you think they would be?'

A shrug. 'Either way, it's a good place to wait.'

'What are we waiting for?'

'*We*'re not. I need you to stay here while I go back to Brighton.'

Harry stared at her for a moment, but could read nothing of value in her expression. Finally she produced a smile, a peace offering of sorts.

'I've gotta check out of my hotel. And I might run past your place one more time. In fact, give me your keys and I'll pick up a change of clothes for you.'

'And what am I meant to do in the meantime?'

'Keep an eye out for their cars. Eat something. Try to relax a little.'

He snorted, as if the very idea was ludicrous.

'Actually,' she said, 'there is one other thing you can do.'

A couple of minutes later he was standing in the car park, listening to the traffic thundering past on the A23. As he watched Ruth drive away he couldn't shake off the feeling that he was being played for a fool. At the same time, it didn't feel like he had much choice: there was no one else who could help get his wife and daughter back.

He looked down at his phone, the number keyed in and ready to go. He didn't think much of the task she had given him, but decided it best to get it over with.

The phone rang eight or nine times, long enough for the jitters to subside. Just as he was about to cut the connection, a woman answered.

'This is Keri. What can I do for you?'

'Ah, Keri, hi. I, er, I wondered if I can see you some time?'

He was stammering, sweaty of palm and sixteen again, but the woman seemed unsurprised by that. Her voice was warm, friendly rather than seductive, and once again confounded his expectations. She sounded well-educated and intelligent, with a soft Midlands accent.

'Well, I'm not available tonight. Tomorrow I can do twelve o'clock, midday.'

'Midday? Right, okay, yes.'

'An hour?'

'Er, yes, please. Um, whereabouts are you?'

'Thetford.' A hint of suspicion audible in her voice. 'How did you hear about me?'

'A friend recommended you. Sorry, I'm new to this. I meant, where in Thetford?'

'Not far from the centre. Look, you call again tomorrow, at eleven, to confirm the booking. Then I'll text the address. Safety and discretion are important, for both of us.'

He could tell she was smiling, which at least meant she'd bought his story. That was something, even if he hadn't managed to get a specific address. He thanked her and rang off, wondering if Ruth would regard his effort as a failure.

He'd know soon enough – assuming that she was coming back. It had crossed his mind that he'd already outlived his usefulness.

This particular Little Chef, because of its proximity to Brighton, wasn't one he'd visited before, but he was familiar enough with the chain. The dining room was quiet, with only half a dozen tables occupied, mostly by travellers in ones and twos. Harry gave them all a careful appraisal during the brief wait to be seated.

He chose a table by the window, where he could see if any suspicious cars came or went. Studied the menu and ordered a cheeseburger and fries, along with a coffee and some water.

It was mid-afternoon, the sky outside still bright but fading fast, in the poignant manner of late autumn. There wasn't much traffic to monitor, and while he was glad of that, it soon made him restless. His mind kept drifting back to the early hours of Thursday morning, trying to analyse why and how his life had been turned upside down.

The answer, he knew, lay in their failure to notify the police. He tried to craft a different narrative, where he rolled out of bed and watched the van drive away and then called 999. Police cars raced to the scene but the men in the van, still loitering in the area, spotted the flashing lights and realised that Harry had disobeyed their instructions …

No good. How about: he and Alice got back to sleep, but in the morning they went to a police station and gave detailed statements. Except that Alice couldn't bear the thought of describing the sexual assault, so they agreed beforehand to leave that part out. Then, while being interviewed separately, inconsistencies started to appear, and the police became suspicious …

Harry sighed. It was futile trying to re-imagine the past. For better or worse, this was the path they'd taken. There was no *Sliding Doors* scenario available to them here.

A second delivery, Alice had said. But what had possessed her to take the package across to number 43? If she'd phoned him at work, he could have come home and together they might have been able to plot a course of action; something that wouldn't have led to all this … turmoil.

His food arrived. He ate with a fierce appetite, then ordered more coffee and tried to make it last. Time was beginning to drag, and it didn't help that every few minutes he called Alice and got bounced to voicemail.

At first he thought better of leaving a message, but then he succumbed.

'Alice, it's me. I love you. Call me when you can, please.' His voice was choking up; he struggled to finish: 'We'll get through this, Alice. I know we will.'

TWENTY-EIGHT

At first it didn't feel like proper sleep. For a long time Alice felt she was aware of the engine noise, the movement of the car and the burr of tyres on the road, but although she kept trying she found it impossible to open her eyes.

What came back to her were the long-ago journeys of her childhood: the family holidays to Scotland or the Lake District where her father, a history teacher, had insisted on a five a.m. start, Alice stuck in the middle seat between her squabbling older brothers; Mum in the passenger seat playing peace envoy, doling out sweets to buy silence.

And now Alice was studying the back of her father's neck, counting the little grey hairs that curled over the top of his collar while wishing she could speak out and tell him how much she loved him; how much he meant to her. Puzzling over the fact that somehow she knew he was dead …

It took her a second to register that her beloved dad had been gone for nearly nine years; a few more seconds to recall how and why she had come to be travelling like this, with a stranger at the wheel and Evie in her carrier rather than a proper child seat.

Renshaw was concentrating on the road with an expression of grim satisfaction. They were still on a motorway, enclosed by trees, only now they appeared to be travelling west, towards the setting sun.

Feeling groggy, she rubbed her eyes, ran a hand through her hair. 'Where are we?'

'The M4, just past Reading.'

Alice sat up with a jerk. According to the dashboard clock it was twenty past three.

'I can't have been asleep for that long?'

'Oh, you were.' He gave a chuckle. 'You snored, too, from time to time.'

'I take it you've decided where to go?'

'I have an idea, at least. An old friend who can give us shelter.'

Alice said nothing. She didn't want to be visiting anyone Renshaw knew. She didn't want to be on the M4. She wanted to be in Brighton, with her own friends and her family close at hand. She wanted to be with Harry, and to know that everything was all right between them.

She shivered. The trees by the roadside were tinged with gold. The sky was a rich but strangely melancholic shade of dark blue. Back in Lavinia Street lights would be snapping on in the homes of her neighbours: bright rectangles of warmth and comfort. And here she was on this cold open road, heading into the unknown.

She fought off a sudden urge to cry. *What am I doing here?* she asked herself.

What have I done?

Ruth had been gone for an hour when Harry resorted to browsing a display of tourist leaflets. He paid his bill and used the gents, where he found a discarded property magazine tucked behind the taps. He took it with him out to the lobby and browsed through it, aware that they really might have to sell up. Perhaps it was time to get out of Brighton, find a nice rural location: Hassocks or Stenhurst; somewhere with good schools for Evie …

At the back of his mind he was still preoccupied with what Ruth had told him about Vaughan and his gang. It was a struggle to come to terms with the fact that his settled family life had been derailed by a collision with such vicious criminals.

Then there was the worrying aspect of Ruth's refusal to explain why her husband had been investigating Laird in his own time. He was brooding over that when his phone lit up with an incoming call. The name in the display produced first disappointment, then guilt. It was his mother.

He was tempted to ignore it, but then he wondered if something had happened to her or Dad. Could they have been targeted, somehow?

'Harry? Are you all right, love?'

'Fine. Why?'

No answer. Harry had the impression she was conferring with someone. His dad must be standing at her shoulder. Neither of them would think to put the call on speaker.

'What about Alice and Evie? Are they with you?'

Now it was his turn to hesitate. 'What's up, Mum?'

'Harry, please. Where are you?'

There was no mistaking the anguish in her voice. *She knows*, he thought.

'Uh, just outside Brighton. I've got a meeting, Mum, and I don't—'

'I'm at your house.'

His heart jumped. They'd given his mum a set of keys when they moved in, so she could be there to oversee builders and take delivery of furniture while they were both at work.

'Okay,' he said, in what he hoped was a neutral tone.

'I was in town and I'd bought a few things for Evie, so I thought I'd pop in and surprise Alice. What I found was her handbag in the lounge, and the change bag upstairs, and no sign of either of them. Where are they, Harry?'

Her voice was dissolving into tears. That sense of another presence grew stronger, and Harry instinctively turned to the door, as if to flee from it. Movement outside caught his attention: Ruth's Corsa was speeding into the car park.

A man voice's came on the phone: 'Mr French, I'm Detective Inspector Thomsett. Can you please confirm that your wife and daughter are safe and well?'

Reeling, Harry said, 'Of course they are. Look, what is this? What are you doing at my home?'

'Are they with you?' The detective remained calm, not reacting to Harry's bluster. 'I'd like to speak to Mrs French, please.'

The Corsa pulled up and Ruth jumped out. She'd changed her appearance: back in the dark wig and trench coat. Her urgency broke his concentration.

'No, she's, uh … They're not with me right now.'

'Then can you tell me where they are? Your mother here wants to know that all three of you are safe.'

'Why wouldn't we be safe?' His voice was still too high, too strained. He was pushing through the door when Ruth saw him. She jabbed a finger at his phone.

'Is it the police?' she mouthed. And when he nodded dumbly, she grabbed his arm and hustled him away from the building. 'Turn the phone off. They might be tracing your location.'

'What?'

'I'll explain in the car. Now come on.'

The detective was speaking again, but Harry said, 'The connection's going, I'm sorry …' and cut the call.

*

He powered the phone off and followed Ruth to the car. 'My mum just rang me. She's at my house, with the police.'

'I know. I was in Lavinia Street when the cops turned up—shit!'

Harry frowned. A second later he heard it, too: a distant siren.

'That's not because of me?' he asked.

'Maybe not, but we can't take the risk. Get in the back. Lie down.'

Ruth slowed a little as they left the car park. With some difficulty Harry squeezed through the gap between the seats, tumbling forward as Ruth reached the roundabout and accelerated from the junction, swinging the car to the right. Harry glimpsed a police car speeding towards them.

'No way of knowing if that's coming for us,' Ruth said, 'but best stay where you are for now.'

She wanted to know about the nearest town, Burgess Hill. Did it have plenty of banks?

'I guess so. Why?'

'Cashpoint. They might not freeze your account, but they're likely to start monitoring the use of your cards. Aside from mobile phones, it's the easiest way to trace someone. From here on it's cash purchases only.'

Harry was stunned by the implication. 'Are you serious?'

'Afraid so. You're a fugitive now, Harry.'

TWENTY-NINE

Alice deliberated briefly before deciding that the blunt approach was best – or certainly no worse than any other.

'What exactly is going on here? I need to know.'

Apparently untroubled by her tone, Renshaw gave a couple of slow blinks. 'It is a conversation we must have, but not at this moment. I am unaccustomed to these motorways.'

Alice's next question was interrupted by a sharp cry from Evie. She looked as though she'd been awake for a while, and had lost patience waiting for her mother to notice.

'My daughter needs a feed. A clean nappy.'

'Of course. You feed her naturally, do you?'

'Yes,' Alice said, thinking: *No way am I doing it here, in front of you.*

'At the next services, then. We are close.'

A few minutes passed without any confirmation of that. For most of the time the motorway was bordered by tree-covered slopes, so uniform in appearance that it was like driving against a looping background in an old movie. Harry would have come up with a more vivid landscape than this, she thought wistfully.

At last there was a sign for Chieveley services. Alice was doing her best to keep Evie occupied but the baby kept arching her back, squealing at a volume that made Renshaw cringe.

'She can't help it,' Alice said crossly. 'It's a miracle she's been quiet for this long.'

Renshaw didn't look as though he agreed, but evidently thought it wise not to antagonise her. In a bold attempt at small talk, he asked what Harry did for a living. He seemed fascinated by her description of the special effects business, even when she was virtually shouting to be heard over Evie's cries. He didn't once ask whether Alice had a career.

They were at least half a mile from the junction for Chieveley when Renshaw began signalling, the car slowing to less than forty miles an hour. Alice could hear a very large vehicle behind them but she didn't dare look round. She gripped the door handle, bracing herself for an impact.

Finally they veered on to the slip road and a gigantic haulage lorry thundered past. Renshaw tentatively followed the directions to the large, busy car park. He aimed for a row of spaces in the far corner and switched off the engine with evident relief. As if to taunt him, Evie stopped crying at that exact moment.

Alice glanced out of her window, wondering what would happen if she jumped out now and ran away. It wasn't a particularly rational response – or even a sensible course of action, when she thought about it: more a primeval instinct just to flee from the whole nightmarish predicament.

She heard a click as Renshaw released his seatbelt. Another click as he released hers, too. As if he'd read her mind, he said, quietly: 'I cannot stop you. Even with the infant, I expect you are faster than me. If you scream, people will come to your aid. And you will have signed my death warrant.'

*

There was no melodrama in his voice. No sense of exaggeration. Alice believed him.

'No offence,' she said, 'but I don't want to be here. I want to be at home. Even if that's not possible right now, at least tell me when it *will* be possible.'

'I cannot. There are too many factors. And you should not return until it is safe, you must agree with that?'

'Then what about Harry? Because he's not safe, is he, especially if that woman is something to do with them?'

Renshaw conceded the point, then added, 'Perhaps there is another explanation. For instance, could it be that your husband has taken a lover?'

He said it so matter-of-factly that for a moment she felt winded. She had to swallow, take a breath. 'No, he hasn't,' she answered, but she was blushing furiously and she wasn't sure if she detected a hint of doubt in her voice.

She struggled out of the car, shivering in the cold air. Evie's pramsuit was warm enough, thankfully, but Alice had left the house wearing a light jacket. And she had no money on her, no cash or credit cards.

'May I have my phone back?'

Regretfully, Renshaw shook his head. 'I would prefer to keep it for now. It allows me a measure of protection.'

That was absurd – for him to feel he was in any way at *her* mercy – but Alice didn't argue. She needed him to buy nappies.

Taking the rucksack from the back seat, he hooked it over his shoulder and locked the car. They joined a stream of travellers making their way into the building, and no one gave them a glance. Alice realised they must look like three generations of the same family: father, daughter, granddaughter. Even the thought of it seemed like a dreadful insult to her actual father, who had died of brain cancer when he was only fifty-two.

Their first destination was the shop, where she was able to find nappies and wet wipes. Renshaw spared her the humiliation of having to ask him to pay. He turned away from her as he opened his wallet, but not before she'd spotted a thick wad of notes.

He escorted her to the baby change room and said he'd make his phone call while she dealt with Evie. They would meet outside once she was finished.

Alice felt an indescribable relief to be alone with her daughter. The poor girl was now starving, and fed greedily for ten minutes before pausing, exhausted by the effort. Alice winded her, then changed her nappy. It was full to bursting, but fortunately hadn't leaked into her clothes.

She let Evie lie bare-legged, giving her a chance to stretch after so long cooped up in the carrier. Blowing on her tummy made her writhe with pleasure, and Alice was struck by the natural resilience of an infant: so long as you fed her, kept her clean and warm, Evie didn't really care about anything else.

After another quick feed Alice put her back in the carrier while she herself used the toilet and tried to freshen up a little. She'd now been in the baby change room for nearly half an hour. She was surprised that Renshaw hadn't lost patience and knocked on the door.

Maybe he's abandoned me here, she thought, and then asked herself: *Would that be better, or worse, than to find him waiting outside?*

When she came out, Renshaw was nowhere to be seen. At first her stomach lurched with panic at the many challenges now facing her. Twenty past four on a Friday afternoon and she was stranded, over a hundred miles from home, with no money and no phone. Where could she turn for help? Was there some way she could get a bus, or a train?

God, was I always this pathetic, she scolded herself, *or has motherhood addled my brain?*

It was a question that, for better or worse, she wouldn't have to answer, because at that moment Renshaw emerged from a shadowy alcove that contained several fruit machines. He beamed at her, pressing his hands together in silent applause.

'My friend has agreed to put us up.'

Alice gave this news a guarded smile. 'Oh. Good.'

'The baby fed well, I hope?' Renshaw patted his stomach. 'Now we will do the same.'

Alice was taken aback by the change in his demeanour. He seemed an altogether more charming and jovial man than the one who'd snapped and snarled at her earlier. Even so, she held her ground as he turned towards the cafe.

'I'm prepared to come with you, but there's one condition. I have to speak to Harry again.'

She waited, horrified by the thought that passersby might assume this was a father-daughter spat. But this was the approach she'd decided on while feeding Evie, and it was non-negotiable.

Renshaw made a sucking sound with his tongue and teeth. 'Very well. May I suggest you wait until we leave here?'

Alice frowned. 'So we eat, and then I can phone him?'

'Correct.'

'All right. But I mean it. I'm not going anywhere till I've spoken to him.'

Feeling slightly sore that she'd been outmanoeuvred, she followed him to one of the food counters. The dining area was crowded and noisy, with the clatter of crockery and the scrape of chairs on the wooden floor. A dismal setting for a meal, and yet the sight of hot food made her stomach growl with desire.

'So where does this friend of yours live?'

'Nerys is in a village called Cranstone, in Gloucestershire.'

'Isn't that miles from here?'

'Not too far, according to her. And tomorrow I will drive you and the baby to Gloucester. I will also bear the cost of the rail fare to Brighton.' He spoke as if Alice should be overwhelmed with gratitude. 'Remember, though, that it may still be dangerous to go back.'

'I'll take my chances,' Alice said. 'I'm not sure about staying overnight, either. I want to see what Harry says first.'

She expected an argument, but he inclined his head. 'Very well.'

'Anyway, is this friend of yours aware that I have a small baby with me? Only that could come as a shock.'

'It will be no problem, I assure you.'

'Does she have a family?'

'She is widowed. I believe there is a son, but he will be grown-up now, no doubt living elsewhere.' He smiled fondly. 'Nerys is a good woman. We worked together once.'

'Oh? Doing what?'

'I am a doctor. Nerys was my assistant.'

Alice couldn't help gaping at him. She recalled one of the men on Wednesday night mentioning Renshaw's title, but had assumed it was fake, along with the other names he used.

'How did you get mixed up in something like this?'

'The answer is simple. My job – my vocation – is to help people. All my life, this has been my guiding principle. To help. But this time I made a mistake. I helped the *wrong* people.'

THIRTY

Harry remained crouched in the back of the Corsa until they found a safe place to stop, in the car park of a leisure centre on the edge of Burgess Hill. On the way there, Ruth described how she'd checked out of her hotel and then driven to Lavinia Street.

'There was a police car outside your house, so I parked on the corner and had a look at number 43. The back door had been forced. I went inside, had a look around ...' She paused. 'Renshaw had set a trap in the kitchen. Bleach. From the look of it, one of Laird's men could have suffered some nasty burns.'

'Oh, Jesus. This is the guy who's got my wife and daughter ...'

'He has no reason to harm them. The trap was self-defence, which is understandable in the circumstances.'

Harry thought about the hammer he'd kept beneath his pillow and found he couldn't disagree. When Ruth pulled up he got out of the car, stretched his cramped limbs and returned to the front seat.

'I fucked up, didn't I?' he said. 'The police must have responded to my 999 call.'

'Could be. They take domestic incidents a lot more seriously than they used to.'

'This isn't a domestic—'

'No, but that's the way it looks to them. Abduction by strangers is rare enough when the victim is a child. It's almost unheard of for a mother and child to be taken together. But vengeful fathers turning violent on their families? That, I'm afraid, happens with depressing regularity, week in, week out. Which makes you the first and strongest suspect.'

'My parents won't believe I've done anything to them. Neither will Alice's mum.'

Ruth made a sceptical noise in her throat. 'Maybe your mother got worried and called the police?' Ignoring the look of horror on his face, she said, 'You can hand yourself in, Harry, but you won't be able to tell them where to find your family. And without evidence the police won't give your story any credence.'

'Not even with Renshaw's house … ?'

'Where's the proof of a connection?' she shot back.

Harry nodded. Cautiously, he said, 'You could corroborate it for me, couldn't you?'

'No.'

'Why not?'

'It just wouldn't work. Trust me. The only thing that's gonna help you is having Alice and Evie reappear, unharmed. And right now I can't make that happen any more than you can.'

Smarting at what felt like another dressing-down, Harry gave her directions to the town centre. Ruth pulled into a bus stop while Harry ran to the nearest ATM. He had a couple of cards, and used them to withdraw a total of six hundred pounds, all the time wondering if this was a huge overreaction. He was aware that the police could trace the use of a bank card, but would they really do so on the basis of a single muddled phone call?

Back in the car, they took a different route out of town, heading north towards Haywards Heath. Ruth wanted to know if he'd spoken to Keri.

'Yes. But I didn't get her address.' He relayed the conversation, expecting disappointment, but she only nodded impassively.

'Tomorrow at twelve is good enough.'

'There's no way I can go up there …'

'All I want you to do is call Keri tomorrow, get the address and text it to me. Then I'll go see her, and you can focus on your family.'

That didn't seem unreasonable, so he said, 'And what about tonight?'

'Crawley.'

'Why Crawley?'

'Foster and Bridge were booked into the Hickstead Travelodge on Wednesday night. What I didn't mention was that I saw them checking out on Thursday morning.'

Harry turned in his seat to stare at her. 'So telling me to keep a watch out for their cars, that was just bullshit?'

'Everyone likes to feel useful.'

'Not if they're being taken for a fool.' He waited till she glanced in his direction. 'I'm finding it hard enough to trust you as it is …'

'Like I say, Harry, that's a decision you have to make. I can drop you right here if you want, but the chances are you'll be in a police cell by morning. And Alice and Evie might still be missing.'

Harry turned away in disgust. After a moment he felt her hand on his arm.

'I'm sorry. You've gotta understand that I'm not used to collaborating. I tell you only what you need to know, because that's what my instinct says I should do. The same way your wife didn't tell you about the parcel. And you didn't tell her about me.'

'And look at the mess it's caused, us not being straight with each other.'

Ruth said nothing for a second, then she nodded. 'All right. Let's talk some more about this parcel.'

'Which one?'

His question made her gasp. Her hands tightened on the steering wheel. 'Say again?'

'I thought you'd overheard Alice, on the phone. She said there was another parcel – well, *package* was her exact word.'

'I only heard a few snippets.' Ruth pursed her lips. Her gaze remained fixed on the road but her mind, Harry sensed, was somewhere else entirely. 'A package, that's what she called it? Not parcel.'

'No, though I don't suppose there's much difference.'

Ruth pondered. 'Go back to the first one. How did she describe that?'

'Just a standard A4 envelope, quite thick and solid. We thought it might have been …' At the last moment he changed his mind, and said: 'Paper, or something.'

Ruth wasn't fooled. 'Paper, as in money?'

'Possibly. She didn't open it, if that's what you're thinking.'

She shook her head. 'I'm not accusing your wife of anything. Money sounds like a plausible thing for them to be chasing. But the second delivery … to me, the word "package" suggests something smaller.'

'Maybe. Hopefully I can find out soon, if I'm able to speak to her.'

'Can't use your phone,' she reminded him, and when he started to protest: 'Don't worry. I have one you can borrow.'

Harry grunted his thanks, but he was preoccupied by the memory of his last conversation with Alice. 'What I can't work out is why she tried to give the thing to Renshaw. If she'd called the police instead, we wouldn't now be in this fucking mess.'

'No, but you might have been in some other fucking mess, maybe a much worse one.'

Her tone was so dark that Harry didn't push the issue. Right now he didn't want to contemplate anything worse than this.

THIRTY-ONE

Alice had fish and chips and ate about half of it. Setting her cutlery down, she earned a disapproving look from Renshaw.

'You don't care for the food?'

'No, it's quite nice. I'm just … my stomach's churning.'

Renshaw had already wolfed down a steak pie, but evidently had room for more. He speared one of her chips with his fork and said, 'Anything else you remember?'

She shook her head. 'No. That's it.'

During the meal he'd peppered her with questions about the ordeal on Thursday morning, and the subsequent visit by Warley and Cassell. But he had ignored Alice's own questions, gesturing at his plate as if to make plain that his hunger took precedence over her curiosity.

After devouring a few more chips, he sat back and patted his belly. 'Proper hot food. A rare treat, indeed.'

'How long have you been living like that?'

Renshaw squinted as he did the calculation. 'Almost fifteen months.'

'And you didn't leave the house at all?'

'Once a week, late at night, to stock up on food and keep the car running. Thank heaven for Asda, and twenty-four-hour opening.' He snorted. 'But there were many difficulties. The rubbish piled up, because I could take only small amounts out with me. Organic waste I washed down the toilet, using a bucket to flush because the cistern was too loud. I had no lights on, except for one room which had foil on the window. No heating but for one electric fire. For hot water I had to use a kettle, because the pipes were too noisy.'

'How did you find it in the first place?'

'I knew the owner, a long time ago. She lives abroad, and agreed to say nothing about my presence there.'

'And what about the escape route?'

'It was planned from the beginning. I ascertained that my neighbour lived alone and was frequently out of the house. After breaking through I went next door regularly to make sure there were no nasty surprises.'

'I can't believe Lawrence didn't know you lived there.'

He blinked slowly a couple of times, as if offended. 'Did *you* know I lived there?'

'No,' she conceded. 'And no one else has ever mentioned it.'

'People today exist in a bubble of their own selfishness. It is quite easy to be invisible in a street such as yours.'

He said it with a measure of scorn. Alice felt an urge to defend her community, but now she had him talking there were more important things to discuss.

'Who are they? And why are they so determined to find you?'

'I told you, I worked for them.'

'You were employed as a doctor, by criminals?'

He glowered at her incredulous tone. 'Yes. I wished to retire, but they would not permit that.'

'Why didn't you go to the police?'

'And become an informer? Ha! You think the police will keep me safe, year after year? You think I would get a new life, a new identity, the way it happens in the movies?'

Alice sighed. It was exactly what the two men had warned them.

'But the parcel on Tuesday,' she said. 'It was full of money, wasn't it?'

Renshaw sat forward, resting his elbows on the table, and laced his hands together. He wore a defiant gaze as he said, 'It is a fraction of what I am owed.'

'Weren't you taking a big risk, having it delivered to the wrong address?'

'The risk came from venturing out in daylight. But I chose the destination well. Your number, 34, is my number reversed. An understandable error. I judged that you were trustworthy, and as a new mother there was a high probability that you would be home when the package arrived. That way I could intercept it swiftly, before you became curious.'

Alice suppressed a shudder at the thought that Renshaw had made a conscious decision to involve her – and that the decision had been prompted by Evie's presence in the house. He must have been watching her for weeks.

'What was in the envelope today?'

His expression became guarded. 'Insurance,' he muttered, checking his watch. 'We should go.'

'Hold on. I want to know who sent them.'

'It was a man called Hasan Mansur. I saved his life once. He did this to repay me, at great risk.'

'So he stole money from them?' Alice frowned. 'How did he manage to send two packages, if the gang came after the first one?'

'He waited many months for the right opportunity.' Renshaw looked sombre. 'On Monday I received a text, saying the first package had been sent. There was another text on Wednesday, to say Hasan would be sending the second item that night. Since then, nothing.'

'So you think they found out about it on Wednesday?'

Renshaw nodded. 'Hasan must have been forced to reveal the address I gave him. I cannot blame him. But perhaps he kept from them the existence of the second package.' A sigh. 'Either way, he is almost certainly dead by now.'

There was a brief interruption from Evie, who burped in her sleep and then smiled. Renshaw shifted in his seat, eager to be away, but Alice couldn't leave it there.

'What are they involved in, precisely? Drugs?'

'A little. Not so much, these days. They have legitimate enterprises that flourish now, but also some illegal gambling. Other entertainments, too. Prostitution.'

Alice recoiled in distaste. 'And you were part of that?'

'I helped to look after the young ladies,' he said indignantly. 'These are not cheap whores touting for business on the streets. It is a high-class operation.'

'Maybe. But we're still talking about a group of men profiting from the exploitation of women.'

He gave her a withering look. 'You think prostitution will fizzle away because middle-class feminists disapprove of it? Huh. Some people do not have the same comfortable choices that have been available to you.'

'I know that—' she began, but he cut her off.

'And do you know that for many it is an informed choice? That what you call exploitation can be something they find enjoyable and rewarding? For these women, the real exploitation is to toil for forty or fifty hours a week in factories or shops. Stocking shelves at four a.m. in Asda.'

'You can't compare that with prostitution. And whatever the motive, the idea of women having to sell their bodies for sex is repulsive.'

'Only because you are English, and the English are sexually repressed.' He gave her a thin, knowing smile, which caused Alice's face to burn red.

It was almost a relief when he stood up, until she remembered that another, far more important confrontation was looming.

The Friday evening rush was well underway. Fighting through a horde of travellers at the exit, Alice experienced a desperate longing to spot someone she knew, someone more reliable who could offer her shelter for the night.

'I need to call Harry,' she reminded him.

'Yes, yes. At the car.'

Outside it was quickly growing dark, and bitterly cold. A glitter of frost was already visible on some of the cars. Alice shivered, unable to shake off a conviction that Renshaw would fail to keep his word.

He unlocked the car, opened his door and then stopped, realising that she had made no move to get in.

'What?' he asked.

'I was thinking, why don't I ask Harry to come and get me?'

'From here?' Renshaw's eyes narrowed. 'But the woman? If she is working for them ...'

'I don't think Harry's that naïve. Besides, I'm willing to take the chance.' Seeing the doubt on his face, she said, 'You'll be long gone by the time they get here, so it's no risk to you.'

Another pause. She could almost see tiny cogs whirring inside his head. At last he shrugged, and produced Alice's phone.

'Very well. But make the call from the car. It is too cold out here.'

On that point Alice didn't argue. Renshaw started the engine and turned the heating up, then handed her the phone.

With a heartfelt sigh, he said, 'I realise that my own situation has been weighing so heavy, I failed to give enough thought to what you must be feeling. I want you to know I am truly sorry.'

Alice nodded, taken aback by such an effusive apology, and the fact that he had agreed to her suggestion. The possibility of being reunited with Harry, perhaps within an hour or two, lifted her spirits enormously.

She looked down at her phone and saw that the display remained dark. She pressed the power button again. Nothing happened.

'Weird,' she murmured to herself. She had seen Renshaw switch her phone off earlier, and she was certain it had been charged as normal last night. She'd had a few problems before with some of the background apps draining power, but thought that had been sorted out. 'Battery's dead.'

Renshaw clicked his tongue. 'I find such gadgets are often temperamental. Please, use this.'

He produced a battered old Nokia. Still puzzled, Alice took it and keyed in Harry's number from memory. It diverted immediately to voicemail.

She checked the number, reading it aloud, then dialled again. Voicemail. *What was going on?*

'A problem?' Renshaw asked gently.

'He's not answering.' There were horrible images crowding her mind: Harry held prisoner by the men from Thursday morning; Harry in bed with this mysterious woman …

'We must go now.' Renshaw moved to put the car in gear.

'But I could still wait here …'

'And what if he does not answer?' He offered a smile. 'Stay if you must, but this is no place for your infant. Nerys will look after us; you have nothing to fear.'

Alice sighed. She knew in her heart he was right. Being stranded at the services wasn't an appealing prospect, especially when she had no money and no working phone.

'I'm sorry, I didn't mean to be rude. I just want to be back with my husband.'

'Of course. And you should text him now, to say you are well. Tonight, perhaps, we can arrange for you to meet him somewhere.'

'What if I sent him your friend's address?'

'Ah. I would prefer to keep that to myself.'

'Because of this woman with Harry?'

'Partly it is that.' Renshaw seemed to be wincing as he spoke. 'Also, if you do not know this information, they cannot later extract it from you.'

Alice had a minute to dwell on the comment while she helped Renshaw negotiate a route out of the services and back on to the motorway. At one point he ignored the lane markings and was nearly side-swiped by a van. It was only when they were trundling west at a steady fifty miles an hour that she felt it was safe to compose a text. The archaic phone was a struggle to use, so she kept the message brief.

Harry, this is Alice on Renshaw phone. Me and Evie fine. Staying at R friend in Gloucs, hope to call u later to collect us. Let me know who u r xx

Checking the text to be sure it had sent, she spotted the error. She had intended to say: Let me know *how* you are. Would he perceive that as a dig at him, because of his mystery companion – and did she even care if that was his interpretation?

Or was she just very tired, and lonely, and prone to overthinking everything?

'Done now, yes?' Renshaw said, after she had conspicuously failed to return the phone. She was hoping against hope that Harry would call straight back.

Evie began to squirm, screwing up her face and moaning in her sleep. There was a bowel movement coming, Alice guessed. She put the phone down between the seats, and while she was trying to make things more comfortable for Evie, Renshaw deftly returned it to his pocket.

It took a while to settle the baby, Renshaw grumbling about the effect on his concentration. Finally Evie was calm again, apparently having passed nothing more than wind.

'What was in the bucket?'

The question just popped out before Alice could consider the wisdom of asking it.

Renshaw shifted in his seat, and the car gave a corresponding wobble. 'It was bleach.'

Alice gasped. 'So you might have … disfigured him?'

'Do you care?'

She hesitated. Her immediate reaction was to feel sickened by the idea, but then she had to remember who they were talking about here: not innocent victims, unfortunate bystanders, but men with knives and guns who had terrorised her family. Just the image of Evie being hauled from her crib produced a surge of fury, as intense now as when it had happened.

'No, I suppose not,' she said.

THIRTY-TWO

In return for telling her about the parcels, Harry was given a little more information: yesterday Ruth had followed Foster, Bridge and another man to a hotel in Crawley, a shuttle bus ride from Gatwick airport.

'I don't know if they're still there. Probably not.'

He frowned at the regret in her voice. 'Isn't that a good thing? I mean, are we following them or hiding from them?'

'We're doing both, Harry. We need to stay on their trail—'

'*You* need to stay on their trail. *I* need to find my wife and daughter.'

'Yeah, but right now we have no clues as to where they've gone. Until we do, this is as good a place as any to stay tonight. As long as we're careful.'

He saw how serious she was when they reached the hotel, a huge and rather ugly modern construction close to the town centre. They drove into the car park beneath the building, and the way Ruth scouted it made the earlier search at Hickstead seem cursory by comparison. She appeared to stare at every number plate, as if committing it to memory. The tension unnerved him, but it also made him cross that he'd been so easily fooled before.

Finally she parked in a space close to the exit and told him the plan. She intended to book them in, then summon Harry so that he could go directly to the room.

'The fewer people who see you, the better. Once you're inside I'm going to pop out to get some stuff from the shopping mall along the road. And I want to make a call, see if I can check out those fake cops.'

She fetched a small suitcase from the boot and unzipped the pocket at the front. To Harry's surprise, she handed him a cheap Samsung phone.

'Please don't use it without asking me first. I'll call you in a minute with the room number.'

He nodded, feeling increasingly like a child in the care of an over-protective guardian. When Ruth shut the door, he thought for a second that she might instruct him to lock the car for his own safety.

He spent the next ten minutes listening to the tick of the cooling engine and the rumble of passing traffic. Then the phone trilled.

'Room 224,' said Ruth. She described the layout of the hotel, and how to avoid coming to the notice of the staff at reception.

As it was, there were a couple of off-duty flight crews waiting at the check-in desk, so nobody paid Harry any attention as he hurried through the impressive atrium that dominated the ground floor of the main building. Ruth met him at the lifts, explaining that they could only be operated with the key card.

'I booked just the one room. Best save money where we can. It's twin beds, though.'

'Oh.' Harry dreaded to think how Alice would greet the news that her husband intended to spend the night in a hotel with another woman.

'Don't worry,' Ruth added wryly. 'I'm not going to jump your bones, as we say in Yorkshire.'

The room was bland – beige walls and a plain blue carpet – but it was a reasonable size and in good order. The en suite looked decent, too.

He gave Ruth her car keys but was reluctant to hand over the phone. 'Can I use this to contact Alice?'

'You mean you haven't called her already?'

Ruth grinned as she said it, so he replied with the same tone of amused irony: 'I thought I had to get your permission.' After all, if they were going to be stuck in this room until morning, it was better that they got along. 'I was thinking, if she was able to contact the police and let them know she's all right ...'

Ruth looked sceptical, but didn't veto the idea. 'Can you get her number without switching your own phone back on?'

He tapped his head. 'It's in here.'

'Go on, then.' She eased past him, and he had a foretaste of the awkwardness that lay ahead: washing, undressing, lying awake in the dark. 'While you do that, I've got to put a parking ticket in the car, then do some shopping. Do you want me to buy some food, or we could get room service later?'

'I'm not hungry, thanks.'

'Okay. I might pick up some snacks.' She looked at her watch. 'I should be thirty, forty minutes max. You've got your own key card, but I'd advise you to stay here in the room. And don't use the phone other than to call your wife.'

'I know, I know.' He shooed her towards the door. 'I won't think for myself any more. I've learned my lesson.'

Maybe he had, Ruth thought, and maybe he hadn't. At heart Harry seemed like a good man, and certainly likeable enough – and yet she was aware of a constant nagging irritation when she was with him.

The reason, she deduced, was that she felt a sense of almost parental responsibility towards him. The age gap was probably no more than ten or fifteen years, but added to the imbalance in their respective life experiences, that was more than enough for a mother–son dynamic to form.

That's what you don't like, said the critical voice in her head. *That he seems so young and innocent. So unlike you.*

She propped the parking ticket on the dashboard, then walked out of the hotel into the glare of artificial lights. Above them, night had fallen, and the air was cold and crisp. Her breath emerged in clouds of steam. A perfect night for bonfires and fireworks, baked potatoes and hot toddies.

In another life, she thought.

The main road dipped beneath a bridge and then rose, but it ran straight enough to make out the shops, less than a quarter of a mile away. There was a lot of slow-moving traffic, pumping clouds of exhaust into the air. A lot of pedestrians about, too, mostly people traipsing home from work.

Ruth quickened her pace. She was still fretting about Harry, and how he would adjust to his new status as a fugitive. She knew the unreality of it would keep clawing at him, impairing his judgement, which was why she needed to get back before he did anything foolish.

Shouldn't have left him the phone, she was thinking as a car slowed alongside her. It was a Peugeot estate with three occupants: two males and a female. And there was a detachable blue light on the roof, of a type Ruth hadn't seen for a while: these days most unmarked cars had lights concealed behind the front grille.

As these thoughts passed through her head, she made the mistake of breaking her stride. It meant that the man who emerged from the passenger seat was able to step directly in front of her, holding up a warrant card, while the woman climbed out of the back, a baseball cap hiding her face.

For one long wasted second it struck Ruth that these people might be genuine police officers. But the man wasn't dissimilar to Harry's description of DI Warley, and the woman – that wise voice in her head was now shrieking at her – *the woman was Sian Vickery.*

'Come with us, please, madam.' The man took hold of her arm and Ruth couldn't pull away because Vickery was on her other side, hemming her in; both displaying their ID wallets for the benefit of any witnesses. Some of the passersby were frowning, some smiling, but none seemed in any doubt as to what was happening here. A masterstroke, tactically speaking.

'What are you— no!' she blurted, at this point still more humiliated than scared. After warning Harry to stay alert, she'd been careless herself, and all because she thought it would be quicker to walk to the shops than drive.

She shouted: 'Help me, please! They're not real pol—'

'Come on, madam.' Vickery sounded firm but not unfriendly. 'The doctors warned us you'd say that.'

They hustled her towards the car, the man subtly applying far more pressure to her arm than was necessary. Ruth cried out, hoping to gain a measure of sympathy, but Vickery grabbed hold of her hair and wrenched the wig from her head.

There was a horrified gasp from the onlookers: all their prejudices confirmed in that single act.

Vickery tossed the wig into the footwell and slid along the back seat, pulling on Ruth's arm as Warley shoved her into the car. He got in last, shutting the door behind him. Vickery had taken something from her pocket – Ruth caught the flash of a needle – but by now the car was moving, all the doors and windows tightly shut, and the sharp stab of pain in her arm told her it was futile to struggle. She was theirs now, and no one who'd witnessed her abduction would think they had seen anything other than an unruly woman trying to resist a legitimate arrest.

THIRTY-THREE

The journey to Gloucester took far longer than anticipated, and the mood in the car became tense and fractious. Even with Alice studying a road atlas and issuing clear instructions, Renshaw had a habit of trundling past important junctions, or turning left when she had distinctly said right.

Just north of Cirencester they came off the A417 by accident, and then continued on a succession of winding narrow lanes, all of them woefully short of illumination and road signs. As poor a driver as he had been in daylight, Renshaw was even worse in darkness. Alice was almost tempted to offer to take the wheel herself, except that it would mean Renshaw holding Evie, and she couldn't allow that. It was bad enough that Evie wasn't in a car seat to begin with.

Eventually they located the village of Cranstone, which appeared to be little more than a handful of pale stone cottages with a matching church. Then Renshaw confessed that his friend lived another mile or so further on. He pulled up and took out his phone to call for directions.

'Can I see if Harry's texted back?' Alice asked quickly.

Sighing, Renshaw checked the display, then showed it to her: nothing. He made the call and there was a brief conversation. Alice noticed that several times he said *I*, not *we*.

'I have not mentioned you yet,' he admitted when she pressed him on it. 'But it will be no problem, I assure you.'

This time, crawling through the darkness, Renshaw managed to locate the correct turning on the first attempt. He drove down a lane that was barely wide enough to accommodate their car. Tall hedges loomed over them on each side, stray branches clawing the car as they passed.

There were only a handful of properties along here, set so well back that they were all but invisible. Most had name plates fixed to the gateposts, which Alice read aloud for Renshaw's benefit.

'High View … The Old Lodge …'

'Beech House,' Renshaw muttered. 'We need Beech— ah!'

He braked sharply beside a set of open gates. Alice couldn't see a name anywhere, but Renshaw seemed to feel this was the place. He turned on to a gravel drive, and gave a small exhalation as the property came into view. It was a substantial-looking farmhouse built in Cotswold stone. Five or six bedrooms at least, Alice guessed.

'Not what you were expecting?'

'It's …' Renshaw began, then hesitated, as if he wanted her to believe he knew Nerys better than he did. 'She has done well,' he said ruefully. 'Very well.'

There was a spacious parking area in front of a double garage, but no other vehicles in sight. Renshaw parked and got out, telling Alice to stay where she was. Presumably he wanted a chance to explain to Nerys that he'd brought along a couple of additional guests.

He'd left his door open and the air coming into the car was icy cold. Alice snuggled Evie against her but she knew they couldn't wait here long, or they'd both freeze. But as Renshaw reached the house, the front door opened and a woman emerged, wearing a black knitted dress over black leggings. She was in her late fifties, well-built rather than fat, with a distinctly hourglass figure. She had a rounded face with a pale complexion, and dark wavy hair.

Ignoring Renshaw's order, Alice began the task of manoeuvring her way out of the car without waking Evie. The woman noticed her at once and gave Renshaw a quizzical look. For a second her amiable expression gave way to something quite fierce, and Renshaw seemed taken aback by it.

'Nerys, I am so sorry. I will explain.'

The woman nodded, rather neutrally. Renshaw made to embrace her but Nerys caught his arms at the wrists and held them while she turned her head to one side, allowing him to place a kiss on her cheek.

'It's just for one night?' Her voice was low-pitched, with a soft Welsh accent.

'One night. I promise. Tomorrow, Alice here can return home on the train.'

He was trying not scowl as Alice joined him. Nerys offered her a weary but welcoming smile.

'Hello, I'm Nerys.' After shaking hands with Alice, she gently touched the carrier. 'And who's this little sweetie?'

'Evie.'

'Evie? She's adorable. Now, you must come in, out of the cold.'

She waved Alice into the house. Renshaw was turning towards the car when Nerys, still in a mild tone of voice, asked quietly: 'No one followed you here?'

'No. I'm certain of that.'

'I hope so, Edward. I've put the past behind me. I thought you had, too.'

*

The comment had a faintly bitter edge to it, but Alice could see why Nerys was so keen to keep her new life firmly separate from the old, if this house was anything to go by.

She was in an entrance hall so spacious that it wasn't cramped by the presence of a bureau and a couple of easy chairs. Its centrepiece was a wide staircase, and there were doors to several living rooms. The decor and furnishings were old, and in some cases slightly tired, but in a way that was entirely sympathetic to the age and style of property. From the kitchen came the delicious aroma of fresh baking.

Alice could hear a TV playing in the nearest of the living rooms. She recognised it as the six o'clock news: a reminder that right now she and Harry ought to be at home, bathing Evie, getting her ready for bed, then settling down to usher in the weekend with pizza and maybe a glass or two of wine ...

'It's a beautiful home,' Alice said, wondering if her relief was evident. She'd been anticipating somewhere a lot more basic.

'Oh, it's a bit ridiculous, really, me on my own in a place this size. But it's the sort of house I always set my heart on, you know? And my son's often round – his kids just love it here.'

'How many grandchildren do you have?'

'Four, now,' she said proudly. 'The latest probably isn't much older than your wee darling ...'

There was enough of a question in her voice for Alice to say, 'Evie's eight weeks, and already has a mind of her own.'

'Don't they all?' Nerys winked. 'Still, us girls have to take charge from an early age, don't we?'

They made small talk while Renshaw unloaded the car. He trudged in with the rucksack on his back, the bag of nappies in one hand and a heavy-looking duffle bag in the other. That, presumably, had been stashed in the boot, ready for a quick getaway.

Nerys peered at the carrier bag as Renshaw passed it to Alice. 'Is this all you have?'

'We left in a hurry,' Alice said.

'Let me get settled, and I will tell you the story,' Renshaw said.

Nerys gestured to the front room. 'Help yourself to a drink while I show Alice to the nursery.'

'Nursery?' Alice queried.

'Oh, yes. It's where the youngest ones stay when they sleep over. Well, not the babe, Mikey, yet. He's almost twelve weeks, and won't be parted from Mummy.'

She climbed the stairs at a brisk pace, explaining a little of the house's history. In the thirties it had been owned by a world-famous naturalist with a brood of eight children, and later by a cinematographer with an Oscar to his name.

'My husband's in the film business,' Alice said. 'Special effects.'

The words were out before she'd had a chance to consider the wisdom of revealing too much about herself and her family.

'How fascinating. I can't believe some of the things they can do nowadays. And I love those animations, like *Toy Story* and the one with monsters. Mind you, my granddaughters watch *Frozen* so often, I think there ought to be a support group for us grown-ups!'

Alice laughed politely and made noises of agreement while admiring the landing. As with the hall, it was wide enough to accommodate a bookcase and an antique writing desk.

The nursery was no less impressive. It was a vast room, containing both a double and a single bed as well as an old-fashioned crib and a huge wardrobe, painted white and decorated with a pattern of climbing roses. A similar design had been hand-painted on one of the walls, feeding into a large mural of a woodland scene, complete with bubbling stream and verdant meadow. Various mythical creatures frolicked along the riverbank: nymphs and fairies and fawns. The other walls were painted cream, while the ceiling was decorated with a sumptuous *trompe l'oeil* sky with white fluffy clouds drifting overhead. Pre-motherhood, Alice might have regarded the whole thing as a bit sickly and overdone. As a newly sentimental parent she adored it.

'This is absolutely … amazing!'

'You can see why it's a hit with the children, though I have a devil of a job stopping Betty from embellishing it with her crayons.' Nerys was bustling around the beds, plumping pillows and turning back the covers. 'Now, I can make up the crib if you'd like, or would you prefer Evie to share the double with you?'

'She'll be fine with me. I don't want to put you to any more trouble.'

'It's a pleasure, honestly. The bathroom's right next door. Why don't I leave you to freshen up, and when you're ready, come down and have something to eat and drink.'

'Sounds great. Thank you.'

Nerys paused in the doorway. The thoughtful look on her face gave Alice a little jolt of alarm. She was about to ask what was wrong when Nerys snapped out of it, smiled broadly and left the room.

Alice stood still for a moment, taking a few deep breaths while she tried to come to terms with the day's events. Yes, it had been horrific, but she and Evie had come through it, physically unscathed. Now they were somewhere comfortable and safe.

Time to look on the bright side. There was only tonight to endure: tomorrow, all being well, she and Evie could go back to their normal lives.

Evie wriggled, moaning softly. Easing her out of the carrier and taking off her pramsuit, Alice wandered across to the larger of two windows and drew back the curtain. The room overlooked the back garden, but there was little she could make out in the darkness: a wide lawn, hedges and trees, a couple of vague shapes that might have been a shed and a climbing frame or swing. There were no lights anywhere, nothing to indicate the presence of neighbouring homes or farms. She pictured the acres of wild open countryside that must lie beyond the garden, and thought: *What an idyllic setting.*

And then it struck her: perhaps Nerys had chosen to hide away from the world for exactly the same reason as Renshaw.

Alice might be safe here for the time being, but that didn't mean she could let her guard down.

THIRTY-FOUR

Alone in the hotel room, Harry decided to take a long shower. The pleasure was diminished somewhat by the prospect of having to dress in the clothes he'd been wearing all day, but at least it left him feeling moderately fresher than before.

Afterwards he sat on one of the beds and stared at the phones in his hands. His own was still switched off. The Samsung, loaned to him by Ruth, steadfastly refused to bring him an incoming message. He'd sent three texts to Alice's phone and called her half a dozen times, and all he'd got was voicemail.

What really ate at him was the thought that his own phone might hold the message that would ease all his fears. But Ruth had warned him not to turn it on, in case the authorities tracked his location. That seemed like overkill to him. Ridiculous.

Aware that his willpower was slipping away, he placed the phone on the unit by the TV, then returned to the bed and played around with the remote control. He found BBC1, where the six o'clock news had just got underway.

He frowned. He wasn't sure precisely how long Ruth had been gone, but it had to be getting on for an hour.

That meant she ought to be back any minute. He comforted himself with the knowledge that at least he hadn't done anything stupid in her absence.

Yet.

*

After a while he muted the TV volume. He didn't want to hear about other people's problems; nor was he interested in what the TV companies classed as entertainment at this time of the evening.

But his tetchiness was a warning sign. If Ruth wasn't here soon he might not be able to resist using his phone.

Then it hit him with brilliant clarity. Ruth wasn't coming back. She must have found another way to locate Keri, and so Harry, having served his purpose, had simply been discarded.

He grabbed his trainers and the key card, then noticed Ruth's suitcase on the floor by the bed. Why had she brought it in here, if she was intending to do a runner?

He hesitated, aware that the combination of stress and solitude might be causing him to overreact. It was all too easy to think the worst.

Fortunately there was a straightforward way to find out.

He passed several other guests on his way through the atrium, but no one paid him any attention. He took the steps down to the car park and felt only a queasy satisfaction at the sight of the empty bay where Ruth's Corsa had been parked. Another couple of minutes and he had surveyed the rest of the car park and verified it beyond doubt.

Ruth was gone. He was on his own.

Returning to the room, he tipped the contents of her case on to the bed. It was mostly clothing: underwear, t-shirts, a spare pair of jeans, plus a toiletry bag with just the basics for a few days away. A second wig, this one with reddish, wavy hair. There was nothing essential: no paperwork or identifying documents, no keys or money or personal items. Everything here could be quickly replaced – and evidently the cost of doing so had been a price worth paying to be rid of him without further complication.

Of course, he still had the phone she'd given him, which held her number from when she'd called with the all-clear from the hotel room.

He rang it, and a recorded voice informed him that the mobile was switched off. There was no option to leave a message.

He slumped on to the bed and considered his options. First he wondered if something could have happened to her. But that was almost too terrible to imagine.

The desire to check his own phone was now overpowering. As for being tracked, his understanding – admittedly garnered from TV cop shows – was that the signal could be triangulated using the nearest base stations. Given that his location was right in the centre of Crawley, pinpointing this hotel must be next to impossible.

'Worth the risk,' he murmured to himself. He powered up the phone, and a series of quiet chimes announced that he was a man in demand. He had a stack of missed calls and three voicemail messages: one from Sam at work and two from his mum. Wiser to ignore those, he decided.

He switched to texts. Five messages, the first a junk thing about concert tickets. One from Sam, wishing Alice a speedy recovery, which made no sense until he remembered his earlier lie about the migraine. One each from Alice's mum and his own mother, while the remaining text was from an unfamiliar number. Maybe the detective who'd spoken to him on the phone?

Braced for disappointment, he opened that next and was rewarded with a surge of relief.

Harry, this is Alice on Renshaw phone. Me and Evie fine. Staying at R friend in Gloucs, hope to call u later to collect us. Let me know who u r xx

Alice was okay. They were both safe and well, and free to come home. Harry wasn't sure why Alice hadn't been able to text him from her own phone, but that seemed a minor detail in the circumstances.

He read it again. This time the last line made him frown. *Let me know* who *you are.* He hoped it was an error, rather than a dig at him for holding back information.

Still puzzling over it, he happened to glance at the TV and saw a familiar location on screen.

Lavinia Street.

The sight of his home on the local news came as an almost physical blow. Harry reeled back in shock, hoping desperately it was a coincidence: something else had happened in Lavinia Street to attract the media's attention …

He restored the volume in time to hear an improbably handsome man, identified as Detective Inspector Thomsett, issuing an urgent appeal for Brighton filmmaker Harry French to make contact with Sussex Police. They cut to a head shot of Harry, taken from the LiveFire website, while DI Thomsett explained that, following calls to the police made from the property earlier in the day, they now had serious concerns for the welfare of Harry, his wife Alice and their infant daughter.

Another picture: this one of mother and newborn, taken by Harry's mum. He felt a shudder of revulsion at the thought that she must have supplied the photo. Did that mean she was willing to think the worst of her own son?

Back to the studio, where the presenter solemnly reiterated the plea for him to get in touch. She sounded faintly disgusted, as if his guilt were already beyond doubt.

But it wasn't, was it? He had a message from Alice to prove she was unharmed.

He was pondering how best to approach DI Thomsett when he spotted the flaw in his plan. The text had been sent from an anonymous mobile. As evidence that Alice and Evie were safe and well, it was useless.

He punched the mattress in frustration. He was back to his original plan: get Alice to ring DI Thomsett.

His own phone was toxic, but before switching it off he took a note of the number Alice had used, keying it into the Samsung. Then he rang the number, but there was no answer. *Of course there wasn't.*

He texted: *Alice, it's Harry. I'm having to use a borrowed phone, too. Will explain all soon. If this really is you, tell me where we went for that weekend before Evie came along. And tell me you really are safe! I love you. Harry xx*

For good measure he tried Ruth's number again, but no one answered. That sealed it: he was alone. Wanted by the authorities, stranded in a traveller's hotel in Crawley, a wad of cash in his pocket but no idea how it could help him.

A wanted man. He tried out the phrase, reciting it several times in the hope that it would sound absurd, but all it did was make him more afraid. How could he possibly help Alice and Evie if he was on the run from the police?

THIRTY-FIVE

Alice fed Evie for a good twenty minutes, then let her lie on the bed in just her nappy, taking great pleasure at the sight of her daughter kicking and punching the air with her chubby limbs. For an old house it was remarkably warm: the heating seemed to be on full blast. The air in the room was a little fusty, but nicely scented by the ageing timber furniture. Lying next to her daughter on the double bed, Alice soon began to feel drowsy.

She stirred at the sound of a car starting up. Wrapping Evie in her pramsuit, she hurried along the landing and watched from the window as Renshaw inexpertly guided his car into the garage. It seemed like an unnecessary precaution – unless it meant that, even here, he didn't feel safe from his pursuers?

Jittery again, she tiptoed back to the nursery. She knew she must face her reluctance to join Nerys and Renshaw, but all she wanted to do was speak to Harry and make sure he was all right, then go to bed and put this dreadful day behind her. She no longer held out any hope of being reunited with him tonight, but if she could at least arrange something for tomorrow she'd sleep a lot more easily.

Except that Renshaw had taken his phone back, and her own phone was useless without a charger.

A landline, then? Out here in the wilds the mobile reception was probably patchy at best. Nerys would no doubt rely on a landline, and in a house as large as this, surely she'd have more than one extension?

Alice deliberated for a few minutes. It would be an abuse of the hospitality Nerys had offered to go snooping around the woman's home, and yet Alice knew she would prefer to do that than ask to use the phone. Having spent all afternoon pressuring Renshaw for the right to contact Harry, she didn't have the energy for another battle with Nerys. In any case, there was too much at stake to worry about social niceties.

She waited a while on the landing, listening for movement from below. There were four other rooms on this floor, as well as a narrow staircase that led up to the roof space. She opened each door in turn and found two more guest bedrooms, far more modest in scale than the nursery. There was a large bathroom with a big steel tub and a built-in shower, and then a master bedroom, notable for being considerably untidier than elsewhere. The floor was strewn with discarded clothes, and a small landslide of shoes was piled against the side of a free-standing wardrobe.

There was only the one bedside table. It was home to a tin of boiled sweets, a Sylvia Day novel and a neat black cordless phone.

A floorboard creaked as she walked around the bed, making her wince. From what she could make of the layout, Renshaw and Nerys were most likely in the living room directly below her. She braced herself for an angry reaction, but no one came running. An old house like this, it probably creaks all the time, Alice told herself.

She shifted Evie to her left arm, which provoked a cry of displeasure. Not loud enough to be heard downstairs, she hoped.

Alice lifted the phone from its cradle and put it to her ear. Nothing.

She examined the keypad. Maybe she had to press the call button to open the connection? She tried that, but still there was no dial tone. And yet the charger had a tiny light glowing to indicate that it was plugged in.

The line was dead. Pure bad luck, or something more sinister?

She was pushing her luck to stay in here any longer. And she could hardly go crawling under the bed to check the socket. Returning Evie to her favoured position high on her shoulder, Alice tiptoed downstairs, with an excuse prepared that she always took the stairs slowly when carrying her daughter.

She reached the hall and saw the door to the lounge was ajar. There was music playing quietly – something blandly classical – along with the murmur of conversation. Even before she could make out the words, Alice knew from the tone that this wasn't just idle chatter.

She stopped a few feet from the door and went into a rocking motion, as if pausing to get Evie to sleep. She caught Nerys saying: '… could offer to return the money, and see if they'll—?'

'No. I am owed this. Anyhow, it is also our history. What I know of their business.'

'Well, *I* knew all about it, and they let me retire, didn't they?'

Renshaw grunted. The silence that followed was sheer agony for Alice: the tiniest squeak from Evie and they would know she was eavesdropping.

Then Nerys said: 'Or do you know something I don't?'

In a dismissive tone, Renshaw sidestepped the question. 'Men such as Laird, one does not reason with them. I take it you do not broadcast your whereabouts?'

'I don't, but not because they threatened me. Just plain common sense, that's all. You never know when one of them might …'

She tailed off, presumably because Renshaw had got the message. Evie wriggled and arched her back, and Alice took a step towards the door, and then Nerys said: 'Getting yourself saddled with *passengers*, Edward. What in God's name are you intending to do with them?'

Alice flinched. Her heart was beating so loudly it was a struggle to hear the conversation.

'Put them on a train tomorrow.'

'Oh, and that's the end of it, eh? All nice and simple.' The Welsh accent lent a whimsical note to her scorn. The response from Renshaw was far more subdued.

'There is the possibility of reprisals, when she returns to Brighton. Alas, this is not my concern.'

'Maybe not. But if it was me in this sort of mess, I'd be considering all my options …'

She must have lowered her voice, or moved across the room, because Alice couldn't make out what she said next. But she heard Renshaw's flustered response: 'I didn't—' before Nerys broke in with something else, and then Renshaw, more decisively, said, 'No. No. It is too complicated.'

Complicated, Alice thought. Was that all he could say about the chaos he'd brought down upon them all? Not illegal, or morally wrong. *Complicated*.

Her indignation nearly gave her away. Shifting her weight from one foot to the other, she almost bumped against the door. There was an immediate rustling sound from within the lounge.

Nerys, her voice much closer, as if she was walking out of the room, said, 'I thought by now she'd have—' just as Alice pushed the door open, trying frantically to make it appear that she'd crossed the hall in a single fluid movement.

THIRTY-SIX

Nerys had indeed been approaching the door. At the sight of Alice she shrugged on a friendly manner like a well-worn coat, beaming as she held out her hands towards Evie.

'Oh, isn't she a darling? Do you mind if Auntie Nerys has a cuddle?'

You're not her auntie, Alice wanted to say. But she managed a sickly grin and handed the baby over.

'And she's been fed, has she? Anything else she needs, my love?'

'No.' Alice secretly hoped the baby would take against Nerys and start to wail, as she had a habit of doing with some of Harry and Alice's older relatives, but to her dismay, Evie seemed delighted to be cooed over by this smiling stranger.

Renshaw had taken the interruption as an opportunity to reload his plate. The coffee table in front of him was set out with a pot of tea, two different types of cake, a plate of homemade biscuits and bowls of nuts and crisps.

Nerys saw her looking and said, 'Please, help yourself. If you'd like a sandwich or something, just say …'

'No, we ate at the services, thank you.'

'Edward told me. Hasn't stopped him making short work of my carrot cake.'

'It's my weakness,' he admitted, cutting himself another slice.

Nerys wanted to know if she was all right with tea or preferred something stronger. Alice noticed a glass of dark liquid next to Renshaw's cup.

'Tea's fine.'

The situation reminded her a little of the first time she'd met Harry's family. Everyone on their best behaviour, the conversation polite but brittle in its formality. As on that occasion, Alice found it was actually a relief to eat: if nothing else, it spared her from speaking.

Nerys had good news: her son, Michael, was able to lend Alice some baby clothes.

'He's popping round later. If there's anything else you need, let me know and I'll text him.'

So mobiles *do* work here, Alice thought. But what about the landline?

'That's very kind,' she said, 'but there's no need. We'll be going home tomorrow.'

'Oh, but you know how the little ones can mess up an outfit, whether it's burping up milk or a leaky nappy. And Michael's happy to help.'

Alice could only shrug and smile. She didn't want an argument about it. As she summoned up the nerve to ask another favour, Renshaw had a question of his own for Nerys.

'Your son lives nearby?'

'In Cheltenham. For the schools and shops, really.' She chuckled. 'Robyn, his wife, would never agree to live out here in the sticks.'

Nodding inanely, Alice gestured to get Renshaw's attention. 'Could I check to see if Harry's replied to my text?'

'He has not.' Renshaw tried to stare her down, but Alice held his gaze.

'Could I take a look? Please?'

Under sufferance, Renshaw handed her the Nokia and watched as she confirmed it for herself. Even though it was a crushing disappointment, Alice fought to appear untroubled.

It felt important somehow not to show any weakness in front of them.

'May I try him again?'

Renshaw exchanged a glance with Nerys, who said, 'Good idea. Best if he knows you're safe.'

Renshaw held up a chubby index finger. 'But do not reveal our location.'

'I won't,' she snapped, and then forced a conciliatory smile. 'Thank you.'

It was mortifying to make the call in front of them, but Alice wasn't about to leave the room while Nerys had Evie. Not when that strange comment she'd overheard was still reverberating in her mind: *If it was me in this sort of mess, I'd be considering all my options.*

What could Nerys have suggested that Renshaw felt was 'too complicated'?

Alice listened to the connection go straight to voicemail. Nerys saw the reaction in her face.

'Never mind, dear. You texted him earlier and said you were all right, didn't you?'

Alice nodded. Renshaw already had his hand out. 'If he replies, I will be sure to tell you.'

Alice had no choice but to return the Nokia and trust that Renshaw would keep to his word. It occurred to her that he still had her phone, so she asked for it back.

'But the battery is dead.'

'I know that.' She asked Nerys: 'Do you have a charger for an iPhone, by any chance?'

Nerys squinted in the manner of someone addressed in a foreign language. 'Um, no. I've got a Samsung, I think it is, if that's any good to you?'

Alice shook her head, then held out her hand to Renshaw. 'I'd still like to have it, though.'

'Very well.' He passed the phone to her, a peevish smirk on his face, as though her behaviour was completely irrational.

Then again, she thought, perhaps it was. It seemed like she couldn't be sure of anything at the moment, including her own judgement.

She drank a cup of tea, ate a biscuit and tried not to resent Nerys's natural rapport with Evie. They talked about the trials of childbirth, the stresses of motherhood. Renshaw contributed little. A couple of times Alice saw him glance at Nerys and then look away.

When his glass was empty, he refilled it himself from a bottle of rum that had been sitting on the floor beside the sofa. Nerys pressed Alice to have a proper drink, but she resisted.

'Sure?' Nerys said. 'I've got some wonderful pear cider.'

Thankfully, Evie chose this moment to emit a whine of displeasure. Alice pretended to groan, but she was thinking: *thank God thank God thank God!*

'Uh oh, someone's tired. Time for bed, I think.'

'Come back down once you get her off,' Nerys said as she handed her back. 'Have a proper drink with the grown-ups.'

'Thanks, but I'm pretty shattered myself.'

Nerys tutted in sympathy, but didn't press Alice to change her mind. Probably keen to discuss those 'options' that Nerys wanted Renshaw to consider.

Poor woman can't win, Alice thought as she fled the room. She's either *too* hospitable, or not hospitable enough.

Back in the sanctuary of the vast bedroom, she tried to analyse what she'd overheard. Renshaw and Nerys had been in the same line of work, which presumably meant providing medical support to a criminal gang. Nerys had been allowed to retire, but Renshaw hadn't. Did that mean Nerys was less intimately connected to the illegal side of the business? Or was she simply more trusted than Renshaw?

And what about her sarcastic reaction when Renshaw said he'd put Alice and Evie on a train tomorrow: *All nice and simple.* Well, why wouldn't it be? Did Nerys think it was unlikely to happen?

Alice puzzled over it for a while, and concluded that it was probably only her current insecurity that had cast the comments in such a sinister light – and that, after all, was quite understandable in the circumstances.

Sleep on it, she told herself. Go through it again in the morning.

After using the bathroom, where she took a dab of Nerys's toothpaste and brushed her teeth with her finger, she undressed and got comfortable in the big double bed. Evie grizzled and wouldn't settle, so Alice fed her to sleep. Another contravention of the Ideal Mother's Handbook, but she was past caring about that.

She wasn't sure what happened next. A noise seemed to startle her awake, and yet she could have sworn that she hadn't dozed off. It was pitch dark in the room, even though she'd left the curtains partly open. She had to move in close to Evie to see that she was fast asleep.

The noise, Alice thought, might have been the crunch of tyres on gravel. She had no idea how much time had passed. It could have been minutes since they'd gone to bed; it could have been hours. Normally her first instinct would be to check her phone, but right now that was only a sleek but useless rectangle of plastic.

Listening hard, she made out the distant thud of a door closing. And voices, maybe?

This must be the son. Nerys had said he would drop by, so there was no need to worry. And yet it was unsettling, the thought of another stranger in the house. It prompted her to consider the possibility she'd been trying so hard to dismiss as absurd: that she was here not as a guest, but as a prisoner.

A few minutes passed in silence, then came the creak of floorboards. A tap on the door.

'Alice?' Nerys said in a loud whisper. 'Alice, are you awake?'

Feeling about eight years old, Alice clamped her lips together and said nothing. Nerys called once more, waited, then walked away.

Slowly, Alice let out her breath. She couldn't have said why she hadn't answered, and now wasn't the time for yet more self-interrogation. She wanted only to sleep, so she pulled up the duvet and buried herself beneath it: like her eight-year-old self, scared of the dark and hiding from the monster in the closet.

THIRTY-SEVEN

Well, who'd have thought it? His dull Friday evening had been transformed into a whirlwind of excitement and intrigue – and by his mother, of all people.

He'd taken the call in the kitchen. It was almost seven o'clock and the kids were bleating and squawking around him, the normal bedtime rules abandoned on Friday. Robyn was bottle-feeding baby Mikey, helping five-year-old Betty with a puzzle and discussing best friend traumas with seven-year-old Chloe: all this while also making pasta and meatballs, as well as a vegetarian stir fry for Betty. The eldest – thirteen-year-old Ronald, who since his grandfather's death had insisted on calling himself 'Jay' – was locked in his bedroom as usual.

After mouthing, 'Only Mum,' and receiving the customary half-serious grimace, Michael had slipped away to his study. That was the beauty of honesty, he thought later. Robyn didn't expect her mother-in-law to have anything interesting to say, so she wouldn't want much in the way of a report on the conversation.

Domestic duties kept her confined to the kitchen while Michael hurried upstairs and helped himself to a selection of little Mikey's clothes. He sneaked the bag into his car, then went back inside and concocted a story about an enquiry from Revenue & Customs.

'It's to do with a partner on one of Dad's dodgy sidelines, from the 1980s. Something the chap's done now might be explained by his – and Dad's – activities back then.'

'What's that got to do with your mother?'

'Apparently Dad had her down as a director. It was during one of their truces. Anyway, she's in a right tizz about it, so I said I'd pop over.'

'Now?' Robyn gestured at the meatballs, which did, he had to admit, smell delicious.

'No. It'll wait till after dinner.'

'Why doesn't she ask her accountant for advice? She can easily afford the fees.'

Robyn said it in a mild enough tone – and it was undeniably true – but still there was a moment where Michael longed to punch her in the face.

Instead he shrugged, and in an equally reasonable voice said, 'Better if I can save her a few quid.' And he winked. 'Remember: we'll get it back eventually.'

Michael Baxter was a man of habitual secrecy, a trait he'd inherited from his late father, whose fortune was undoubtedly boosted by his inclination to tell the tax authorities only what he thought they needed to know; as such, the tale Michael had spun to his wife was all too plausible.

Now, however, it was becoming apparent that his mother was no slouch in the secrets department, either. She hadn't explained much on the phone – just that an old colleague from her nursing days needed a room for the night. Oh, and he had a young woman and a baby with him. Nerys claimed she didn't know the full story, not right then, but she'd get it.

'And I might need your help. The situation with my pal Renshaw is a bit … volatile.'

Hmm. Arriving at the house at a little after nine, having been delayed by a succession of slow drivers and the aftermath of a three-car shunt on the Cirencester Road, he quickly formed the view that 'volatile' was something of a euphemism.

This man Renshaw had a hunted air about him. He radiated tension as Nerys made the introductions, and there was a wariness, a feral look in his eyes that only started to dim once they'd sat down. Michael had been served a mug of hot chocolate, made just the way he liked it. Renshaw, for his part, was self-medicating with a bottle of dark rum, which Michael decided was not a bad thing. Good tongue-loosening properties.

'Nerys tells me you have four children.'

'That's right.'

'And you are close, you and your mother.' Renshaw was nodding, as if it was a statement rather than a question. He frowned at Nerys. 'And yet, I seem to recall you said it was difficult, the relationship …'

'It was. With my first husband – Michael's father – we went through a very bitter divorce. At first I was going to have custody, until Ronald decreed that his son would have the best education money could buy.'

'Trouble was,' Michael chipped in, 'he'd only fund it on the condition that I pledged loyalty to him.'

'A *pledge*?' Renshaw echoed.

'That's what it was, effectively,' Nerys said. 'He had to disown me, his own mother.'

Michael said, 'But we talked it through and decided it was the best thing for us both, in the long run.'

Renshaw looked amazed. 'And you were, how old?'

'Eight.'

'Always had a wise head, this one,' Nerys said approvingly.

'I used to sneak away to visit Mum in the holidays. Told my dad I was staying with friends. He thought I hardly had any contact, but in fact we were talking most weeks.'

'I was usually rushed off my feet, anyway. So it worked out perfectly.'

'Of course, Dad was already quite ill.'

'Diabetes,' Nerys explained. 'Ronald and I actually met in a hospital canteen, did I never mention that? So we knew that, for all his money, his long-term prognosis wasn't very good.'

'Just a matter of time,' Michael said, 'though he actually lasted years longer than anyone expected. We even had to pretend the grandchildren never saw Nanny Nerys, didn't we?'

'Ronald was a vindictive bugger. He'd always sworn I'd never get a penny, you see? He died thinking Michael had been brainwashed into agreement.'

'I was the sole heir.' Michael illustrated his freedom with an expansive wave of his hand. 'I could do whatever I liked with the money.'

'It's Michael I have to thank for all this.' Nerys made exactly the same motion to indicate the house, only hers was slightly less co-ordinated. Clearly she'd been imbibing along with her new house guest.

Renshaw made a poor job of concealing his envy, 'An impressive home, indeed. A pity you have not met someone else ...'

'Oh, I did. Not long after I retired.'

'Clive,' Michael said, as if the name itself was a sour taste.

Nerys clicked her tongue. 'It proved to be a mistake.'

'So you are twice divorced?'

'He died.'

A beat of silence, Renshaw nodding to himself as he digested the news. 'A pity,' he said at last, 'that he was unable to share in your good fortune.'

'Well, there you go,' said Nerys. '*Life's a bitch*, isn't that what they say?'

Michael decided that they had revealed more than enough to put Renshaw at ease: it was time to reverse the direction of travel, conversationally-speaking. He said, 'My mother's always been vague about her working life. You're the only one of her colleagues that I've met.'

Renshaw gave Nerys a quick, uncertain look, then said, 'It was a small team.'

'But not NHS? Some kind of private care?'

Renshaw nodded. 'Quite run-of-the-mill.'

'Doing what, exactly? What was your role?'

'A doctor.' Renshaw was bristling, his pudgy face bright red above the grey fluff of his beard. He didn't like this line of questioning, but a subtle nod from Nerys told Michael that he was authorised, for now, to go on pushing.

'A doctor? Wow. What did you specialise in?'

'I was a GP, originally. I worked in several locations. Inner cities, some truly horrendous places. Just as I was becoming jaded, I was offered a new … opportunity. Your mother, I knew from her days as a midwife. She too was eager for something different.'

'So who employed you?'

'Ah …' Renshaw heaved out a sigh, set down his glass and rested back on the sofa.

'That question, I'm afraid,' said Nerys quietly, 'brings us to the reason why Edward needs to stay here tonight.'

Renshaw nodded wearily, then shut his eyes, as if he could barely compose an answer.

'As with your late father, our employer demanded absolute loyalty. But there were criminal elements to some of his businesses – elements which your mother and I knew nothing about.'

Yeah, right, Michael thought. As if his mother would work for someone and not acquaint herself with every little weakness, every scam. That was one of the things that had so infuriated his father: the way Nerys had been able to root out every skeleton in his closet. Given that ability, it was little wonder that her own secrets had been buried so deeply.

Playing along, Michael said, 'So what are we talking about here? A *gangster*?'

The question was directed at his mother, who nodded.

'Rather a melodramatic term, but that's what he is at heart, yes. A gangster.'

Renshaw sighed again. 'And now it seems that, quite inadvertently, I have made an enemy of this man. I am so very grateful to Nerys here, for the refuge she has offered me.'

THIRTY-EIGHT

So that's you. What about the woman, and her kid?

This was the question Michael was itching to ask, but he could see that Renshaw was exhausted, tetchy, and half drunk. A look from Nerys confirmed it: *leave him for now.*

While Nerys escorted Renshaw upstairs, Michael fetched a bottle of Grolsch and paced the room until his mother returned. He felt a pleasant tingle in his stomach; a sense of nervous anticipation.

She came in, turning to push the door to, but not shutting it completely.

'We need to hear if either of them comes down.'

He couldn't help but grin: she was ahead of him there.

'I'm trying to imagine what kind of criminal organisation needs its own in-house medical team.'

'You'd be surprised.'

'Would I?' He grunted. 'Actually, I'm not sure how I feel about this. I suppose I was shocked, at first, but not really surprised.' He flashed a smile. 'I'm more annoyed that I didn't worm it out of you at the time.'

She said nothing until she'd helped herself to a fistful of cashew nuts and settled into an armchair. 'I don't think many children give a thought to their parents' careers, as long as there's food on the table, and money when they need it.'

'You're saying I didn't show an interest?' He pulled on his bottom lip while he trawled his memory. '*Did* I show an interest? I must have done.'

'We met up so rarely, there were better things to talk about.'

'Like Dad and his pneumatic girlfriends.'

'And that.' She met his gaze. 'But when you did ask, I used to lie.'

'Mother!' he exclaimed, with mock outrage. 'Lying to your son and heir!'

'It's not a game, Michael. You'd do well to remember that.'

Chastened, he said, quietly, 'I just can't believe you led this sort of … double life, and I never cottoned on to it.'

'I took the view that the less you knew, the better it was for you.'

'But you used to be so disapproving of Dad's financial she-nanigans.'

'Only because I thought he'd get caught – and then look at the trouble you'd have been in.'

'Well, that makes sense.' He came and perched on the side of her armchair. 'So why am I here, exactly?'

'First, you need to understand that I wouldn't involve you if I had any other choice. You and the grandchildren, you're all I've got …'

Her voice choked up a little. Sometimes she did it for effect, especially if Robyn was competing for his time and energy, but in this instance it seemed genuine.

'He sprang it on me. Called up this afternoon and said he needed a room for the night.'

'He didn't mention the woman or the baby?'

'Not a word. And he didn't say the problem was anything to do with Nathan Laird. Otherwise I'd have told him, quite frankly, to swivel.'

*

'Nathan Laird,' Michael repeated slowly. 'What is he, a Tony Soprano character?'

Nerys didn't crack a smile. He watched her pushing the nuts into her mouth, one at a time, like some kind of burrowing animal.

'Edward knows not to cross a man like Laird, that's what worries me. Sneaky little sod.'

'What, Laird?'

'Renshaw. He was burnt out as a GP when Laird picked him up. He'd been done for embezzlement. Kept moving practices because he was so rude and dishonest. And he used to assault the patients.'

'Sexually?' Michael asked; more interested now.

'Not really. Just rough with them. Though it *was* often the young females,' she added, as if that had only just occurred to her.

'And what do you think he's done now?'

Nerys pursed her lips. 'It's serious, goes without saying. But I know he left the organisation last year, around April or May, it was, because one of Laird's people emailed, asking if I'd be interested in going back with them.'

'And you didn't tell me?'

'Wasn't relevant. I turned them down flat. Didn't need the hassle, or the money.' A bleak smile. 'I also made it clear I wasn't any fan of Renshaw's, and I'm bloody glad I did. But they never gave a hint that he'd caused them trouble.'

'So where's he been all this time? And can you please tell me what he's done to piss them off?'

'He's taken money, he admitted that much.' Another snatch at the bowl of nuts. 'But there's more to it. He knows something he's not supposed to know.'

'What, like, market sensitive stuff?' Michael was taken aback when she looked at him as though he was a pitiful idiot.

'No. Like something he can use to destroy them.'

'Can't he give it back?'

Her scorn went up a level. 'If somebody takes a secret from you, there's only one way you can be sure they won't blab.'

Michael was silent for a moment, both overwhelmed and worried about making a fool of himself again.

'*Murder?*'

'You have to understand that Nathan Laird isn't some common-or-garden thug,' Nerys told him. 'He's a businessman, every bit as much as your father was.'

Michael raised his eyebrows. Like most successful entrepreneurs, his father had always had a touch of the street brawler lurking within him.

She went on: 'To start with, it was drugs, I think. This was years before I joined them. Gradually it all became more legitimate. Gambling, clubs and pubs and what have you. Laird keeps himself very clean, but there are people who'll do the messy work for him.'

She paused, but Michael knew she had more to say.

'The thing is, if Laird hears that I've given shelter to Edward, that'll be me written off. I'm a traitor. Worse than that, a threat.'

'And Renshaw knows this, I suppose?'

'Oh, yes. You can bet he does.'

Responding to the stress in her voice, he placed a hand on the back of her head, gently stroking his fingers through her hair. 'So, in effect, we're bound up in this now, whether we like it or not. What do we do about that?'

This earned him a grateful smile – because he'd said *we* – and then she was sombre again.

'This secret, whatever it is, must be bloody valuable. And like I say, we're hung for a sheep as a lamb. The challenge is how we put Laird's mind at rest, and give him back whatever it is Edward took – 'cause he's *got* to have some proof – without making ourselves the sort of liability I just mentioned.'

She closed her eyes, enjoying the massage, as he asked: 'The sort that has to be eliminated?'

'Mm. Exactly.'

'Well,' he said drily. 'That *is* going to take some finessing.'

She laughed, more at his dry delivery than at the comment itself.

'And there's the woman,' Michael added. 'Where does she fit in?'

'No idea, yet.' A wariness crept into her voice. Her eyes opened and she sat forward. She knew what Michael was asking, and he thought: *Sod you, then.*

He stood up. 'What's she like, anyway? Is she my type?'

A snort. 'They're *all* your type, Michael.'

'How old? Tall, short, slim, curvy?'

'She's about thirty. Quite pretty – and smart with it, I'd say. Light brown hair. Same height as Robyn, but slimmer, narrower at the hips. Maybe a size ten. Good legs, I would think.'

'I'm liking the sound of this. And married, yes?'

'Yes, but hubby doesn't know where she is. Edward let her send a text, using one of his phones. He took Alice's phone when they stopped at the services and made sure to drain the battery.'

'Clever old fox, your friend Renshaw.'

'He is. It means the husband has seen a message that Alice is safe, but the only way he can contact her is through Edward's phone.'

Nerys confided that, as a further precaution, she'd disconnected the landline after showing Alice and her daughter to the nursery.

'The last thing we want is the police turning up, and Alice claiming she's being held here against her will.'

'Is she likely to do that?'

'I think she trusts Edward, more or less. And I laid on the charm with a trowel. But it's important that we control her ability to communicate, at least till we've decided where this is going.'

Michael nodded. 'Okay, so let me get this straight. When Alice texted her husband, she couldn't tell him her destination?'

'Apparently all Edward said was near Gloucester. No specifics.'

'So nobody knows where she is?' He could barely contain his excitement. 'And, uh, *what—*' His voice had gone thick; he cleared his throat. 'I mean, what are the possibilities here, do you think?'

Nerys fixed him with a steady gaze. In that moment he could see exactly how his father had fallen for her: she was a perfect combination of tough and pragmatic and – well – sexy.

'If it's my honest opinion you want, Michael, I'd say the sky's the fucking limit.'

THIRTY-NINE

Ruth woke to utter darkness. A pounding headache. Her mouth so dry it felt like her throat might crumble into dust.

But she remembered it all: that was something. No cognitive impairment; just a burning shame that she had been taken so easily.

Within a few minutes she had ascertained that she was alone in her captivity. She was in some kind of large metal box: a shipping container, possibly. There was rough matting on the floor, which stank of old sweat and rotten meat. Ruth wasn't restrained in any way, so she could kneel, and then stand, making sure there were no injuries she'd overlooked.

A weak slap against the side of the container produced a dull metallic echo. Clearly they were not concerned if she made a noise. Had to be somewhere remote.

Her head was woozy, so she dropped to her hands and knees once again and crawled around the perimeter, looking for something to use as a weapon. Her hands grew sticky from the dirt and grime that covered the matting. The stench was revolting.

She didn't hold any hope of finding a way out, but neither did she expect to find a torch. And yet there it was, unmistakable in shape, waiting in the far corner for her to discover it.

A penlight. Not big or heavy enough to hit someone with. Still she gripped it for a second, comforted for only as long as it took to understand why it had been placed there.

Something they wanted her to see.

They probably thought she'd understand that, and perhaps try to resist; but knew that curiosity would prevail.

As indeed it did.

Ruth had already guessed: she just hadn't admitted it to herself. The smell told her what it was.

She pressed the button and a thin beam of light illuminated the floor at her feet. She moved it around in a slow circle, then directed the beam on to each of the four walls in turn.

Blood. Dried to black in splashes on the walls. Dark puddles of it, congealed on the matting.

This was a warning: *See what we can do*.

See what we can do to you.

Harry didn't have a great night. Every time he suppressed his anxiety enough to make sleep possible, another guest would slam a door, flush a toilet or trundle past his room with a wheeled case that seemed as loud as a Formula One car.

By six o'clock he'd given up, and made a final weak coffee from the tray of complimentary beverages. Then he showered again, slowly massaging his scalp beneath a stream of blissfully hot water. It wasn't much of a struggle to decide what to do next, simply because his options were so limited to start with.

He was ready to go by six thirty, leaving a five-pound tip for the cleaner. He knew Ruth had paid up front the night before, so he had no qualms about not checking out. He felt slightly bad about leaving her case behind, but only slightly.

No one paid him any attention as he left the hotel. It was another fine and bright day, the sun just appearing; with only a little high cloud creeping in from the west. A deep frost sparkled on the cars and the grass verges. Harry shivered as he walked. His shirt and tailored jacket had been fine yesterday for work; not so good for travelling on a freezing cold morning.

Crawley's train station was only a couple of minutes from the hotel. He kept his head down as he entered the station from East Park Road, on the opposite side to the main building. He used a self-service machine to buy a ticket to London Victoria, and was glad to see that, being a Saturday, the platforms were virtually deserted.

He crossed the tracks to the booking hall, intending to buy a newspaper. There was a plastic stand outside the small café, but Harry stopped abruptly when he saw the front cover of the local paper, the *Argus*. His own photograph occupied almost a quarter of the page, below a screaming headline: BRIGHTON MAN SOUGHT IN DISAPPEARANCE OF WIFE AND DAUGHTER.

He turned and bolted, certain that anyone who glanced at him would immediately make the connection. The only saving grace was that in the picture he was clean-shaven, whereas now he had several days' growth of stubble.

He stood at the far end of the platform, telling himself that his fellow passengers wouldn't notice him: they had their own lives, their own preoccupations. When the train arrived he leapt aboard and kept his face turned to the window. The journey passed in a mist of panic, and he arrived at Victoria unable to recall having had a single clear thought in the previous forty-five minutes.

The concourse was quiet here, too. Harry decided to risk using the ticket office. He needed information on the best route to Thetford, and figured it was unlikely that many people in London would have been scouring the news about Sussex. He didn't want to contemplate the possibility that the hunt for him had interested the national media.

The woman who served him was pleasingly indifferent. Harry paid for his ticket in cash, wondering if later the police would examine CCTV and trace the relevant transaction.

Tough if they did, he thought. He wasn't an expert; he wasn't a spy or a secret agent. He didn't even know what he hoped to achieve by going to Norfolk.

All he knew was that Alice and Evie were lost to him – and Ruth, despite her vanishing act, seemed like his best hope of finding them. And this woman, Keri, was his only link to Ruth.

FORTY

There was no good reason to delay the inevitable, so Ruth elbowed the side of a container a few times. She heard a shout, and felt the thud of running feet.

A series of clunking noises warned her that the door was opening. Even when she shielded her eyes with her hand the intrusion of daylight was overwhelming. She had to turn away, which suited her captors just fine.

'Shut your eyes! Kneel down, hands behind your back.'

She glimpsed a large man in black overalls and a clown mask, holding a gun in one hand and a canvas bag in another. Another man behind him, smaller, in a full-face balaclava. Beyond them, a patch of waste ground, mud and brambles and the beginnings of wide open country. The sky was the palest shade of blue, studded with dabs of cloud, and gloriously beautiful; a mackerel sky.

She weighed up her odds and didn't care for them. She offered no resistance as handcuffs were applied and the canvas bag placed over her head. They bundled her outside, steadying her when she caught her toe on the lip of the container.

The morning was bitterly cold, but after the foul atmosphere of the container it was a joy to shiver and gasp in the fresh air. It had the salty tang of the coast, and as she was manoeuvred into the back of a van she heard the far away cry of a seagull.

East Anglia, she thought. Back on their territory.

She was made to lie face down. The man in the clown mask stayed with her, his gun pressed into the small of her back. She had a feeling this was Niall Foster, one of the men who'd terrorised Harry French and his family earlier in the week.

She'd been thinking about Harry a lot. She hoped he was still safe in Crawley, furious at her perceived betrayal. Better that than the alternative – that he too had been spotted, snatched, and was now languishing in captivity himself. Or dead.

She wasn't taken far: she estimated the journey took about twenty minutes, on roads that rarely allowed for high speed. There was very little traffic noise, and no conversation except for one brief exchange. The driver had shouted in a strong Glaswegian accent: 'You copping a feel back there?'

'Shut it,' the other man said. Quite a rich voice: definitely Foster.

'Ah, I don't see the harm. Looks tasty enough, for her age. Are they decent tits, 'cause it annoys me off how the bras make 'em seem—'

'I said, shut it.'

A couple more minutes and they turned right, then took a sharp left and bumped over some sort of minor obstruction before slowing to a crawl. The engine noise changed, echoing as they moved inside. A garage door clanged shut. The pressure of the firearm eased slightly.

'Don't try anything,' the gunman told her. 'There's no escape from here, and you just heard my friend. If you misbehave, rape is only one of our options.'

Ruth thought he was bluffing, but she couldn't be certain. In any case, she had no plans to fight back until the odds in her favour were improved – or until she was left with absolutely no choice.

She was directed through an internal door, into a building that felt blissfully warm and well-kept. Her feet sank into deep carpets. There was a pleasant scent of fresh flowers and, even more appealing, fresh coffee.

After being manhandled up two flights of stairs, still with the gun at her back, she was taken into a large room with a wooden floor and made to kneel on a soft woollen rug. The smell of the coffee made her delirious with longing. Assuming it was around seven in the morning, she'd gone more than eighteen hours without food or drink.

The gentle clink of cup on saucer suggested a certain refinement, in line with what her other senses had told her about this place. She felt sure she was in a large, well-appointed home, owned by a man with taste and good judgement – in some matters, at least.

Her heart was thumping at the thought. After so many years, to be this close now …

Finally the canvas bag was removed from her head, though the handcuffs stayed on. She was in a sun lounge that doubled as an office. There was a range of furniture of Indian design, including a sideboard, a desk and a couple of bookshelves. Most of the shelves contained lever arch files rather than books.

The light in here was comfortably muted; the blinds closed on what was obviously an impressive picture window. A sea view lay beyond it, she suspected.

Aside from herself and the men who had brought her here, there was only one other person in the room. And it wasn't who she'd hoped to find.

FORTY-ONE

'Hello, Mark.'

'Ruth. Wish I could say it's good to see you.'

'Likewise.'

It had been eight or nine years since she'd seen Mark Vickery at close quarters. He'd aged pretty well, she had to admit. Always a slim man, he had perhaps lost a few extra pounds, and was in danger of looking gaunt. But his hair was a darker brown than ever, styled in a side parting, and some of his teeth looked whiter and straighter than she remembered.

He was sitting behind the desk, dressed in a white shirt and a pale blue V-neck sweater. There was an unlit cigarette in his right hand, which he twirled, restlessly, between his fingers. A silver MacBook sat before him.

'There,' he said. 'Pleasantries over in no time. Now, why don't you explain how you came to be working with Renshaw?'

She knew her frown of confusion would be only mildly realistic. Name recognition tended to produce an unmistakable signal.

'I'm not. I have no idea who he is.'

'Then what were you doing in Sussex?'

'Following Foster and his buddies.' Burying her relief that they didn't seem to know about her recent alliance with Harry, she nodded towards the man in the clown mask. 'I was hoping they could lead me to your boss.'

'*I'm* in charge here,' Vickery snapped. But he shifted uncomfortably as he spoke, glancing at the laptop as though it was an autocue. 'Tell me what you know about Renshaw.'

'I know you're searching for him. That's all.'

'Renshaw has stolen something from us. He had help. A man called Hasan Mansur.'

He paused, watching for her reaction. The name was vaguely familiar, but this time Ruth gave nothing away.

Vickery said, 'Hasan came to a messy end, in the place where you spent the night.'

Ruth tried to maintain a look of disinterest. 'I wouldn't have thought you had the stomach for torture.'

'Things have moved on since you were last a part of our lives.' He gave her an icy smile. 'Oh, I do hope you enjoyed your time away?'

'Very refreshing, thanks. But I saw for myself that people like you don't really change.'

That wasn't entirely true. For one thing, Vickery seemed more confident, more at ease with himself than Ruth remembered. And he'd dropped the silly attempts to speak with an Estuary accent, reverting to the clipped, privately educated voice of his Surrey childhood.

'Renshaw used a cut-out to take receipt of a parcel Hasan sent him. Some young couple with a baby. Because of that, he eluded us again, and now the family have disappeared as well.' Another glance at the laptop. 'I believe you know more about this than you've admitted, so either you tell me right now, or you'll suffer the same fate as Hasan.'

This time Ruth made him wait. She stretched out, leaning a few inches to her left. To retain eye contact Vickery had to turn his head slightly.

'One problem. Torture only works if the victim has the information you want. And I don't. You know that, and so does Nathan.'

'I've told you—'

'Mark, he's listening to this and feeding you instructions through that earpiece you're wearing. So stop treating me like a fool – both of you – and listen to my proposal.'

Vickery looked furious, probably toying with the idea of tearing out the earpiece and telling Foster to go to work on her right there and then.

But he couldn't. Because he wasn't running the show.

'You think you're in any position to make a deal?' he said at last.

'Yes. I don't have what you want, but I *do* know how to get it. And without my co-operation, what I know is useless to you.'

'Go on, then.'

'Renshaw has one of the innocent neighbours with him. A woman called Alice French. I agreed to help her husband find her.'

'Why … ?' Vickery began, but Ruth shook her head.

'Doesn't matter. The fact is, I can find the husband, Harry, and monitor his communication with Alice. Renshaw let her speak to Harry once, so he might do again. If he does, I can find out where he is.'

'So we're supposed to let you go, and trust you to lead us to Renshaw?'

'Yeah. I don't care who he is or what he's done. He's nothing to me. But if I find him for you, I want something in return.'

'What?'

'Laird knows.'

That really pissed him off. Vickery listened to the voice in his ear, his fists clenched on the desk.

'In that case, my guys are coming with you.'

Ruth glanced round. The masks had come off and she'd guessed right about the gunman: Niall Foster. The Scottish man had the same slight build as his usual partner, Darrell Bridge, but he was much older, in his fifties, with a scrawny, undernourished look and thinning grey hair.

'The name's McBride, hen,' he said with a leer. 'Look forward to seein' more of you.'

Ruth ignored the comment, addressing Vickery. 'They have to stay in the background. If Harry gets a whiff of their presence he'll be gone. I can't afford to lose his trust. Neither can you.'

Laird must have said something, for Vickery let out a bark of laughter. Ruth gave him a quizzical look but Vickery, when he spoke, wasn't talking to her.

'Yeah, she is.' Now he met her gaze, still replying to Laird, but speaking loudly for Ruth's benefit: 'Oh, it will be a pleasure, if she doesn't come up with the goods.'

FORTY-TWO

Country sounds nudged through her dreams: the busy squawk of chickens, the growl of a passing tractor. There were rooks or crows cawing on the roof. From far away came what might have been the crack of a shotgun. A dog barked three times – and then the memories came rushing back. She knew where she was, and how she had come to be here.

But was it safe?

She'd fallen asleep, unable to decide for sure, and vaguely recalled waking a couple of times in the night – once on autopilot while she fed Evie and changed her nappy – but she had refused to let herself dwell on it. Now, looking around the nursery in the soft grey light of morning, the answer remained stubbornly out of reach. It felt as though she'd entered a fairytale world: enchanting, outwardly benign, but with just a hint of menace below. Menace that could be expressed in one simple question: *Would she be permitted to leave?*

A knock on the door made her jump. Remembering her reluctance to answer the night before, she swallowed, moistened her dry lips with her tongue and called out: 'Yes?'

The door opened, Nerys pushing it with her hip because she had a mug of tea in one hand and a large plastic bag in the other.

'Not too early, I hope?' And when Alice frowned, Nerys saw the baby was still asleep and whispered, 'It's about ten past eight.'

Alice gave a start. 'Oh my God! Really? Evie's never slept that late before.'

'Ah, but this room is special. Didn't I tell you my grandchildren love it here?'

She put the tea down, then showed Alice the contents of the bag.

'Michael called in last night with some outfits for the little one. I came up, but you must have been out cold by then.'

'Mmm,' Alice lied. 'I was exhausted.'

'I thought you might be glad of a change of clothes yourself, so I've sorted a few things. And feel free to have a bath, if you want.'

Alice nodded and thanked her. Nerys was gazing, rapt, at the sight of Evie. 'Isn't she just *perfect*, the little poppet. Oh, Michael brought you some formula milk, just in case stocks are running low!'

She laughed gaily. Alice forced a smile. 'I'm fine, I think.'

'Good. Well, in that case, it's *you* that needs refuelling. And having guests gives me the perfect excuse to make eggs and bacon, the works. How does that sound?'

'Lovely,' said Alice, thinking: *Anything to make you go away.* 'But is it all right if I have a bath first?'

'Of course. And don't rush. Enjoy the lie-in while you can, that's what I'd do.'

She shut the door quietly behind her, and Alice realised that something about the woman made her tense, even when Nerys was radiating good cheer.

Evie was stirring. After taking a sip of tea, Alice wriggled back down in the bed, placing her face close to Evie's so that she wouldn't miss a moment of the waking ceremony. It was a precious experience to observe the little frowns and twitches, the gentle exhalations and pursing of lips: the infant equivalent of a warm-up routine.

Smiling down at her, Alice was reminded that the official advice cautioned against co-sleeping: Harry's mum thought that was a lot of nonsense, while her own mother said it was for the best. *Welcome to motherhood, where everyone has an opinion on everything.*

There had been a few instances – especially at first, in the hospital – when that had fazed her; Alice was in no doubt that some of her confidence had ebbed away, which she put down to the absence of the day-to-day challenges and interactions of her job. The period at home before the birth had been a strange and difficult time, a kind of frustrating 'phony war' when she'd burned through a lot of energy doing nothing: like an athlete who has prepared too early for a big race.

It had made her appreciate how much of her self-esteem was derived from her career, and that in turn fuelled concerns about the effects of a prolonged spell at home. She feared that her new, more insular existence could become so comfortable, so familiar, that one day she'd wake to find she was willing to settle for being – as she guiltily put it – 'just a mother'.

Nothing wrong with that, except that she'd worked hard to qualify as a dental hygienist. It was a role that carried many of the risks and responsibilities inherent in dentistry (albeit with a fraction of the prestige) and she took pride in her ability to do it well. It required a strength of character to work in such close proximity to strangers, delving into one of the most intimate parts of the body. And you had to be emotionally robust, as well – in the deprived area of Brighton where she'd first practised, she had regularly inspected the mouth of a new patient and seen immediately that half their teeth were beyond saving. On other occasions, working in tandem with the dentist, she was able to alert patients to the suspicious red or white patches that could be the pre-cursor to oral cancer. It was a job that made a difference to people's lives, and she didn't want to let it go.

But there's also you: after a tiny burp, Evie's eyes prised open, recognised her mother's face and lit up with a pure, instinctive joy that was just about the most beautiful thing Alice had ever seen. She blinked away sudden, silly tears. Tears of love and guilt.

When you've been blessed with a beautiful, healthy child, wasn't it unspeakably selfish to mourn what you might be losing of yourself?

Michael left the house at seven-fifteen, having constructed a story that there was more paperwork to review before they could reply to the Revenue; not only that, but his mother was coming down with flu, felt sorry for herself and wanted him there for the comfort, blah blah blah.

Robyn gave no sign that she doubted his word: she was accustomed to him skipping out on the flimsiest of pretexts. In many ways her passivity was a blessing, and yet there were times when he longed for her to rant and rage, to accuse him of something. Give him a reason to fight back – or save him from himself.

He promised to be home to take Chloe to football training, but he'd already decided to avoid that as well. By then Robyn would be at Betty's Saturday drama school, taking Junior with her, but he was sure one of the other parents would come to the rescue. Only Jay had the privilege of sleeping the morning away before his guitar tutor came to the house for his midday lesson.

He arrived as Nerys brought in the day's eggs from the chicken coop. She'd already been in to see Alice, but hadn't woken Renshaw, preferring to wait until she and Michael had discussed tactics once again.

'I need to be certain that you're happy to go on with this.'

'I am. Don't worry.' He gripped his mother by the arms and kissed her firmly on the cheek. 'A challenge will do me good. Life's been too easy since the old man popped his clogs.'

She nodded. 'Alice will be expecting Renshaw to organise her train home. We have to convince her to hold off till the afternoon, at least.'

'I can help there.' Michael set out his idea while Nerys made him coffee. They agreed that she should take tea up to Renshaw and talk to him privately.

'I get the feeling he's wary of you,' Nerys said. 'He'd have been expecting to find me here on my own. Vulnerable.'

Michael couldn't help raising his eyebrows. As if his mother was ever vulnerable, alone or otherwise.

'And you'll talk to Laird this morning?'

'If I can. More likely his lieutenant, Vickery.' She paused. 'The other issue, if we're going to meet him, is where we do it. I don't want him knowing where I live.'

She left him with that thought, and he couldn't help marvelling at how swiftly they'd adjusted to the roles of co-conspirators. Just like the old days, really, when he'd fooled his father into believing that Nerys no longer featured in his life. Since then, what risks he'd taken had been confined mostly to matters of personal gratification. The little empire he'd inherited had flourished without the need for any questionable activity – thankfully, since everything was too drearily well-regulated nowadays to make it worthwhile. So this was probably the closest he'd ever been to such overt criminality, and he congratulated himself on how well he was adapting to it.

Nerys was back a few minutes later. She winked.

'He's happy to go with our plan. He can't seem to look ahead more than a few hours at the moment. If you ask me, he's completely deluded, thinking he can get away with this.'

'Suits us. The more deluded, the better.'

'Oh, and he says he slept like a baby, isn't that sweet?' A derisive laugh as she took a bagel from the breadbin and stood it upright to cut it open. In a deceptively offhand tone, she said, 'Ronald's holiday home at Symonds Yat, you haven't sold it, have you?'

'You know I haven't.' Michael felt wounded by the suggestion that he'd do such a thing behind her back.

'It's nice and private, that's what I was thinking. But is there anything that could link it to me?'

He considered. 'No. The holiday home is officially owned by the business, whereas for here I used a shell company. Completely anonymous, the way you wanted.'

'Good.' She dropped the bagel halves into the toaster and pushed the lever down.

Michael, waiting in vain for an explanation, rooted in the cupboard for jam to accompany his bagel. 'How will it help, when Renshaw knows where we live?'

'Renshaw's easy to handle. I'm a lot more worried about Laird.' A sigh. 'And Alice, of course.'

'On that subject,' he said carefully, 'and just to be clear, are we going to keep her here against her will? If it comes to it, I mean.'

'If it comes to it,' Nerys repeated. 'Let's hope it doesn't, eh?'

FORTY-THREE

Evie fed for a few minutes, while Alice found her attention drawn back to that fleeting moment in the early hours of Thursday morning when she had denied the existence of a parcel. Was it a purely instinctive reaction, borne of panic, or had there been some degree of calculation? A desire to take on responsibility for the secret, in order to keep Evie and Harry safe?

If so, she hadn't had nearly enough time to gauge the risks properly. But perhaps her actions this week were driven by the need to forge a measure of independence, a way of demonstrating to herself that she was more than just 'the little woman at home with baby'. Certainly her headstrong – if not downright reckless – decision to take the second package across the road to Renshaw could be seen in that light.

'And now we're all paying the price,' she murmured to herself, unable to hold back the battery of questions that followed: *Is Harry safe, is he okay, has he been duped by another member of the gang … ?*

With Evie taking a break, Alice stood up and winded her, then opened the curtains to take a first look outside in daylight. The view made her gasp. The back garden stretched half the length of a football pitch, it seemed, the wide lawn sparkling with frost. To one side there was a chicken run next to a couple of sheds, a swing and a trampoline for Nerys's grandchildren and a large vegetable patch at the bottom.

Hedges and a high fence enclosed the garden, but Alice could see a little of the countryside that lay beyond: fields and trees in the muted yellowy browns of autumn.

She opened the window, braving the cold for a taste of country air: damp grass, manure and wood smoke. What perfection to live somewhere like this with Harry and Evie and perhaps one or two more siblings; safe enough to let the kids go roaming over the fields …

At first the only sound was the whine of a light aircraft. Then a clattering nearby caught her attention, and Nerys emerged from the henhouse, incongruous in thick dressing gown and wellington boots. She was holding what looked like a plastic mixing bowl.

Alice moved back out of sight, shaking her head in wonder. Eggs freshly laid this morning: it was surely too good to be true.

She shut the window and carried Evie around the room, chatting brightly about the day ahead. 'We'll have a bath, and breakfast, and then Mr Renshaw will drive us to the station to get a train back to Brighton. Back to Daddy! Won't that be nice?'

Unless something's happened to Daddy.

No. Alice couldn't let those fears take hold. She had to believe he was okay.

Because if he wasn't, the fault lay with her,

She heard a car out front and might have gone to investigate, but Evie was suddenly agitated. Hungry again.

After a longer feed, Alice looked through the bag of clothes and found a vest, t-shirt and dungarees that should just about fit Evie. As for herself, the selection wouldn't be winning any fashion awards – some plain but new M&S underwear, grey trackie bottoms, a white t-shirt and a black zip-up Adidas fleece – but they were infinitely preferable to wearing her own grubby clothes.

Next came a bath: lukewarm, for Evie's sake, but still a pleasure. By the time they'd both dried and dressed Alice had begun to fear she was taking liberties with Nerys's hospitality.

Eager as she was to leave, Alice was in no hurry to go downstairs. But it had to be done – if nothing else, she was starving.

The nerves were magnified when she saw a silver Range Rover parked on the drive. Descending the stairs, she followed the sound of voices, only for conversation to cease as she reached the kitchen door.

Nerys was standing by the sink, her broad smile directed first at Evie, then Alice. For the man seated at the large oak table, it was the other way round. He gave Alice a long, intense appraisal, his glance at Evie merely an afterthought.

'This is my boy, Michael,' said Nerys, somewhat unnecessarily. The physical resemblance was clear enough, even though her son was tall and lean where Nerys was short and curvy. He had the same dark hair and olive skin, the same blue eyes and expressive mouth. He was wearing black jeans and a navy blue cashmere sweater; his attractively mussed-up hair giving him a slightly wild look, like a smouldering vampire from an American TV show.

Michael's teeth, Alice noted from a semi-professional viewpoint, were white and straight and evenly spaced. His smile, even when it didn't quite reach his eyes, had the kind of power that made female knees go weak. It struck Alice that at university – at any time before she met Harry, for that matter – she might have been bowled over by a man like this.

The kitchen, too, was the sort that Alice had always coveted, down to the handmade timber cabinets and the big oak dresser.

It was almost surreal, the irony that she was staying somewhere so beautiful as a result of such harrowing events; forced now to rely on the kindness of strangers whose motives were impossible to fathom.

Invited to sit, Alice took a seat at right angles to Michael. She'd been prepared to hold Evie and eat one-handed, but Nerys fetched her grandson's Fisher-Price playmat and set it on the floor beside Alice. It was in a safe corner of the kitchen, and the jungle animals dangling from the overhead gym looked like they would be a useful distraction, so Alice agreed to try Evie on it while she ate.

Nerys was in bustle mode, making a fresh pot of tea, tidying away the plates and mugs they'd already used and cajoling Alice into having a larger and larger breakfast – fried tomatoes, mushrooms, baked beans – while teasing her son for requesting scrambled egg on toast when he'd already had a bagel.

'I was up early.' His voice was slightly more nasal than Alice had expected, with the type of neutral accent that generally denoted an expensive education. He gave her a heavy-lidded look. 'My youngest is only three months, but he seems to be teething at the moment. Not good.'

Alice smiled. 'Still got that to come, unfortunately.'

She already knew that parenthood made it ridiculously easy to engage in small talk, and so it was here. And if the conversation faltered there was always Nerys to chip in with an irreverent comment, sometimes prompting Michael to raise his eyebrows and offer Alice a conspiratorial grin.

But even as they chatted away, Alice continued to be flustered by his presence. There was an energy about him, a charisma that made it feel as though he'd been brilliantly superimposed onto the kitchen: one of LiveFire's CGI creations that seemed hyper-real within this ordinary domestic setting. When Nerys went off to wake Renshaw, Alice was half inclined to jump up and follow her out of the room. Michael slouched in his seat and regarded Alice with a playful little smile, as if he knew exactly the reaction he was provoking.

He treated her to a few horror stories about childcare until Nerys returned, wrestling a wicker laundry basket through the doorway and chuckling about the fact that Renshaw had overslept. According to the small digital clock on the oven, it was nearly nine thirty.

Alice felt another stab of alarm. She couldn't quite rid herself of this irrational urge to flee. But that was silly, wasn't it?

Evie was staring in fascination at Michael, as if puzzled by his lack of interest in her. With the food almost ready, Alice set her down on the playmat, where she flailed happily, grabbing at a blue elephant and smiling whenever she made contact with it. Nerys clucked over her briefly, checked on the bacon and said, 'Two minutes, if you like it crispy,' then knelt at one of the units and started to load the washing machine. The task didn't register properly with Alice until she caught a flash of red material.

'Nerys … is that my t-shirt?'

The door had already shut, Nerys groaning as she rose to her feet and turned the dial. Alice heard a thump and a gurgle as the pump engaged and began to draw water.

'They'll be done in no time.' Nerys winked. 'I know you'd much rather go home in your own clothes, freshly washed, than in my tatty things.'

Alice opened her mouth to protest but realised it seemed so churlish. How could she insist on leaving soon without coming across as ungrateful?

Nerys briskly rubbed her hands together. 'Now, with your breakfast – toast or a bagel, my love?'

FORTY-FOUR

Michael spotted the flash of panic. Alice was caught, pinned like a butterfly to a board, but she clearly didn't want to acknowledge it.

Physically, the woman wasn't a disappointment at all. Great features, lovely hair, and a pretty good body considering the age of the baby. So Michael ramped up the charm, and wasn't deterred by its lack of effect: quite the opposite, in fact.

Then Renshaw mooched in, looking like a tramp in the ancient dressing gown that Nerys had found for him. He nodded brusquely and sat down. Michael gave him a cool glance, and tried not to resent the fond greeting offered by Nerys.

She's playing a role, remember. Keeping him sweet.

No one said much while they ate, but Michael could feel the anxiety radiating from both of their visitors. There wasn't a lot of warmth in evidence between Alice and Renshaw, and yet to Michael it seemed that Alice should have been a lot angrier about her predicament. He said a silent prayer that she wouldn't turn out to be as passive as Robyn. He wanted resistance, a spark of something.

Finally she dredged up the nerve to ask Renshaw what time he was driving her to the station. The old man glanced first at Nerys, who had insisted on taking the baby when she started squalling.

'Uh, later this morning.'

'And you're sure there's been no message from Harry?'

'No.'

Alice went to speak again, but Michael jumped in: 'Where are you going, anyway?'

'Brighton.'

'Oh, really?' A pause while he pretended to think. 'I have to be in Folkestone tomorrow. My company has a depot there. It would be no problem to give you a lift.'

Alice was shaking her head. 'No, that's very generous—'

'You're more than welcome to stay tonight,' Nerys chipped in. 'To be honest with you, that train can be a right mare.'

'Even on a Saturday?' Alice asked.

'Oh, yes. Much better by car, especially with this little darling to look after.' Nerys planted a kiss on the baby's head. Michael was sure he saw Alice flinch.

He tipped his chair back, balancing on the rear legs. 'Actually, I could go over tonight instead. Got a friend in Tonbridge who'd put me up.'

Alice looked distressed, the pressure of their generosity wearing her down.

'No, I can't put you to all that trouble.' She looked from him to Renshaw, and then to Nerys. 'Could we find out the train times, please?'

The silence that followed her request quickly became unbearable. Returning home by train was only what Renshaw had suggested, but Alice remembered the sarcastic retort from Nerys – *All nice and simple* – and felt convinced that they were going to refuse. And then it would be laid bare, the undeniable truth: she was a prisoner here.

It was Michael who broke the tension. 'Sure.' He popped out to the hall and returned, tapping the screen of an iPhone 6. 'Gloucester to Brighton, here we are.'

'Ah!' Alice exclaimed. 'Do you have the charger for that?'

'Not on me, I'm afraid.' He moved alongside her, leaning on the table with one elbow almost touching her arm. Alice could see the timetable, but the text was too small to read without shifting closer. He seemed to realise that, his hip gently bumping against her.

'Your best bet is the 2.17 to Paddington, though you have to change at Swindon. Then the Tube to Victoria and you reach Brighton at half six.'

'Four hours,' Alice murmured. Was she being ridiculous, refusing the offer of a lift?

She peered at the phone to check for other options, but Michael had scrolled to bottom of the page.

'It's about sixty pounds.'

Nerys made a clicking sound, as if slightly cross. 'Michael's happy to give you a lift—'

'She wants to go by train, Mum.' Another bump of his hip, letting her know he wasn't offended.

'Thank you.' Alice expected Renshaw to grumble about the cost, but the look he gave her was one of regret; perhaps even concern. Then Nerys moved into his line of sight and he looked away.

'Any more toast for you?' she asked. 'Tea or coffee?'

Renshaw shook his head. Alice also declined, standing up to reach for Evie, who still wasn't quite asleep.

'I'll take her for a nap, if that's okay?'

'Course it is, my love. You got the whole morning free now, haven't you?'

Michael had faded from the conversation. His phone had been put away, and Alice didn't want to push her luck by asking to borrow it. He was staring at his watch, which she noticed was a chunky Breitling; worth a fortune, probably.

'I'll be off soon, Mum. Playing taxi for the kids.' He shot Alice a laser beam smile. 'That'll be you in a few years.'

'Oh God, I know. It was nice to meet you. And thank you for the loan of the baby clothes.'

'Not a loan – keep them. We have plenty.'

They shook hands. She was a little surprised, almost taken aback, when he made no attempt to kiss her. From Renshaw there was another meaningful glance, but once again it made no sense.

Hurrying into the hall, she was startled by a thud against the front door. Several envelopes clattered on to the floor and the shock nearly caused her to cry out – a vivid reminder of what had got her into all this trouble.

But there was an opportunity here. Slow to spot it, she'd begun to turn for the stairs and stopped, first making sure Evie was safe in her grasp, then knelt awkwardly and flipped one of the envelopes so she could read the address.

A noise behind her. Alice jerked upright and found Renshaw motioning at her to wait.

He said quietly, 'Once the baby has slept, we should take a walk.'

'A walk?' For a moment the proposal seemed as unlikely as a trip to Mars.

'Nerys tells me it is beautiful here. And you have time to pass before your train.'

Alice couldn't argue with that. And the thought of escaping the house was certainly appealing, even if it meant putting up with Renshaw. She also had the impression that he wanted to talk to her in private.

She nodded. 'Give me half an hour.'

FORTY-FIVE

After arriving at Victoria, Harry took the underground to King's Cross, where he boarded the 8.44 train to Ely. An hour's journey across the flat green and brown agricultural landscapes of East Anglia: England's own little slice of Iowa.

The day grew milder but not much lighter. All traces of last night's frost had vanished, and the sky wore a caul of grey cloud. A day as dull and flat as his own spirit.

He rang Renshaw's phone several times, with no success. Same with Ruth's. Then he noticed his battery level was fast reducing. Having no way to recharge it, he was forced to give up. He shut his eyes and tried to relax into the rhythm of the train's motion, telling himself that this whole experience was a wrong turning. Soon he would back up, rejoin Alice and Evie and resume life as normal.

At Ely, waiting for the connection to Thetford, he found a quiet spot on the platform and made the call to Keri. The phone rang for a long time, and when she answered she sounded distinctly cool.

'I suggested you phone at eleven.'

'Sorry, I just—'

'I prefer my clients to follow instructions. That's better for us both.'

'Yes, I'm sure. Uh, I rang because I'm going to be in Thetford sooner than I thought. I wondered if we could meet an hour earlier?'

She sucked in a breath, prompting him to add: 'Look, I can pay extra if—'

'The rate's the rate. I'm not a rip-off merchant.'

'No. Sorry.' He snorted. 'I'm making a total hash of this.'

'You sound nervous. Is it your first time?'

'God, no! I'm thirty-two. I have—' He stopped, unwilling to mention Alice.

Keri was laughing softly. 'I mean, your first time with an escort. I didn't expect you to be a virgin – although I can cater for that, if you are.'

'Oh. Right. No, I'm not. But yes, it is my first time.'

Another pause, but he sensed he'd won her over.

'I'm in a block called Milton Place, just off Painter Street. It's not far from the centre.' She gave him directions. 'I'll text you a few minutes before eleven with the apartment number.'

'Okay. Are you always this careful with your address? Only it seems a bit … long-winded.'

'Maybe it does. But you're not me. This is the way I work, and it's not negotiable. See you at eleven.'

He was in Thetford by ten forty. His paranoia had receded just enough that he could walk through the station and not feel that everyone was looking at him, but it had changed how he viewed the world. All he saw now were traps, threats, danger.

There was a biting wind from the North Sea, cutting through his jacket with ease. He set off along a quiet residential street, and nearly missed the turning he needed to reach Painter Street.

By ten to eleven he was waiting by a short terrace of stone-built cottages. Across the road, Milton Place was a more recent development of several three-storey buildings, almost but not quite brutalist in design, painted an unappealing cream and brown.

Harry tried not to look conspicuous, but felt his purpose must be blatantly obvious: *Man visiting prostitute! Man visiting prostitute!*

Or maybe he wasn't. Maybe she'd rumbled him and had no intention of responding—

The phone buzzed. *Flat 14.*

He practically ran to the main entrance and pressed the button for number 14. The double glass doors clicked and he pushed one open and walked inside. The communal area felt freshly painted, the carpet thick and springy: a new conversion, maybe.

The third floor was whisper-quiet, as if the whole place was empty. Harry couldn't decide whether that should reassure him or exacerbate his nerves. He imagined unseen eyes tracking him along the corridor. It felt like a terrible error, now, to visit this woman under false pretences. He wasn't at all sure that his acting skills were up to the task.

He knocked on her door and faced the spyhole, trying to wear a relaxed, guileless expression. The door opened and he was greeted by an attractive woman in her late twenties, wearing a black cocktail dress with just a hint of cleavage on display.

Keri was slim and extremely tall, thanks in part to a pair of six-inch platform heels. Her hair was long and wavy, light brown in colour, and her make-up was subtle and effective. In short, she was a world away from Harry's preconceptions. Take a couple of inches off the heels and she could be a City lawyer at a high-powered function.

She smiled. 'Come on in, Harry. How did you hear about me?'

'Uh, a friend.'

He stepped into a narrow hallway, and was hoping he wouldn't have to elaborate when he heard a trilling noise. It took a quizzical look from Keri to make him realise it was his own phone.

He fumbled it from his pocket. The number was the one Ruth had used last night.

'I'm really sorry, I have to take this.'

'Don't worry.' Keri indicated a door behind him. 'I thought you might want to freshen up.'

Nodding, he entered a small but immaculate bathroom, and shut the door before answering the phone.

'Ruth?' he hissed.

'Yeah, sorry I had to run out—'

'Where the hell did you go?'

'I spotted one of their cars and went after them. Then my phone ran out of juice and I've only just had a chance to power it up. Let me come and get you now.'

'I'm not in Crawley. I came to Norfolk.'

'Why?' It took her only a second to work it out. 'Don't tell me you're going to see Keri?'

'What else could I do? Yesterday that was what you wanted.'

'The plan was to get her address. But I don't actually need her any more, so don't bother with a meeting.'

'Ruth, you owe me an—'

'Yeah, yeah, I know. I can be there in about an hour. Meet by the statue of Thomas Paine, in King Street.'

She rang off, leaving him angry and bewildered. How was he going to explain this to Keri? It was bad enough that he'd deceived his way into the flat in the first place. Then he thought: *Huh*.

Why should he listen to Ruth, after the way she'd treated him?

He joined Keri in the living room, where she was sitting on a long L-shaped sofa. The room was tidy but characterless, predominantly beige and sparsely furnished, with no photographs or personal items on view. Keri's posture seemed quite guarded:

legs crossed, her hands clamped at her sides, as if to stop herself from fidgeting.

'I assume we settle the, er, financial aspect first?'

'Please,' she said, a little tightly.

Harry counted out a hundred and fifty pounds, his hands trembling. When he held the money out to her, she sprang up and swiped at him, a weapon suddenly in her right hand. It was a telescopic steel baton, and it struck a glancing blow to his arm. He dropped the money, stumbling back out of range. What a fool: he was being robbed. The oldest trick in the book ...

'You bastard! Ruth Monroe sent you here, didn't she?'

'What?' Now he understood: she must have been listening at the door. 'No, look. I'm sorry—'

'Where is she, waiting outside? You know she's a fucking lunatic, don't you?'

Her eyes were bright with tears. She maintained an aggressive stance, the baton raised to strike. Harry had no idea how to pacify her, so he took the blunt approach instead.

'She says you had an affair with her husband. But she's not waiting outside, and she doesn't have your address. I promise.'

He kept his hands up, palms out, until Keri relaxed slightly. She lowered the baton, then kicked off her shoes, instantly becoming six inches shorter, as well as more human, somehow.

'What else did she tell you?'

'That her husband had been a police officer. He was investigating a man called Nathan Laird, and because of that he was murdered.' He faltered, only now thinking of Ruth's attempt to dissuade him from seeing Keri. 'Or is any of that not true?'

'Greg was killed. Nobody knows for sure who did it.'

'But Laird might have been responsible?'

'Maybe. I prefer not to dwell on it, thanks.'

Harry scrutinised her carefully. 'Okay ... so what am I missing?'

With a scornful sigh, Keri dropped back on to the sofa. 'There's a lot she hasn't told you.'

'Really?'

'For one thing, at the time of his death Greg wasn't her husband. They'd split up years before.' A lot of emotion in her voice now: bitterness and grief. 'And I doubt if Ruth happened to mention *why* they split, did she? Or what *she* was doing while Greg was risking his life on her behalf?'

'No. She didn't.' He waited.

And waited.

'Please, Keri. What?'

'She was in prison.'

FORTY-SIX

Evie, for once, might have slept the morning away. She looked sublimely relaxed, motionless but for her bottom lip, which trembled with each exhalation.

She'd had about twenty-five minutes when there was a tap on the door. Alice opened it to find Renshaw, looking like the Michelin man in a quilted jacket over a thick sweater.

'Oh!' Alice exclaimed. 'I'm not ready.'

'Leave the baby if you must, or bring her in the papoose. Either way …' He tapped his watch. This was the short-tempered, impatient Renshaw back again.

So what had caused the change of mood? Alice pondered that question while she carefully dressed Evie in her pramsuit and placed her in the carrier. Evie grumbled and squealed, but didn't quite wake up. Suspecting that a bowel movement was due, Alice picked up a nappy and a pack of wipes, and put them in a nappy sack.

She followed Renshaw downstairs, wishing they were leaving for good. She'd toyed with the idea of asking Michael to take her and Evie to Gloucester station, but was deterred by the thought of what it might signify if he refused.

There was no sign of Nerys and Michael, although she could hear someone moving in the kitchen. The Range Rover was still on the drive. Spotting a couple of winter coats on a stand by the door, Alice decided to borrow a Barbour waxed jacket, large enough to give Evie some extra protection from the elements, and with a pocket for the nappy and wipes.

She was glad of the coat as soon as they stepped outside. The sky was filling with high cloud and the wind had a moist, raw feel to it, blowing in gusts from the west.

Without saying a word, Renshaw tramped into the lane, then turned on to a footpath leading across the fields that she'd seen from the nursery window. Alice followed, abruptly deciding that she'd had enough of his moods.

'I should have heard from Harry by now. There's no way he wouldn't be trying to get in touch with me.'

'I told you—' he began, but she spoke over him.

'To my mind it means one of two things. Either you're lying to me and not passing on his messages, or, for some reason, he isn't able to communicate.' She paused to let this sink in, and saw him nodding gravely.

'The woman he was with,' he muttered. 'Perhaps she was not to be trusted.'

'In that case, he's in danger. You have to let me call the police.'

'Impossible. No police.'

'How did I know you were going to say that?' She laughed, coldly. Renshaw strode on, skirting a puddle with a thin crust of ice on the surface. He was breathing hard, staring at the ground as if he wanted to forget she existed.

'Why are you so anxious this morning?' she asked him. 'Were you aware that the landline doesn't work?'

At this, he jerked upright. 'No. But it does not surprise me.'

'I assumed you were scared of the gang finding you here. But that look you gave me at breakfast … it's Nerys you're worried about, isn't it?'

Again, Renshaw said nothing, but he wore a sombre expression.

'I don't get it,' Alice said. 'If Nerys was up to something, why let us come out like this?'

Renshaw indicated the ploughed field to their right, a meadow to their left; a lonely copse of tall thin trees up ahead. 'To reassure us, perhaps? There is nowhere we can go from here.'

'All right, but …' Alice bit her lip for a second. 'Don't take this the wrong way, but after what happened yesterday, aren't we both likely to be prone to paranoia?'

'Possibly. But my instincts say otherwise.' He hesitated, struggling to put his thoughts into words. Evie started squirming in her carrier, screwing up her face. *Right on cue*, Alice thought.

Renshaw said, 'If I had come to Nerys alone, I believe she would have helped me, and asked for nothing in return. But the presence of her son …' He narrowed his eyes, not maliciously; almost with regret. 'Your presence, too. It changes things.'

'I don't understand. In what way?'

But Renshaw only shook his head. 'No. Forget I said this.'

By kneeling on a chest of drawers in one of the spare bedrooms, Michael was able to follow their progress along the track. He thought their body language might tell him something, but there wasn't much to discern from this pair of roly-polys: Renshaw waddling along in his padded winter coat, Alice bulked out by the presence of the baby carrier.

The door creaked. Michael didn't look round until his mother chuckled.

'Very dignified.'

'I want to see where they go. She's taken your coat, cheeky bitch.' No comment from Nerys, so he said, 'What did you find?'

'Nothing. Clothes, most of them in a horrendous state. No paperwork. And no money.'

'So he's hidden it somewhere?'

'Or he's got it on him.'

The coat. With a groan, Michael gently butted his forehead against the glass. Renshaw and Alice were almost lost from sight now, heading for the wood that marked the boundary between two farms.

'What if they're doing a runner?' he said.

'Calm down. He's got no reason to leave the car behind. If he's kept the money with him it's only 'cause he knows we'll search his room.'

'So why go out in the first place?'

'Could be a test, to see how we react. And that's not a problem, really. Anything to keep them relaxed.'

Probably right, Michael thought. He could no longer see them so he climbed down, bruising his knee in the process.

'Did you find the number for this Vickers, or whatever his name is?'

'Vickery. I have a number, but I'm not calling till I've worked out how to play it. Ideally I need a bit more out of Edward first. If we just knew the *nature* of the leverage that he's got over Laird.'

'But if you push him, surely he'll guess what we're up to?'

'The bigger problem is handling Vickery and Laird.' She sighed. 'We're tapdancing on a tightrope. The last thing we want is to make an enemy out of Laird, and yet we've got to know something about Edward's little scheme, because that's where his value lies.'

Michael spotted a glint in her eye. 'I take it you're hatching a brilliant plan?'

'Not really. But when they come back, it'd be a lot better if you weren't here – at least, not officially.'

'What do you mean?'

'You make him nervous. Like I said last night, he's more, what is it … *pliable* if he thinks I'm on my own.' She saw he was wounded by this, and pouted back at him. 'Don't worry, there'll still be a chance for you to have your little pleasure, I dare say.'

Now he had to fake incomprehension. 'What are you implying?'

'I'm not stupid. I've seen the way you look at her.' She was grinning – fortunately – as if her disapproval was based only on the fact that he'd made it so obvious.

'Why? How *do* I look at her?'

'Like a wolf, Michael. A ravenous wolf.'

FORTY-SEVEN

Harry was stunned, and didn't mind Keri knowing it. *Ruth had been in prison …*

After being granted permission to sit at the far end of the sofa, he said, 'Ruth just tried to persuade me not to talk to you. Now I can see why.'

Once he was seated, the tension in the room eased a little. Keri gathered up the fallen money, shuffled the notes into a neat bundle and handed them back to him. Then she sat down, carefully placing the baton within easy reach.

'Who are you, anyway? You're not police. And not her toyboy, surely?' This last was said with a caustic smile.

He proceeded to explain what had happened to his family over the past three days. The mention of Renshaw's name brought a little gasp of recognition, but she gestured for him to carry on. He rushed through his story, concluding with Ruth's sudden disappearance last night.

'She wants to meet me later today, but first I need to know why she was in prison.'

'I can only tell you what I managed to pry out of Greg. She beat someone up, left them in a coma. As for who, or why, he couldn't say any more than that.'

'Couldn't – or wouldn't?'

She narrowed her eyes. 'What does it matter?'

'Just wondering if … well, if Greg had a reason to portray her in a bad light.'

'Playing the old sympathy routine to get me into bed?' Her eyes flashed mischievously. 'You're forgetting how I pay my bills. Greg didn't have to tell me a thing. If you're asking whether he had his own secrets, yeah, I'm sure he did. But I can't blame him for being reluctant to discuss his ex-wife. Her ending up in jail wasn't exactly easy for him.'

'I bet it wasn't. Did they have kids?'

'No. They'd tried for years. I suspect Greg wanted them a lot more than Ruth did.'

'Right.' Harry had to clear his throat before his next question. 'So, um, when you slept with him, was it a, uh, professional transaction?'

'Did I fuck him for money? Actually, at first I did. I found out later that paying for it made him feel less guilty.'

'Why? Hadn't he split from Ruth by then?'

She snorted. 'It wasn't that. He was guilty about trying to use me to get to Laird.'

Harry rested his head back while he tried to assimilate all this new information. Keri regarded him solemnly.

'She's bad news, Harry. I don't just mean the prison thing. It's the pressure she put on Greg, even after they split up. Nathan Laird was her obsession, and being behind bars didn't reduce that one bit. She made sure it became Greg's obsession, too.'

'But why? What is it about Laird … ?'

'Some sort of grudge, going back years, that's all I know.'

'Didn't you ask Greg?'

'Of course. He said it wouldn't be fair to tell me. Whether he meant fair to me, or fair to Ruth …' She threw out her hands,

at a loss to explain. 'Ever since she was released, at the end of
last year, she's been trying to track me down. She won't take no
for an answer.'

'But why? I mean, why does she keep pursuing you – assuming
it's not bitterness over you and Greg?'

'She's convinced that I'm holding back on her.'

'But if you knew anything significant, surely you'd have already
told Greg?'

'Well, I was far from happy that he'd deceived me. But yeah, he
was a good guy, and I would've helped him if I could. The fact is,
I couldn't: simple as that. He accepted it right away, but Ruth …
I don't understand why, but she won't leave me alone.' Her voice
choked and she sniffed, laced her fingers together and twisted
them back and forth. 'Times like this I really wish I still smoked.'

She offered Harry a drink, and when he asked for water she
fetched a glass for herself as well. As Keri returned to the sofa,
he realised he was averting his gaze every time she crossed or
uncrossed her legs.

He asked: 'The stuff she told me about Laird, is that all true?'

'Pretty much. He has a whole range of business interests, some
less legal than others.'

'Including the escorting?'

'Yeah, but even that's conducted at a pretty exclusive level, so
it isn't likely to bother the authorities.' She sat forward. 'I can't tell
you about Laird's early years, but if he was still involved in drugs,
robberies – heavy-duty stuff – I think there would be far more
official interest in him. More than just poor old Greg, snooping
around to keep his ex-wife off his back.'

'So what kind of information was Greg looking for? Did he
want Laird's address? His financial records? What?'

'All of that. Where he lived, whether he was in contact with any of his family. Who he trusted. I think Ruth wanted anything she could get.'

Harry's next question was about Renshaw. He was shocked to learn that the man was genuinely a doctor.

'The girls operate mostly on their own, or maybe in pairs,' Keri explained. 'They work out of rented apartments in practically every big town in East Anglia, as well as further afield, in London, Manchester, Birmingham. Renshaw's job was to take care of their medical needs – contraception, regular testing for STIs, that sort of thing. I knew of one or two who had drug problems when they started, and Renshaw helped them get clean.'

Harry shook his head, mystified. 'With what Ruth has told me about Laird, I'd wondered if he was involved in trafficking. You hear so much about women being brought over from Eastern Europe …'

'And it happens,' Keri said. 'It's slavery and torture, and the men responsible ought to be going away for life, rather than the pathetic sentences they get at the moment.'

She took a sip of water, a quick smile acknowledging her vehemence on the issue.

'But the women who worked for Laird were mostly British, along with a few Europeans: Spanish, French, Scandinavian. There was no coercion – or not that I saw. And, for the most part, they looked after us.'

She gave him another smile, but it was uneasy, almost a grimace.

'So why did you leave, if it was such a good set-up?'

'Lots of reasons.' She looked uncomfortable. 'For one thing, I needed a break. And I had a dissertation to write. So …'

She shrugged. Harry felt there was more to come, so he pushed gently.

'And Laird was okay about you leaving?'
'He was fine with it. Completely fine.'

Another silence. This time Harry waited, said nothing, and finally she spoke again.

'If you must know, I got pregnant, about a year ago.' She issued a long, thoughtful sigh. 'Occupational hazard.'

'Really? You just mentioned contraception—'

'Condoms split. The pill isn't a hundred per cent effective. I'd had a tummy bug around the time it happened, so maybe that was the reason.'

'And what did you … ?'

'I didn't.' She swallowed, a little too heavily. 'Miscarried, at seven weeks. Afterwards … well, I was in no state to work. It seemed like the right time to get out. So I did. Ran home to Mum with a story of a relationship gone sour, licked my wounds for a couple of months, then got myself together.'

'So why come back? Especially if this is Laird's territory?'

'I like this part of the world. It's been my home for most of my adult life. And I have nothing to fear from Laird.'

A slight wobble in her voice made him frown. 'You're sure about that?'

'Look, there was hardly any risk in talking to Greg, because I trusted him to be discreet. But Ruth would sell me out in a heartbeat. If she comes near me, and then they get to hear about it, I'm finished.'

FORTY-EIGHT

Alice pushed Renshaw on what he meant – how had her presence changed things? – but he wouldn't be drawn. Her attempts to get an explanation were hampered by Evie as she became more and more agitated, her little feet pummelling her mother's body.

They'd skirted the fields that lay behind Nerys's home, the muddy path becoming sticky as it thawed. Now they were entering the copse of trees. Very quickly the light dimmed; the breeze dying away beneath the golden-brown canopy of leaves.

The trees were mostly beech, tall and wide with smooth grey bark. They walked over a thick carpet of fallen leaves, the surface dry and crunchy with a layer of mulch beneath. At the first clearing Alice stopped to focus on Evie, who was still writhing and complaining loudly. She lifted her out of the carrier and sniffed.

'I need to change her nappy.'

Renshaw looked set to object, but nodded instead. 'Very well.'

Shrugging off the coat she'd borrowed, Alice laid it on the ground and set Evie down on top of it. As she undid the pramsuit, Renshaw grunted unhappily and backed away, as if the noise and smells emanating from this little creature were more than he could bear.

Well, tough, Alice thought. She was growing equally weary of Renshaw.

After changing the nappy, she bagged it up, and said, 'You don't trust Nerys, but what is it you think she's going to do? Betray you to Laird?'

'I … I would not go that far.' He was kicking idly at a pile of leaves, his hands thrust in his pockets like a bored adolescent. 'The son, Michael … he has the eyes of a predator, does he not?'

He has his mother's eyes, Alice thought, but she opted not to say so. She lifted Evie up, kissed her gratefully for co-operating, and placed her back in the carrier. Then she picked up the bag with the soiled nappy.

'I'll take this back with me,' she said, in answer to Renshaw's frown. 'Unless we find a bin.'

'Here.' Before she could react, he had taken it from her, only to turn and fling it into the undergrowth. She let out a cry of protest, and he raised his hands to placate her. 'There are more important things to consider.'

'I know that. Don't lecture me.' A moment of angry silence. 'Look, why don't we just pack up and go? Isn't that the best option for both of us?'

'Is it?' He turned, looking coldly amused. 'For both of us?'

'Yes.' She refused to be taunted. 'What are you worried about, really?'

He gave a slow blink, studying her carefully. 'You are an intelligent woman. I see that now.'

It was such a patronising comment that Alice could only laugh, a reaction which Renshaw interpreted as a modest denial.

'I mean it. What did you do before the baby came along?'

'I'm a dental hygienist,' she said, and added sardonically: 'Thanks for asking.'

'A useful occupation,' was Renshaw's only comment, which suggested he wasn't very interested. He'd placed his foot on a fallen log and now it shifted unexpectedly, causing him to stumble. Alice muffled a snort of laughter. To conceal his embarrassment,

Renshaw knelt down and fiddled with his shoe, pulling the lace free and retying it.

Noticing that Evie was sleepy again. Alice took long, exaggerated strides across the clearing, jogging the carrier up and down to enhance the rhythm of her movements.

'What now, then?' she asked as Renshaw stood up. 'Because we can't stay out here all morning.'

'I agree. But I propose that you wait for a short time, while I go back to speak with Nerys.'

Alice thought he was joking. 'Why? What difference does it make if I'm not there?'

'I have a reason. An important one—'

'Yes,' she interrupted, 'and as usual you won't tell me what it is. Well, I've got an eight-week-old baby here, and soon she'll need feeding again.'

'I know, but—'

'No, I've been far too patient up to now, far too meek and fucking reasonable, and I've had enough.' She was gratified that the obscenity shocked him into silence. 'All I want is to get on a train home. I should never have been talked into waiting till this afternoon, so if you want me out of the way, call me a taxi right now and Evie and I will be gone.'

'With no money?'

'I'll bloody well—' She broke off; swallowed.

What *would* she do?

Renshaw sighed. 'Becoming emotional won't help.' He took a step towards her, glancing both ways as if checking to make sure they were alone; one hand still deep in his pocket.

Alice tensed. Had he lured her out here in order to kill her?

*

Another step closer. Alice wrapped her arms around the carrier, working out if she could outrun him.

Then he prised something from his pocket and dropped it at her feet. A packet of yellow paper. The size and colour were unfamiliar, so it took her a few seconds to register what it was.

Money. In euros.

Another bundle came from the same pocket. Two more from the opposite pocket. He unzipped his coat and produced another half dozen packets, these ones purple, in solid bricks. Lastly came a strong carrier bag, which he unfolded and placed next to the pile of money. Ignoring her, he knelt down and filled the bag.

'How much ... ?' It was all Alice could manage.

'About half a million, in two-hundred- and five-hundred-euro notes. Barely enough to establish a new life.' He stood up and held the bag out to her. 'And too dangerous to convert in this quantity. I will have to leave the country, but first I need a few days to make the arrangements.'

He was still offering the bag but Alice wouldn't take it. Irascibly, he dropped it beside her.

'You feel this money is tainted, no doubt. That is good. It means you can be trusted not to run off with it.'

'What?' Alice stared at the bag. 'How long do I wait?'

'An hour should be sufficient.' A smug smile. 'You understand now? It is not that I need *you* away from the house. It is that the money must be safe while I speak with Nerys.'

'Ah hour,' Alice repeated miserably. 'And then what?'

'If I am satisfied she can be trusted, I will fetch you, and this afternoon you take the train home. If Nerys gives me reason for concern, then we take the car and leave right away. I will drive you to the station and give you money for a ticket.'

She nodded grimly. Renshaw was already turning away when she called: 'Hold on. What if you don't come back within the hour?'

His eyes narrowed slightly, as if he'd been hoping she wouldn't identify that particular scenario. He reached into his trouser pocket and produced the phone he'd been letting her use. He pressed a few buttons, then tilted the screen in her direction.

She peered at the text: *Alice, it's Harry. I'm having to use a borrowed phone, too. Will explain all soon. If this really is you, tell me where we went for that weekend before Evie came along. And tell me you really are safe! I love you. Harry xx*

The relief was indescribable: Harry was okay.

Then came the shock. The suspicion. 'When did you get this?'

'It was sent last night. There were other messages, attempts to reach you, but I deleted them. This I put in a folder, so you would not see it.'

Alice remembered how she'd been allowed to check the phone in the living room. She felt a tear come to her eyes and hated herself for it.

'And what about my iPhone?' She saw the truth in his eyes. 'You wore out the battery, didn't you, so I'd be forced to rely on you?'

He nodded. 'I am truly sorry.' Then, to her surprise, he thrust the Nokia into her hand. 'You do not trust me, and you were right, in many ways. But I trust you, Alice. Keep this. Please wait an hour. If I do not return, you are free to call your husband, the police, anyone you wish.'

'So I make my own way home? And what about all this money? How do I explain—?'

'I *will* be back within an hour.' A gesture at the bag. 'This guarantees it, I assure you.'

FORTY-NINE

Michael dutifully complied with his mother's instructions. He drove towards the village and left the Range Rover in a cul-de-sac, about a ten-minute stroll from the house.

Walking back, he called Robyn to apologise. Somehow she had dropped Betty at her drama class, rushed Chloe to football, then made it back in time to see Betty take part in a display of modern dance.

'And Junior was all right with that?'

'Oh yes, he adores our little car journeys, although there is something funny. A couple of his outfits are missing. You know those purple dungarees my sister bought him?'

Michael grunted, not interested. 'I'd better get back to Mum. I'll be home as soon as I can.'

A soft laugh. 'Oh, no hurry, darling. Your mother comes first.'

He analysed her tone for traces of sarcasm and found none. Then Junior squealed in the background and Robyn said she had to rush, blew him a kiss to pass to Nanny Nerys and rang off.

'Nanny Nerys' was grimly excited when he reached the house. She'd managed to get hold of Mark Vickery.

'I said I'd heard he's looking for Renshaw, and that I might know where he is. Vickery played it cool but I could tell he's interested. *Very* interested.'

'Did you talk terms?' It worried Michael that his mother had chosen to make the call in his absence. He wondered if she still had reservations about confiding in him – and that was the real reason he'd been sent to move the car.

'Not yet. But Vickery will know I'll be expecting a reward of some kind.'

'So now what?'

'Sort out your hiding place,' Nerys said, with a grin so wicked that it made her look ten years younger. 'And then wait for them to come back.'

He studied her for a moment: those big eyes glowing with vitality. 'You're getting a kick out of this, aren't you?'

'I don't know about that. I'd be a lot happier if Renshaw had never got in touch, but since he has …' She shrugged. 'A change is as good as a rest, isn't that what they say?'

They didn't have to wait long. Nerys was upstairs, tidying the nursery, when she shouted down to him: 'Edward's on his way across the field.'

In the kitchen, Michael was idly flicking through the *Mail.* He threw it aside when she called out again: 'Alice isn't with him.'

He raced upstairs, joined Nerys in the guest bedroom and watched Renshaw marching along the path. Was it his imagination, or did Renshaw look slightly less rotund?

'Where is she?' he asked. 'What's he done with her?'

Nerys grasped his arm and spoke in a soothing voice. 'And the baby, remember? He can't have harmed them.'

'But what if he's let them go?' Michael knew he sounded hopelessly bereft, a boy whose most treasured toy has just been snatched by the school bully.

Tutting, Nerys eased him away from the window. 'We'll have to see what he says, won't we?'

Initially she'd been reluctant for him to do anything other than wait in an adjoining room, but Michael had insisted on staying close to the action. Having decided that her country kitchen was the least intimidating place to speak to Renshaw, they'd cleared space for him to hide in the old-fashioned pantry. It meant he had to crouch below a shelf of tins and dried pasta, hemmed in tight by the side walls. The door was held shut by a roller catch, but the slightest pressure would open it. The air reeked of stale onions. Within seconds Michael had a dusting of flour on his face and had to pinch his nostrils together to suppress a sneeze.

A minute or two passed before he heard them come in, his mother referring to Alice when she said: '… could have gone upstairs, if you'd wanted to talk in private. It's a big house!'

'No. It is better if she and the infant are well away from here, until this is agreed.'

'I see,' Nerys said. 'And what's to agree?'

A chair creaked: Renshaw sitting down. Michael heard a cupboard open, mugs being placed on the worktop.

'Several things. I cannot believe you have failed to spot the potential here. Their value.' He paused. 'Your son has gone now, yes?'

'Yes. Why?'

'I … I do not think it wise to involve him. This should be between us. Only us.'

The rush of water into a kettle obscured Renshaw's next comment, but Michael heard his mother grumbling: 'My conscience is clear. I gave those girls the best possible care.'

'And yet, you have told your son nothing.'

'Because it's ancient history. Now, why don't you get to the point?'

A soft, menacing chuckle from Renshaw. 'The point, Nerys, is that this is not ancient history at all. The threat from Laird is real. I had hoped for sanctuary here, but I fear it would not be safe to stay.'

'Nonsense. And I'm offended, frankly, that you could say so.'

Michael smiled. His mother sounded so indignant that he felt a momentary pang of sympathy for her position – as if she wasn't intending to betray Renshaw for the right price.

Renshaw went on, unrepentant: 'It is better that I leave. But I will need money.'

'You've got money, haven't you?'

'It is not sufficient. Clearly you have done very well here. This peaceful life in the countryside, it must be worth a lot to keep it this way?'

'What are you saying, Edward?'

'To keep silent about your present location, I must have some help towards my own retirement.'

Over the fizz of a boiling kettle, Nerys gave a spluttering laugh. 'And if I don't pay up?'

'Please. Such things are ugly to discuss. Let us agree quickly on a deal, so that we remain friends. You also keep the, ah, "merchandise", do not forget.'

Nerys said nothing. Michael could hear her making the tea. Finally she spoke, in a calm, reasonable tone.

'How much do you need?'

'As much as you can spare. Two, three hundred thousand …'

'Are you serious?' Nerys laughed again. 'D'you think I have that sort of cash lying around?'

'Entirely possible. Your late husband's business was, what, antique importing?'

'More or less. And Michael's added a retail arm – a dozen shops now. But cash flow is really tight. The recession's been hell for—'

'Nonsense. This is a high-end market, and as we both know, the rich are richer than ever. I would be amazed if you or your son did not have a rainy day fund, hidden away from the taxman.'

Silence. Michael struggled to picture his mother, speechless with shock.

'Also, I require a better car. Your son's Range Rover would be ideal for my purposes.'

'Edward …' Nerys exhaled impatiently. 'You can't just roll up here and make all these demands.'

'No? Then you would prefer it if Nathan Laird "rolls up here", following a tip-off that you helped me escape?'

FIFTY

So there it was. No doubting where they stood now, Michael thought. His mother's warnings had been entirely vindicated.

Almost through gritted teeth, by the sound of it, she said, 'This is bloody unfair, Edward. You haven't even told me why you're in so much trouble.'

'You know what you need to know.'

'Bullshit. I'm not giving you a penny till you tell me why Laird's so desperate to find you.'

Renshaw huffed and puffed a bit, but it couldn't have escaped his attention that she'd as good as capitulated.

'There was one particular transaction.' He said it carefully, as if to avoid incriminating himself. 'It was not my intention to do so, but I learned the identity of the customer.'

'I don't suppose you'll tell me who it is?' Nerys asked.

He must have shaken his head. 'He wanted not just one, but two, three … a regular conveyor belt, to be used for—'

'I get it,' said Nerys quickly. She sounded cross, Michael thought, and it struck him that the interruption was to prevent him from overhearing the full details from his position in the pantry. 'I assume you've got proof, otherwise it's just the kind of rubbish that goes flying round the internet every day.'

'I have proof. Hidden well, in case you were wondering.' He sniffed. 'You will have searched my room, no doubt?'

Nerys made regretful noises. 'I appreciate why you've had to be so suspicious, but to act this way with *me*, after all the years we've known each other …'

There were kitchen drawers opening and closing as she spoke, and she sounded upset but also slightly distracted – occupied with her domestic tasks – to an extent that probably invited Renshaw to pay scant attention to her complaint.

'I am no fool, Nerys,' he growled. 'It is clear your life here is worth everything to you. I am being generous giving you the girl. Now you either take the deal, or answer to Laird.'

From Nerys, a long troubled sigh. Then she said, 'Well, you certainly strike a hard bargain, Edward.'

What? Michael couldn't understand why she wasn't arguing her case more forcefully, but then came a strange scuffling noise, the harsh scrape of a chair, and Renshaw let out a cry. It was cut short by a hard, heavy clonk that was unmistakably an act of violence: the sound of a solid object striking something hard, but also something wet and yielding.

After kicking the pantry door open, there was a second when Michael couldn't move. He had to force himself to relax, folding his arms in tight before he could pitch forward, but he forgot to duck his head and caught the sharp edge of the shelf as he tried to stand up too soon.

Dizzy and reeling from the pain, he took in the nightmarish scene before him. Nerys was behind Renshaw's chair, a rolling pin in her hand: the cartoon battle-axe's weapon of choice. She'd swung at Renshaw's head but he must have ducked away; his right cheek and eye socket had been smashed and there was blood streaming down his face.

Nevertheless he was still in one piece, still conscious; able and willing to fight back. With an agonised roar he lurched out of his chair and made to grab the rolling pin, but there was blood on the weapon and his hand slipped, giving Nerys time to lift it out of his reach. She smacked it down on his head, a direct strike this time. The noise made Michael think of a pumpkin being hollowed out for Halloween.

Renshaw pitched forward, off the chair, and landed on his knees. His one good eye swivelled and rolled and came to focus on Michael. His mouth opened, perhaps to appeal for mercy, but all that emerged was another thick gout of blood.

'Mum—' Michael began, but she didn't hear him. She swung again. Blood and hair and what might have been skull fragments flew across the room. Spots of blood landed on Michael's face and he whipped his head away in disgust, spitting and brushing at his cheeks. He heard a thud: Renshaw flopping on to his belly. But he wasn't lying still. He rolled from side to side, clawing at the kitchen tiles with blood-streaked fingers, his feet making a frantic cycling action as if trying to get away.

Renshaw let out a long, eerie moan, like a wild animal caught in a snare, and somehow managed to get on to his elbows and knees, bumping against Nerys as she rose to land another blow. Her feet slipped in his blood and made her stumble; she grabbed the table for support but dropped the rolling pin. It landed with a noise like a bomb going off, and Michael shouted something but he had no idea what, because it was too much to take in – this was his mother, for Christ's sake, beating someone to death in front of his eyes – and still Renshaw wouldn't give up: he went on screeching, trying to lift his ruined head and stay alive another second.

'Finish it!' Nerys shrieked. 'Michael, finish it!'

At first he didn't have a clue what she meant. Then he understood.

She was asking *him* to do it.

Stricken, he shook his head.

I can't.

Her expression, for only a split-second, was one of the purest contempt. With a weary sigh, she bent over to retrieve the rolling pin, then planted a foot on Renshaw's spine and forced him to lie flat. She pulled a chair alongside him and sat down, taking the weight off her feet while she leaned forward and clubbed him half a dozen times, her fatigue, by the end, making her look almost bored. Michael turned away, gagging at the sudden dreadful smell in the room.

'He's soiled himself,' Nerys muttered. 'Often happens, at the point of death.'

Michael hurried to the sink and spat, then ran the tap and splashed his face, wiping and wiping until he felt sure he must be clean.

'He's dead,' he murmured in disbelief. 'He's really dead?'

He hadn't intended to phrase it as a question, but there was a short, sarcastic laugh from Nerys.

'Are you trying to be funny?' She wiped her own mouth with a long, slow drag of her sleeve, like a workman at the end of a hard day. 'Look at him. He's basically lasagne from the neck up.'

FIFTY-ONE

Harry checked the time. Soon, he had to decide whether he was going to meet up with Ruth. But the conversation with Keri had left him more confused than ever.

'Why do you think they're chasing Renshaw?'

'He was a prickly man, had quite an ego. I can easily imagine him feeling he was worth more than they paid him, so maybe he had his hand in the till.'

'Any idea where he'd have gone?'

'Sorry, no. It's ages since he left – well over a year. Vickery's sister, Sian, took over his role, even though she had no qualifications whatsoever.' She gave him a cryptic glance. 'Another good reason for me to get out.'

Harry decided he had nothing to lose in being blunt. He leant forward, placed his hands on his knees and said, 'I have a feeling there's something you're not telling me.'

'There's probably a lot,' she shot back. Then her tone changed, became reflective. 'You know, I do this because it can be fun, it really can. Being independent means I can pick and choose, and seeing two or three guys a week gives me the income to fund my master's degree without incurring any debts. Okay?'

Harry nodded. 'Makes sense, I suppose.'

'There are some lovely men out there, but also a lot of evil-minded bastards. Hence the precautions today.' A long pause. 'Occasionally, when I worked for Laird, there'd be gossip about girls who'd suddenly disappeared. We'd hear that they had gone back home, or run off with a rich client. In some cases it may have been true – or it was a cover story because they'd got pregnant. Some even came back after a while. But other times … it sounded like bullshit.'

'Didn't it worry you, what the real reason might be?'

Keri dipped her head, then pushed her hair back, scraping it away from her face. For a moment she looked like she could sleep for a year and it wouldn't be enough to revive her.

'Yes and no,' she said at last. 'Yes, because here I am, working solo and taking a hell of a lot of care with my personal security. No, because in this game you can't give in to nerves, rumours, irrational fears.'

'And is there anyone else – former colleagues of yours – who could say whether there's any truth to those rumours?'

'I doubt it. Otherwise Greg would have found out, and acted on it. Instead he ended up dead.'

Harry considered that, and then said, 'Unless he's dead because he *did* find out?'

Keri seemed to pale at the suggestion. 'I don't think so. I—' she began, and thought better of it. 'No.'

'Keri, please. There's something else. I know there is. What is it?'

She deliberated for a moment, then rose and left the room. She returned with a local newspaper, dated the previous day, folded it to an inside page and thrust it into his hand.

The main headline was: **BODY PARTS FOUND ON SUFFOLK BEACH**. It described the discovery of a dismembered corpse on a beach near Lowestoft. Subsequent investigations had identified the remains as Hasan Mansur, aged 28, of no fixed address, a low-level criminal with a string of convictions for theft, drug-dealing and assault.

'He worked for them,' Keri said. 'It's Hasan I thought of when you mentioned Renshaw.'

'You think there's a connection?' Harry inhaled sharply. This was even worse than what Ruth had told him.

'I hope not. I don't want to think Laird did that to one of his own people.' She gulped a mouthful of water and nearly choked. 'Four or five years ago there was some kind of dispute, with a rival gang. Hasan was brought to Vickery's one night with a gunshot wound. At death's door is how I heard it. Renshaw, who'd only trained as a GP, ended up performing surgery on him, and managed to save his life.'

Harry squinted at her, disbelieving. 'On his own?'

'Pretty much. There was a woman who worked with him at the time.' She pursed her lips in thought. 'Nerys-someone. Nasty old cow.'

'Either way, this Hasan would have been in debt to Renshaw.' Harry found himself reliving the ordeal on Thursday morning, and the threat to cut his daughter's throat. The idea that the same men could be responsible for an atrocity like this made him feel sick. 'If he wasn't killed by the people who are hunting Renshaw, who else might have done it?'

She gazed at him, bleakly, and finally shrugged. 'I don't know.'

'And if Laird did this,' Harry went on, 'then he must have killed Greg as well.'

Another shrug. Maybe she was numb to it, after years of association with these people, or maybe she truly believed she was safe. But to Harry, these revelations were a terrifying confirmation of the danger that Alice and Evie were in.

He checked his watch again. 'I need to go.'

'You're meeting Ruth?'

'Yes,' he admitted. He was unsure whether to mention that Ruth had said she was no longer interested in Keri, and settled for promising not to reveal Keri's address. 'After what you've told me, I'm kidding myself to think she's serious about helping me. But it's not as though I have any other options.'

'Well, it's your decision. Either way, I'm sorry about your family,' Keri said. 'I hope you find them soon.'

He stood up, stretched, realising how tired he felt. Keri followed him out to the hall, where he stopped abruptly.

'Ruth gave me the impression that she doesn't know anything about Renshaw. Would you have mentioned him to Greg?'

'I think so. It wasn't a secret that they had a doctor on the payroll.'

Troubling over this, he moved back to let her past him. The door to her apartment boasted a spyhole, a security chain and two hefty bolts.

Keri spoke again, quietly: 'Please remember what I said about Ruth. All she cares about is herself.'

'Seems to me that all she cares about is getting even with Laird. If only I knew *why* …'

Keri hesitated before speaking, then said, 'This is just my own gut feeling, okay, but sometimes I wondered if it stemmed from an old relationship.'

Confused, Harry said: 'Between … ?'

'Ruth and Laird.'

'Ruth and *Laird*? No, that can't be …'

'Like I say, I have nothing to substantiate it. Just … well, that needle of jealousy you'll often see in a guy when he's talking about a rival. I got that from Greg, a little.'

Harry was lost for words. As he stepped over the threshold, Keri placed her hand on his arm.

'Be careful, Harry. Don't get caught in the crossfire.' And she leaned forward and kissed him on the cheek.

He took the stairs to the lobby, Keri's warning ringing in his ears. But he was hardly worried for himself: nothing mattered now except locating his family before the gang caught up with them. He was tormented by the thought of being too late, of finding nothing but dismembered bodies.

King Street lay in the centre of town, which meant busier streets. This time it wasn't the fear of recognition that haunted him so much as the sight of carefree families out enjoying their weekend. Ruth had played him for a fool, and it would have been all too easy to give in to resentment and rage. But for the sake of his wife and daughter he was determined to stay in control.

He checked the time: eleven forty-five. Staring at the phone, he experienced a sudden impulse to call the number he had for Alice. No doubt it was still switched off, but it wouldn't hurt to try.

His heart lurched when he heard a ringing tone. Then it stopped. Half a second before he realised the line hadn't gone dead; then an uncertain voice said, 'Hello?'

Harry nearly dropped the phone.

FIFTY-TWO

With Renshaw gone, the first thing Alice did was note the time: just after eleven o'clock. The phone's battery was down to a single bar, and there was only a very weak signal.

She roamed the clearing for a few minutes, testing various locations to see if the signal strengthened. At times it did, but probably not enough to make or receive a call. Kicking through the fallen leaves, she spotted tiny white blobs – mushrooms – and had a crazy image of herself, gone feral, abandoned in the woods and foraging for food.

No, she wouldn't let it come to that, or anywhere near. But she was skating perilously close to self-pity, until a sudden, vicious voice in her head spoke up: *You caused this, remember. This is the choice you made.*

She cut off the voice by slapping her own cheek: an act of madness, if anybody had been present to witness it. But it had to be silenced.

For now, preservation was the goal: hers and Evie's. Preservation at all costs.

Evie was grizzling, refusing to be pacified. Finally, Alice gave in. Making sure she was unobserved, she sat on the driest log she could find and fed her daughter until Evie conceded that, no, she wasn't hungry any more, and yes, she probably would benefit from a mid-morning sleep.

Alice felt certain that someone would stumble upon them at any moment: a lecherous farmer, or a group of ramblers disgusted by public nudity. But feeding passed the time, at least: once she'd returned Evie to the carrier it was almost twenty to twelve. The phone, when she checked, had no signal whatsoever.

She decided to walk to the edge of the copse. It meant taking the money, the bag heavy enough to drag painfully on her arm. She followed the path until the field came into sight. By leaning to one side she could just make out the hedge that marked the perimeter of Nerys Baxter's property.

There were a couple of dog walkers in the distance, but no sign of Renshaw. She hoped he wouldn't make her wait the full hour—

The phone rang. She looked at the number before answering, and couldn't believe her eyes.

'Harry?'

One word, then the connection was cut. Had someone grabbed the phone?

Harry stopped dead on a narrow pavement outside a pub, oblivious to the activity around him. In that instant the meeting with Ruth meant nothing. All he could think about was this brief moment of contact with Alice, snatched away from him.

He dialled again, feeling so powerless that it reminded him of dreams where he was horribly late for a meeting and yet his legs refused to move.

Should he call the police? But would they be prepared to launch a search on the basis of a single phone call? *And from a fugitive, remember …*

He set off, so preoccupied that he almost didn't realise the phone had been answered.

'Harry? Are you there? I lost the signal.'

'Where are you? Are you safe? Is Evie—'

'Harry, listen! In case the phone dies on me. I'm staying at a friend of Renshaw's, near Gloucester. Her name is Nerys Baxter. The address is Beech House, Mercombe Lane, Cranstone. But the turning is actually about a mile beyond the village. Have you got that?'

Harry repeated it back to her, terrified that the details wouldn't stick. 'I'll come and get you,' he said, but she interrupted him again.

'I'm getting a lift to the station this afternoon. It'll take about four hours to Brighton.'

'Not with Renshaw?'

'No. He's doing his own thing.'

'Good. If I'm not there first, take the train and I'll meet you somewhere en route.'

'Oh, yes, please.' The words came out on a long, heartfelt sigh. 'It's been okay here, but … they make me uncomfortable.' She sniffed. 'Are you really all right? Who was that woman yesterday?'

'No one, honestly. But there's a big problem.' To escape the glares of the pedestrians he was obstructing, he crossed Whitehart Street and took refuge in the entrance to a church. 'The police came to our house. They've somehow got the impression that I might have … done away with you or something.'

'*What?* That's ridiculous.'

'I know, but right now my face is plastered over the media in the South East. If anyone recognises me I'm going to be hauled into a cell. Can you phone the police and get them off my backs? You need to speak to a DI Thomsett.'

'I'll try. What's his number?'

'Shit.' It was on his own phone, which was switched off. Powering it up would take precious seconds, and then there was the risk of being traced …

Alice jumped in with a suggestion: 'I'll call my mum. She must be frantic with worry. Just remember, Beech House, Mercombe Lane, Cranst—' There was a burst of interference. '—losing you,' he heard her cry, and it made him shudder.

'I'm coming to get you, Alice,' he yelled, as if his determination could overcome the weakening signal, the hundreds of miles between them. 'I'm coming—'

But she was gone. Harry stared at the phone, urgently mumbling to himself – 'Beech House, Mercombe Lane, Cranstone' – over and over, while a new sense of resolve began to harden in his mind.

Whatever the reason for Ruth's sudden reappearance, Harry was certain of one thing. She was damn well going to help him now.

Alice moved again, lugging the stolen money with her. By the time she found a stronger signal she'd accepted that it made no sense to call Harry back, no matter how much she wanted to hear his voice. Before the battery went flat she ought to phone her mother, as promised.

She dialled the landline, aware that Mum often ignored her mobile if the caller's number was unfamiliar. But it was answered immediately, as if the handset had been snatched from its cradle. Her mum had lost her husband at a tragically early age, and there'd been no one else since, so the fear of losing her daughter and youngest grandchild must be unimaginably traumatic.

Alice felt tears in her eyes: she'd just about held it together when speaking to Harry. Could she do it again?

'Mum, it's me. I'm all right.'

There was a brief but deafening shriek; other voices in the background, questioning, concerned, hardly daring to interpret the reaction as good news.

'Harry?' her mother said. 'Did he—?'

'He's fine, too. So is Evie.'

'Oh, thank heavens.' She gasped for a breath. 'Jill and David are here now, waiting for news.'

Harry's parents. So he hadn't been exaggerating, Alice realised. They really had thought the worst.

She said, 'I'm so sorry, Mum. It's been a terrible misunderstanding.'

'So Harry's there with you? Jill's desperate to speak to him—'

'Mum, please. I need you to do something for me.' She used the stern tone reserved for patients who'd ignored all previous warnings about the calamitous state of their teeth and gums. 'No questions, no arguments: just do it, please.'

FIFTY-THREE

It was five to twelve when Harry turned into King Street, passed the church and almost immediately found the statue of the great radical thinker, Thomas Paine. It was positioned in front of an imposing Georgian building that now housed the town council. There were benches either side of the statue, but Harry was too restless to sit down and wait for Ruth.

He should have been elated at the thought of being reunited with his family, possibly within just a couple of hours. And yet he had a lingering fear that it wouldn't work out the way he hoped; a suspicion that Alice, once again – and no doubt with the best of intentions – had failed to tell him the full truth.

He'd wandered up the steps into the car park of Kings House when someone whistled. He turned as Ruth emerged from the churchyard, and had an unsettling thought that somehow she had followed him.

'Harry.' She wore her customary half-smile: a little weary, a little impatient. 'I wasn't sure if you'd come.'

He nodded, deciding to say nothing and see if she offered an apology.

'Ah,' she said. 'You're mad at me. Okay. The reason I ran out last night—'

'I'm sure you have a very good explanation, but I probably won't believe it.'

She raised an eyebrow. 'So Keri changed your view of me? I thought she would.'

'Yeah, but that's irrelevant now. I need you to drive me somewhere.'

'Oh?' Now her expression changed: wary, but interested.

'I've heard from Alice. We're going to get her.'

'Where is she?'

'Gloucestershire. Where's your car?'

'Off Magdalen Street. It's not far.'

She led the way at a pace that was just short of jogging, the two of them weaving in and out of the shoppers along the pedestrian thoroughfare. Ruth had a barrage of questions: how and when had Alice been in touch? Was she still with Renshaw? Where exactly had they chosen to hide?

Harry ignored them all, fighting his natural instinct to be helpful, until Ruth began to fume.

'I get that you're sulking, Harry, but this isn't a very mature att—' She broke off and slowed at the same time, causing him to bump against her shoulder, then nudged him and increased her pace. 'Hurry.'

'What was it?'

She indicated a side street to their left. 'I saw a car down there. It looked familiar.'

'Were you followed here?'

'I didn't think I was. Come on.'

The car park was a small open space tucked between two rows of rear gardens. It had room for no more than twenty-five or thirty cars, and was about half full. There was no one in sight – or so he thought.

Ruth's Corsa was parked at the far end, in the shadow of a couple of overhanging trees. It took Harry a moment to see the man standing just beyond the car.

DI Warley. At least, that was the name he'd given Harry on Thursday evening.

Ruth swore softly under her breath and broke into a run. Warley hadn't yet seen them approaching, but he turned at the sound of the bleep that unlocked the car. Ruth was sprinting towards him with the keys in her hand, Harry trailing in her wake.

'Ruth!' It was all the warning he could muster: he didn't have time to point out that Warley might be armed.

'Just get in,' she shouted. Warley had moved to intercept her but she seemed undeterred, running to face him head on. He looked bemused by her decision, grinning slightly, his hands curling into fists.

She was faster than he could have expected. In a blur of movement her foot caught Warley on the knee, her hands struck him in the stomach and neck and then somehow she was behind him, forcing his right arm behind his back, his injured leg buckling. She dragged him out of sight between her car and its neighbour, then grabbed the driver's door as Harry ran round to the passenger side.

'Is he … ?'

'He won't stay down for long. And he's not alone, remember.'

She slotted the key into the ignition and started the engine, pulling on the seatbelt with her left hand.

'Buckle up. This won't be pretty.'

The Corsa lurched backwards, skidded to a halt, then stuttered in a half circle as Ruth used a couple of empty bays as a small short cut to the exit. She had to brake sharply as someone stepped off the pavement into her path. Harry was thrown forward, hands slamming on the dashboard, then they were moving again, with Harry struggling to fit the seatbelt into the clasp. He glanced back and saw Warley making a stumbling run towards them. A

Mercedes had turned into the one-way street and was slowing at the entrance to the car park.

Harry gasped. 'I think they're in a Mercedes.'

'Better get a move on, then.'

They turned right into Castle Street, back to the roundabout they'd just passed on foot, took a right and then a sharp left, into a narrow road that didn't look as if it went anywhere much.

'You know where you're going, yes?' he asked.

'Of course,' she snarled. 'Now let me concentrate, will you?'

The road widened a little, which Ruth took as a cue to drive recklessly fast. Then they reached a junction with a much busier road and were forced to slow down.

Harry looked back once or twice and saw no sign of the Mercedes. That might have been a small mercy but Harry, once he'd recovered from the initial shock, was furious.

'How the hell did that happen?'

'I don't know. I thought I'd managed to stay under their radar.'

'Well, it wasn't me, I'm certain of that.' He twisted to look behind him. 'Are they following?'

'Not so far.'

'We've got to be sure, for Christ's sake. We can't afford to lead them to my wife.'

Ruth began to speak, then thought better of it. Harry let her drive in silence for several minutes. He adjusted the wing mirror on the passenger side so he could keep an eye on the road behind. They passed through a couple of traffic light controlled junctions; on the long straight stretches in between Ruth overtook whenever she had a chance.

'Where did you go last night?' he asked.

Ruth shook her head irritably. 'Not now.'

'I want to know how they found you. They just tried to attack us back there, and you're not even—'

He broke off and turned to stare at her. Ruth went on looking at the road ahead. He reviewed the fight he'd just witnessed; the speed and elegance of it, like a perfectly choreographed setpiece …

'This is bollocks.'

'What?'

'You're lying to me. You've probably been lying to me the whole time.'

'Not *all* the time.'

'But this? The fight back there …'

A reluctant nod. 'Staged. He's not coming after us, because he doesn't have to. There's an Audi waiting for us up ahead.'

'So you were told to come this way?' Harry realised that he was gripping the edges of his seat, as if he expected Ruth to crash the car on purpose.

Thank God he hadn't revealed Alice's location.

'I'm sorry. I had no choice.'

'You've lured me into a trap?'

Her silence confirmed it. She accelerated up to a roundabout, and Harry saw a blue Audi parked up on the grass verge to his right. The driver was male, unfamiliar. The woman in the passenger seat was possibly the other fake detective, Sian Vickery.

'So what happens now?' he asked.

'It depends,' Ruth muttered, as though the question didn't particularly concern her.

'On what?'

'On whether you're any use to me.'

FIFTY-FOUR

For what seemed a very long time, Michael couldn't move at all; not even when the slaughterhouse smell of the kitchen became overpowering. What held him in place was a concept, a single word, blaring out like some lurid headline:

BLOODBATH!

This was a bloodbath. A victim whose head had been smashed to pieces, causing the grisly contents of the skull to explode across the kitchen. The sight of it left Michael shaky, cold inside, his limbs rubbery and useless. There was a strange prickling inside his head, blurring his thoughts, a little like the prelude to a bad case of flu.

He expected his mother to be similarly disorientated, and yet Nerys looked only mildly perturbed, as if a pigeon had shat on her clean washing.

'The stupid bloody pillock,' she muttered. The vehement tone brought out her native Welsh accent. 'To go and blackmail a man like Laird, and then try to drag me into it with him. The stupid, *stupid* pillock.'

Michael had to make a huge effort not to spill his guts, even while his mind was in disarray. 'I assume we're not going to … report it?'

A snort. 'You want to dial 999, do you?'

'No. But if it's what *you* want. I mean, you could claim it was self-defence. If I wasn't here, say, and he got violent with you …'

Nerys grinned slyly, as if she saw what he was really getting at. *If I wasn't here …*

'I'm not trying to get out of this. I'm just saying, it's an option.'

'No, Michael. It isn't. Look at him. You think a jury's going to believe *this* was self-defence?'

She was right, of course. Michael's shoulders sagged. He hadn't felt this slow-witted in his mother's presence since he was about six years old.

'So what, then?'

'Cover our traces, first of all.' She moved around the table and inspected his clothes. 'You're clean, I think. Best go and fetch your car.'

He tried to object but she wouldn't listen.

'Mine's too small to fit him in the boot.' She studied the body again. 'Before you do that, have a look in the garage for me. I'm sure I've got extra strong bags for garden waste. And there's a set of overalls I bought for Clive and never threw away …' She paused briefly; refocused: 'Get the car, then change into the overalls. I'll run your clothes through the machine, just in case.'

Michael's attention wavered at the mention of Clive Saunders. He had been Nerys's second husband for less than a year when he died of a heart attack, only a matter of weeks after the death of Michael's father. He was recalling how, at the wake, he'd remarked on the unfortunate timing: the fact that Clive hadn't lived to share the financial bonanza that was coming Nerys's way.

'Shame,' she had agreed at the time. 'But that's the way the cookie crumbles.'

Now he stared at her, barely able to believe what he was about to say.

'Have you done this before?'

*

She looked askance at him. 'Oh yes, I make a habit of bludgeoning people to death in my kitchen.'

'I don't mean this method, specifically.' He held her gaze for long enough to see the warning in her eyes: *Don't ask.* He added, 'I'm not judging you. If anything, I think I'd be … reassured if you had. And very impressed.'

His gambit failed. She said coolly, 'There's a lot you don't know about me, Michael. Let's leave it at that.'

'All right.' He turned away, murmuring to himself: 'Garden bags. Overalls. Fetch the Range Rover.'

Nerys too was almost speaking to herself. 'We'll clean up the worst of it, then fetch the girls …'

Michael frowned. *Girls?* For a dreadful moment he thought she was referring to her granddaughters.

'Oh, Christ,' he whispered. 'Alice.'

FIFTY-FIVE

Her mother listened to Alice's request. She was happy to comply, but it wouldn't do any good.

'The detective made it quite clear, he needs to speak to you himself. I've got his mobile number here.'

Relenting, Alice agreed to try. At least it gave her an excuse to terminate the conversation before Harry's parents came on the line.

She rang the number, and the signal cut out just as she got a connection. She had only a sliver of battery power left.

On the second attempt he answered straight away. 'DI Thomsett.'

'This is Alice French. I understand you're worried about me.'

'And your daughter.' His voice was warm, concerned, and Alice felt a sudden irrational urge to cry.

'Evie's fine. We both are. There's just been a … a misunderstanding. Harry hasn't harmed either of us. He wouldn't do that. So you can call off the search for him … please.'

'We'd like to, Alice. Just one thing: the number you're calling from isn't the one we have for you.'

'No, I had to borrow this phone. From a friend.' The word caught in her throat. 'Mine's out of power.'

'I see.' Still cautious. 'The problem, as I'm sure you appreciate, is that I have to be sure I am actually speaking to Alice French.'

*

It made her gasp, this glimpse of a detective's worldview: the idea that Harry might not just do away with his wife, but also arrange for an imposter to throw the police off the scent.

'I've just spoken to my mother. She'll confirm that I'm the real Alice.'

He chuckled lightly. 'Of course. And may I ask where you are?'

'In the Gloucester area.'

'Staying with a friend?'

'Yes.' She heard a wobble of uncertainty in her voice and knew he wouldn't miss it. 'Look, are all these questions necessary, because I'm low on battery?'

'We have to be certain. I'm afraid I need you to call in at the nearest police station, along with Evie. And take some form of ID.'

'What?'

'So we can be sure you're not speaking under duress. It's a formality, I assure you.'

Alice sighed. It made perfect sense, and he had her best interests at heart: but still …

'Look, I'm planning to be back in Brighton this afternoon.' She wanted to add that Harry might be with her, but feared it would provoke questions about his whereabouts.

'Are you? That's even better. Call me when you get home, and with any luck we'll have this wrapped up by tonight.'

'Thank you.' To her relief, Evie squealed loudly enough for Thomsett to hear. 'I've got to go, sorry.'

Thomsett said goodbye, adding that he hoped to hear from her again soon. Alice rocked Evie back to sleep, wondering if she'd done enough to keep Harry out of custody. Her mother would corroborate her identity – although, Mum being Mum, she'd probably complicate matters by declaring that Alice didn't know a soul in Gloucestershire.

She decided to return to the clearing. Waiting this close to the field made her uneasy. If someone came past and started asking questions about what she was doing here, or what was in the bag … She imagined having to tell Renshaw that she had been mugged: his precious money gone. It almost made her smile.

With the cloud thickening, it was gloomier now under the trees, the air damp and chilly. A bird was chirping from not too far away, but otherwise there was silence. Alice stashed Renshaw's bag behind a tree stump and attempted to sit down. She had to descend in extreme slow motion, hoping to fool the built-in altimeter that woke her daughter whenever you tried to rest while holding her. The instant she made contact with the seat, Evie opened her eyes and gave her an accusing stare.

'All right.' Sighing, Alice stood up again. Evie shut her eyes and went back to sleep.

A gust of wind blew through the trees, causing dry leaves to lift from the ground and settle back, like soil being scattered on a coffin. Alice shivered. Checked the phone and saw that the battery was all but dead.

It was gone twelve. He ought to have been here by now.

'Hurry up, Renshaw,' she whispered. 'Hurry up and get me out of here.'

FIFTY-SIX

Harry stewed, impotently, while Ruth drove at a steady fifty in a line of traffic on the A11, level fields and thin woodland on either side of them. The Audi kept on their tail at a relaxed distance, six or seven cars back. Harry knew that what he'd said to Keri still applied: he was in a position where he had no alternative but to trust Ruth – *consider* trusting her, at least – or go it alone.

'How long have you been working for them?'

'Less than ninety minutes.' A sidelong glance at him. 'I mean it. This only came about because I screwed up. They spotted me as I left the hotel in Crawley. The only saving grace,' she pointed out, 'is they didn't see me with *you*.'

'Right.'

'Same deal, Harry,' she said airily. 'Believe me or don't believe me. But this is the truth. They bundled me into a car and gave me a sedative. One of them took my keys and found the Corsa, while the others drove me here, to Norfolk. I woke up in a shipping container, awash with the blood of another victim of theirs. A man named Hasan—'

'Mansur,' Harry finished. 'His remains were found on a beach at Lowestoft.'

'Yeah. Well, this morning I had an audience with Mark Vickery – and Laird, I think, was listening in from somewhere else. Now I'm heading for the same fate as Hasan unless I give them what they want: namely, Renshaw. I managed to convince them that I could find him, using you.'

Harry snorted. 'You sold me out?'

'No, let me explain. That was the only bargaining chip I had. It meant I could live to fight another day.'

'So why the pretend ambush?'

'I suggested that, to rebuild your trust after my disappearing act last night. Which I've just owned up to, by the way.'

'Yeah, except this might be a double bluff.'

'Do you think it is? Because that's not the vibe I'm getting from you.'

Unwilling to confirm her intuition, Harry said nothing. His gut instinct was to believe her, but when he thought about it rationally, he couldn't explain why. Perhaps only that he had a desperate need to trust *someone*.

They drove for another ten or fifteen minutes, through a landscape that was both attractive and rather monotonous, Ruth declining several opportunities to overtake. They crossed several junctions, Harry noting signs for various quaint-sounding places like Elveden and Tuddenham, and then they became snarled up in roadworks.

'So,' Ruth said at last. 'The address?'

He couldn't help but groan. This was what she had meant by being 'of use' to her.

'You honestly expect me to tell you? So you can find Renshaw – and then what? Hand him over to Laird? In the meantime, what happens to me, and my family?' He flapped his hand dismissively. 'You don't give a toss about us.'

'That's not entirely true. And this is no time for petulance, Harry. You're going to tell me the address—'

'Or what? You'll hurt me?'

She laughed. 'No. You'll give it to me, because you don't want me to die a slow, horrible death. And because you know that, without me, you won't get to Gloucestershire and find your family.'

He said nothing. After a minute she reached out and patted his leg, making him flinch.

'Relax, will you? This is a breathing space, right now.'

'We're being followed, remember?'

'Yeah.' She pondered for a moment. 'Guess I'd better do something about that.'

They reached a major roundabout with four or five exits. In the past few minutes the Audi had leapfrogged several other vehicles and was now only three cars back.

As she pulled out on to the roundabout, Ruth suddenly cut across in front of the car to her right. Harry saw that the road ahead widened into a dual carriageway, and guessed that was the reason for her decision. Now she would be able to put on some speed.

Instead, she slowed to the point where the car behind, already aggrieved at the sudden lane change, blasted its horn. Ignoring it, Ruth braked harder, then wrenched the wheel to the right and bumped two wheels up on to the low kerb of the central reservation, which formed a triangle between the two carriageways and the roundabout.

Harry shouted out in alarm as Ruth accelerated into the path of the oncoming traffic, forcing her way back on to the roundabout. The Audi had been unable to react in time: Harry saw it change lane but by then the triangle of paved central reservation had given way to a steel safety barrier. Their pursuers had no way of turning until the next junction, whenever that was.

Ruth took the first exit, heading north through more woodland. She seemed unruffled by the manoeuvre.

'You nearly killed us,' Harry muttered.

'Not really. It was pretty slow-moving traffic. Could have totalled the car, at worst, but even that wouldn't have been fatal.'

Harry swallowed, not wanting to imagine being trapped in a mangled wreck. Ruth accelerated past an elderly Nissan, checked her mirror carefully, and then pronounced them free of their tail. She tapped out a playful little tune on the steering wheel, as if it were a beloved percussion instrument.

'So … where to, Harry?'

Finding Alice was a major priority but not the only one, Nerys reminded him. They had to think carefully. Be methodical.

Like when you smashed his skull to pieces, Michael could have said.

Ignoring the smell and the filth, Nerys crouched down and searched Renshaw's pockets. She found a cheap phone, a set of keys and a wallet. The wallet contained a couple of hundred pounds in notes and a single credit card.

'It's *got* to be here somewhere. You heard him say he's got evidence. Why isn't it here?'

'Definitely not in his room?'

'I searched it from top to bottom.'

'His car, then?'

She nodded glumly. 'We'll have to check.'

'You do the car. I'll have another look at his room.'

They were back in the kitchen within a few minutes: empty-handed, despondent. Nerys stared into the middle distance, her lips a thin white line.

'I don't believe this. I *do not* frigging believe this.' She stared at Michael, her eyes cold, not really seeing him. 'Alice,' she said at last.

'You think he's left it with her?'

'Must have done. I wonder if he gave us a cock-and-bull story about her being an innocent bystander. Perhaps she was his accomplice all along.'

'Even more reason to find her then.'

A flash of panic crossed his mother's face. 'They might have set a time limit. If he's not back within x minutes, she makes a run for it.'

Michael felt his heart beating faster. 'Where would she go?'

'Most of the paths in Westcombe Wood lead to a track across the northern edge, which runs parallel to the Elkstone Road. From there she could hitch a lift.' A gulp. 'Or maybe they've got another car?'

'Oh, shit.' Michael turned towards the front door. 'How do I get there?'

'Up Hall's Lane, then you're on the A435 for about thirty seconds. Left just past The Eagle pub. There's a parking area right at the top of the wood.'

'No problem,' Michael said. 'I'll find her.'

And he meant it. He was buzzing as he left the house, his senses heightened, all the fear and regrets pushed aside: utterly absorbed by the thrill of the chase.

FIFTY-SEVEN

Alice was cold and hungry and miserable. An hour, Renshaw had said. He was twenty minutes late. Based on his agreement earlier, she was free to do what she wanted.

Except that her phone was nearly dead, she had no car, and no money other than a bag of high-denomination euros. If the police found her now, they might well take her for a drug smuggler.

The peculiar stillness of the wood was playing on her nerves. Both light and sound were eerily muted. Occasionally she made out some far distant engine, or a dog barking, but mostly there was silence, punctuated by sudden tiny noises from close by: a snap or click or rustle that her jittery mind perceived as someone sneaking up on her.

It took her some time to identify the sounds as the soft patter of rain. Another minute or two before the first drop made it through the trees and landed on her head.

She shivered. It seemed ludicrous to be sitting here, getting wet, just to indulge Renshaw's paranoia. Why on earth would Nerys want to rob him, anyway? She and her son had pots of money.

From behind her came the snap of a twig breaking. Startled, Alice stood up and peered into the trees. No one there, as far as she could see.

The rainfall grew more intense, a busy chatter of noise. Like a whole crowd was whispering to her: a warning, or a threat.

She tried to focus on positive thoughts. Harry was on his way here, so she didn't have to rely on Renshaw or Michael Baxter to give her a lift to the station. Another couple of hours and Harry could drive them home.

The brief conversation had made her all the more desperate to be reunited with him. Together, as a family, they would meet DI Thomsett and tell him everything, and hope that he could offer the help they needed to stay safe.

In a new, decisive frame of mind she grabbed the bag of money and set off along the path. It was ridiculous to stay out any longer. She would return to the house: at the first sign of danger she'd give Renshaw his money back, then walk into the village. Even a bus shelter would be a better place to wait than here.

The rain was tumbling down when she reached the edge of the wood. It woke Evie, who let out a thin cry of displeasure. Alice faltered, beset once again by doubts. Why hadn't Renshaw come back? He'd said it himself: the money guaranteed his return.

So where was he?

Something was wrong. In that instant Alice knew it, with a certainty as cold and unpleasant as the rain.

At the edge of the tree line she peered across the muddy field. It wasn't long before she spotted movement in the bushes at the rear of Beech House. A figure stepped into view, clad in a long coat and a headscarf.

Nerys. It had to be. But she'd emerged from her garden as furtively as a burglar, glancing around as if worried about being seen. Alice couldn't think of any reason for Nerys to act that way, unless—

The woman's head came up. Her body stiffened with concentration as her gaze locked on the path into the wood: there was a moment of distant but unmistakable eye contact, before Alice turned and fled.

*

Michael had sprinted all the way back to the Range Rover, and even managed to enjoy the exertion: so much more satisfying than the sterile, comfortably tailored environment of a gym, having to adjust to the uneven surface, his movement hampered by his bulky winter clothes, cold air in his lungs and rain on his face. Exhilarating.

Truth be told, he was in remarkably good spirits all round. It made him wonder if he should have given free rein to the darker side of his character years ago.

Women were his obsession, and had been for as long as he could remember. In his teens and twenties he had been driven by lust, the thrill of the chase; the triumph of conquest. But then it became a compulsion, almost beyond his control. He'd slept with one of the bridesmaids the night before his wedding. He slept with his wife's cousin. He slept with the women he employed, and the women he met during the course of his working day. He slept with women at his gym and women he picked up in bars and hotels, both away on business and only a few miles from home.

Most of the time, it was absurdly easy. He had a gift for it. But over the years, he noticed how the pleasure was diminishing for precisely that reason. To increase the challenge, he started targeting women who weren't interested. Who *really* weren't interested. And a few times – the frequency escalating in recent years – he'd fucked women who hadn't in any way, shape or form consented to being fucked.

He unlocked the car, flung his jacket on the back seat and drove away. He was tempted to go flat out but made a conscious effort not to draw attention to himself. And thoughts of self-preservation led to the question he hadn't yet asked his mother. Once they caught Alice – and Evie – *what happened then?*

Nerys had virtually conceded that he could unleash that dark side of his, hadn't she? It made him wonder what she'd gleaned from their past conversations. He often talked to her of his exploits – it was no fun to bottle it up, but his male friends only got jealous, and Robyn couldn't really be expected to listen. He'd never even hinted at the '*no means yes*' side of things, but perhaps he hadn't had to: it was clear now that Nerys was a woman of supreme gifts.

If he had his fun and afterwards there were ... complications, well, he guessed that Mother would know what to do. But the idea of having her there, as an accomplice. Wouldn't that make him feel ... hmm ... *uncomfortable*?

Maybe. Maybe not.

'Don't go there,' he muttered aloud. But it lingered at the back of his mind, a disquieting fantasy where Nerys was in the room with him and Alice – watching them, at least. On some level the concept still appalled him, but he sensed that by frequently revisiting the idea he could acquire tolerance to it, the way that taking rapid sips of scalding hot coffee soon makes it bearable, then acceptable, and finally delicious.

Delicious. That was the perfect word.

Michael licked his lips.

Alice didn't really know why she was running. A voice inside her head kept appealing for reason. This was a pretty stupid reaction, wasn't it, to be blundering through the trees, her feet slippery on the wet ground, no purpose or destination other than to get away from Nerys; no reason beyond an instinct that the older woman had been moving with some vaguely sinister intent.

But there was Renshaw, don't forget. He was long overdue to retrieve his precious money.

That was when Alice remembered the bag. In her panic she'd dropped it as she began to move. Its loss troubled her for a second or two; then her foot caught on a protruding root and she almost went down. She recovered only by hitting the ground with one hand, badly jarring her wrist. Poor Evie was pitched into a violent descent and then wrenched upright again. She wailed, not unreasonably, and a couple of birds took flight nearby.

In her desperation Alice had left the path, figuring that the trees offered her better concealment. But it also made the going a lot tougher, and the weight of Evie in the carrier was a factor she hadn't considered, especially on rough terrain made treacherous by tree roots and fallen branches.

And then Michael appeared in front of her, almost from nowhere. Only later did she consider the noise they'd been making, especially with Evie sobbing. It must have been ridiculously easy to find them.

She slithered to a halt, then tried to change direction; dodging sideways, as though she were some kind of agile teenage gymnast, rather than a thirty-one-year-old woman weighed down with a baby. But she pushed off too quickly and nearly ran headlong into a tree. She swerved to avoid it but lost her footing and slid into a shallow ditch, a natural hollow that, if you scooped out the mulchy leaves and loose earth, would have been just about the perfect size for a grave.

FIFTY-EIGHT

Harry checked the wing mirror for the fourth or fifth time. Still nothing.

'Okay, we lost the Audi. But what about the other car, the Mercedes?'

'I suppose they could get a message to the driver, but they won't pick up the route I intend to take.'

As Ruth spoke she was turning off the main road, into what seemed little more than a track through the forest. Harry sighed.

'How do I know this isn't just another trick to gain my trust?'

'I guess that's a decision only you can make, Harry. But do it quickly.'

Moments later, she pulled up in a shallow lay-by. Harry wondered if she was intending to kick him out if he didn't give her the information she wanted. But she simply reached across him to the glove compartment and took out a road atlas.

'Gloucester's not an easy place to reach from here. We're crossing the spine of the country, so all the major routes run north–south.'

Harry had a look for himself. She was right, but he doubted if a train would be any quicker. Short of commandeering a helicopter, they were looking at two or three hours to get there – by which time Alice and Evie should, with any luck, be on their way home.

'Head towards Cirencester,' he told her.

'Thank you.' She handed him the atlas and pulled out of the lay-by.

'I want some proper answers now. For a start, why have you only been pursuing Laird for the last few months?'

Ruth kept her eyes on the road, but she looked bemused. 'I haven't. What do you mean?'

'Prior to this year, tell me what you were doing.'

He crossed his arms and waited, studying her face for any indication that she was about to lie to him. After a long pause, Ruth exhaled slowly.

'I was behind bars, Harry. Is that what you wanted to hear?'

It threw him that she gave up the truth so freely. Trying not to bluster, he said, 'You committed a serious attack on someone, according to Keri. Is that true?'

'You are *so* far out of your depth here, Harry. And I'm not saying that to be rude, or to hurt you.'

'Just tell me, please.'

'Okay. Okay.' She sighed. 'A long time ago I worked for the security services. My area of expertise was organised crime. There's a lot of crossover with terrorism, especially in the area of money laundering, identity theft and so on. As a result of that work, and particularly an undercover operation that I was involved in, I made a series of very bad – *incredibly* bad – decisions that led, years later, to all this.'

'The feud with Laird, or whatever it is?'

'Feud?' She tapped the steering wheel with one hand. 'Good a word as any, I suppose.'

Her attention seemed to drift away, but he was too impatient to allow her more than a few seconds.

'And the person you attacked? Was that to do with Laird?'

'Not directly. It happened years after the … the flashpoint with Laird.' A dark glance told Harry he wasn't welcome to interrupt. 'I'd gone through a tough time. What I should have done was resign, or retire on health grounds, but instead I took a less stressful job, working on a surveillance team. A watcher.'

She sketched out the basics of a long, complex operation to monitor the activities of a man suspected of smuggling gold coins to finance terrorism.

'In the course of our surveillance, it became apparent that the man was also a violent and prolific paedophile. There was evidence that he'd been abusing children for more than twenty years, but our lords and masters ruled that this couldn't be allowed to jeopardise the enquiry. I was assured that these crimes would be investigated in due course, but only when they'd gathered every crumb of information on the gold smuggling.' She snorted. 'Priorities, eh?'

'What did you do?'

'Took matters into my own hands. I made certain that he was never able to contemplate sex with anyone, ever again.'

Harry nodded, as neutrally as he could. 'And did you get caught?'

'I thought I'd engineered a little window in the surveillance, but it turned out I was wrong. One of my diligent colleagues spotted me, and felt obliged to "do the right thing".' There was heavy irony in her voice.

'I'm surprised I don't remember this being in the news. The media would have gone crazy.'

'They never got the chance. Officially, I was a mentally unstable citizen who'd attacked a man after a drunken argument about money. The victim went along with that, of course, and so did his lawyers. All the evidence of his paedophilia was quietly spirited away, and I spent the next four-and-a-half years at Her Majesty's Pleasure.'

Harry let her take a break from what was obviously a difficult subject to discuss. They'd passed through several villages and were now on the A142, heading south to join the A14. The sky overhead was growing darker, a few spots of rain appearing on the windscreen. Miserable weather. He thought of Alice, stuck in a house with people she didn't like. What had she said? *They make me uncomfortable.*

'Tell me about Greg,' he said. 'I can't understand why he risked so much, digging into the affairs of a man like Laird. Keri says he went on with his enquiries while you were in prison.'

'That's right.'

'But why, when you two had split up?'

'Because he was a good man. Genuinely a good man.'

'Okay.' Harry waited. And couldn't help but laugh at her failure to elaborate. 'Please, Ruth. I only want to know what he was trying to find.'

She shook her head. Struggling with frustration, Harry aimed what he knew was a low blow.

'Keri suggested there might have been a relationship once.'

'What?'

'Between you and Laird.'

'Did she?' Ruth sounded intrigued, rather than offended. 'I always thought there was an element of competition in her attitude towards me. Part of the reason she seduced Greg.'

'Hold on.' Harry was confused, not least because she seemed to be admitting to the relationship. 'Competition for what?'

'She was Laird's favourite for a time. She probably didn't admit that, did she? As with most guys in his position, Laird liked to sample the merchandise. In Keri's case it became quite serious – until Laird lost interest. That was why Greg worked so hard to befriend her. He thought she'd know more than the other girls.'

'*He* thought? Don't you mean *you* thought?' Harry, annoyed by Ruth's attitude to Keri, was in no mood to go easy on her. 'Because Greg was doing all this for you, wasn't he? A favour that cost him his life. So there must have been a very good reason.'

'There was,' Ruth conceded. 'Laird took something from me.'

'Okay.' *Now we're getting somewhere*, he thought. 'I know I keep pressing, but given what's at stake here – the danger my family are in – I have to understand what's motivating you.'

'My son,' Ruth said brusquely. 'That's what motivates me, all right? Nathan Laird took my son from me.'

FIFTY-NINE

Alice didn't lose consciousness – or at least she didn't think so – but there was a moment of overload, when the fear and panic and adrenalin obscured her ability to process the world around her.

And then she came back to find she had rolled over, somehow, and was lying in the soft depression in the earth, staring up at a canopy of golden leaves, the rain dripping hard on her face. Her arms were still enfolded around the carrier: they ached from the effort of taking her weight, protecting Evie from being crushed as she fell. But had she succeeded?

She held her breath until Evie made a sound; a shuddering gasp. Tiny feet prodded her in the stomach. *What are we doing, Mummy? Get up!*

Then Michael's face loomed above her, still disgustingly handsome despite the sheen of rain and sweat on his forehead. He wore a wide-eyed expression of horror.

'Alice, oh thank God! You're alive!'

As he reached out, her whole body convulsed. She pushed his hand away but he leaned in, grabbed her arm and squeezed it tight.

'Don't fight, Alice. You're safe, Evie's safe, I promise. Just relax …'

'Leave me alone!' She went on struggling but it was hopeless, lying on her back, with Michael angled over her. So she froze instead, the way an animal will freeze in the face of a predator it cannot defeat.

Michael gazed at her, and for a moment there seemed to be a real hunger in his eyes. Then he released her arm and rested back on his knees. His chin dropped to his chest as he took several huge breaths.

'Thank God. We were so worried, Alice. So worried that Renshaw had done something terrible.'

Michael hadn't given any thought to what he would say when he caught her. He rarely bothered to plan out his encounters with women. Better to keep it loose, rely on his ability to read the character and the moment.

He'd done that now, quite brilliantly. In an instant, he had it all there in his head. He was ready for any question, and his manner conveyed precisely the right degree of relief and concern for her welfare.

Alice stared at him, still wary but wanting so much to believe: he could see it in her eyes. Her genuine emotions were as near to the surface as his own fake ones.

'He went back to the house.'

Michael nodded. 'We didn't realise at first. The garage door wasn't locked, so he sneaked in that way.'

He paused, partly because he required a few more seconds to assemble the next part of his explanation. He bought that time by offering his hand, though he was careful not to touch her.

'Let me help you up. Are you sure you're not hurt?'

She ignored the question, but the baby had recovered from the shock of the fall and started bawling again. Although Michael wasn't too worried about anyone coming along in this weather, he didn't want to push his luck. They could do without the noise.

'I'm sorry,' he said. 'By the time we realised he was in the house, he'd gathered up his things and was ready to leave. The bastard's run out on you, I'm afraid.'

By now she'd relaxed a little, and seemed willing to hear him out. A drop of rain hit her in the eye and she wiped it away, then gingerly took his hand and struggled to her feet. She looked disorientated, confused, but not afraid.

That was good, he thought. That was essential, in fact.

Alice didn't know what to think. The impulse to flee had been so instinctive: could she have got it wrong? It was Renshaw who'd used the word 'predator', but Michael was a family man, with a wife and four children. *Young* children.

'The money,' she murmured. Michael didn't hear her, because of Evie crying. She lifted the carrier enough to be able to kiss and stroke the baby's head, gradually soothing her. 'What about the money?'

'What money?'

'In euros. A lot of money. Renshaw left it with me.'

Michael frowned, turned and examined the short distance she'd travelled before she fell.

'No … I dropped it, earlier.' She felt foolish now, realising how wild and eccentric she must appear.

He shrugged. 'It's probably counterfeit. Otherwise he'd hardly have left it here with you.' He pushed a hand through his hair, a foppish gesture that sent a spray of rain over his shoulder. 'I'm so sorry, Alice. It wasn't till he drove out of the garage that we realised you weren't with him. Then, like I say, we started to fear the worst …'

He tailed off, because Nerys was hurrying towards them, lugging the carrier bag in both hands. Her face was flushed and glistening with rain. Something about the way the headscarf concealed her hair, while emphasising her features, made Alice think of a fairytale witch.

'They're both safe!' Michael cried. 'It turns out Renshaw didn't hurt them. Isn't that a relief?'

Nerys made a noise that might have signalled agreement. She looked decidedly vexed.

Michael said, 'I was telling Alice about Renshaw doing a runner. Is that the money?' He indicated the bag. 'It's almost certainly fake. That or he's got so much he didn't need this any more.'

Nerys nodded vaguely, as if reluctant to express an opinion. She studied Alice for a moment, and produced a thin smile. 'What a bunch of drowned rats we are.' After handing the bag to Michael, she touched the carrier. 'I had visions of this little mite coming to harm, all because of that ghastly man.'

'I thought he was your friend?' Alice said.

'More a colleague. I can't say I knew him that well, to be honest.' Nerys turned and began to walk away, giving Alice little choice but to follow. 'I stepped in to help him, because that's my nature. I don't turn people away.'

'Heart of gold,' Michael said, in a way that implied it was a burden he'd had to bear. 'But people take advantage.'

Nerys was in rueful agreement. 'They do. Abandoning you out here, it was wicked of him. He didn't care one bit if you both ended up with pneumonia.'

Michael, yet again, was amazed by how swiftly his mother had adapted to the cover story he had laid down for them. He let her take command, following with the bag while she escorted mother and baby along the path.

They walked as quickly as the conditions would allow, the leaves mushy beneath their feet. The rain made a tremendous noise as it hit the leaves, but they didn't appreciate the protection offered by the wood until they emerged into the field. Here the rain was slanting down like strings of glass beads.

'Couple of minutes and we'll be back in the warm,' Nerys shouted.

Michael didn't hear Alice's response but he was watching her face. At first she seemed distressed. Then he saw a visible effort to set her fears aside. It wasn't surrender, as such – but surrender was what it amounted to.

She was theirs.

Alice clung to a vague hope of encountering someone else on the way back, someone who could serve as a witness, at least, even though she kept assuring herself that there was nothing to be afraid of. Their account of Renshaw's departure was perfectly plausible – so long as you accepted that the money was something he could readily abandon.

She wished that she'd taken a closer look at the banknotes. But would she have been able to distinguish a forgery? She knew nothing about large euro notes.

Perhaps Michael sensed what she was brooding about, for as they came to the end of the footpath he nudged his elbow against her arm and said, 'You and Evie are okay, so who cares about Renshaw, eh? You can get cleaned up, then I'll drive you to the station for the train at twenty past two.'

She nodded, muttered her thanks. Perhaps that was for the best: get to the station, at least, then speak to Harry again. But the immediate priority was to make sure Evie was warm and dry – and for that Alice knew she had to endure another hour or so in their company.

The lane was deserted, and it took only a minute to reach the house. Alice wondered vaguely why they hadn't gone in through the back garden.

Nerys opened the front door and stepped inside, kicking off her boots in a well-practised motion. She urged Alice to follow and not worry if she got mud on the carpet. Alice's shoes were filthy, her jogging pants soaked and splattered with mud. Hopefully by now her own clothes had been washed and dried.

It was only when Michael shut the front door that her senses picked up on some anomaly. She couldn't say what it was, but it provoked a shudder of unease. Nerys was using the headscarf to wipe her face, while Michael still faced the door. A surreptitious click told her he was locking them in.

Alice sniffed, and knew at once which sense had alerted her to danger. She'd had enough medical training to identify the smell of blood. For a second her mind seemed to shut down, and when she came back Nerys was saying: '... run you a nice hot bath,' and Michael was promising tea and toast and warm towels, and neither of them was able to stop her when Alice broke away and ran towards the kitchen.

The door was half open. A body lay in a pool of blood on the floor beside the table, but the head – Renshaw's head, it must be – was no longer recognisable as human.

She took it all in: the blood splatters on the kitchen cabinets, on the bin and the fridge, a lump of white hair attached to a fragment of his scalp, lying on its own just a couple of feet from the doorway.

She turned, not at all sure that her legs would obey the command to run. In any case, Michael and Nerys stood shoulder to shoulder, blocking her path. Michael wore a regretful smile, while his mother's face was a picture of hard, calculating hostility.

And Nerys was holding a weapon, a short-bladed paring knife.

Alice took a step backwards, putting her on the threshold of the kitchen. Nerys tutted.

'Back door's locked and bolted. You won't get out that way.'

'And we're not going to hurt you,' Michael said. 'Are we, Mum?'

'Not if she does as she's told.'

Alice fought to stay calm. She managed to nod. 'All right.'

'Good.' A tight smile from Nerys. 'Now give me the baby.'

SIXTY

Laird had taken her son. In terms of what might have been motivating Ruth, this went way off the scale. Having pressured her so much for answers, Harry now felt reluctant – even ashamed – about questioning her further.

His silence prompted a bitter laugh. 'What's up, Harry? You wanted to know. I told you.'

'I'm staggered. I don't know what to say.'

'Well, how about if you take over driving for a while, and I'll do my best to explain?'

She pulled up on the verge, a mile or so from the A14. It was still only raining lightly but there was a lot more to come, judging by the skies to the west. Harry got out of the car and automatically checked his phone. Nothing more from Alice.

Once Harry had rejoined the traffic, Ruth described how she had first heard of Laird in 1998. He'd grown up in a well-to-do part of Surrey, but had been banished from the family home when in his late teens: the classic underachiever who fell in with the wrong crowd. By his mid-twenties he'd served a couple of short prison sentences: one for fraud, one for aggravated assault. Then he joined a Far Right group that had a lucrative sideline importing drugs – mostly hallucinogenics and other so-called 'club drugs'.

'I was asked to help infiltrate the gang, by posing as the girlfriend of another undercover officer. At that time there were very few female officers with the training and experience for this sort of work.' She snorted. 'Not to mention the appetite for it.'

'But you did – have the experience, I mean?'

'I'd been seconded to the Met for several undercover roles in the past and discovered that I had a flair for acting.'

Lying, Harry thought, just as Ruth seemed to read his mind.

'Or lying, you might prefer to call it. Amounts to the same thing.'

After a couple of months the male officer had been forced to withdraw from the operation because of personal issues. Ruth opted to stay in place and her handlers agreed, since by now she had formed a bond with Nathan Laird.

'He was far and away the most intelligent member of the group. Charismatic, ambitious, and extremely good-looking. He made it clear that he was attracted to me, so I decided to make use of that.'

'You slept with him?' He frowned. 'Hold on – is that even allowed, when you're undercover? I remember a big outcry a few years back—'

'There's a valid argument about the betrayal of trust, I suppose, especially if the people you're deceiving are essentially innocent of any crime. That wasn't the case with Laird.' She seemed irritated that he had raised the point. 'It's a fine line. Until you've been in that situation, you've really got no right to judge.'

'I can express an opinion—'

'I didn't mean *you*, specifically. Anyway, this was purely my own decision. It was never officially sanctioned. And boy, did I pay for it, in the end.'

She turned her head away from him, staring out of the window.

'To this day I don't know how I got pregnant. I suspect Nathan sabotaged my contraceptives. He's the most perceptive man I've ever met. His intuition could be terrifying, it was so sharp.'

'What do you mean?'

'I think he knew from the start that I was undercover. But he played along, had his fun with me. Never gave me a hint of anything incriminating. And then, the final insult: he got me knocked up.'

Harry, once again, was subdued by the sheer weight of the tragedy she was describing.

'Did you … I mean, weren't you tempted to … ?'

'Have an abortion? Yeah. I thought about it. My dad was raised a Catholic, a pretty half-hearted one by the time I came along, so religion wasn't much of a factor. And yet … I couldn't destroy an innocent life. I was young, healthy, I had a good salary. Keeping it seemed the right decision.'

'And Greg?'

'We weren't together at that stage. He was a colleague, first of all, then a close friend. I'd known for a long time how he felt about me, but I …' She heaved a breath in, and out again. 'To be brutally honest, I didn't feel the same way about him.'

'So what happened?'

'Greg and I discussed it. He was desperate to be a part of my life, and more than willing to raise the child as his own. We agreed that our families would be told the father was a previous boyfriend of mine. We told our bosses the same thing, though I'm sure they had their doubts. They'd turned a blind eye to the fact that I'd slept with Laird, but it terrified them, the idea that one day the truth might come out.'

'You were safe from Laird, surely? He wouldn't have known your real identity.'

'So I thought. Once the pregnancy was confirmed I abandoned the undercover role right away. From Nathan's perspective, he just woke up one day and I was gone.'

There was an air of finality in her voice, and it made him shiver.

'I don't know how, but he found out who I really was. Found out where I lived. He turned up when I was seven months pregnant.' A short, bitter laugh as she gazed into the past. 'I could have killed him that day,' she said wistfully. 'I wish I had.'

'What did he want?'

'He said he knew the baby was his, and he'd come to claim it, like a TV or a piece of jewellery, left at the pawn shop. If I refused, he would take me to court, and he'd also make it public that I got pregnant while working undercover. He guessed – rightly – that my bosses would go crazy if I caused a scandal.'

'And that was more important to you … ?'

'No! Christ, no. But it was clear that, even if I fought him and won, I wouldn't ever be rid of him. I wouldn't be safe, and neither would my child.'

After that, they both seemed to welcome a break in the conversation. Ruth went on staring out of the window and Harry drove in silence, mulling over what he'd heard, trying and failing to make sense of it. The rain grew strong enough to need the windscreen wipers on. He thought the hypnotic sweep of the blades might have calmed him, but they didn't.

It was gone one o'clock. Harry dug his phone out of his pocket and checked it for messages. Nothing. He offered the phone to Ruth.

'I want to check Alice is okay. Will you ring her for me?'

'If you like.' Instead of putting the phone to her ear, she held it at chest height for Harry to hear. It went at once to a recorded message: the phone was switched off.

When Harry sighed, Ruth attempted to reassure him.

'She called you earlier, and she wasn't in any trouble then. Try in a few minutes.'

No sooner had she said that and the phone buzzed; a different noise this time.

'Is that her?'

'No. That's mine.' She switched phones, glanced at the number, then answered curtly: 'Yes?'

Once again she held the phone out for Harry to hear. It was a man's voice, far from amused.

'I'm disappointed in you, Ruth. What are you trying to prove?'

'Nothing.'

'Then let Sian and Niall catch up. Where are you?'

'Can't say. Sorry.'

'You will be, Ruth. Once we've dealt with Renshaw we'll be dealing with you, too.'

Ruth made a scoffing noise, but the man spoke over it.

'Oh, we know where he is. That means our deal is off the table.'

A brief pause. Harry was expecting Ruth to respond forcefully, but she seemed lost for words.

The man said, 'Which way are you heading? West, is it?' He laughed. 'Just keep going. I'll be in touch.'

The line went dead. A long sigh from Ruth.

Harry said: 'Was that Laird?'

'Vickery.'

'He knows where Renshaw is?'

'Relax, Harry. He's bluffing.'

'How can you be so sure?'

'That was the whole point of the call – to keep me off-balance.'

It struck Harry that she sounded a lot more confident now than when she'd been talking to Vickery.

'All right, but if he isn't bluffing, Alice and Evie could be in serious danger.'

'Harry, I know this is stressful but try—'

'Call her again. Please.'

As she waited for the call to connect, Harry glanced at the speedometer and saw he was doing ninety-five. Not wise on a two-lane road in the rain.

'Still switched off.'

Harry gave a helpless moan. 'What are we going to do? We're still so far away.'

'Remember, it's not just us in that situation.'

'What?'

'The only hint he gave me is that they're heading west. Now Renshaw's in Gloucestershire, and this morning I was with Vickery on the east coast. Bluff or not, he and his men have to get across the country as well.'

'Oh.' Such a simple point, and yet Harry had completely failed to take it into account.

It reassured him, but only slightly. And not for long.

SIXTY-ONE

They had Evie. *They had Evie*. That fact had plunged Alice into a despair so deep that her own death meant nothing by comparison.

At first she'd tried to struggle, there on the threshold of the kitchen, until Nerys put the knife to her throat and hissed a reminder that she should take note of the new reality. And with his corpse lying only a few feet away, Alice couldn't ignore what they had done to Renshaw.

She couldn't ignore what they might do to her. Or to Evie.

Drawing a promise from Nerys that the baby would not be harmed, Alice had allowed the other woman to release the carrier and take Evie into her arms.

Evie screamed ferociously at first, but calmed once Nerys took her and swiftly made for the living room. Alice went to follow but Michael grabbed her by the shoulders. Too agitated to fight, she collapsed to her knees, pleading incoherently for Evie. For mercy.

'She'll be fine,' Michael said. 'Now come on. Let's get cleaned up.'

He had manhandled her towards the stairs. Weeping softly, she strained to hear what Nerys was doing, listening out for Evie's cries, but the only sound was the rain, pummelling on the roof; the harsh rattle of it against the windows.

She was taken into the bathroom, where Michael made her undress. When she faltered he grabbed the waistband of her jogging pants and wrenched them down. Her pleas to be left alone only angered him.

'Do as you're told and nothing's going to happen. How hard is that to understand?'

'All right, I'm sorry.' Then her legs nearly gave way; she let out a moan. 'Don't hurt her, please.'

'We won't. I give you my word.'

'R-Renshaw.' She felt bile rising; swallowed it down. 'Why did you kill him?'

Michael shook his head, as if the question had no merit, and gestured impatiently. 'Come on, clean up.'

She tried to stare him down. The voice in her head was saying: *Be strong for Evie, be strong for Evie, be strong for Evie,* but it couldn't quite drown out that other, reproachful voice: *This is the choice you made.*

'I'll have a shower, but can I do it alone?'

'No. You'll lock the door.'

She'd lost this battle but there would be other, more important ones to come. There was a flimsy plastic shower curtain, which she pulled along the bath. Michael dropped the toilet seat, then sat down on it. She couldn't read much from his expression. There was some lust there, she thought, but maybe a hint of distaste, too. Or was that wishful thinking?

Cringing, she turned her back on him and finished undressing. She could feel his gaze on her skin. As she put one foot into the bath she lost her balance and stumbled, righting herself. She glared at Michael as he leaned forward to steady her.

'Give me some privacy, please!' she snapped, and to her surprise he sat back and averted his eyes.

He said nothing as Alice, her hands shaking uncontrollably, puzzled over the old-fashioned shower unit with its mixer taps. At last she had the water flowing, bitterly cold to begin with, making her shiver and gasp until she'd adjusted the temperature.

'You okay in there?' The way he chuckled, they might have been a couple of friends on a camping trip.

Revived a little by the stream of hot water, she felt ready to engage with him again.

'Why are you doing this?'

'What, letting you clean up?'

'You know what I mean. You have to call the police.'

'And say what?'

Alice went to speak but saw she was arguing this from completely the wrong perspective. An innocent perspective. And whatever Michael might turn out to be, he was not innocent. The proof of that lay in the bloodied mess in the kitchen.

Michael added: 'None of us asked for this to happen. It's all a ... a misunderstanding.'

'Perhaps you're right. But you don't have to make it any worse.'

'Who says we're going to? That's just you leaping to conclusions, I'm afraid.'

She couldn't help marvelling at his tone; gently mocking, as though she was the one with the screw loose.

'Why has Nerys taken Evie?'

'To give you a chance to have a shower. Stop getting so upset, will you? Mum's a trained nurse, and a *midwife*, for God's sake. I bet she's delivered more babies than you've had sexual partners!'

His laughter scared her. She switched off the shower and used the clammy plastic curtain as a shield, extending one arm towards him. 'Pass me a towel.'

'Playing hard to get now, are we?' He tutted. 'That works for me.'

In that one phrase, his intentions were crystallised. She couldn't delude herself any more: she'd known, deep down, what he wanted, had known it from that moment in the woods.

Alice was silent; afraid that whatever she said would either encourage or antagonise him. For a few seconds she stood, immobile, listening to the mournful drip of water from the shower head. The question now was whether she fought, or just submitted.

What was best for Evie?

Finally he grabbed a towel from the rail and shoved it into her hand. She wrapped it as tightly as she could under her arms and pulled the front of it higher over her breasts.

Michael was waiting as she pulled back the shower curtain and climbed out, arms folded tight, a wry look on his face.

'You know, most women would give anything to be alone in a bathroom with me.' He let her absorb this, before adding, gravely, 'You don't realise how lucky you are.'

Before they left the room he unhooked a velour dressing gown from the back of the door. They crossed the landing into one of the smaller guest bedrooms. Michael shut the door behind him and leaned against it.

Alice patted herself dry without removing the towel, then turned to face him. With a thoughtful, distracted air, he pulled the belt free of the dressing gown, looping one end around his fist as if holding a whip.

Here it comes, said a voice in her head. It shocked her, that any part of her mind could be so matter-of-fact. She was preparing. Steeling herself to endure whatever it was that needed to be endured – for Evie's sake.

He threw the dressing gown at her. 'Put this on, then sit down next to the radiator.'

Confused, she turned away to put the gown on, wrapping it tightly around her body, and quickly used the towel on her hair. She followed his instructions, sitting below the window with her back to the radiator. Michael knelt beside her, looped the robe's belt around one of the radiator brackets and then used it to tie her wrists together.

Alice tried pleading with him again. 'I need to be with Evie. You're a father. You must understand.'

'Of course I do. And it'll be soon.'

'But how soon? She'll be hungry. Please, Michael … there's no need to do this.'

He stood up. As he backed away he gave her a shockingly contemptuous look. 'I really don't like it that you have such a low opinion of me.'

'But I'm—'

'I can see it in your face. And I don't like it,' he repeated, with quiet menace.

Michael left the room but he was back almost immediately, holding the mobile phone that Renshaw had given her. He thrust it out for her to see.

'Where did you get this?'

'Renshaw.'

'You stole it from him?'

'No. He gave it to me … to call my husband. But the signal wasn't strong enough.'

'I don't believe you.' His eyes narrowed. 'Does anyone know you're here?'

She hesitated, unable to work out which was the better answer. Say no, and she was at his mercy. Say yes and he might take her somewhere else.

Or kill her there and then. And Evie, too ...

He didn't wait for an answer. Instead he went back to the subject of Renshaw: 'How come he trusted you enough to give you the phone?'

'Because I wasn't a threat to him, I suppose.'

'And he left the money with you.'

'It's counterfeit, you said.'

He made a spitting noise. 'Christ, you're gullible. I want to know what the two of you agreed. It's not just the money you were keeping, is it?'

She frowned. 'What do you mean?'

'You hid it somewhere. We've searched your room. We've searched Renshaw. I've looked through your clothes and drawn a blank. So where is it?'

'Where is *what*?'

'The evidence. The leverage Renshaw has over the people chasing him.'

'I don't—' She faltered as an image of the second delivery flashed into her mind: the tiny padded envelope. 'I haven't got anything.'

He stared at her for a long moment, and she saw how the anger changed him, made him someone that even his mother might not recognise. He glanced at his watch, then pointed at her.

'I'm going to give you some time to think about this. To think about the wisdom of holding out. And when I come back you'd better be ready to tell me the truth.'

SIXTY-TWO

They circled round Cambridge, reeled in the county of Bedfordshire, crossed the M1 and drove parallel to it for a few minutes before turning west again, still on the A421, then began to negotiate a seemingly endless sequence of roundabouts through Milton Keynes. Mile after mile of dual carriageway, bordered by neat grass verges and screened by trees on either side, the horizon crushed by heavy skies, leaving only a vague suggestion of a world beyond this road.

The rain came down harder but Harry barely reduced his speed: he couldn't afford to. Somewhere, behind them or even – God forbid – up ahead, Vickery and his men might also be racing towards the same destination.

But it didn't matter how fast he drove, how many risks he took, they still weren't eating up the miles quickly enough. At first he had Ruth trying Alice's number every ten minutes, then every five, then every two.

Finally she snapped. 'No, Harry. That's enough for now.'

There was a tense, brooding silence. Ruth leaned into the back and found a bottle of water. She offered it to Harry, who took a swig, then she drank herself.

'What was Laird's motive for wanting your son?'

Ruth snorted, as if to say: *We're back to that.*

'Probably lots of things. Revenge. Greed. And just sheer bloody-mindedness. What's his is his, so he's gonna have it whether he wants it or not.'

'You agreed?'

'Not straight away. Again there were hours, days of talking it over with Greg. It was way too late for a termination, of course – I suspect Laird timed his approach to make sure of that. Greg kept saying that he'd support me, whatever I opted to do, but the final decision had to be mine.'

Another of her bitter chuckles, this one with more than a hint of self-loathing.

'You know, it says something about the kind of person I am that I doubted how Greg felt about it. I thought that deep down he wanted me to hand the baby over. I judged him by my own lousy standards, you see?'

'And did that affect your decision?' It was about the least painful way of phrasing the question.

'Not really. Though I knew I owed Greg a lot. Without his support I would have …' Her voice had grown hoarse. 'Well, I don't like to think what I'd have done.'

'But you gave your son to Laird?'

'No, I managed to negotiate with him. We agreed that I should nurse Benjamin for the first two years. It would spare Nathan all the unrewarding stuff, the sleeplessness and the daily grind.'

Harry snorted, thinking of a couple of occasions when he'd joked about finding someone else to take on the first exhausting phase of parenthood.

'When he accepted, I thought I'd won. In those two years he was bound to change his mind, get bored with the idea, hopefully even go to jail or end up dead. Every night I willed, I prayed, I *begged* for his death. A heart attack, road accident, murder: I didn't care which.'

'You must have been tempted to make that happen?'

'Oh God, yes. But Nathan anticipated that, as well. He vanished from all his usual haunts. I couldn't find him anywhere, couldn't contact him. And because of that, I even started to believe my wish had come true.' She gave a hollow laugh. 'But it hadn't. When the two years were up he reappeared, demanding that I stick to the deal. By this point he'd gone at least partially legitimate, and his mentor, Kenny Vaughan, had been put away for life.'

She took a sip of water. Rested the bottle on her thigh, her thumb toying with the lid.

'There was nothing I could do. Ostensibly he was a successful businessman, his past convictions spent. He insisted that his name be on the birth certificate. He could afford to hire the best lawyers – and contesting it would have ruined all our lives, he'd have made sure of that.'

A sigh. Another sip of water.

'I had to let Benjamin go, albeit with lots of safeguards: Nathan agreed to let me have regular access, he promised never to move abroad; all kinds of conditions designed to reassure me, keep me compliant …'

Harry nodded gloomily. He could guess what was coming next.

'He didn't keep to a single word of the agreement. He just vanished, even more thoroughly than before. That was the last I ever saw of either of them.'

'You have no idea what happened to him?'

'That's why I'm here, Harry. Following any lead to Laird, because only he has the answer.' She tried a laugh. 'You can't believe the soul-searching I've done. For a year or two I was a basket case. I didn't sleep, didn't eat, didn't properly connect with anyone. Poor Greg stuck by me, helped me the best he could. He thought the answer was to have our own children. I went along with it, because I felt it was the least I could do. But when it didn't happen I was glad, in a way. That's a terrible thing to say, because I know it broke Greg's heart. But I didn't deserve another child. I'd had my chance and blown it, hadn't I? In my head I wasn't just a bad mother, I was the worst mother of all time.'

'I don't think so,' Harry said, but it was an inadequate attempt at consoling her. Despite everything she'd said in mitigation, when he thought of the pain it was causing him right now, to be separated from Evie, he found Ruth's decision inconceivable, no matter what the circumstances.

'How old would he be now?'

'Fifteen. Fifteen and three months. Sometimes I can picture him so clearly. A big strong teenager. I can see just what he's like, I can almost hear his voice …' She sniffed. 'Other times I try to imagine him and there's nothing. He's only a blank shape. A ghost.'

She choked up, then just as abruptly rubbed her eyes and her nose, and was in control of her emotions again.

'I look back now and I can't understand how it happened. How could I have agreed to let him go? It was a different person who made that decision, that's what I tell myself. It's ironic, Harry. You'd probably think I must be so hard, to do something like that. But actually I was soft then. I was afraid of a fight. The person I am now is much harder, with only one mission in life. To make good the damage, any way I can.'

It was one thirty-five. At this rate Harry guessed they were still at least an hour away, maybe ninety minutes. Should have rented a—

'Oh shit,' he breathed.

'What?'

'Vickery and the gang. They've made a lot of money, right? I mean, they could charter a helicopter, if they had to?'

'It's not very likely—'

'Jesus, Ruth, they terrorised us the other night. They've killed one of their own men, Hasan, because he helped Renshaw. You seriously don't feel this is important enough to warrant a helicopter?'

'I'm sure they're bluffing about the address.'

'I can't take that risk. We should call the police.'

'Harry, that's not a good idea.'

'I don't care. It can be an anonymous call.'

'They'll dismiss it.'

'Then we give them a false name.'

'But what are we reporting?'

Harry sighed, not just angry but frustrated that her objections had some genuine weight.

'Look,' he said at last, 'I know the address. I can say I've seen what looks like an intruder. A suspected burglary. At least that means they'll check out the house.'

'And if Vickery's men *are* there, you could be sending some poor local cop to his death.'

'If Vickery's men are there,' Harry reminded her through gritted teeth, 'I want someone – anyone – who might be able to help my wife and daughter.'

Ruth didn't agree, exactly, but her protests ceased when he moved into the left-hand lane and started searching for a place to pull over.

'Give me the address. I'll do it.'

She used her own phone. After he'd recited the address, she dialled 999 and claimed to be a resident of Cranstone who'd just seen what looked like a burglary at Beech House. She lied smoothly about her own name and address, and sounded remarkably convincing.

Afterwards, she exhaled heavily. 'I don't think that was a good idea.'

'Better than doing nothing.' He thought for a moment. 'How are we going to know what happens?'

'We're not. Not until we get there. You have to accept that, I'm afraid. We've done all we can.'

SIXTY-THREE

The room they'd chosen for Alice was the only one with both a
door and a window that could be locked. Once she was secure,
Michael used one of the other rooms to change into the overalls
Nerys had found for him. He also allowed himself a little time
to savour the image of Alice climbing into the shower.

Downstairs, his mother was a whirlwind of activity. She'd
changed into old clothes and put on a plastic apron, fetched the
waste bags and filled a bucket with hot water and bleach, made up
a bottle of formula milk and was now feeding Evie while studying
the chaos in the kitchen, planning the clean-up operation.

'Did you find it?'

'No. It's not there.'

'Bloody hell, Michael, we could be up shit creek without it.'

'I know. But you're the one who …' He gestured at Renshaw's
body.

'You heard him trying to blackmail me. I'm not taking that
crap from anyone.'

'No, but you could have waited till we knew where the
evidence was.'

'Easy to say now.' She was seething, all the more irritable because
she knew he was right. 'Once he'd admitted to having something,
I thought it would be easy to find. What has Alice told you?'

'Not much. I think she's holding back on us.' He showed her
the phone and she gasped.

'Did Alice have that?'

'She says Renshaw gave it to her. She claimed she couldn't get a signal, but I've just checked the call log. She's lying. There are lots of attempts to reach her, as well as three outgoing numbers. Two mobiles and a landline – area code 01273, which is Brighton, I believe.'

'Family?' Nerys mused. 'But no 999 calls?'

Michael shook his head. 'I suppose, if she didn't feel threatened, she might have called to reassure people.'

'Let's hope so. What time were they?'

He checked the phone. 'Between half eleven and twelve.'

'Well, then. That's two hours ago. If she'd summoned the cavalry I bet they'd be here by now.'

He nodded, partially reassured. 'There's still the issue of people knowing she's here.'

'But no proof,' Nerys reminded him. 'As long we make sure there's no trace left of any of them, we just deny it.'

Michael pondered this as he watched the baby suck and gasp, suck and gasp. The bottle was almost empty.

'So we're … we're going to do away with them?'

A shrug. 'With any luck that'll be Laird's problem, not ours. But right now they're a bargaining tool, both of them.' She tipped the baby back to take the final dregs of milk. 'You need to get your skates on and fetch the car. How long will it take?'

Michael groaned. In all the excitement he'd forgotten that the Range Rover was parked in Westcombe Wood.

'Ten or fifteen minutes, if I run.'

'You *have* to bloody run. While you're doing that, I'll make a start on the clean-up.'

*

Alice listened obsessively to every sound from below, but she could hear very little over the rain. Within a few minutes of Michael leaving her, she thought an outer door might have slammed. Then nothing.

Why wasn't Evie howling? Alice was plagued with fear that she had been hurt. Just to contemplate it made her head swim; her breathing became shallow and rapid, her skin coated in a clammy cold sweat. She pulled on the cords and felt them give, a little, but not enough to free her hands.

She wondered if Harry was on his way here. Would he remember the address she'd shouted down the phone? Would he find the place in time?

It seemed like such a faint hope to cling on to – and one that she hardly deserved. She despised herself for dismissing Renshaw's concerns about Nerys and her son.

Ugh. Even the thought of Michael made her shudder. The way he looked at her …

She heard the sound of a key turning in the lock. The door opened and Nerys came in, Evie held expertly in one arm.

Alice's heart leapt. She started to speak but Nerys shushed her.

'Don't. She's asleep.'

'Is she all right?'

'Starving,' Nerys said, her voice scornful. 'She drained a whole bottle. Nearly nine ounces.'

'What?'

'I gave her some SMA.'

'You …' Alice was staggered; for a moment the reality of her predicament forgotten. 'You gave her formula milk?'

'Yes, and it's a good thing I did. The poor mite's obviously underfed.' She sniffed, disapprovingly, and indicated Alice's breasts. 'Must be poor quality milk in there.'

Alice couldn't respond. In the scheme of things it was a trivial issue – what mattered was that Evie was alive and well – and yet it came as such a terrible affront to her own sense of motherhood, her capability.

'At least let me cuddle her, please? I won't try to escape.'

'Course you will. Anyway, you don't need to cuddle her. She's perfectly all right on her own.'

Alice was helpless as Nerys settled Evie in the centre of the single bed. Then the woman turned and knelt down before her.

'When you were out for your walk, Renshaw gave you something else, didn't he? Along with the phone and the money.'

'No, he didn't.'

Nerys reached out and took hold of Alice's left ear, pinching the lobe between her fingers, digging her nails into the soft cartilage. Alice winced.

'He didn't! I promise you!'

Nerys pinched tighter, and twisted, forcing Alice's head down. 'You're lying.'

'I'm not. I'm not.' Alice sucked in a breath, unable to credit that such a small manoeuvre could be so agonising. She swallowed, and said, 'There was … He had a tiny envelope, maybe with a USB stick or something.'

'That's it. Go on.'

'He put it in his pocket yesterday morning, when we escaped from the house in Brighton. But I never saw it after that, I swear to you.'

'On Evie's life, you'd swear?'

'Yes! I swear, I don't know where it is.'

Nerys said nothing but she held on, twisting, for three, four, five long seconds, Alice writhing with the pain, desperate not to cry out and frighten Evie.

Then Nerys let go. 'I don't have a lot of time for torture – problem is, I'm too nice.' She gave Alice a sickly smile. 'But those men who were chasing Renshaw? They'll get the answers out of you.'

Michael was still sweating profusely when he parked the Range Rover on the drive. He'd worn a coat to conceal the overalls, fearing the sight of them might be a little incongruous while he was running across a field.

And run he had – till his lungs burned from the effort. He'd ignored all the cramps and twinges in his ankles and calves and knees; he'd run through the pain and eventually, in the middle of the wood, he felt his second wind; that blissful moment when the lungs seem to expand and glow with pleasure at the exertion. He might have just kept going, sprinted past the car and on over the countryside, his only goal to put distance between himself and the house, himself and the mess he was in …

But he couldn't. Nerys needed him as never before. And after this – provided they could negotiate an exit route that kept them both out of jail – his mother would be in his debt forever.

She'd have to do anything he wanted.

Anything.

By the time he got back she had worked wonders. The house reeked of detergent rather than blood. Renshaw's body still lay in the kitchen, but now it was trussed up in three layers of thick plastic, held in place by loops of packing tape. It looked like a cartoon mummy: something from *Scooby Doo*.

Nerys was still mopping up, but the worst of the blood and gore had gone. The washing machine was running, hot suds sloshing against the porthole, erasing the blood from their clothes. She looked grimly satisfied with her progress.

'Alice has admitted that Renshaw had evidence. A USB stick, she thinks it was. She says she didn't see what he did with it.'

'Do you believe her?'

Nerys wavered. 'I'd love to think she was lying, but it's unlikely.' She did have some good news, of sorts. 'I've spoken to Vickery again. They're coming by helicopter, so I need to get my skates on.'

Michael frowned. 'Did you warn him that Renshaw's dead, and that we don't—'

'What do you take me for? I'm hardly going to show my hand this soon. Renshaw must have hidden it somewhere here, in the house. We've *got* to find it.' She frowned as he started to move. 'Where are you off to?'

'To search for the mem—'

'Not *now*. Good God!' She gestured crossly at the body. 'Go and reverse your car up to the front door. Close as you can get.'

Turning away, he was trying to figure out where in the house Renshaw might have secreted the memory stick, and only dimly registered the sound of an engine as he crossed the hall. He was reaching for the front door when he heard something more distinct: a car door slamming.

He made a detour to the nearest window. Peered out, and it felt like he had to clench every muscle in his body to prevent his insides from collapsing.

'Mu-um!' A long, half-broken syllable, part hiss, part croak.

'What is it?'

'Police. A fucking cop car.'

SIXTY-FOUR

Michael had never in his life felt even a tenth as scared as he was now. He stared at his mother, stricken by the knowledge that she too had finally met her match. There was no way out of this.

But Nerys displayed no panic. 'Wait in the kitchen. Don't make a sound.'

She removed the apron, balled it up and threw it on to the floor. Michael was moving past her when a thought occurred to him.

'Alice, and the baby … ?'

'She's on the other side of the house.' A deep breath. 'Get a knife. Be ready to come if I call.'

They both heard movement outside, what sounded like a single figure approaching the door. Then the footsteps receded.

Puzzled, Nerys leaned into the dining room and peeped out. Her body relaxed. She gave Michael a smile and hissed: 'Kitchen. Go!'

Michael obeyed, but he left the door open a couple of inches. He needed to hear this.

He needed to be prepared to attack. Or run away.

Nerys thought she'd recognised the man peering around the side of the house. It meant she was calmer as she opened the front door, but it also left her somewhat conflicted.

Jack Fryer wasn't a bad man. It would be a shame if she had to kill him.

He'd heard the door open and was ambling towards her, his expression untroubled. He was in his early fifties, thickset and balding with a big nose and an oddly impish demeanour for a middle-aged police officer.

'All right, Jack?'

He smiled, and she saw relief in his eyes, which was rather strange.

'Hello, Nerys. You know, I thought this was your place.' He stopped on the lower step, hands on hips. 'We had reports of an attempted burglary.'

'Oh? When was this?'

'Ten, fifteen minutes ago. Woman rang on a mobile saying she'd seen someone trying to break in.'

Nerys was able to look convincingly baffled. 'And you're sure it was my address?'

'That's what she said. I had my doubts, because her name didn't ring a bell. And I reckon I know everyone who lives in these parts.'

Nerys tutted along with him, agreeing that it was most unlikely that someone had just been passing: Mercombe Lane was a dead end, after all.

'Just odd that it was a woman. Prank callers, they're normally males, or young girls.' He snorted. 'Who you been upsetting?'

'Upsetting?' Nerys flashed her eyes at him. 'A charmer like me, Jack? I don't upset anyone.'

'No. Probably means I've been given the wrong address.' He sighed. 'Definitely all right round the back, are you?'

He shifted sideways, only half a pace, but it sent a bolt of alarm through her.

'No one's been in the garden. I was here all morning.'

Jack indicated the Range Rover. 'New car, is it?'

'Belongs to my son. I'm using it for a couple of days.'

'I didn't think you'd stolen it, Nerys.' He grinned – but was he also peering at her a little more closely?

She concealed her nerves with a chuckle. 'How's your golf these days?'

'Lousy – as always.' He stared hard at her left hip. 'Nerys, is that blood?'

She looked down and saw a pinkish smudge on the old slacks she'd worn for the clean-up. She rubbed at it, dismissively, with her wrist.

'Just had to kill a lame hen,' she explained.

'Oh, sorry to hear that. I've got myself some new Marans. Slow to lay at first, but blimmin delicious when they do.'

He patted his belly and launched into an enthusiastic comparison of the various breeds he'd kept over the years. At one point, while she listened, Nerys made a soft spitting noise and removed an imaginary scrap of feather from her tongue. It was a gesture he would know well, and it reinforced her cover story at a subliminal level.

Finally he departed, almost but not quite brave enough to kiss her on the cheek. She promised to contact his wife, Joan, to arrange a game of badminton at the social club, and stood in the doorway until he was back in the car.

Michael stayed in the kitchen for a few more seconds. Even as his brain accepted the reality of their close escape, his body still wanted to collapse from the shock.

'Did you hear all that?' Nerys asked.

'Most of it.' He joined her in the dining room. The patrol car had driven away.

'Bit of a coincidence, isn't it?' she said. 'A woman reporting a burglary.'

'Alice, you mean?'

'If Alice had access to a phone she wouldn't muck around with a story about a break-in.' She looked sombre. 'No, I wonder if it was someone she spoke to earlier.'

'But why?'

'No idea. Testing the water in some way.'

'You could have asked who'd reported it.'

'I didn't want to seem too interested.' She fretted over that. 'Perhaps I should have, but we can't worry about that now. Let's get that body shifted.'

'Oh my God!' Michael went pale. 'A minute or two later and he'd have rolled up just as we were putting Renshaw in the boot.'

Nerys stared at him for a moment, looking as shocked as he was; then, abruptly, she started to laugh.

'We can count ourselves lucky, then, can't we?'

Another ten minutes and Nerys was ready to go. Renshaw's body, bent at the waist, had been placed in the boot. His duffle bag and rucksack were dumped in there as well, and all covered by an old picnic blanket.

Nerys put the bag of money in the front passenger footwell, then locked the Range Rover and returned to the kitchen for one final inspection.

'The bedroom will need a deep clean, but I can do that tonight or tomorrow.' She crouched down, peering beneath the kitchen cabinets. 'While I'm gone, can you finish up in here?'

Michael blanched. 'I thought you wanted me to search … ?'

'You can do both, can't you? It's only a bit of cleaning. It won't kill you.'

'I know.'

'Good. One more trip upstairs …' Nerys paused, as if to choose her words carefully. 'You know that Alice mustn't come to any serious harm in my absence.'

'Who says I'm going to hurt her?'

A look passed between them. Nerys pursed her lips, then said, 'You're welcome to question her some more. Don't worry if you can't get answers. I'm sure Laird's men will see to that.'

'Then why not take her with you?'

'Do you want me to?' She smiled, having called his bluff. 'Like I say, I want her here for insurance. But be ready to bring her to Symonds Yat, if and when, okay?' A glance at her watch. 'I should be there by half three at the latest.'

'Yes. Look, er, Mum—' He felt a sudden loss of nerve, and it must have been evident in his expression. She pressed the tip of her finger against his lips.

'Don't worry, darling. We're on the home straight now. Just find that dratted USB thing, will you? And by tonight we'll be rich. We'll be free.'

Michael nodded, but as he watched her climb the stairs, he thought: *I'm already rich.*

And until this morning I was free.

SIXTY-FIVE

The decision to make an emergency call didn't bring as much relief as Harry had hoped. Ruth was categorically opposed to ringing Gloucestershire police for an update, and Harry reluctantly accepted that decision.

When they returned to the discussion about Laird, Ruth admitted that she'd been slightly economical with the truth on one point. Vickery and his team hadn't reappeared in the way she'd described before. In fact their operations had flourished – albeit with no sign of Laird at the helm – during the years that Ruth had languished in prison.

'You said that Laird was listening in this morning. So he is still on the scene?'

'In the sense that he makes the big decisions. But his physical location – that could be anywhere in the world. I doubt if even Vickery knows.'

'Really?'

She nodded. 'I remember, years ago, he joked that his ideal routine would be to stay every night in a different bed. I thought he meant to have a different woman – and he probably did mean that, as well. But he likes to stay on the move.'

'And you have no idea what happened to your son?'

'I have no solid information.'

'But?'

'It's possible that Nathan gave him away.'

'Laird gave away *his own son*?'

Tight-lipped, she nodded. 'I think he might have sold him.'

She explained that it had been a morbid preoccupation for years. There was no evidence to support it, but wouldn't anyone in her situation fear the very worst?

Then, during her time in prison, she happened to hear a rumour. A woman in for drug offences had a friend who'd worked as one of Laird's escorts.

'She'd got pregnant – accidentally, or so she thought. Later she realised her contraceptives had been tampered with.'

'The same as you?' Harry blurted.

'Possibly,' Ruth said. 'Anyway, the woman just assumed she'd have an abortion. *She* didn't want a baby, and she couldn't imagine her employers being pleased. But Vickery persuaded her to reconsider. Once the baby was born it was taken from the mother and never seen again.'

Harry didn't comment for a minute. He was thinking of Keri, her pregnancy and subsequent miscarriage, and he feared Ruth's reaction to what he had to say.

'How much do you know about Renshaw?'

'Very little. Why?'

'Just … it surprised me that you seemed so vague about him, despite all the effort you've put into investigating Laird.'

'Yeah, and I've also told you how hard it is to get meaningful information.'

Harry conceded the point. 'According to Keri, Renshaw was a doctor. His job was to look after the girls. He organised contraceptives, checked them for STIs and so on.' He cleared his throat. 'If they deliberately wanted pregnancies, he would be perfectly placed to make that happen.'

Ruth was nodding rapidly: a signal to stop talking. Her face was pale, bloodless. After a long silence, all she said was, 'It all fits.'

'I'm sorry. I asked Keri if she'd mentioned any of this to Greg and she was fairly sure he knew about Renshaw—'

'But Greg didn't tell me that.' She swallowed heavily. 'And I can see why. Because I'd make the connection right away.'

'You told Greg about this rumour in prison?'

A nod. 'The moment I heard it, I thought: that's what Benjamin is to Laird. A commodity. And Greg knew it, too, which is why he went to such lengths to hunt Laird.'

'But you don't actually know that he gave his own son away, do you?'

She was shaking her head, dismissing his attempt to offer comfort.

'In our hearts, we knew.'

It was twenty to three when a sign for Cranstone appeared. They turned off the A435 and drove for another two miles along a narrow road, threading their way between rain-dulled meadows and gloomy copses. Apart from a truck that nearly ran them off the road they encountered no other traffic.

Ruth's phone rang. She listened for a few seconds, then moved the phone to her left ear. Harry had no hope of hearing the conversation.

'But—' It was her only contribution. A few more seconds and she flapped a hand at him. 'Stop the car.'

'What?'

'Pull over. Quickly!'

There was a steep grass bank to their left, so Harry swerved across the road and drove two wheels on to the narrow grass verge.

He'd barely come to a halt before Ruth discarded her seatbelt and jumped out of the car.

He watched in the rear-view mirror as she strode away, the phone at her ear. He considered following her, then changed his mind; a battle underway in his thoughts.

I have to know.

I don't want to know.

While he waited, he checked his own phone. No messages. He tried Alice again. The phone was still switched off. What did that mean?

Ruth had come to a halt, her right arm pressed against her stomach. She stood very still, oblivious to the rain, making no gestures that might hint at the nature of the call.

Unless the lack of movement was a clue in itself.

Two long minutes passed. Then she put the phone away and hurried back, almost running, only to stop again and take cover at the rear of the car. There was a tractor approaching. It had to scrape the bank to get past the Corsa, the driver's sneer quite easy to read: *idiot townies*.

Finally she was back in the car. Harry didn't think he could bear to ask, but he managed a single word: 'Vickery?'

'No.' She sounded distant, almost shellshocked. 'It was Nathan.'

'Nathan *Laird*?'

'He wants to see me. He says … he says Renshaw's being brought to them, somewhere near Ross-on-Wye.'

'What about Alice? Is she still with Renshaw?'

Silence. Ruth sat slumped, head down, eyes unfocused.

'Ruth!' he said again. 'Where is Alice?'

'Still here, I guess. I asked him. He said they're not interested in her.'

At this, Harry dared to allow himself a small measure of relief. 'Does that mean she's safe?'

'I don't know. But I have to go to Ross-on-Wye, right now.'

He saw how pale she was, saw she was trembling.

'Ruth, what has he told you? Is it about Benjamin?'

'I'll drive, Harry. Get out of the car.'

'Not until I know what's happened. I can't go anywhere else if there's a chance that Alice could still be here.'

He waited, fighting his anger, but Ruth said nothing. He reached out and grasped her upper arm. She flinched, but didn't look up.

'I don't care about Renshaw. I *need* to find my wife and daughter. You must understand that better than anyone.'

'I do.' Now she turned, taking in the physical contact between them, and made eye contact with a deep probing gaze that felt like she was scooping out his soul. 'I'm so sorry.'

'Why? Sorry about what?'

'It's not just Renshaw they're getting,' Ruth said. 'It's Evie.'

SIXTY-SIX

She described the call in more detail, but Harry could barely take it in. He felt like he was hearing Ruth's voice from the bottom of a deep well.

'They've done a deal with whoever was hiding Renshaw. It sounds like Evie was included in that deal. A kind of bonus for them.'

'You're not serious. Please tell me you're not …'

'I'm sorry. But we still have time to stop it.'

'Laird will sell her, the way he did—'

'We don't know for certain.' She regarded him sadly. 'Don't fall apart now, Harry. We have a lot to do.'

He nodded, wiped his eyes and sniffed. 'Where have they told you to go?'

'I don't have the full address. They're not stupid. Someone will be watching the main road into town. When they see me go past they'll call me with instructions.'

'But you're walking into a trap.'

'Of course I am. This is their big chance. I've been an irritant to Nathan for years, and now I'm handing him an opportunity to deal with me once and for all.'

'There must be some way—'

'No. If I don't do as he says, Evie will suffer.'

'He said that? Laird threatened my daughter?'

A solemn nod. 'So if you were gonna persuade me to think again, forget it. Deep down you don't want to talk me out of it, and you shouldn't feel guilty about that.' A quick, bitter smile. 'I deserve whatever I get.'

Harry had no idea how to respond. He was struggling to accept that the woman sitting beside him – a woman he should be wary of trusting – was now the only person who could save his daughter's life.

'What about Alice? What's happening to her?'

'I don't think they even know where she is.'

'So it's possible that she's still here, in Cranstone? We've got to check the address.'

'You can. I need to get going.' She paused, giving him a look of almost maternal concern. 'You have to prepare yourself for the possibility that it's too late for Alice.'

'I know that,' he said tightly. But he was lying. He couldn't even begin to accept that he might never see his wife again – any more than he could accept the same of his daughter.

And now he had to choose between them.

He stared straight ahead, almost hypnotised by a drop of rain sliding down the glass.

'Should I stay here or go with you?'

'If you come with me, I'll have to drop you off outside of town. They're expecting me to come alone.'

'But I ought to be there. Couldn't I help in some way … ?'

She smiled, as if sparing his feelings. 'I'm probably better doing this on my own.'

He didn't take offence. If anything, her honesty helped him deal with the most agonising decision he'd ever faced. Allowing Ruth to go alone made him feel he was abandoning his daughter, who was more precious to him than anyone on earth. And yet, to drive away when Alice might be here in Cranstone, desperately in need of help … how could he even think of leaving her to her fate?

'I know it's a lousy choice, Harry. I'm sorry.'

He nodded brusquely, and put the car into gear.

The village was no doubt quite pretty but made little impression on Harry. He checked the odometer as he passed the last house, remembering what Alice had said: about a mile further on.

He pulled over to let a couple of impatient drivers race past, rolled slowly around a bend and finally spotted a narrow opening that might have been Mercombe Lane. As he drew alongside he searched in vain for a road sign, but decided this must be it. There were no other junctions in sight.

He pulled up in the road and put the hazard lights on. They got out of the car, Ruth hurrying round to the driver's side. Harry moved back to let her get in, but first, unexpectedly, she drew him into a quick embrace.

'I'll do my best for Evie, I promise.'

Harry didn't trust himself to speak. His eyes shining with tears, he stood at the side of the road and watched Ruth drive away, then crossed over and set off along Mercombe Lane.

SIXTY-SEVEN

Alice fought like any mother would, when Nerys revealed what she intended to do. Alice fought, she screamed and struggled, but it did no good. Worse than that, she became so frantic, so distraught that she hyperventilated to the point where she passed out.

When she came round she was alone. The room was empty, the door shut. She listened for movement downstairs, or cars outside, and heard nothing. Nerys had gone, she guessed. But was Michael still here?

Alice hardly cared any more what he might or might not do to her. Compared to losing Evie, it was irrelevant.

A long time seemed to pass before he came in. He was dressed in dark green overalls, and he looked sweaty and dishevelled. After seeing her recoil, he sniffed his armpit and grimaced.

'Uh oh. Better have a shower.'

'Michael, please,' she called to him. 'Tell Nerys to bring Evie back.' He hesitated, and she knew what she had to say: 'Do that for me and I'll give you anything.'

'Oh?' He pretended to be intrigued, raising his eyebrows and taking a step closer. She could smell him now: the armpit routine hadn't been a joke.

'I mean it. But you have to save Evie.'

Still smiling, he shook his head. 'You don't get to bargain with me, Alice. You should have worked that out by now.' He indicated her position on the floor. 'I can do whatever I like. And I will.'

She regarded him with contempt. 'You think I care? You think that scares me, after what your mother's done? You're pathetic.'

He looked disappointed. 'Oh, Alice, that's just unnecessary, when I've gone out of my way to be kind.' A wink. 'Quick shower, then I'll be back.'

He talked the talk, Michael was thinking as he stripped off in the bathroom. But could he walk the walk?

This wasn't like the other occasions. Normally there was alcohol involved, and sometimes drugs. Usually the *ambience* was suggestive of sex, in some way – plush hotel rooms, low lighting, background music – and both he and the woman in question were relaxed and on good terms, at least to begin with.

But this was about as different as you could get. And without Evie's presence to act as leverage, Alice might feel she had nothing to lose. As much as it would enhance the experience if she fought him, any scratches or bites would be difficult to explain away to Robyn, when he was supposed to have spent the day reviewing paperwork with his mother. And then there was the risk of leaving DNA on her body.

You won't get away with this, a voice kept telling him. *Just because your mother keeps saying so, doesn't mean it will all turn out fine.*

He put that out of his head and stood under the shower, soaping his body and trying to focus his thoughts on the pleasure to come. As he dried off he wondered about fetching a bottle of vodka and making her drink a few shots. It might soften her up, make her more co-operative.

He considered just wrapping a towel around his waist, but decided it left him feeling vulnerable. Instead he trooped downstairs and retrieved his clothes from the tumble dryer. He'd followed Nerys's instructions and searched all the hiding places he could think of, but hadn't found Renshaw's memory stick. Then he'd made an attempt at cleaning up the kitchen, but would be the first to admit he hadn't done the job as thoroughly as she would have done it.

Good enough for now, he decided, when there were far more pressing matters on his mind.

Alice was resigned to Michael's return. If he intended to rape her, it would mean coming close – and that might give her a chance to get free.

Hearing the rattle of the key in the lock, she took a deep breath. The door opened and he entered the room. His hair was wet, mussed up by hand, and he was back in the clothes he'd worn this morning, freshly washed. He was also holding her clothes, neatly folded.

'All lovely and clean,' he said, 'so you can get dressed again.'

Her heart leapt. 'Now?'

He sucked his teeth, and said, 'Well, *afterwards* works better for me.'

Despite the levity, she thought he looked slightly apprehensive. She took that to mean he wasn't nearly as comfortable with this set-up as he tried to make out. Perhaps she could use that to her advantage.

He sat down on the bed and looked her over. 'Mum told me you saw Renshaw with something. A memory stick, probably.'

Spotting an opportunity, Alice said, 'He must have hidden it somewhere close at hand. Why don't I help you look for it?'

'Ha. Nice try.' He shook his head, his gaze crueller than before. 'Why did you kill him before he gave it to you?'

The question hit a nerve. 'I didn't kill him. It was a mistake.'

'Well, so is this, and I think you know that.' Alice steeled herself and said, 'My offer still stands, Michael. Bring Evie back, and I'll submit to you. I won't fight.'

He looked offended. 'What do you mean, "submit"?'

She gave him a withering glance, but said nothing. He got up, planted his feet apart and stood before her.

'I saw the way you eyed me up this morning, in the kitchen. Why are you scared to admit that you find me attractive?'

'*What?*' His arrogance was astounding. 'How can you possibly imagine that I'd fancy *anyone* in a situation like this? You'd have to be … *insane*.'

'But you do fancy me. I saw it in your eyes, and I'm never wrong. Besides, it's a well-known fact that danger makes people horny—'

'You've taken my daughter!' she yelled at him. 'Your fucking psycho of a mother is threatening to *sell* my daughter to a bunch of criminals, and *you* helped her.' She took a couple of breaths, lowered her voice. 'You can still do the right thing. Call her and persuade her to bring Evie back to me. If you don't, and you try to lay a finger on me, I swear I'll do everything I can to hurt you. Give me one chance and I'll have your eyes, your balls, anywhere I can get.'

It must have been a convincing performance, because Michael took an involuntary step back. He studied her, at first disturbed by the outburst, then fascinated, and finally – to her horror – aroused.

He pulled the belt from his jeans. Stepped forward again.

'I'll take that chance.'

It took nearly ten minutes for Harry to jog down the lane and reach the end, where he realised that somewhere he had passed Beech House. Wiping rain from his face, he knocked on the door of a square stone bungalow and was given directions by a woman who peered at him as if he were potentially an axe murderer.

Beech House was about a hundred yards back. The gates were standing open and the driveway was empty. All the windows were shut. No sign of life. Harry wondered if the police had followed up on Ruth's phone call: if so, presumably they'd found nothing untoward.

He crossed the drive, intending to knock on the front door, but at the last moment he veered away, making for the far corner of the house. Some instinct told him it was better not to announce his presence just yet.

The back garden was fenced off, with a gate blocking the path along the side of the property. Both fence and gate were a good six feet high. The gate, predictably, was locked.

Harry jumped up, grabbed the fence with both hands and scrabbled, feet slippery from the rain, and managed in an ungainly way to haul himself up. A pause to check there was no one watching, then he dropped down on the other side, just a few feet from the back door. The glass panels revealed an attractive farmhouse kitchen, complete with a large oak table. There was a set of overalls crumpled on the floor, and a mop leaning against the worktop.

Harry felt his heart rate increase. He tried the door but it was locked. And it was sturdy: not something he could force without tools.

Agonising over what he should do next, he wandered into the back garden and then stopped, abruptly, as he realised that a sound had come from deep within the house.

A scream.

A woman's voice.

SIXTY-EIGHT

First, he used his belt to lash her across the face. The pain was intense, but Alice was too shocked to react. The skin on her cheeks was numbed by the impact of the leather, but she felt a trickle of blood from her nose.

Michael looked almost as shocked as she did, as if he hadn't quite believed he had it in him to act like this. But she'd goaded him into it, hadn't she, and now he had called her bluff.

Alice was still reeling when he untied the cord from the radiator bracket, wrestled her face down on the carpet and tore the gown away from her. He tied her wrists again, behind her back, then lifted her under her arms and dragged her, naked, on to the bed. She let out a long, piercing scream – she knew the house was too remote for it to be of help, but thought it might at least unsettle him, bring him to his senses.

'You don't want to do this, Michael.'

'Save it.'

'Listen to me, please—'

'I *deserve* this!' he shouted. 'All the shit I've been through today, this is my reward.'

He moved to the foot of the bed and took hold of her feet, stroking them gently for a second or two before gripping them firmly and forcing her legs apart.

From downstairs came a loud crash: the sound of shattering glass, followed by a heavy impact. Michael jerked upright, glaring at Alice as if she could explain it. She met his gaze, wanting to gloat that his plans had been disrupted, but in truth she was no less afraid.

That fear was just as evident in Michael. As he turned away she caught him murmuring a single word.

'Fuck.'

Harry found a stone birdbath on a plinth in the middle of the lawn. It must have weighed about seventy pounds. Holding it in both hands, he staggered back to the house and somehow found the strength to hurl it through a set of timber-framed doors. None of the subtlety with which Laird's men had gained entry to his own house the other night.

He ran into the house and immediately heard movement upstairs. A door slammed, a man's voice snarled something Harry couldn't make out.

He reached the bottom of the stairs as a man appeared on the landing – he was in his late thirties, tall, dark-haired – and stared at Harry in confusion.

'Who are you? Get the fuck out of my house.'

He descended a couple of stairs, then stopped. Harry climbed up one step, mirroring the other man's aggressive posture.

'I'm looking for my wife—'

'I told you to get the fuck out of here,' the other man shouted over him. 'I'll call the police!'

'Alice French,' Harry growled. 'Where is she?'

'I don't know what you mean.' He dug in his pocket, showed Harry a mobile phone. The ploy might have worked, if not for a tiny wavering doubt in the man's eyes.

'I heard a scream,' Harry said, then he shouted: 'Alice? Are you here?'

The response was a muffled cry: 'Harry!'

Michael saw how the husband reacted to Alice's voice and tried to gauge what sort of an opponent Harry would make. In terms of their age and build, there wasn't a lot in it. Michael had a tactical advantage, standing above his adversary, but that was squandered when Harry was first to move, springing up the stairs with frightening agility. In a panic, Michael hurled the phone at him. It struck Harry squarely in the chest. He grunted but didn't slow down.

Michael turned and bolted along the landing. He wasn't a natural fighter, and guessed Harry probably wasn't either. What he needed was a weapon to tilt the playing field in his favour.

As he passed the spare bedroom there was a thump against the door, and Alice cried out her husband's name. Michael skidded to a halt, torn between finding scissors that he hoped might be in the bathroom cabinet, and preventing Harry from releasing Alice: two against one, he could do without.

Harry had seen his opportunity and made for the bedroom, forcing Michael to abandon his quest and run back along the landing. He took Harry by surprise, thudding into him before he could turn the key. Harry stumbled into a bookcase, trying to shove Michael away, and the two men fell to the floor in a tangle of limbs, punching and clawing, knees and feet working to gain traction on the carpet.

All Michael could think about was a weapon. He managed to land a few blows to Harry's face and then break free, throwing himself forward, towards the stairs. He crawled a couple of feet before Harry landed on him, the impact forcing the air from his lungs. Harry grabbed at his hair, his neck. In a fury, Michael opened his mouth and clamped down on Harry's fingers, catching two of them between his teeth and biting hard enough to draw blood.

Harry gave a cry of pain. In response Alice started shrieking, kicking and battering at the door. Michael spat blood from his mouth as he rolled and kicked his way along the landing. Reaching the top of the stairs, he was able to drag himself forward, but Harry wouldn't let go, clutching at his shirt, now on top of him again, ignoring every kick, every blow, trying to wrestle him into submission.

With one last great effort, Michael got up on his knees and lurched forward, Harry now clinging to him like some hideous parasite. He must have realised what was going to happen – but the same could have been said for Michael.

For just a fraction of a second both men were stationary, perfectly balanced on the lip of the stairs, and then in an ungainly tangle they slithered and bumped and rolled down the stairs, taking out some of the spindles in the process and landing in a heap at the bottom.

Harry knew you could die from a fall down the stairs. He also understood that this man wanted him dead.

As he fell he could still hear Alice calling his name, and he clung to the sense of joy and relief that she was alive. It helped slightly to lessen the pain from practically every muscle, every limb, and the intense throbbing from the bite wound on his fingers.

The blood on his hand hampered his ability to grab hold of anything that could slow his descent. Maybe that was the reason Harry came off worse, or maybe it was just bad luck. But on the third step from the bottom his body slid almost sideways, his head struck the newel post and he blacked out.

*

At first Michael didn't realise what had happened. He was lying with half his body beneath Harry. He too was dazed and in pain: raw agony in the case of his right ankle. But that was forgotten when he wriggled an inch or two and saw that Harry remained motionless.

Michael eased his body free and managed to right himself. His head spun as he climbed to his feet; another bolt of white-hot pain when he set his right foot down. Barely able to put any pressure on that leg, he hobbled towards the kitchen, glancing back when he heard Harry let out a weak groan.

Still alive, then. But in no state to offer resistance.

A new sound penetrated Michael's consciousness as he reached the kitchen, but it wasn't one he could comprehend right now. The survival instinct took precedence, and Harry fucking French was the one major threat to that survival.

The kitchen offered units and a table to help bear his weight. He reached the cutlery drawer, picked up a knife with a wide serrated blade and staggered back as fast as his busted ankle would allow.

In his mind it all slotted easily into place: kill this intruder, stash the body in the garage for Nerys to deal with later. Then some thoroughly-deserved R&R with Alice.

All perfectly straightforward. Just forget the sound that didn't fit in. Forget the fact that when he returned to the hall, Harry was on his hands and knees, coughing and retching. Another second or two and the fucker would be back in the fight.

For a moment Harry didn't know where he was or why he hurt so badly. All he knew was that something terrible had happened

– *was happening* – and that he needed to be alert and capable of defending himself.

Easier said than done. A wave of nausea assaulted him as he tried to get up. The temptation to collapse back to the floor was overwhelming; how wonderful if he could just close his eyes and lie still …

Then he heard harsh breathing; glanced up and saw the man who'd attacked him, limping badly but coming in fast, a knife in his hand.

Harry couldn't move far but he managed to straighten up, raising an arm to protect his face and leaning back to avoid the path of the blade. Still the knife caught him on the forearm and he felt it go deep. Having lunged while off-balance, his attacker stumbled and Harry saw his chance. His other hand whipped out and caught the man's wrist, squeezing and twisting until the knife fell from his grasp. Then he drove his right fist into the man's groin, dimly aware of blood pulsing from the slash wound on his arm.

He was on his feet, raining several more blows and forcing his opponent to retreat. The man's ankle gave way and he fell, Harry going with him, sitting on his chest and pinning him to the floor. The knife was only a few inches away and he scooped it up. Someone knocked on the front door but Harry didn't pause, raising the knife in his right hand. This was kill or be killed, and that was what he had to do—

More thumping on the front door. A woman's voice called out: 'Nerys? Michael?' The letterbox clattered open, tiny hands reaching inside, and a child shouted: 'Nanny! It's us!'

Harry froze, the knife poised over the man's chest, blood dripping from his elbow. This man was Michael, he realised. And outside was Michael's wife, his daughter.

He looked down at the stricken face and knew he couldn't go through with it. No matter how ferocious his rage. No matter what Michael had done to Alice or Evie.

He couldn't take a man's life when his family were just a few yards away.

Michael didn't move as Harry lifted himself up and crossed the hall. He was aware that he'd had a lucky escape, but didn't fully understand what had happened. The intensity of the fight had caused a kind of static in his brain: only now were his senses returning to normal.

He could hear the girls calling for their grandmother. Harry reached the door, the knife in his hand. Michael felt a jolt of alarm until he saw Harry pause, then hide the knife on top of the coat rack. He opened the door and stepped back, turning away as if concerned that the sight of him was going to be a shock.

And it was. Robyn gaped at Harry for a second, then spotted Michael on the floor. By then Betty had bowled inside, failing to register that the door had been opened by a stranger. She skidded to a halt when she took in the state of her dad, and the blood splashed everywhere. Upstairs, Alice was shouting and kicking the door.

'Betty!' Robyn had gone white, tottering on the step with Junior in her arms.

Harry retreated from her, palms up. It might have been a calming gesture, if not for the blood streaming down his arm.

'Daddy?' Standing beside her mother, Chloe was equally pale. The shock caused her to let go of the tureen in her hands. It crashed to the ground in an explosion of porcelain and a cascade of vegetable soup. As Michael struggled to his knees and reached out for Betty's hand, her pretty five-year-old face crumpled with sorrow and she threw herself into his embrace. He held her tight, as any father would, but he knew that this was the moment he had lost them all.

SIXTY-NINE

Nerys felt aggrieved with the whole world, her mood so bleak that even the pleasure of driving her son's new Range Rover did little to alleviate it.

Why was it that no matter how clever or devious you were, no matter how well prepared, things only ever went about ninety per cent right? She'd been around long enough to know this, of course, but that didn't make it any easier to bear. Because here and now, that ten per cent bad luck had the potential to ruin everything.

Whenever the traffic allowed, she pushed the Range Rover up to sixty or seventy on the A40, as fast as she dared without attracting attention. In a dim corner of her mind lurked the possibility that another motorist would carelessly turn across her path and take Nerys's fate out of her hands. But she wasn't by nature a negative woman, so she kept such thoughts at bay and took extra care to anticipate the actions of other drivers.

She passed beneath the last echoes of the rain storm and the sky began to clear, the clouds separating as if clawed apart by invisible hands. West of Gloucester the landscape changed, became greener, wilder; most of all, steeper. Cresting one summit, a glimpse of gorgeous peachy light made her sigh. It was going to be one of those drab, miserable days that ended with a glorious sunset – turning nice when it was too late to enjoy it – and that just about summed up Nerys's luck at the moment. Even the weather was taking the piss.

*

She was at Symonds Yat by three fifteen. The holiday home
had been in her ex-husband's family for years, so she had a few
memories of summer weekends she'd spent there when Michael
was a child. A couple of those memories were happy ones, but
most were not.

To reach the property she had to negotiate a number of narrow
roads on the southern bank of the river, and inevitably she became
snarled up in traffic, backed up behind some stupid out-of-season
caravan. The lack of motion disturbed Evie, who until then had
been sound asleep in little Mikey's car seat. Nerys sang lullabies
to her, and soon she was sleeping again.

The final approach took her up a steep winding road for nearly
a mile, close to the Symonds Yat rock. The house sat on an acre
of land, most of it covered in trees, but the front garden had been
cleared to allow magnificent views of the meandering river valley.

Nerys pulled up at the gates and at first couldn't find the manual
release. They were supposed to operate electrically, but Michael
hadn't got the keyfob on him. Another bad omen, if you wanted
to be swayed by such things. Nerys told herself she wouldn't.

Finally the gate was open. After driving through, she decided to
close it behind her. She wanted her visitors coming in as slowly as
possible, giving her time to assess what kind of a threat they posed.

No more than three of you, she had stipulated to Vickery. *Turn
up mob-handed and I'll call it off.*

Unknown to them, there was another way out of the property,
along a narrow unmade track that ran between the trees and
rejoined the road almost half a mile on. Nerys eased the Range
Rover past the garage, round to the rear of the house, and parked

it out of sight next to a long low outbuilding, which Ronald had at one stage turned into an art studio for some ludicrous bimbo of a girlfriend.

Her plan was to wait in one of the bedrooms, armed with the binoculars she'd thought to bring with her. From there she could safely monitor their arrival. If anything gave her cause for concern she would be in the car and out the back way before they'd made it up the drive.

She'd told them four thirty, so she still had about an hour. The house was in darkness, except for a single light downstairs, kept on for security purposes. Once she was inside she'd make a restorative cup of tea – plenty of sugar – then let Michael know she'd arrived safely.

She lifted Evie out of the car seat and picked up the bag which contained nappies, spare clothes and some formula milk. She had to walk round to the front, because the keys were in a lockbox fixed to the outer wall.

The air here felt cool, with the fresh wintery tang of pine trees. The sky had the pale, glassy sheen of mid-afternoon, hastening towards dusk. A few birds sang in the trees, but apart from that and the distant hum of traffic it was quiet here. A peaceful scene.

So why did she feel so jittery?

Maybe because it felt like trespassing, she told herself as she found the lockbox. This had always been Ronald's place. She had never much liked it, never felt truly comfortable here.

Evie had woken again. She squalled until Nerys had retrieved the keys and straightened up. The front door had two locks, and it was a struggle to open them while simultaneously joggling the baby up and down.

With the door open, Nerys pushed it with her foot and picked up the bag of baby stuff. She stepped inside and peered into the gloom, searching for the light switch and wondering why the alarm hadn't started to beep. According to Michael she had twenty seconds to enter the five-digit code. Why wasn't it—

A shadow moved behind the door and took on solid form: a man in dark clothing, with a gun in his hand. She saw him and tried to retreat but someone else had come out of the living room and looped a rope around her neck, choking her as he yanked her backwards. A third assailant – a woman – moved alongside and wrestled the baby from her grasp. Only a few seconds after unlocking the door and already her plans were in tatters, her escape route redundant, her hopes of success crushed to a bitter paste.

That damn ten per cent, she thought. *Gets you every fucking time.*

SEVENTY

At first nobody moved or said a word. The only sound was the sobbing of the two young girls. The baby stared at them in astonishment, then decided to join in.

Harry kept his eye on Michael as he edged backwards, looking for something to help stem the bleeding. The bite wounds on his fingers weren't as bad as he'd feared, but the cut on his forearm was too deep to ignore.

Michael was still hugging one of his daughters, while staring at his wife with an expression of abject sorrow – or perhaps it was self-pity. The bizarre tableau was broken by a loud pounding from upstairs; Alice screamed his name and the woman in the doorway gave a start.

'Who's that?' she demanded of Michael.

It was Harry who answered. 'My wife.'

He snatched a fleece from the coat rack and clumsily wrapped it around his arm, squeezing the wound as tight as he could. He hurried upstairs, calling out: 'It's me, Alice. I'm okay.'

He found the key on the floor and unlocked the bedroom door. Alice had stood back as it opened. When he saw her, Harry's first reaction was to embrace her but Alice reacted oddly, immediately turning her back on him, as if ashamed of her nakedness. Then he saw that her hands were tied at the wrists.

'They've taken Evie,' she said as he untied her. 'That bitch Nerys has Evie.'

'I know,' Harry said, then realised he would have to explain. But first, just for a moment, he wanted to hold her.

To his great relief, she allowed him to take her in his arms. She'd had a nosebleed, and there were abrasions on her face, but otherwise she seemed unharmed.

'Did he … ? Has he hurt you?'

'Not like that,' Alice said. Then, as they broke apart, she said, 'Where is Michael? Did you kill him?'

Despite everything, Harry was a little shocked by the vehemence of her tone.

'No, I didn't. But you're safe. It—'

'Oh my God, what happened to your arm?'

Now she was further back, Alice had noticed blood seeping through the material he'd wrapped around the wound.

'Michael did that?' she asked as she pulled on the dressing gown. 'We mustn't let him get away.'

'He won't,' Harry said. 'His wife's here.'

She inspected his arm and told him it needed to be dressed properly. He didn't protest as she hurried him along the landing. Halfway down the stairs she caught sight of Michael being comforted by two young girls. A woman stood nearby, glaring at him.

Hearing them come down, the woman turned. Alice spotted the baby in her arms and let out a yelp of shock, even as she registered that it wasn't Evie. For a moment it felt like a cruel trick had been played on her. This was Michael's youngest child.

'You're Robyn?' she asked.

The woman looked disgusted; from the way she glanced at the dressing gown, Alice wondered if she thought this was some kind of sleazy affair that had culminated in a violent dispute.

In her fury, Alice forgot about the presence of young children and shouted, 'Your husband's a murderer!'

Michael tried to bluster: 'This is all lies. Seriously, you mustn't believe anything she—'

'No,' his wife snapped. 'I want to hear it.'

A strange, artificial calm descended on the house, all four adults suddenly aware of the need to project a more reassuring air for the sake of the children. But Harry was determined that this wouldn't prevent him from getting the answers he wanted.

He and Alice kept up the pressure to move swiftly. Within the space of a couple of minutes, Michael's daughters had been packed off to the lounge to watch TV and eat sweets. They were also entrusted, for a short time, with their baby brother.

Robyn shepherded her limping husband in the direction of the kitchen, only for him to swerve towards a small sitting room, where he collapsed into an armchair. Harry perched on the arm of a sofa, while Robyn fetched a first aid kit and helped Alice clean and dress the wound on his arm.

As the two men glowered at each other, Alice set out what had happened over the past twenty-four hours. She described how Renshaw had left her in a nearby wood, returning to the house to talk to Nerys.

'That's when I found out he didn't really trust her. And he was even more worried about you.'

She indicated Michael, who shook his head irritably. He couldn't look Robyn in the eye.

'He didn't come back at the time he'd agreed. Then I was caught by Michael and his mother. They brought me back here, and I saw Renshaw's body in the kitchen. They'd ... butchered him.'

Robyn was stunned. 'Is this true?'

Michael, misty-eyed, was still shaking his head. 'It was Mum. She just went berserk. Honestly. I didn't have a chance to stop her.'

'Now she's taken our daughter.' Alice held Robyn's gaze, making sure that every word sunk in. 'Evie is eight weeks old, and Nerys intends to use her as a bargaining chip in a deal with this man Laird.'

Harry, at this point, decided not to add what he knew. He turned his attention to Michael.

'Call your mother. Get her back here, right now.'

Michael exchanged a glance with Robyn, then found his phone and dialled. In the silence, they all heard a recorded voice informing him that the call could not be connected.

'I don't know what's happened.' Michael checked his watch. 'Perhaps she's stuck in traffic.'

Harry sighed. 'The address, then? Tell me where she's going.'

'It's not that simple,' Michael began. He seemed to be rapidly gaining in confidence, and Harry guessed why that might be.

'Listen, you might think you can talk your way out of this. Just because we haven't called the police doesn't mean you're in any less trouble. If you don't tell me where she is, I intend to change your mind by force. And then *I'll* call the police.'

Alice nodded, standing beside Harry with her arm around his shoulders.

'You've cleaned it up, but I bet you weren't thorough enough. The blood was everywhere.'

Catching what might have been doubt in Robyn's eyes, Alice said, 'You need to know that your husband was getting ready to rape me. He made me take a shower, then tied me to a radiator in the bedroom. He told me that the danger I was in ought to be a turn-on.'

Robyn flinched. She wouldn't look at Michael when he whispered: 'It's not true. Her clothes were soaked from the rain, that's all.'

'Tell them where they can find their little girl.'

'But, darling, they're lying—'

Robyn took a step forward and slapped his face so hard that his lip started bleeding. Harry moved closer, in case Michael tried to retaliate.

'God knows, all the times you've pushed your luck. But this …' Robyn threw up her hands and Michael recoiled, anticipating another blow.

'When I think of the sacrifices I made for you. The nights when I knew you were screwing someone else while I cried myself to sleep. Four children I gave you. Four children, three miscarriages and God knows how many times I turned a blind eye to your cheating … well, it ends right now. It ends with you paying for what you've done. You and that witch of a mother I've been pretending to like for seventeen years.' She raised her voice: 'Now tell them where their daughter is!'

In defeat, Michael exhaled noisily through his nose. 'Symonds Yat,' he said.

'Our holiday home,' Robyn queried.

'Is that near Ross-on-Wye?' Harry asked.

Michael nodded, then gestured wearily at his wife. 'Get me a pen and paper. It's better if I draw you a map.'

SEVENTY-ONE

Nerys regained consciousness in unfamiliar surroundings, which she belatedly recognised as the holiday home in Symonds Yat. The air had a fusty smell, and the walls were spotted with mould: perhaps her skinflint son wasn't running the heating as often as he should.

She was a lot more reluctant to consider why she was lying in this room, or why she was in so much pain. Someone had hit her, probably more than once, and obviously hard enough to knock her out. She had a bitter, disgusting taste in her mouth: blood and bile.

And she was not alone. This took her a minute or two to comprehend. The man in the corner was an old colleague of sorts; not one whose company she'd ever relished.

'Darrell … Bridge?' Her voice sounded harsh, strained. Everything hurt.

The man grunted, shifting position a little closer to the window. She could see angry red sores covering almost half of his face.

'Been in the wars,' she said.

He grunted again. 'You? Or me?'

The door opened and Mark Vickery joined them. His hair was a shade darker than the last time she'd seen him, but otherwise he seemed unchanged: as smooth and over-groomed as ever.

Without preamble, he snarled at Nerys: 'Renshaw's dead.'

Nerys moistened her lips before she spoke. 'No choice.'

'You delivered us a corpse. Since when was that the deal?'

She tried a shrug. No bones broken, she decided, though she felt like she'd been run through a mangle.

'On the run from you, wasn't he? I found him, brought him here.'

'Yes. But it wasn't just Renshaw we were after.'

'Who, then?'

Vickery scowled. 'Don't be obtuse, Nerys. Not who but *what*.'

'You got the money. It's all there, I hope, because—'

Because he left it with the woman, Nerys had been about to say, till she clammed up just in time.

Thinking about Alice reminded Nerys of the baby. She'd had it when she came here, but they had taken it from her. She considered asking after its welfare, then decided not to bother. Truth be told, at this stage she didn't give a toss about the baby.

Vickery was still waiting. 'Because?'

'I mean, I don't want you assuming I helped myself. I wouldn't do that, Mark.'

'Of course you wouldn't. So who's been helping you?'

'No one.' She winced, pretending it was the pain rather than the speed of her answer. Too fast, when until then she'd been faking a bit of confusion.

'You bashed Renshaw's brains in on your own? Trussed him up and tossed him in the Range Rover all by yourself? Nice car, by the way.'

'Mmm.'

'Registered to MBB Imports Ltd. That would be the business owned by your son, Michael?'

'He … I mean, I borrowed the car. He doesn't know anything about this.'

'I beg to differ, Nerys. There's a conspiracy here, involving three of you, at least. You got greedy, that's clear enough. What did you think, that we'd overlook the data just because you delivered a body and a bag of cash?'

'D-data?'

'It's what we want, Nerys. More than Renshaw. More than the money. It's what we're going to kill you to retrieve. But before we kill you we'll wring out every last thing you can tell us.'

'I don't know about any data. I promise you, Mark. What's that mean, anyway – data?'

'Information, Nerys. A client list, loaded on to one of those little flash drives. Ringing any bells?'

Nerys shook her head, wildly, sending little gobbets of snot flying across the room. She knew how badly she'd misjudged things. There was no point claiming to have the evidence, or to know where it was. All she wanted now was to protect her son, her grandchildren.

'Well, no matter,' Vickery said cheerfully. 'Obtaining the truth is the job of Darrell here, with your old friend Mr Foster to supervise. Darrell's no friend of Renshaw, as it happens. Got a nasty burn thanks to the bad doctor. But since he can't make Renshaw pay for the pain he's endured, he'll have to settle for taking it out on you instead.'

'Mark, please. I came here in good faith, you can see I did …'

'We need the client list. Tell us where we can find it, and everything's hunky dory.'

'I don't have it. I'll say it till I'm blue in the face—'

'Why are we here, Nerys?'

The question threw her. 'You know why.'

'I mean this precise location.' Vickery sniffed, gave the room a disparaging glance. 'Owned by the business, is it?' He smiled. 'We haven't tracked down the paperwork yet, but we will. You can save us the bother by telling me your home address, and who you're working with.'

Nerys thought about it, then set her expression to one of resolute determination.

'I can't do that.'

'It'll save you a lot of pain.'

'My home's private. But not because I've something to hide. I haven't. I'm telling you, on my word of honour. Yes, I searched Renshaw. I searched his car, his clothes, and I found nothing. If I had, I'd be offering it to you now, wouldn't I?'

'You've left it with someone. Your accomplice.'

'No. I haven't … I mean, there isn't anyone else. It's just me.'

'Final answer?'

'Final answer, I swear to you.'

With a sigh, Vickery turned to Darrell, who was slouching like a teenager outside the headmaster's office.

'Niall all set?'

'Should be.'

'Good.' Vickery brushed imaginary dust from his palms. 'Go to work on her.'

SEVENTY-TWO

Alice quickly got dressed, the urgency of Evie's absence like a humming in her brain, an oppressive vibration that kept every nerve on edge. Her fears for her daughter were so intense that she couldn't properly dwell on them for more than a second or two at a time.

Back in the sitting room, Michael was explaining the layout of the rough map he'd drawn. Harry wanted to know how far away they were.

'It's usually about an hour, depending on the traffic,' Robyn told him.

'Or how you drive,' Michael muttered. He checked his phone again. 'Still nothing from Mum. I texted her, like you asked.'

Robyn chipped in: 'The reception's not great out there, to be honest.'

'What about a landline?' Alice asked, but Harry vetoed the idea.

'If Laird is already there, we don't want him forewarned. It's too risky.'

That sounded slightly lame to Alice's ears, and it solidified the doubts she'd been harbouring for the past few minutes.

There was something Harry wasn't telling her.

The suspicion evident on Alice's face hurt all the more because Harry knew he was about to make it worse.

He snatched up the map and said, 'I need to make a call. Are you okay to wait here a minute?'

He didn't like leaving Alice alone with Michael and Robyn, but when she gave her assent he shut the door behind him and called Ruth. It took her a moment to answer, and there was road noise in the background. She was still driving.

'Harry? You okay?'

'Yes, I'm good. Alice is here, and she's all right.' He gave her a brief précis of events, then told her the address of the holiday home and described the layout of the property as Michael had detailed it.

'That's great, Harry. Helps me a lot.'

'Where are you?'

'A couple of miles out from Ross-on-Wye. Probably twenty minutes or so to Symonds Yat.'

'Oh.' He realised he was expecting a miracle: he wanted her there right now. He wanted confirmation that Evie was safe.

'I know what you're thinking, Harry. Call the cops and they might get there sooner. But Laird's men will have guns, so you'd be sending unarmed police to their deaths. You'd have to warn them, and it'll take longer than twenty minutes to put together a full armed response. And then you've got all the risks of a shoot-out, with Evie being caught in the crossfire.'

'So what, then? What are you going to do?'

'They don't realise that I know the address. That gives me a big advantage. My plan is to sneak in, and if I can get to Evie I will. If I can't, I'll get back out and call the police myself.'

'And you promise that? You promise Evie comes first, no matter what?'

'I promise, Harry.'

Harry wavered, remembering how often he'd been given reason to doubt her word.

'Don't let me down,' he said, and ended the call.

Harry returned looking so exhausted, so profoundly anxious that a little of Alice's remaining hope for her daughter drained away.

'We need to go there now,' he said. 'That means borrowing a car.'

'Here.' Robyn produced a set of keys from her jacket and handed them over.

'Another thing,' Harry said. 'I need you to make sure your husband doesn't warn anyone that we're coming.'

'That's all very well,' Michael complained, 'but what about my mother?'

'She takes her chances,' Harry said.

It was clear that Robyn agreed. She thrust her hand out: 'Phone.'

Scowling, Michael surrendered it to her. As she turned away he tried to stand up. His foot wouldn't bear his weight and he cried out, sinking back into the chair.

'I think my ankle's broken. It needs X-raying.'

'Later,' Robyn said, as blunt with him as Harry had been.

In the hall there were sounds of distress coming from the other living room. Robyn hurried out and returned with her infant son. The sight of him was too much for Alice. She crossed her arms over her breasts, aware of how much they ached. With tears in her eyes, she said, 'Imagine hearing your baby crying, needing you, and you can't go to him because someone's stopping you.'

To her credit, Robyn didn't look away. She asked quietly: 'When you've got your daughter, are you coming back here?'

Alice shrugged, though she understood what Robyn was getting at.

'I don't know. But I think the police will have to be involved at some stage.'

Robyn was silent for a long moment. Then she nodded. 'Yes.'

'I'm sorry,' Alice said. 'I can see how difficult this must be, when you have so much to lose.' She reached out and grasped Robyn's hand. 'I wasn't exaggerating earlier. I really believe he would have raped me.'

Robyn seemed about to speak, then changed her mind. She nodded again.

Harry waited at the door while Alice and Robyn talked quietly. Only a few seconds, but it felt like far too long. He was boiling with frustration, and let some of it out as Alice joined him and they left the house.

'I should have bloody killed him. He's not getting away with this.'

'He won't. But finding Evie is more important.'

Harry unlocked Robyn's car, which turned out to be a brand new Range Rover. Her husband had an identical one, according to Alice.

'His and hers Rangeys,' she muttered ruefully.

'Can we trust Robyn, do you think?' Harry asked as they climbed in.

'I think so. As much as you can trust anyone.'

He frowned. Her tone was decidedly cold.

'Meaning?'

'You're hiding something. It's about Evie, isn't it? Or that woman who was with you?'

'Actually, it's both.' He started the engine and pulled away, tentative at first, unsure if the big 4x4 would handle differently to the cars he was used to driving. There was a pulse of pain from his arm as he turned the wheel, but he decided it wasn't bad enough to hamper him.

As well as concentrating on the road, he also had to sketch out Ruth's background and the reasons for her involvement, as well as explaining why he'd agreed to let Ruth go to Symonds Yat without notifying the police. Alice didn't react quite as fiercely as he'd expected, but nor did she hold back on her scorn.

'It sounds like Laird has been a step ahead of Ruth the whole time, and yet you still seem to put more faith in her than you do in the police.'

'It's not a straightforward decision. I think Ruth will do her best for us. And she's made a valid point about the risks of a standoff. Do you want to be watching behind a barricade as armed police storm the house with our daughter inside?'

A violent shudder from Alice told him the answer was no. A moment later he felt her hand on his leg, the weight of it warm and comforting.

'There's nothing we can do but hurry,' he said sadly, 'and pray it works out all right.'

Michael was resting back in his chair, eyes shut, when he heard the front door close. All things considered, he felt pretty good. His ankle was hurting, but not as badly as he'd made out. He thought it was probably a nasty sprain; not a fracture.

He'd nearly had a heart attack when Harry turned up like the proverbial white knight. Another when his own wife and kids appeared – although, as it turned out, they'd performed essentially the same function for Michael, saving him from death or jail.

It was what he'd needed, he told himself now. He had been foolish, even reckless, allowing Nerys to pull him off course. Now Robyn was here to set him on the right path once more.

Best of all, there was no sign that the police would become involved. Harry and Alice appeared to have their own reasons to go it alone, which suited him fine. He allowed himself to mull over the possibility that all his problems would be solved by some bloody confrontation at the holiday home. Was it asking too much that the whole lot of them could end up dead? Harry, Alice, Nathan Laird ... and even his own mother.

If that happened, and the police rolled up at Symonds Yat to find a bunch of bodies – including Renshaw's – there was every chance that Michael could plausibly deny all knowledge and get away with it. So what if his mum had borrowed his car? He'd had no inkling that she was caught up in something unsavoury.

In fact, Officer, I spent the entire day with my darling wife, Robyn, as she'll be only too happy to confirm ...

He'd better get the house cleaned a lot more thoroughly, just in case. Robyn could help there, he thought. So could the kids, for that matter.

He pictured his daughters in Mrs Mop overalls and headscarves, scrubbing the kitchen floor. A laugh escaped just as Robyn walked in. She had Junior in her arms. The girls were out in the hall, talking to each other with only a fraction of their normal exuberance.

Michael tried to wipe off his smile but it wouldn't quite go; his lips went on twitching. A great burden had been lifted and he felt giddy. Euphoric.

'Have you got my phone?' he asked.

'You're not having it.'

'I just want to check—' He broke off, his wife's face made almost unrecognisable by the depth of loathing in her expression. 'But-but ... all that stuff you said, it was just for show, wasn't it?'

'No.'

'Oh, come on.' He laughed again, derisively, and started to get up.

'*Stay there!*' she hissed.

'Darling …' he began, switching to a placatory manner, because Robyn had turned and was ushering the girls in to join them.

In a bright, lively voice, she said, 'Sit with Daddy, will you, girls? He's feeling poorly, and needs to keep very still.'

Then, unseen by the children, another venomous glare at Michael as Chloe and Betty clambered on to his lap.

'And make the most of it,' she added. 'Daddy might have to go away soon.'

SEVENTY-THREE

After speaking to Harry, Ruth stopped briefly to check her map. Laird had instructed her to go to Ross-on-Wye. Guessing that someone would be posted on the A40 to watch for her approach, she took a succession of minor roads instead.

She felt remarkably calm about the prospect of finally meeting Nathan – perhaps because deep down she suspected it wouldn't happen. The fact that he'd made the phone call didn't guarantee his presence.

On the other hand, if Harry was right about it being a trap – and she thought he was – it seemed likely that Nathan would be there to revel in his victory.

It was almost four p.m. when she spotted the turning for the house. She drove past, noting that the landscape around her was densely wooded, with only a handful of properties dotted over the hillside. A bit further on she found the track Harry had mentioned and parked out of sight of the road.

This morning, after Vickery had made a deal and given her car back, Ruth had fully expected it to have been searched. But if it had, they'd missed the compartment for the spare wheel where she had concealed her little box of tricks, which included a length of nylon yacht rope and a folding sheath knife with a four-inch blade.

Retrieving them now, she set off through the trees towards the holiday home. It was cold and dark up here, although the sky overhead held perhaps another thirty minutes of twilight. Once she broke from the cover of the trees she would be fairly easy to spot. Which meant taking things slowly.

That would be fine, if this was only about confronting Laird. But there was also Evie to consider.

She reflected on that pledge to Harry. Hadn't she known from the start that it was a promise she would struggle to keep?

For Nerys, it felt like a lot of time passed very quickly. Or maybe it was a short time that passed very slowly.

Or it was both. Or neither. Nothing made sense any more.

She was trying so hard to hold it together, when really she ought to just let go. That was the answer. Let go.

She could deal with the pain, just about, but not the fury. The fury that everything had gone so very wrong – and it wasn't over yet. There was more to come.

Some of her fingers had been broken, and now they were on fire: burning, yet cold. She was shivering, even while the sweat burst out on her forehead and rolled down her temples.

She was in the dining room with Niall Foster and Darrell Bridge. They had placed her on the table, stacking the chairs in the corner to give them more space. The way they worked, quietly industrious, reminded her of tradesmen she'd employed over the years. Plumbers, electricians, joiners. At one point Darrell had actually whistled, though that might have been to block out the shrieking from their victim.

Eventually the door opened. Vickery was back.

'Still nothing?'

From Foster's grunt, you might have thought his expertise was being called into question.

Vickery came as close to Nerys as he dared. 'Tough old bird,' he said.

'Too right I am,' she gasped, almost choking on the blood in her throat. 'And you … don't even have the guts to watch, do you?'

'Tell us where it is, Nerys. Then you can rest.'

'Wanker! Wish they'd let me take you on.' She caught Foster smirking and addressed him: 'Pay good money to see, to see that, eh? Me against this … this little prick.'

Foster didn't react but Nerys laughed anyway, and coughed up a lot of blood. Bristling at the insult, Vickery went away.

So did Nerys, in a manner of speaking, and when she came back someone else had joined them.

She wasn't completely certain it was Nathan Laird. But the voice sounded familiar, and the expensive aftershave was true to form.

He crouched very close and whispered in her ear, apologising for what she'd been through, expressing such tender concern for her wellbeing that tears trickled down her cheeks.

'I st-stayed loyal,' she told him, more than once. It was vital that he understood. 'Could've sold you out, but I never … never did.'

'I know.'

'Some of those little 'uns were … were heading off to good homes, parents who'd love them. But some weren't. And I—' A spasm of pain. 'I kept my mouth shut, either way.'

'That's true. You did.'

Her body jerked as he touched her. He started stroking his hand through her hair; gently finger-combing. It felt so extraordinary that she managed to relax; for a moment the agony was forgotten, set aside. This could have been her son, tending to her wounds.

'L-like that girl, as well. Marisha, was it? I did … all I could to save her. Even in hospital she probably wouldn't … wouldn't have made it.'

'That's a fair point.'

'Still, I guessed you'd keep something … to hold over me. Wouldn't blame you, Mr Laird. But when all this happened, Renshaw turning up … I saw a chance to get things clear. That's all … all I want, you see. A clean slate.'

'Don't worry, Nerys. The slate is almost clean.'

'And the baby – I mean … that's an extra. From me to you. G-goodwill.'

'It's much appreciated. But now you must tell me where you were hiding Renshaw, so we don't have to punish your grandchildren.'

'My … ?' Her eyes opened briefly.

'Michael and Robyn's children. I expect it was Michael who lent a hand? We have his address now. We can go there instead, if you'd prefer? Talk to Michael, and Robyn. And the children.'

'No.'

After she'd given up her own address, she heard him issuing instructions to Foster and Bridge. Nerys wanted to interrupt, to say how important it was that no harm came to Michael or the children, but speech had become impossible.

There was a feeling of pressure on her throat that wouldn't clear. She opened her eyes again and found Laird's upper body looming over her. His forearm was resting on her throat and he was pushing down, harder and harder until black stars exploded in her eyes, and the world with Michael and her beloved grandchildren and everyone else in it began to slip away.

SEVENTY-FOUR

Ruth moved cautiously through the trees, grateful that the earlier rainfall had softened the leaves and made them quieter underfoot. After ascending a steep ridge she came to a perimeter fence comprised of posts and railings, topped with barbed wire. She used a fallen branch to press the barbed wire low enough to climb over, then slowly advanced.

As the trees thinned out, she could see the edge of a lawn, about sixty yards away. Then the house came into view. It was a substantial white stucco and grey-slate building, with a garage on the side nearest to Ruth and some kind of annexe behind the garage. A Range Rover was parked between the two buildings.

The main gardens lay beyond the annexe, and ran right out to the edge of the gorge itself. More trees enveloped the steep slopes, which dropped to the river valley hundreds of feet below.

She moved on a little further, then stopped. Now she could see the outline of another structure, possibly a summer house, screened by shrubbery on the far side of the lawn. She thought she spotted a silhouetted figure moving out of sight at the front of the structure. It was gone before her eyes could register what they had seen, leaving Ruth to wonder if she had imagined it.

She paused, taking a moment to steady herself while she assessed her options. She could hear leaves rustling gently around her, as

well as the distant, almost subliminal rush of the river. An owl
hooted suddenly, not too far away, and it seemed to Ruth like a
call to arms.

There were plenty of lights on in the house, but all the windows
were covered by curtains and blinds. From this position Ruth couldn't
see how many vehicles were parked out front, so she edged away to
her right, tracking parallel to the side of the house. Here the trees
gave way to a small area of cultivated plants and bushes. Beyond
that was another thin section of grass, and then a wide driveway
that opened out to a parking area directly in front of the house.

There were two cars here: identical E-class Mercedes, probably
rented from wherever they'd flown in. Ruth felt a little frisson.

She crept out of the trees and crouched down behind a large
hydrangea. There was still too much light in the sky for her
liking: another half hour and it would be much easier to move
without being seen. But it was a bit too long to wait, unless she
was willing to disregard her commitment to Harry.

Noises at the house caught her attention. The clunk of a door
opening; low muttering voices. Two men hurried out and made
for one of the Mercedes. She recognised them both: Niall Foster
and Darrell Bridge. Bridge had what looked like a port wine
birthmark on his face, which puzzled Ruth until she remembered
the booby trap in Renshaw's kitchen.

She smiled grimly. Bridge was a man who deserved to suffer.

Their urgent departure was a puzzle, but one Ruth welcomed.
The odds against her had just improved a little.

She waited till the car's engine had faded completely, studying
the house the whole time. Half a dozen windows, four of them with
faint illumination behind the curtains. No movement anywhere.

A glance upwards. The sky was the rich blue shade of the ink she'd used in her fountain pen at school. For a second she was transported back to that era: for a second she could remember what it was to be wholly innocent and innocently brave, untainted by life and experience.

This moment, she understood, was the last point at which she could change her mind, turn away, retreat.

She thought about what – or who – might await her, inside the house. Vickery, and at least one or two others. She thought about Evie, too, and the responsibility she had assumed on Harry's behalf.

But mostly she thought about Benjamin, and the way that losing her son had hollowed her out, leaving a great black hole in her consciousness.

She rose slowly, took one last look around, then sprinted to the entrance, stepping lightly from grass to the stone paving that led up to a small open porch. An old pair of boots and a broken umbrella had been left to the mercy of the elements.

The front door was as sturdy and well-protected as Ruth would expect of a holiday home in a remote location. There was no way she could break in without making a lot of noise.

She put her head to the door and listened carefully, but heard nothing inside. Keeping low, ducking beneath a couple of windows, she crept to the far side and listened again, then risked a quick look round the corner. A path ran beside the house, bordered by bushes and a few thin trees. There were soil and water pipes fixed to the wall, suggesting that the bathroom and kitchen were on this side.

Better still, about halfway along she could see a doorway, and a vertical sliver of timber that might be the edge of a door, suggesting it was open.

Ruth was about to investigate it when her senses picked up a threat from somewhere. She moved back out of sight. Moments later she heard the soft thud of footsteps on grass. Someone was approaching the house, possibly from the summer house in the garden.

A louder tapping sound as the shoes hit the path for several paces, and then stopped. She waited to hear a door open or close, but nothing happened.

She counted off five seconds, then decided to take a look.

It was Mark Vickery. Fortunately he had his back to her. He was wearing the same shirt and trousers as this morning, with the addition of a grey silk waistcoat. He seemed perfectly relaxed, anticipating no danger as he loitered on the path.

She watched him take a small box from his pocket and consider it for a moment: cigarettes. With a gentle sigh, he flipped it open and upended the box, tapping a cigarette into his palm.

'Can't quite kick the habit?'

Vickery jumped, the box falling from his hand as he spun, completely unprepared, and Ruth landed a savage punch to the side of his neck, just below his left ear. She followed up with a kick to the groin, and then a blow to the temple as he was falling. Vickery went down like a sack of cement.

Wasting no time, she grabbed his feet and dragged him into the bushes. Cut a length of the rope and used it to tie his hands and feet. He was already coming round, trying to speak, so she sliced through his waistcoat, removing a long strip of material to use as a gag.

He stared at her, wide-eyed and struggling to focus. Even with the gag, he was making a lot of noise, whining in his throat.

'Bad idea.' Ruth jabbed the knife at his forehead, opening a small but nasty cut. 'One more squeak and I'll come back and kill you.'

Vickery flinched, squinting at her as if he was only now registering who she was. Evidently he took her threat seriously, for he shut up.

As she'd guessed, the back door was standing open. Ruth scooped up the cigarettes and tossed them into the bushes, then stepped into the house.

The kitchen was a good size, a bit dated, and hadn't seen much use lately – other than today's visitors helping themselves to tea and coffee. A couple of dirty mugs sat on the unit, and there was a sprinkling of sugar on the counter next to a recently boiled kettle.

The kitchen door was open, showing a gloomy hallway. As she moved towards it, the floor creaked beneath her foot. She almost stopped, but knew that would make it worse.

'Mark?' It was a woman's voice: Sian Vickery, Mark's sister.

Knife at the ready, Ruth hurried along the hall and saw four rooms leading off it. Two doors were open and two were shut.

The first doorway revealed a dining room. The body of a plump, dark-haired woman was lying on the table. This must be Renshaw's former colleague, Nerys. Both the table and the floor below it were splattered with blood, but Ruth wasted no time checking to see if the woman was alive.

The other open door led to a lounge at the front of the house. There was a TV playing quietly – a property show – and another sound which Ruth couldn't place at first. Then she realised it was a baby, grizzling in a sort of low-level way, as if too weary to make a proper fuss.

More of the room came into view, but she couldn't see Sian Vickery. She could, however, see the baby, lying on a hard wooden floor in front of a stone hearth. The fire wasn't lit, but still it shocked Ruth: the image it evoked was that of an offering, a gift to placate a higher power.

What she did next was foolish in the extreme. Obeying some long-dormant maternal impulse not to leave an infant where it could come to harm, she strode into the room and had fully cleared the doorway before her other, more primitive instinct reasserted itself.

Trap.

Sian had hidden behind the door. A neat move on her part, but she probably hadn't had time to find a weapon: she would have to hit or claw at Ruth, maybe try to wrestle her to the ground.

With yesterday's humiliating ambush sharp in her mind, Ruth darted to her left and turned side on, raising her right arm across her chest. As Sian blundered towards her, Ruth planted her feet and jabbed her elbow with maximum force, catching Sian on the temple. It was a clean, hard strike that felled the woman like a rotten tree in a storm.

Ruth used more of her rope to bind Sian's hands and feet. The woman remained deeply unconscious, so Ruth put her in the recovery position, in spite of a conviction that such care was more than Sian warranted.

The room had been recently colonised, by the look of it: there were nappies and wet wipes and a bottle of white wine, half empty. It must have got boring, watching the baby while the others tortured their victim in the dining room.

Evie had gone quiet. She was lying still, as if concentrating, alert to the change of circumstances. Ruth smiled. Smart cookie, this little girl. Harry and his wife should be proud.

She knelt at the baby's side, moving slowly so as not to startle her. Whispered a greeting, and then gently eased her hands beneath the tiny body before lifting her and holding her against her chest. It felt alien yet completely natural, a long-neglected but never forgotten ability, like swimming. Like riding a bike.

Mother love.

She carried Evie into the hall and stopped, listening hard. She didn't think there was anyone else in the house. She could leave now, she realised.

She *should* leave now, because she had what she came for. The promise to Harry: she'd find his daughter, and keep her safe.

But.

Ruth remembered that glimpse of a figure by the summer house.

She wasn't going anywhere. Not yet.

SEVENTY-FIVE

Harry had swiftly adjusted to driving the Range Rover, though the higher centre of gravity had nearly caught him out a couple of times. They'd also had a horrible near miss – pulling out to overtake just as a car came out of a junction towards them. Alice had to remind him that dying en route wouldn't help Evie at all.

Forty-five minutes after leaving Cranstone, they were skirting around the village of Coleford, approaching Symonds Yat from the south. Michael's map had indicated that this was a quicker route than the A40 through Ross-on-Wye. Harry hoped that wasn't a lie.

In any case, they still weren't going to get there until about thirty minutes after Ruth. By which point anything might have happened.

He hadn't said as much to Alice – in fact they'd hardly spoken at all – but he knew she was thinking the same thing. Their silence had an intimacy to it; the sense of an almost psychic connection that made him feel closer to her than he had in ages. Of course, this was virtually the first time since the birth that they had been together without Evie. Even when their daughter wasn't in the same room, they would be listening out for her on the baby monitor; fretting over the timing of her next feed, her next change; worrying that the snuffling they could hear meant she was coming down with something … always a thousand tiny anxieties to occupy their minds, and now all those mundane concerns seemed laughably trivial.

Was Evie alive? Would they ever see her again? Those questions, those fears, were so all-consuming that they could not be voiced. The closest either of them came to it was when Alice said, 'I keep trying to picture her, and I can't, somehow. I can't see her face in my mind.'

'That's normal when you're under stress,' he said, though in fact he had no idea what was normal in a situation like this.

Alice put her hands to her cheeks, pressing almost savagely against the skin.

'Those nightmares we talked about on Thursday, they're going to come true. Every bad thing all at once.'

'No, they're not. You can't think like that.'

'Why not? Aren't you thinking that way?'

He sighed. 'Yes, I am. But you have to stop me from being negative, and I have to stop you. That's how we'll get through this. It's our only chance.'

He didn't have to add: *It's Evie's only chance.*

It turned out that the woman in the dining room, Nerys, was still alive. Ruth heard ragged breathing, then a feeble cry.

She entered the room, carrying Evie at her shoulder to spare her the sight of what had been done in here. Nerys saw her, though, eyes focusing weakly then widening with … what? Hope?

This was someone who had offered sanctuary to Renshaw and then betrayed him. A woman who had snatched a baby from its mother and brought it here to sell or bargain with.

Nerys tried to speak, coughing up pinkish bubbles as she managed a few words, none of them clear enough to decipher. Ruth was no expert but she could see that Nerys was in a very bad way. Even with urgent medical treatment she might not make it.

But Ruth couldn't ring 999 now, any more than she could walk out of here and return Evie to her parents.

Did that make her, in her own way, just as bad as Nerys? Ruth deliberated for a second and decided that she didn't care what the answer was.

Nerys tried again, her hand beckoning Ruth closer, but Ruth didn't move.

'My son,' Nerys said. 'Son.'

Ruth guessed it was a plea for help – having extracted some information from her, perhaps Foster and Bridge had been despatched to find the man who had helped his mother.

She regarded Nerys for a few seconds, then shook her head.

'You need to keep very quiet. When this is done I'll bring help if I can. But not now.'

Ruth ignored another weak plea as she left the room. She climbed the stairs, confident that there was no one up here but needing to be absolutely sure.

Her intuition was right. Three bedrooms and a bathroom, all empty, the beds stripped for winter. In the room above the kitchen she walked over to the window and carefully peered out. The summer house lay about thirty feet away, facing across the valley. A light from the front was spilling on to the grass.

She descended the stairs slowly, the baby an encumbrance she could do without. She was outwardly calm, as she knew she had to be, but inside there was a degree of turmoil – quite understandably, she thought. The question was: to what extent could it impair her judgement?

Maybe it already has, she reflected as she stepped out of the back door and walked across the garden, helpless with Evie in her arms. *Maybe it already has.*

SEVENTY-SIX

The summer house was a long low building, clad in timber but not dissimilar in size and shape to the shipping container in which Ruth had spent the previous night. The front section was almost entirely made of glass, with a set of double doors in the middle. It was lit by a single lamp.

The interior was large enough for a sofa and a set of aluminium furniture: four tubular framed chairs and a small round table. Nathan Laird was sitting on one of the chairs, a bottle of Evian on the table in front of him, along with a phone and an iPad.

He was wearing a dark grey suit and a white shirt; no tie. His hair was shorter than he used to wear it; close-cropped and greying at the temples, with a pronounced widow's peak. A few lines and wrinkles that hadn't been there before, made more obvious by a deep tan. But the grey hair offset the tan nicely, so although he was looking his age, he was, if anything, even more handsome than before.

He reacted to her approach as if he had fully expected it. As if he had known that his precautions would fail. He studied Ruth in much the same way that she was studying him. He seemed about to rise to greet her, but settled for lifting the Evian in a kind of toast. His other hand went for the phone, tapping a couple of times as he lifted it to his ear.

Someone answered straight away and he told them: 'Get back here. Now.'

*

Ruth waited in the doorway. 'One to one no good for you, then?'

He absorbed the taunt with a lazy smile, and pointedly didn't ask what had happened to Mark or Sian Vickery.

'Come in. Sit down.'

She accepted only the first invitation, moving to the opposite side of the table and standing behind the chair.

'Where are the others? Warley, is it? And the Scottish one.'

'Keeping watch, north and south. I can call them back as well, but Foster and Bridge are the specialists.' He grinned. 'They won't be long. Five or ten minutes.'

'I know. I saw them leave.'

'Well, you were lucky.' His eyes narrowed as he regarded Evie. 'If it's her you came for, why are you still here?'

'You know why.'

He looked genuinely baffled. 'You'd put your head in the noose for something that happened over a decade ago?' Then another unexpected question: 'Where's your friend?'

'What?' For a mad second she thought of Greg, and felt a rush of grief and guilt. But Laird gestured at the baby.

'This one's dad. The family Renshaw used as a cut-out.'

'Harry? I convinced him that he stood more chance of getting his daughter back if he left me to do it.'

'And where is he now, this trusting father?'

Ruth shrugged. 'Waiting for my call.'

Laird looked sceptical. He leaned towards the seat next to him and picked up the gun he'd been keeping out of sight.

This challenged a lot of Ruth's assumptions. She knew Laird as a man who took the utmost care to avoid incriminating himself.

To see him armed, at the scene of a violent crime, was completely out of character.

'Oh, really?' Ruth thought this a fair effort to sound cool, given the circumstances.

'Unavoidable,' he said. 'These are dangerous times, Ruth.'

The gun was a Glock, semi-automatic and lethal at close range. With the garden furniture between her and the doors, she stood no chance of running.

Laird said, 'Why don't you sit down?'

'I'm okay here.'

'Well, you don't look very comfortable with that baby. Why not hand her over?'

'And then you shoot me?'

The question seemed to induce a sudden cry from Evie. Whatever the reason, it caused Ruth to step back, the baby wriggling and kicking with surprising strength.

Laird tutted. 'Give her to me.'

Ruth wanted to call his bluff, counting on the fact that he wouldn't risk shooting when the baby would almost certainly die in the process. But she had underestimated Nathan's capacity for cruelty on more than one occasion, and she was not about to do it again.

'It's a simple choice, Ruth. Both of you in the firing line, or just you. What's it to be?'

Evie yelped again: Ruth had no idea why. Was she hungry, or wet? Or was she scared? Could they sense the threat of violence at this age? Ruth didn't know: she'd been a hopeless mother.

And Laird could read her mind. He watched her clumsy attempts to placate the child and offered a patronising smile.

'What is there to decide?' he asked, his tone vaguely pitying. 'After all, you're not here for her, are you?'

*

The sly look in his eyes was one she remembered well. She felt humiliated by her own need for answers. That she would submit herself to this – and with much worse to come. All he had to do was keep her dangling until Foster and Bridge returned.

Was she really prepared to give up her life, just to know the truth about her son?

She gazed at Evie, whose cries of displeasure had now been reduced to a low-level grizzling. Ruth's arms were aching from the effort of jiggling her up and down.

'What do you want her for?'

Laird looked amused. 'What do you think I want her for?'

'I heard something in Downview.'

'Prison gossip. A lot of stupid people cooped up together, spinning fantasies to pass the time.'

'Maybe. But what I heard was that your girls occasionally got pregnant. Instead of terminations, you "encouraged" them to go to term.'

He laughed at the euphemism. 'They didn't all need "encouraging". Not when there was a very significant bonus to be had.'

'So it's true? And the babies were sold?'

'Adopted, is a better word. Only without all that bothersome paperwork. The girls were consulted.'

'Always?'

'Almost always,' he conceded, with a glint in his eye.

Ruth felt dizzy, the blood roaring in her ears. She shifted her weight, made sure Evie was secure in one hand and grabbed a chair for support.

'Why did you do it?'

'If you spot a gap in the market, it's crazy not to fill it. A lot of wealthy people out there who want to adopt without all the usual rigmarole, the state interference.'

'Or people who'd been turned down as unsuitable?'

'Maybe. They seemed like genuine loving parents, mostly. Desperate for a child they could call their own.' He sniffed. 'Can't say I understand it myself, all this "son and heir" stuff. I couldn't give a toss what happens to a world without me in it. Could you?'

He laughed, boorishly, obscuring any answer she might have given. It startled Evie, who turned towards the source of this noise.

It had startled Ruth, too. Perhaps there was an element of bravado in there, but if that statement held even a kernel of truth, then Laird would have few qualms about disposing of his own son.

Ruth said, 'But people with lots of money and no scruples can get babies anywhere, can't they? The world is awash with unwanted children.'

'Yes, but this clientele tend to want healthy, white, European babies – and western European at that. No one wants Slavs, or gypsy cast-offs. And they can't pass a brown one off as their own child, can they?' He winked at her. 'It's not a politically correct business, you see.'

'Loving parents, *mostly*,' she quoted back at him. 'So not in all cases?'

His shrug wasn't quite as insouciant this time. 'I make it a rule not to enquire too closely about the purposes of the adoption. I mean, they could always lie, if they were planning something unpleasant …'

'And Renshaw was the doctor who helped with this operation?'

'Until he retired. Then he got greedy, and he ended up with something he shouldn't have.' He regarded her thoughtfully. 'And now I'm wondering how much you could tell me about that?'

'Nothing.'

'Well. Foster and Bridge are going to make sure.'

'I don't know anything. If I did, I'd use it as leverage.'

'True.' He sat back in the chair, raising the gun and taking aim at her mid-section. 'Put the baby on the table here, and then we can talk about Benjamin.'

It was a shock just to hear his name spoken aloud. *Spoken by his father*, Ruth had to remind herself, as sickening as that was to acknowledge.

She obeyed quickly, before the guilt could prompt a rethink. The metal surface must have been cold. Evie wailed as she was set down, and Ruth shuddered with self-loathing. For betraying Harry and his wife like this, she ought to be shot on the spot.

'Move back.' Laird jabbed the gun and she retreated, aware that she had just surrendered her one and only bargaining chip.

She reminded herself that it would have been obscene to use Evie in that way. The likely outcome would have seen Laird kill them both. This, surely, was the least bad option.

All Ruth could do now was hope for a miracle.

SEVENTY-SEVEN

They were only a few minutes away when Alice noticed how tense Harry had become. At first she put it down to nerves; then she saw the way he was checking the mirror. She glanced at the wing mirror and saw a sleek black saloon, possibly a Mercedes.

'Are we being followed?'

'Maybe. He pulled out of a turning just now.' Harry slowed from fifty to forty. The Mercedes gained on them a little, but not as much as it should have done.

'Can you see who's inside?'

Harry squinted hard at the mirror, then sighed. 'I think it's Warley.'

'The fake detective?' Alice felt her heart thumping: the onset of panic. 'Do you think he was lying in wait for us?'

'For Ruth, I expect. Hopefully that means she got past him.'

Alice felt there were quite a few optimistic assumptions in that statement, but she chose not to say so.

'What are we going to do?'

Harry was examining the road ahead. It was a single carriageway on level ground, with trees and dense vegetation on both sides. Very little traffic.

'This is risky,' he muttered, 'but worth a try.'

*

With a warning to hold on tight, Harry floored the accelerator. The Range Rover lurched forward and Alice cried out, grabbing the edge of her seat.

He was pushing the car up to seventy and beyond as they reached a shallow bend. Turning into it, he spotted a slight break in the tree line on the left-hand side, just before the end of the next straight section.

'I'm going to pull in. When I do, dive out and hide in the trees.'

As they got closer he saw it wasn't a proper lay-by, as he'd been hoping, but a narrow strip of earth and gravel, bordered by a steep wooded slope. Not much margin for error.

Despite that, he didn't brake till the last possible second. The Mercedes was momentarily lost from view behind him when Harry slewed off the road, still travelling at thirty or more as they bumped and skidded over the rutted surface. He jammed on the brakes, and the rapid deceleration threw him against the steering wheel. Beside him, Alice was clinging to the seatbelt with both hands, her knuckles white.

The instant they were stationary Harry turned off the engine and removed the keys, undid his seatbelt and slipped out of the car in one easy motion. Alice was quicker: with the trees on her side she needed only a couple of steps to be hidden from the road.

Harry ran round the front of the car and glimpsed the Mercedes coming towards him as he darted out of sight. His impression was that Warley was peering over the wheel, confused by the sudden manoeuvre.

He leapt off the edge of the flat ground and slithered down the slope until he saw Alice, crouching fearfully behind a tree.

'What are we doing, Harry?'

He put a finger to his lips, listening for the Mercedes even as he began scanning the ground.

'Help me find something.'

*

He was like a man possessed. Alice still had no idea what he planned to do – though perhaps, she thought, it was better not to know.

The Mercedes was braking hard, tyres squealing as it overshot the lay-by, screeched to a halt and rapidly reversed on to the rough ground behind their Range Rover. Any moment now the driver would be coming after them, and Harry was still kicking frantically through the leaves, explaining nothing.

'Find what?'

'A heavy stick, or— ah!' He scrabbled in the dirt and lifted a jagged lump of rock, the size of a cricket ball.

He started to climb back up. The driver was out of the Mercedes now; they heard the clunk of his door closing.

'Harry, no …' she whispered, but he shook his head.

'We don't have a choice.'

Harry moved slowly, careful not to make any noise. He was helped by the slow, rumbling approach of a lorry. He felt the vibration of its wheels through the ground, and by the time it had passed his head was almost level with the lay-by.

The Mercedes had parked just behind the Range Rover. Warley was making a slow circuit of the vehicle. He paused at the driver's door, then moved round to the passenger side. Now he was less than two feet away.

As Warley peered into the car, Harry stepped up from the slope and brought the rock down on the back of his head. It was only as the man crumpled to the ground that Harry realised how easily he'd acted – without the slightest sense of remorse.

He called to Alice, then checked Warley for a pulse. The man was still alive, bleeding from a gash on his scalp. Alice joined him, briefly resting her hand on Harry's shoulder.

'I can't believe you did that.'

'Neither can I, actually.'

With her help, he dragged Warley along to the Mercedes, stopping once to crouch out of sight as a couple of cars drove past. Then Harry retrieved the keys from the ignition and opened the boot. Lifting the unconscious body proved to be a struggle; made worse when Warley began to stir. In desperation, they shoved him in and slammed the boot shut.

Harry locked the car and threw the keys into the undergrowth. He held Alice close for a second.

'Thank you,' he said. 'You know I couldn't do this without you?'

'I think you could,' Alice said, and her voice held an uneasy mix of admiration and concern.

Back in the Range Rover, they checked the map and realised they must have gone past the property. Harry did a swift U-turn and drove back, Alice craning forward to see the turning that would now be on the right-hand side of the road.

Before they noticed the driveway, they saw the car screaming towards them. Another Mercedes.

Harry slowed, tensing as he waited for the car to rush past them. But the Mercedes was also braking; without indicating it veered on to the wrong side of the road, then took a sharp left into an opening obscured by trees and a bank of grass. Harry spotted two men inside the car.

Alice gasped. 'That driver was at Renshaw's. I think he's the one from the other night, with the knife.'

'I guess this is the place, then,' Harry said, and he turned across the road, following the other car on to the driveway.

SEVENTY-EIGHT

'Did you get me pregnant on purpose?'

Laird was about to reach for Evie. Now he paused, giving Ruth a sidelong glance.

'Say that again?'

'I was always careful, when we were together—'

'Sure you were. That was all part of the plan. To entrap me.' He made sure she was at a safe distance, then put the gun down and picked up the baby, cradling her with a natural ability that cut Ruth to her core.

'And you knew that, didn't you? Right from the start you made sure I got nothing useful.'

'It wasn't straight away, but yeah, I had a feeling something wasn't right.'

'So you impregnated me, as punishment?'

'What you did to me was no less brutal. Worming your way into my life. Pretending to care about me. I was only a young guy, and a lot more tender-hearted than you give me credit for. When I realised what you were up to, I hated you for it. I thought you deserved everything you got.'

Now he had Evie in his left hand, gently rocking her calm. His right hand rested on the table, close to the gun.

'And what about giving Benjamin away? When did you come up with that idea?'

He shook his head. 'You're leaping ahead here. First, let's talk about how quick you were to abandon your maternal responsibility.'

Ruth winced, as if slapped. 'That's not true.'

'When I said I wanted him, you couldn't get him off your hands soon enough.'

'That's not true! That's a horrible—'

'Bullshit, Ruth. I never for one second thought you'd agree to hand him over. Any normal mother would move heaven and earth to keep their kid in a situation like that. So what if a load of stuffed suits at the Met went ballistic? You shouldn't have given a damn about that.' He leaned forward, his gaze hard and unflinching, giving emphasis to his next words: 'Your own flesh and blood, Ruth. That ought to have mattered more than anything.'

Ruth felt robbed of the ability to speak. Her brain was frantically winding back, trying to reassess. Could there be an element of truth in what he was saying?

She swallowed, dry-mouthed. 'Are you telling me that you didn't really want him?'

'No, I did. Sort of. But not as much as I wanted to fuck with you. I never seriously expected to end up with him.'

'I was scared,' Ruth protested, her voice too high, too emotional, 'because you'd made it clear you could come and take him any time you wanted. If I'd fought, there would have been reprisals. People I loved, people I cared about. That's why I let him go – and I did it, believing you would let me have access to him, the way you agreed.'

'If that's what you tell yourself, fine,' he sneered. 'You're good at seeing what you want to see.'

'What do you mean?'

'Greg, for instance. He was quite happy with the arrangement.'

'You're lying.'

'You think he wanted another man's kid in the house? *My* kid? Dream on. All the time he spent later, sniffing round my businesses, that was just to earn brownie points. He'd have done anything to hang on to you.'

'I'm only too aware of what he did for me,' Ruth said bitterly.

She was bracing herself to accuse Laird of Greg's murder when his phone bleeped. She watched him carefully, conscious that if he picked up the phone he wouldn't have a hand free to grab the gun. But Laird was wise to the danger and adroitly touched a couple of buttons, putting it on to speaker.

McBride's Scottish voice said, 'Boss, I can't get hold of Mark.'

'Don't worry about it,' Laird muttered.

'Warley's not answering, either. He there with you?'

'No. Just keep a close eye out for the cops.'

Laird ended the call before McBride could respond, then glared at Ruth. She sensed that he wanted to ask her about Warley, but instead he checked his watch.

'Foster and Bridge will be here any second.'

She ignored the reminder – the threat – and responded with a question: 'Did Greg know about this scheme of yours, to sell the babies?'

'He might have got a whisper or two.'

'And is this where the idea originated? With what you did to me? Taking Benjamin and selling him to God knows who.'

Laird frowned. Evie, now awake, reached out and tried to swat at his nose. He chuckled, and it made his reply sound all the more derisory.

'I didn't sell Benjamin. Where did you get that idea?'

'So you still have him?' Despite everything, she couldn't keep the hope from her voice. It faded as she registered that he was shaking his head.

'I considered it, for a while. A healthy baby, in many ways it's an asset.' He shifted Evie in his arm as if to illustrate the point. 'But in the end I decided against.'

'Then where … ?'

'He's with my sister. Well, half-sister. She had problems conceiving, though she's since had two of her own. Both girls. They adore their older brother.'

Ruth let out a sob. She couldn't help it. Tears made her vision swim out of focus, and she didn't care that Laird was probably smirking at her reaction. Let him feast on it. Let his men beat the crap out of her. Let her world end now, if it had to.

'Is he …' She paused to compose herself. 'Is he aware of what happened?'

'Of course not. He thinks I'm his uncle.'

'So he doesn't know about me … at all?'

Laird shook his head. In a softer tone than she might have expected, he said, 'Better that way, isn't it?'

And Ruth, somehow, found it within her to nod. 'I suppose it is.'

Laird's phone buzzed again: a text. He leaned forward to read it, then grinned.

'They're here.' He looked up at her. 'I hope it was worth it, given what that information's gonna cost—'

He broke off as a terrible booming noise came from the other side of the house. It sounded like a bomb going off.

SEVENTY-NINE

The driveway turned out to be longer and wider than some of the country lanes Harry had driven along today. It ran up a steep incline, veered right, then disappeared over a ridge. The Mercedes was already out of sight.

Harry came to a halt just inside a set of gates.

'I need you to get out.'

'What?' Alice sounded angry as well as mystified.

'There isn't time to explain. Can you follow on foot? Please.'

The tone of his voice must have convinced her. She jumped out, swinging the door shut as he pulled away. If his insane idea had any chance of working, he had to put it into effect right now.

Harry gunned the engine, vaguely wondering if Alice had guessed his intentions. He was hoping this wasn't as dangerous as it appeared. If it was, better that only one of them was hurt.

He barely made it in time. He came hurtling over the ridge and saw the house about fifty yards below him, positioned on a neat plot of land with wilderness on either side. The Mercedes had just pulled up alongside another car parked at the front of the house.

Harry stamped on the accelerator and heard the engine roar. He pressed himself back in the seat and tried to prepare his body for what was to come. By now the men in the Mercedes had heard his approach. The driver was staring at the rear-view mirror, while his passenger made the mistake of turning to glance over his shoulder.

Harry didn't dare look away from his target as he raced down the slope, but he guessed that his speed on impact was around forty or fifty miles an hour.

The noise was astonishing. Apocalyptic. But that was all Harry was able to register before the force of the collision knocked him out.

Ruth identified the ear-splitting crunch and grind of metal on metal as a car crash. A bad one. The odd thing was how close it sounded: not out on the road.

While her reaction was to freeze, Laird grabbed the gun and turned towards the house as if expecting to be attacked. He was holding Evie against his side, trapped beneath his left arm, and she started to wail. The distraction made Laird furious: for a second Ruth thought he was going to strike the baby.

She steadied herself, glad that his focus was elsewhere. She tried to gauge her chances of overpowering him before he opened fire. The honest answer was: not great. But she was also well aware that she had nothing to lose. Once Foster and Bridge got here they were going to kill her, slowly and painfully, while trying to extract information that she didn't possess.

The problem was Evie.

Evie had everything to lose.

Alice ran up the drive, then cut across the grass bank on a more direct route towards the house. It meant she was just in time to see the Range Rover collide with the Mercedes.

Harry did it deliberately, there was no doubt about that. She watched in horror as the front of the Range Rover crumpled against the rear of the Mercedes, which was rammed forward and pushed side on to the house. The wheels hit a low step and the car tipped over, spun a half circle and slammed into the front porch, bringing down a shower of masonry and tiles on to the bodywork.

It seemed like neither of the men inside had their seatbelts fitted; their bodies were thrown around like clothes in a washing machine. As the door frames buckled and windows exploded, Alice saw an arm flop loosely from the passenger side. The sound of the impact slowly reverberated across the valley, and as it died away she realised there were no screams, no shouts or cries for help.

Harry too was slumped in his seat, his head forward on his chest. Alice thought she understood why he had done it – to put two very dangerous men out of action – but still it seemed like a suicidal gesture.

She sprinted down the slope, terrified of what she might find – and only now was she struck by the fact that no one had come from the house to investigate. Did this mean Nerys wasn't here? That *Evie* wasn't here?

To Ruth, Evie's crying had a worn-down, defeated tone that was truly heartbreaking. To Laird, her misery was nothing but an irritation.

Then his phone rang. Sensing an opportunity, Ruth immediately let her shoulders slump. She leaned back, giving him the impression that she was fearful, retreating.

He glanced at her, then at the display. By now he must have concluded that the crash meant bad news. He would want to take the call.

She listened to it ring a second time, then a third. Rather than look at him directly, she faced outwards, gazing at the house, waiting for the telltale movement in her peripheral vision.

On the fourth ring, Laird gave in and answered it. He set the gun down and snatched the phone. Ruth was lightning fast, her right hand whipping out to grab the gun, bringing it up to aim at him even as she darted out of his range.

With a snarl of rage Laird turned towards her. He dropped the phone and almost dropped Evie, too. As he stood up he tipped the table over and sent a couple of chairs crashing towards Ruth. She stumbled and nearly fell but managed to stay on her feet.

Laird edged towards the doorway, glanced that way and then looked down at the baby, making sure she was covering his chest. Evie had been momentarily silenced by this latest shock; now she began to cry again.

'Stay there,' Ruth ordered. But Laird was smiling, seeming relaxed.

'You won't shoot me.'

As if to test that proposition, he backed out of the summer house and stepped on to the lawn. Ruth had no choice but to follow, kicking the fallen chairs out of the way without taking her eyes off Laird.

'A head shot's easy from this distance. Evie will be bruised from the fall, but that's a lot better than what you have planned for her.'

He shrugged. 'I could put her down and you still wouldn't shoot.'

'Really?'

'I meant too much to you, Ruth. I still do.'

She shook her head. 'I hate you.'

'No. You hate yourself, and you deflect those feelings on to me. It's how you cope, knowing you gave your son away just to save your precious career.'

Ruth couldn't understand why he was goading her. 'Put the baby down.'

'No.'

A standoff, in the murky winter dusk.

Evie was crying herself to exhaustion. Taking her in both hands, Laird held her out at chest height, ensuring that his entire upper body was shielded. Ruth could shoot at his legs, but there was no way of knowing how he would react to such an injury. It was too risky, given that he could kill Evie with a single blow.

Even now, even though she had a gun in her hand, he had outwitted her.

The sound of Alice calling his name permeated through the blackness, but it was the pain that brought him back. Harry felt like he'd been dragged into an alley by half a dozen bouncers and given a good kicking. But why?

Alice was struggling to open his door. Finally it yielded with a sound like fingernails on a blackboard. Now Harry realised where he was, but the *why* still eluded him for a second.

'What happened?'

'You bloody nearly killed yourself, you idiot.' Then she took his cheeks in both hands and kissed him. 'You beautiful idiot.'

He released the seatbelt and eased himself out, gingerly, every muscle screaming.

'I knew we couldn't take them on directly. Not when they have knives, guns …'

Without warning he bent double and was violently sick. Alice stayed close, her hand on his back. He could sense how nervously she was looking around.

'Where is everyone?' she murmured. What she meant was: *Where is Evie?*

The question galvanised Harry, who ignored his reeling head and moved with her to examine the wrecked Mercedes. There was a lot of blood and broken glass, and after a quick look he knew two things: the men inside were either unconscious or dead, and Harry had no desire to find out which it was.

The front door was inaccessible, so they followed a path around the side of the house. The back door was open, but as they reached it Alice put a hand up for silence. Harry still had tinnitus from the crash, but gradually he heard what she was hearing.

It was a baby crying.

Their baby crying.

EIGHTY

Ruth kept the gun trained on Laird as he moved another couple of paces across the lawn.

'I want you to put Evie down, very slowly.'

He shook his head. 'Not gonna happen, Ruth. And I warn you, when my guys see you with that gun, you'll be dead in an instant.'

'Shouldn't they be here by now? Don't you think that crash we heard means that something's gone wrong?'

'You'd like to think so.'

When he glanced to his left it seemed like a classic ploy to distract her. But then Ruth sensed movement, looked quickly and found Harry French, battered and exhausted, hurrying towards them. He was accompanied by an equally weary-looking woman that Ruth assumed must be his wife.

Alice French saw Laird first – or, rather, she saw her daughter in Laird's arms – and only then did she register that Ruth was facing them. With a gun.

She screamed, tried to run towards Ruth but Harry grabbed her, then had to withstand her frenzied attempts to break free.

Ruth couldn't afford to lose her focus on Laird. She gestured with the gun.

'Give up, Nathan. You're outnumbered.'

He shook his head. Ruth was determined not to be intimidated by this brazen show of confidence. She steadied her aim, all too aware of how terrifying this must be for Harry and Alice; willing them to understand the position she was in.

Alice had run past the house and stopped at the sight of a man and a woman on the lawn. The man was holding Evie at arm's length, and the woman – Ruth? – was pointing a gun at Evie.

At Evie.

It was a sight that transformed Alice into a wild animal. She wanted to fall upon this woman, gun or no gun, and tear her to pieces.

But Harry restrained her and wouldn't let go, and for a second or two she lost her senses and despised him for that. It even flashed through her mind that maybe this woman, Ruth, was Harry's lover; that they were in this together, plotting against her.

'Give her to me! Put the gun down!'

Laird ignored her. Ruth shook her head. It was left to Harry to explain.

'Alice, stay calm. *He's* the danger. Not Ruth.'

But even now, when he was trying so hard to make her see, wasn't there an undercurrent of doubt in his voice?

Oh God: Harry didn't genuinely trust Ruth. He'd merely pretended that he did – and Alice, foolishly, had gone along with it.

Well, not any more. Not with her daughter's life at stake.

'I'm calling the police,' she told them.

I should just shoot him, Ruth was thinking. *Evie's not my daughter; not my problem.*

And I'm entitled to retribution, aren't I, after what I've been through?

If it was true that Nathan had done the right thing by Benjamin, why the hell hadn't he told her years ago? He could have had a quiet word with Greg, or even – God forbid – have consulted her on the decision to let his half-sister adopt. Instead he'd done everything in his power to torment her.

Laird, like the rest of them, heard Alice's declaration of intent. He didn't seem unduly concerned by it. Ruth was aware of Harry muttering something to his wife, but she couldn't make out the words. Her finger was tightening on the trigger, carefully, smoothly. It had been years since she'd used a firearm, and she was no doubt severely out of practice.

Laird stepped towards her. A single step: not threatening, but purposeful.

'You don't want this baby to die, Ruth.'

'So put her down.'

'Oh, I will. Are you ready?'

'Nathan …'

Teeth clenched in a snarl, he drew Evie back towards him and lowered her to waist level. Only now did they realise what he was about to do.

'Okay, Ruth. She's in your hands.'

And he threw the baby into the air.

Alice was dialling, focused on the phone, when she heard the man speak. His voice was crueller than his appearance suggested. The words were meant only for Ruth, but Alice's attention was caught by the words 'baby' and 'die'.

By the time he spoke again she was running towards them, her phone bouncing on the grass, Harry half a second behind her, but Alice was already too late.

They were both too late.

Laird threw the baby as high as he could. Evie's survival was immaterial: all he cared about was getting away.

Only Ruth was close enough to save her. The impulse to do so, it turned out, was far stronger than any desire for revenge. She threw the gun aside and held out both arms in a cradling motion, almost dancing on her toes as she adjusted her position, making frantic calculations with regard to speed and distance and the angle of descent, all in the space of a few heartbeats.

And when those calculations were complete, when Evie had thudded into her hands and been swiftly gathered in, Ruth toppling backwards with the effort of lessening the impact, landing heavily but nonetheless feeling elated that she had caught the baby safely … when this was done, and the danger had passed, she looked round for Laird and he was nowhere to be seen.

Ruth might not have spotted where he went, but Harry did. At that point he was behind Alice, who ran to Ruth and scooped Evie out of her grasp before realising that Harry wasn't with her.

He was counting on those few seconds to put some distance between them, so that she wouldn't be able to stop him, or make him see reason.

Laird had headed past the summer house and plunged into the undergrowth on the slopes beyond the garden. It was only when Harry reached the edge of the lawn that he discovered how steeply the land fell away, and how dark it was in the trees.

He heard Alice screaming at him to come back but it was impossible to reconsider now. Knowing that she and Evie were no longer in danger, he was seized by a determination not to let Laird escape. He could just about see his target crashing through the trees, perhaps thirty or forty feet away. Laird was well-dressed, and probably wearing thin-soled shoes, whereas Harry wore trainers: on slippery leaves and mud that gave him a slight advantage.

Harry descended with no regard for his own safety, leaping from one patch of ground to another. As well as the darkness to contend with, there were obstacles everywhere: tree roots and low-hanging branches, puddles that concealed deep furrows; the sudden glassy smoothness of the rock that formed the walls of this gorge.

The rational part of his mind knew this wasn't a good idea – he should have stayed with Alice and Evie. But Harry was spurred by a white-hot rage, and it would not be tempered by caution or common sense. This man had used Harry's eight-week-old baby as a human shield. He wasn't going to get away with that.

Harry had narrowed the gap to about twenty feet when it occurred to him that he was unarmed. If Laird saw there was only one man chasing him, he might decide to stop and fight, especially as the ground had begun to level out a little.

Well, if he did, so be it.

Fortunately Laird seemed too intent on escape to spare any time in looking back. He put on a burst of speed, then disappeared so suddenly that Harry thought he must be going crazy. It was like some kind of visual effect: here, not here.

His legs went on running while his brain tried to make sense of it. Laird had been moving far too fast to duck or hide.

The answer came when Harry struck the same patch of mud and weeds, soaked by the earlier rain, and realised that he couldn't stop now if he wanted. He tried taking longer strides, but that only increased his speed.

And then he saw why Laird had vanished. This stretch of slightly flatter ground had effectively formed a ledge, about halfway down the side of the gorge. Even from twenty feet back it was impossible to tell that it ended in a sheer drop. Moving with too much momentum to stop, Laird had simply run over the edge. Now Harry was about to do the same.

EIGHTY-ONE

He had two steps left on solid ground. Harry used the first to change direction, jumping to his right, towards a sturdy-looking tree that grew at the edge of the drop.

His second, final step took him side on, so that even as his weight propelled him into space, his upper body was able to twist round, facing the slope. Then, as he fell, he threw his arms above his head and scrabbled through the muck and leaves, desperately searching for the very things that moments ago he had been trying to avoid.

Tree roots.

His body slammed against the lip of the overhanging ledge, driving all the air from his lungs. His eyes were tightly shut – because he had no wish to witness his own death – and his legs were dangling in the air, helpless to resist the call of gravity. His fingers snagged something thin and sinuous, a cord or a tendon of a main root. It snapped off but he dragged his fingers more deeply into the earth and this time felt the tangle of thicker roots. The weight of his body tore some from the earth, throwing soil into his face as they stretched tight … and tighter still …

But held.

Gripping them with both hands, he pressed his feet against the rock face, searching out any small crevice. Once he had a foot lodged against solid rock he was able to push himself up a few inches, then lift one knee back on to the grass. Still clinging to the roots, he hauled himself to safety.

*

Harry lay for a few seconds, shocked and exhausted, almost incredulous that he had survived. A noise from below caused him to stir. He rose to his knees, wiped his face and spat sweet, mineral-rich crumbs of soil from his mouth.

Another groan. Harry leaned over and peered into the darkness. Laird was crumpled against a tree, about sixty feet below him. He'd fallen over a limestone cliff that actually represented only a short section of the gorge. To left and right Harry could see that the slope continued on much the same gradient as before. Laird had been spectacularly unlucky in his choice of route.

Harry made his way along the ridge until he reached a place where he could safely climb down. He kept a cautious eye on Laird as he approached the body. The only movement he saw was one foot, twitching weakly. At close range it became clear that the man was dying. His head was bent at an awkward angle, and there was a massive wound at the back of his skull, pouring blood into the earth.

And yet there was a small reaction as Harry knelt down. Perhaps sensing his presence, Laird managed to open his eyes a fraction. He registered Harry's gaze and looked vaguely disgusted, as if he'd never thought his end would come so soon, so dismally. Harry felt it would be hypocritical to offer any sort of comfort, so he said nothing.

With difficulty, Laird's mouth formed a word: 'R … Ruth.'

'What about her?'

Laird exhaled, a long juddering breath that had to fight its way out. Somehow, after that, he whispered, 'Sold him.'

'What?'

'Tell her … I sold him.'

His lips twisted into a bitter smile, and he died.

EIGHTY-TWO

Harry heaved himself back up the slope, often having to grab hold of branches to stay on his feet. He forced his aching legs to hurry, knowing how anxious Alice would be; and aware, too, that the danger hadn't necessarily passed.

He spotted Ruth first, a ghostly shadow in a mass of grey and black, creeping through the trees with the gun in her hand. He called out to her in a tentative voice, half afraid that she would turn and shoot; even more afraid that she would somehow guess what he'd just learned. When she saw him, Harry waved and pointed up towards the house. They converged on the edge of the lawn, and by then there was only time to explain that Laird was dead, before Harry was reunited with his wife and daughter.

For the next couple of minutes Ruth hung back at a respectful distance. Finally she coughed to attract Harry's attention. He looked at her, reluctantly, the secret like a lead weight in his guts.

'Alice is insistent on calling the police,' she said. 'Do you go along with that?'

'I think we have to.'

Ruth nodded. 'In that case, I can't hang around. You can tell them you tried to keep me here, but I threatened you.'

He was silent for a moment, lost in thought. Snapped out of it, and said, 'So we are allowed to mention you, then?'

A shrug. 'I'd love it if you didn't, but there's no way I want either of you getting into trouble for this.'

She updated them on what she'd done here, and where the various casualties could be found. She stressed that they should make no mention of firearms until the police were in attendance.

'Otherwise it'll be hours before they even enter the premises, and meanwhile you'll be freezing to death out here.'

Alice had already told her what had happened to Foster and Bridge. Ruth offered to sit in the Range Rover and leave her DNA in the driving seat, so they could claim she was responsible for the collision – otherwise Harry would be open to charges of disproportionate force.

'Juries are going to cut you a lot of slack, but you could do without all the crap that goes with a prosecution.'

Harry thanked her, but said he would take his chances. 'If we start lying we'll just get in more trouble.'

Alice agreed. 'We're not going to lie.'

'Okay,' Ruth said. 'Can I recommend you say that in the confusion you hit their car by accident? Apart from that, you and Alice haven't committed any crimes. You're the victims here.'

Then came the farewells. Alice gave Ruth a quick embrace, with Evie pressed between them. She thanked Ruth for her help but Harry detected a coolness in her tone, reflecting her awareness that it hadn't been straightforward altruism on Ruth's part.

Alice sat down again, desperate to feed Evie. Harry walked with Ruth across the lawn. She dismantled the gun and left the components on the path.

'Laird's death,' she said. 'Definitely an accident?'

'Absolutely. I had nothing to do with it.' He was trembling, he realised, light-headed with indecision.

'I don't mean that. Could it have been deliberate, on his part?'

Harry considered it. 'I don't think so. It was dark, slippery. He just misjudged the terrain, same as me.'

Ruth nodded thoughtfully. Harry felt she was waiting, as if she knew he had more to tell her.

He formed the first difficult sentence in his head and opened his mouth to say it, just as Ruth blurted out: 'He told me about Benjamin.'

Harry gulped. 'Did he?'

'Turns out he viewed the whole, uh, experience very differently to the way I did. *I* was the bad parent, not him.' She sniffed, harshly, and forced a smile. 'Benjamin's been raised by Laird's half-sister. She's bringing him up as her own.'

Harry couldn't speak, so he nodded again. 'Do you ...' He coughed. 'Do you know where to find her?'

'No idea. I didn't even know he had a half-sister. Anyway, Benjamin has a new life. He won't remember anything about me.' She looked him in the eye. 'I can't disrupt that, just for my own selfishness, can I?'

Harry waited through an agonising pause, the emotion churning up his insides, before he said, 'Will it go on torturing you, if you don't find him?'

Ruth gave him what was possibly the saddest, bravest smile he'd ever seen.

'I'll try not to let it. That's the best I can say.'

'Good.'

'Yes.' The smile persisted, against all the odds. 'Nathan's given me a chance for closure. It would be crazy not to take it.'

Harry matched the smile, and knew that the secret had to die with Laird.

'It would,' he said.

EIGHTY-THREE

After a crushing hug of farewell, and thanking her again for saving Evie's life, Harry watched Ruth walk out of sight around the side of the house. Then he returned to Alice and made the phone call. He kept it brief, downplaying the scale of the incident, just as Ruth had suggested.

The first uniformed officers found them ten minutes later. One looked distinctly pale, having tried to administer first aid to Foster and Bridge. Soon there were paramedics out front, along with a second police car. Within an hour that had multiplied to more than a dozen vehicles, once the first officers on the scene established the number of casualties and declared this a major incident.

You're not kidding, Harry thought to himself. After a brief conversation the officer realised he was talking to potential suspects, as well as key witnesses, so they were politely cautioned and asked to change into paper suits so their clothes could be taken away for forensic analysis.

They undressed in the garage, as it was virtually the only part of the property that wasn't a crime scene. A couple of medical staff came to check them over. Harry's wounded arm was given a fresh dressing, and he gratefully accepted some painkillers. One of the crew rustled up nappies and wipes for Evie. Shortly afterwards an officer brought them hot drinks and sandwiches.

Then they had to wait in separate patrol cars, presumably so they couldn't collude. To Harry that felt downright cruel, but he consoled himself with the fact that they were, all three of them, relatively unscathed by their experiences.

As the night wore on they watched a stream of incoming personnel: uniforms and CID, ambulance crews and forensic teams, and even a couple of reporters who got lucky – for a while – before being escorted away. Helicopters buzzed overhead, searchlights roaming the trees, adding to the unreal sense of drama. Now it felt more like a movie set than the site of a genuine tragedy.

It was an interminable wait until Harry and Alice were called to sit with a pair of detectives and give their initial statements. Finally, after nearly three hours, they were allowed to sit together while someone arranged accommodation nearby. The detective explained that they weren't being arrested at this stage, but would be kept under police guard till they'd been questioned at greater length, probably tomorrow. Harry barely listened: he was hugging Alice and holding Evie between them, the poor baby probably mystified by the tears, and the laughter, and the rain of kisses they brought down upon her.

'When can we leave here?' Alice had asked, and the detective shrugged.

'A while yet. There's someone coming to see you.'

That someone was DI Guy Thomsett. He was an affable, well-spoken man in his thirties who, it turned out, had gone to the same sixth-form college as Harry, albeit in different years. They had a couple of mutual acquaintances, and his ex-wife was a patient at Alice's dental practice in Portslade. Small world.

After conferring with the local detectives he returned with the news that he was driving them to a hotel in Ross-on-Wye, where both he and they would be spending the night.

When they drove out they found that the whole area had been sealed off for about half a mile in each direction. An incident room had been set up in a nearby church hall, and the media were out in force. Thomsett warned that the coming days would involve not only hour after hour of meticulous questioning, but also a firestorm of publicity. Help and advice on managing the media would be available if they wanted it – Harry and Alice said they probably would – and a Family Liaison Officer would be assigned to support them. Perhaps they looked dubious, for Thomsett said, 'Everyone reacts differently. What you've been through might affect you for years – or you might shrug it off in a day or two. Until you know which way it'll go, take any assistance you can get.'

Once they were installed at the hotel, the detective arranged for someone to procure some clothes and toiletries. Then he suggested they have a stiff drink and a chat in their room, while Evie slept like a queen in the centre of a large double bed.

Neither of them declined the offer of a restorative brandy. Thomsett drained his small measure in a single gulp, then went through the current status of the investigation.

A body alleged to be that of Edward Renshaw had been found, grievously mutilated, in the boot of a Range Rover, registered to a company owned by a Mr Michael Baxter, of an address in Cheltenham.

Another man, Dean Warley, was found in the boot of a hired Mercedes, approximately a quarter of a mile from the main crime scene. Although he had sustained a head injury, Mr Warley refused medical treatment and was unwilling to offer any information as to how he had come to be there. He was found to be armed, and placed under arrest on suspicion of a number of offences.

At the house, the two men in the wrecked Mercedes were taken to hospital. The latest news was that Niall Foster had to have both legs amputated, while Darrell Bridge had succumbed to his injuries. Both men had long criminal records, and their recent activity was of great interest to several police jurisdictions.

Mark Vickery was found alive, trussed up in the bushes outside the back door. He'd required medical treatment and was now under arrest and regarded as the principal suspect.

His sister, Sian Vickery, had been found inside the house in a similar state: tied up, conscious but confused, and she too had been arrested.

A second woman, Nerys Baxter, was close to death when she was discovered, and went into cardiac arrest in the ambulance. The paramedics managed to keep her alive, but currently her chances of survival were assessed as no more than fifty–fifty.

Finally, the body of Nathan Laird – another person of interest, to the National Crime Agency among others – had been found on the treacherous slopes above the River Wye. Arrangements were still being made to recover the body, which in all likelihood wouldn't happen until morning.

'So,' said Thomsett when that was complete, 'can either of you give me the tiniest clue as to what's going on here?'

They told him the whole story, without embellishment, and with only a few omissions. Thomsett's specific interest was in Renshaw – and what had happened in Brighton. Harry and Alice went through it several times, from each perspective, and kept running into one big unknown: Laird's motive for the hunt.

'It has to revolve around this second parcel,' Thomsett said. 'A flash drive or something similar.'

'That's what Nerys and Michael thought,' Alice agreed. 'Maybe they can tell you more when you interview them.'

'Laird knew, of course,' Harry said. 'Hopefully Mark Vickery does, as well.'

'My hunch is that he'll be claiming amnesia, but we shall see. What he can't tell us, sadly, is where this package is hidden. Only Renshaw knew that.'

The question of reprisals was debated briefly. Thomsett felt it unlikely that they needed to worry. Laird was dead. The Vickery siblings would be held in custody, and every effort would be made to ensure they ended up in prison.

'Still wish I knew what had sparked all this mayhem,' Thomsett said. His eyes gleamed with a hint – just the merest hint – that he suspected there was more they could divulge if they wanted to.

In particular, the lack of information about Ruth troubled him, just as it had troubled the detectives back at the house. Harry had been pressed to recall every tiny detail about the mysterious interloper: her movements over recent days, her past life, her motives. It felt disloyal, he told Alice afterwards, until he realised how little he knew that might actually help track her down. Where did she live? Did she work? Did she own a car? Was she using an alias? He could truthfully say he had no idea.

Turning the tables, he asked Thomsett about Ruth's release from prison: had she been let out on parole, and if so wouldn't the authorities be keeping track of her? What he got back was an embarrassed silence, and the interrogation was over.

Later that night, after they'd spoken to their families, eaten a meal and even managed to relax a little, Thomsett brought news of the police investigation in Cranstone. They had found evidence of Renshaw's murder at Nerys's home, but there had been no sign of Michael or his family. No answer at his home address, either.

Just as they began to fear that he'd absconded, he turned himself in at Cheltenham police station with his wife – and an expensive lawyer – in tow.

'I hope now that Nerys does pull through,' Alice muttered to Harry, 'if only so she can contradict Michael's version of events.'

'Quite.' Wishing them goodnight, Thomsett turned to go. It struck Alice that he looked nearly as drained as they did. His own room was just along the corridor, and she noticed his shoelaces were already undone, as if he were counting the seconds till he could kick them off—

Shoelaces. Why did that … ?

'Wait,' she called, and something in her tone made both Thomsett and Harry turn to stare at her.

'What?' Harry asked.

'I know where it is.'

EIGHTY-FOUR

They didn't go until the next morning, by which time a lot of doubts had surfaced. Alice knew she was going to be very embarrassed if she was wrong, although Thomsett had assured her that it was worth checking. An extensive search of Nerys's property had failed to locate anything that could account for Renshaw's second parcel.

Neither Alice nor Harry had slept particularly well, although Evie had enjoyed a remarkably good night. On Thomsett's advice they ate breakfast in their room to avoid the possibility of encountering the media. Alice thought he was exaggerating until she saw a couple of TV vans parked outside. Word had got out that vital witnesses to the incident were staying here.

They were also held up briefly by a flying visit from the Senior Investigating Officer, to whom Thomsett paid due respect. The man himself exchanged only a few words with them, and seemed to have come along merely to look them over, as if inspecting visitors from some exotic but unsavoury foreign realm.

They travelled in a marked 4x4, driven with lights and sirens for long enough to shake off any pursuing journalists. They were in Cranstone by ten o'clock on a cold, dull Sunday morning.

Alice grew tense as they turned into Mercombe Lane, her experiences here too vivid and painful to repress. Harry clutched her hand and squeezed it tight. She turned to Evie, strapped into a borrowed car seat, seeming to need visual confirmation that her daughter was unharmed before she could truly believe it.

There was a huge amount of forensic activity still evident at Beech House. The 4x4 parked next to the footpath and they climbed out, Alice carrying Evie, Harry and Thomsett and the police driver all waiting for her to take the lead.

A cold wind tugged at her hair as she traipsed across the field. It was a damp and miserable day, the horizons blurred by mist. They passed several groups of walkers, most of whom seemed to be surreptitiously observing the goings-on at Beech House.

The mist was thicker in the wood, actual tendrils of it drifting between the trees like some corny 1970s movie set: Sherlock Holmes or Hammer Horror. Compared to this, the hotel room had been the most blissful sanctuary she could imagine. Alice did her best to focus on the safe, reassuring presence of Harry, Evie, and the police, but still she had to keep pushing away the image of Michael bearing down on her. Would coming here set off the kind of psychological disturbance that Thomsett had warned might afflict them for years?

Added to the worry that she'd got it wrong was a fear that she wouldn't be able to recall the correct place. As it was, the clearing was easy to find. She came to a halt, and tried not to feel self-conscious with everyone's eyes upon her. Evie was grizzling, so Harry took her and started rocking her to sleep.

Alice turned in a slow circle, trying to picture where Renshaw had stood. He'd made some silly patronising comment, then nearly slipped when he put his foot on a rotten log. She remembered him kneeling down, fiddling with his shoelaces. At the time it had seemed perfectly innocuous. She wasn't sure now what had prompted her to think otherwise.

A hunch, she thought glumly. *Just a stupid hunch.*

But then she saw what looked like the right place, the log half-buried in mulch. She hurried over, crouched at the right-hand end and wiped away some of the fallen leaves.

Nothing.

She straightened up, crestfallen. But Thomsett had stepped over the log, and now from the other side he pushed it with his foot. Just an inch or two, but she immediately spotted the corner of a clear plastic bag.

'Hold on,' he said, cautioning her not to touch it. He found a twig and used it to brush off the leaves and muck, revealing a memory stick, wrapped in a plastic freezer bag.

'Bingo, I think,' he said wryly. Taking no chances, he put on latex gloves and placed the package in an evidence bag.

'Thank you,' he said to Alice. 'This could help a lot.'

'I hope so. Will we ever get to know what's on there?'

Thomsett smiled. It was a disarming smile, and Harry had already begun to tease Alice about her susceptibility to it.

'I'd like to say that you will. But I can't guarantee it, I'm afraid.'

EIGHTY-FIVE

The story didn't break for another month. Even when it did, they weren't absolutely certain of the link to that innocuous-looking USB stick.

What led them to suspect a connection was the visit, two days earlier, by DI Thomsett. This was the first contact they'd had since the exhausting round of interviews that had taken place on the Monday and Tuesday following the Wye Valley Killings – as the media had decided to call them.

At the end of that process, Harry had been informed that a number of charges were being considered, and that he would be informed when the investigation was complete. It had been four weeks of constant anxiety. Alice had done her best to calm him, pointing out that the media had portrayed him as a hero – and the CPS would be pretty foolish to bring charges against a man who'd attacked criminals in order to find and protect his missing family.

Harry wasn't so sure. He suspected the authorities might welcome the chance to remind the more vengeful sections of the press that mob rule and vigilante justice had to have their limits in a civilised society. In normal circumstances that would have been Harry's view as well. Not so much if they were going to make an example of him …

*

Returning home had been far from easy, at first. Home is our sanctuary: it's the place we rush back to in times of crisis. But this particular sanctuary had been invaded – violated – with far-reaching consequences. Nights were the hardest, jerking awake to every creak and groan; jumping at shadows; obsessively checking that doors were locked and alarms were set and Evie was safe.

Many times they discussed a quick sale: perhaps they should move to a rented property as a stopgap, then search carefully for a new home? Sometimes it was Harry convincing Alice that they should give it a few more days, in case it became easier to bear; at other times it was Alice persuading Harry that central Brighton was so convenient, so interesting, that moving out of town was sure to disappoint. Whatever the argument, no matter who was suffering the loss of nerve, inertia always won out.

The house over the road was a crime scene for nearly a week, invaded by police officers, forensic staff, journalists and TV camera crews. Neighbours were alternately thrilled and appalled; Clare McIntosh became the unofficial spokesperson for the street, and loved every minute of it. She ended up with far more airtime than either Harry or Alice, which was fine with them.

Then the interest waned, and number 43 was boarded up until, on the instructions of its owner, the builders moved in to renovate, prior to a sale.

And now Thomsett was back. After offering his congratulations on how well they'd borne the media interest, he cleared his throat, as if about to read the nominations at an award ceremony, and announced that he'd had the heads up – he didn't say from whom, exactly – that no further action would be taken against Harry. Official written confirmation would be forthcoming in due course.

The wider investigation into Laird and Vickery's activities was ongoing, but even there Thomsett gave the impression that any prosecutions, if they happened at all, would be rather low-key.

His own hunch, he confessed, was that the enquiry would drag on until the world had lost interest, and then be quietly kicked into the long grass.

'Nerys and her son are giving wildly contrasting versions of what happened at Beech House, but I think we'll get them both for Renshaw's murder. That's something, at least.'

Maybe it was, but once Thomsett had gone they agreed that it didn't make sense. For all the anguish they had caused, Nerys and Michael's crimes had been little more than a sideshow compared to the main conspiracy here.

'They're covering it up, aren't they?' said Alice.

'That's how it looks to me.'

It wasn't wild paranoia to think so – not when they considered the question of Ruth Monroe. Someone had intervened, that first night, Harry guessed: orders from on high. During the formal interviews he had given a detailed account of her involvement, and yet the detectives questioning him had never once indicated that they had any intention of following it up. At times they greeted his tale with outright incredulity.

Nothing had been said about her in the media – the police had specifically warned Harry and Alice to stay silent on that score – and the impression, unofficially confirmed by Thomsett, was that Ruth's prior career threatened to prove too embarrassing to risk pursuing her any further.

So, they stayed perplexed for two days. Then came a news story about a UK-born businessman, a stalwart of the *Sunday Times* Rich List, who inexplicably had leapt to his death from the roof of a luxury apartment block in Dubai.

On the same day, it was announced that a long-serving cabinet minister, with some of the highest approval ratings in government, was resigning with immediate effect, to spend more time with his family. A little odd, given that his grown-up children reportedly had nothing to do with him.

Harry wouldn't have given either story much thought, except that he happened upon an anonymous blog which claimed the two men were linked by certain unspeakable proclivities – and that they had indulged those proclivities via a number of secret and utterly illegal adoptions.

That post had been taken down within six hours, and the whole blog was gone by the following day, never to return.

Nearly six weeks later, with Evie's first Christmas just days away, Harry was conducting the usual last scoot round the house before bed, making sure everything was switched off. Tonight they'd both held out till twenty past ten: an extraordinarily late night by their recent standards.

In part that was because Evie was sleeping better. They'd moved her into the nursery and so far she seemed comfortable with the transition. On one astonishing – and quite scary – occasion she'd slept right through from seven p.m. till five in the morning.

Harry trudged upstairs, feeling tired yet strangely content. Probably because work was back on track, and the Christmas break was coming up, and he couldn't wait to see what Evie made of Christmas morning: all that glossy paper to be crumpled in her lap. Unknown to Alice, he'd bought his daughter a remote-controlled helicopter. He felt sure she'd love it nearly as much as he would.

On the final step he paused. He'd set the new burglar alarm but had forgotten to prop the ironing board against the kitchen door as a little extra precaution.

He thought about going back down, then decided that he couldn't be bothered. They'd be fine.

Alice was already in bed, the light off. Harry climbed in, gave her a quick cuddle, then turned away. He wasn't expecting anything more – because it was a Wednesday, and they'd both had busy days, and a few slightly better nights hadn't yet compensated for the sleep deficit built up over the past three months.

But then he felt her wriggling towards him. 'A cuddle. Is that it?'

'I thought you'd be too knackered.'

'Ohh.' A playful groan. 'What's up, don't you have the energy, old man?'

'Who are you calling "old"?'

And later, when they were lying together, relaxed and drowsy but not quite ready for sleep, he judged that now was the right time to confess.

First he recapped why Ruth had been searching for Laird, and what Laird had told Ruth about Benjamin's new life away from his birth parents.

'The step-sister or whatever she is?'

'Yeah, half-sister, I think. But Laird told me something different.'

She grew sombre. 'What?'

'I went down to him, as he was dying. The last thing he said was, "I sold him." Which is what Ruth suspected all along – that Laird was selling children, regardless of who wanted them, and for what purpose – and that he'd got the idea after what he did with Benjamin.'

'Oh my God,' Alice said quietly. 'You didn't tell Ruth?'

'No. I was going to, sort of. But then she brought up this half-sister thing, and how she'd decided it was better for Ben if she just left him alone.'

Silence, until Alice blew out a sigh. 'And she's really able to do that? Give up her search?'

'Maybe. At the time I sensed she had some doubts, quite understandably, about whether Laird had told her the truth. Now I keep wondering if I should try to get in touch, and set her straight—'

'No,' Alice said. 'You did the right thing.'

'How do you know?'

'I don't, for sure. But bear in mind that Laird might have been lying to *you*, not to Ruth. Perhaps the sister is the truth, and he only changed his story when he realised he was dying. One last act of cruelty, to make sure Ruth suffered for the rest of her life.'

Harry nodded. He'd considered that possibility himself and been unsure, but it sounded a lot more plausible coming from Alice.

She said, 'In the end, we choose what we want to believe. We shape the truth to fit our requirements, because otherwise life would be just too hard to bear.'

'You think so?' Harry asked.

'You said yourself, Ruth had her doubts, but after years of torment she's chosen the explanation that offers her peace. That's a good choice, Harry. Don't give her reason to change it.'

And Harry, who'd had his own agonising choices to make, found that he could not disagree with her.

LETTER FROM TOM BALE

SEE HOW THEY RUN started with a sleepless night. I'd gone to bed at about midnight and was still lying awake when I heard a noise outside; at first I thought it was a cat jumping on to our dustbin. Then the security light came on, and when I got up and opened the bedroom window, a would-be burglar ran away from the back door and disappeared over our fence.

The police attended very quickly, but the culprit was never traced. Afterwards it struck me that, if I hadn't been lying awake, I doubt if either the noise or the outside light would have woken me or my wife. And the brazen nature of the attempted break-in troubled me a lot in the days and weeks that followed. I couldn't help wondering what might have happened had the intruder made it into the house without disturbing us.

What followed was a pattern of very light sleeping which still hasn't quite left me, but it also sparked an idea for a novel, drawing on the many subsequent occasions when I woke suddenly and froze, trying to identify the noise I'd just heard. It reminded me of that other stage in life when light sleeping becomes an exhausting habit – so I thought it only right that Harry and Alice should have a new baby to worry about!

As with most of my novels, this story centres on ordinary people whose lives are suddenly thrown into chaos – and I hope you find it as exciting as I did to discover how they manage to cope with the many challenges that confront them.

If you do enjoy the book, can I ask you to spare a little time to add a rating or a review to the website of your choice? I think most readers are conscious now of the vitally important role that reviews on Goodreads and elsewhere can have on the success of a book. And as I've mentioned in the Acknowledgements, getting that positive feedback makes a tremendous difference: writers work in silence, metaphorically speaking, and a nice review or a favourable comment on social media is the equivalent of an actor or musician hearing applause from the audience.

You can contact me or find out more about my books via the links below, and receive news of my new releases by signing up to my email list:

www.bookouture.com/tom-bale/
www.tombale.net
www.facebook.com/tombalewriter
@t0mbale

ACKNOWLEDGEMENTS

I'd like to thank Keshini Naidoo, my editor, for the time and dedication she put into ensuring that this book is as good as it can possibly be. I'd also like to thank Oliver Rhodes, Kim Nash and the whole team at Bookouture – it's a thrill to be on board!

Similar thanks are due to my agent, Camilla Wray, and everyone at Darley Anderson, particularly Mary Darby, Emma Winter and Rosanna Bellingham.

As always, I'm deeply indebted to my wife, Niki, as well as my family and friends. And since we're hitting the half century in 2016, this feels like the right time for a shout-out to the old geezers who have offered me comradeship and support for four decades or more: Ian Gilburt, Shendon Ireland, Rod Lambert, Stuart Marsom, Denis Sorrill and Ian Vinall. Cheers, guys!

A special thank you to Demetra Saltmarsh, who worked chiropractic miracles on my creaking back: it's been rather an exotic delight to sit without pain (and type without numb fingers) for the first time in over ten years.

Lastly, those of you who have read my previous books will know that this one has been a while coming. I won't bore anyone with the reasons behind that delay but I will say that, as far as my writing career is concerned, the past few years have involved rather more downs than ups. There were times when I wondered if I should pack it in and do something else, but two things kept me on track: the unwavering support of my wife, and the messages I received from readers who had enjoyed my books.

So this is for everyone who took the trouble to contact me by email, Facebook or Twitter; everyone who mentioned my work on their blogs or was good enough to post a review: your positive feedback really did make a difference. Thank you.

Printed in Great Britain
by Amazon